The Arab-Israeli Wars,
The Chinese Civil War,
and
The Korean War

The Arab-Israeli Wars, The Chinese Civil War, and The Korean War

Roy K. Flint
Peter W. Kozumplik
Thomas J. Waraksa

Thomas E. Griess
Series Editor

DEPARTMENT OF HISTORY
UNITED STATES MILITARY ACADEMY
WEST POINT, NEW YORK

AVERY PUBLISHING GROUP INC.
Wayne, New Jersey

Illustration Credits

Page

4   Early Members of the *Hashomer.* Courtesy of Embassy of Israel, Washington, D.C.

5   An Attempt to Restrict Movement in Jerusalem, 1947-1949. Courtesy of Zionist Archives and Library, New York, New York.

10   An Israeli 155-mm Howitzer Made From a Sherman Chassis and an Imported Gun Assembly. Courtesy of Embassy of Israel, Washington, D.C.

12   The Resupply of Rapidly Advancing Israeli Columns. Courtesy of Zionist Archives and Library, New York, New York.

13   Generals Narkis, Dayan, and Rabin in Jerusalem, June 1967. Courtesy of Zionist Archives and Library, New York, New York.

18   Egyptian Engineers Use High-Power Water Hoses to Breach an Israeli Sand Rampart. Courtesy of Embassy of the Arab Republic of Egypt, Washington, D.C.

20   Egyptian Soldiers Transport Heavy Weapons Across the Suez Canal. Courtesy of Embassy of the Arab Republic of Egypt, Washington, D.C.

21   An Israeli Bridge Across the Suez Canal. Courtesy of Israel Press and Photo Agency, Tel Aviv, Israel.

39   Chiang Kai-shek and Wang Ching-wei in Canton, November 1925. Radio Times Hulton Picture Library.

47   The Long March. Eastfoto.

49   Chiang Kai-shek at the Time of the Japanese Invasion of China. Wide World Photos.

54   General George C. Marshall and Mao Tse-tung During Marshall's Visit to China, 1946. Associated Press.

57   Mao Tse-tung With His Army, 1947. Eastfoto.

All other photographs are reprinted courtesy of the U.S. Armed Forces and the U.S. National Archives.

The publisher would like to thank Dr. George Lankevich for the use of his historical library collection, which was the source of much illustrative material. All original artwork was produced by Edward J. Krasnoborski and George Giddings.

Series Editor, Thomas E. Griess
In-House Editor, Joanne Abrams
Cover design by Martin Hochberg

Library of Congress Cataloging-in-Publication Data

Flint, Roy K. (Roy Kenneth), 1928-
  The Arab-Israeli Wars, the Chinese Civil War, and the Korean War.

  Bibliography: p.
  Includes index.
  1. Israel--History, Military. 2. Arab countries--History, Military. 3. China--History--Civil War, 1945-1949. 4. Korean War, 1950-1953. 5. Military art and science--History--20th century. I. Kozumplik, Peter W. II. Waraksa, Thomas J. III. Title.
DS119.2.F56 1987 355.4'2'0904 87-1159
ISBN 0-89529-322-6
ISBN 0-89529-274-2 (pbk.)

10 9 8 7 6 5 4 3 2 1

Printed in the United States of America

Contents

To Thomas E. Griess on the occasion of completing a
contribution unequaled at the United States Military Academy—
the publication of this last volume in his monumental series
on the History of the Military Art

Illustrations

Acknowledgements

In this volume, we have perhaps crossed the frontier between the role of the historian and that of the political scientist in that we have written about reasonably contemporary events without the benefit of the historian's normal cushion of time and reflection. While we do not apologize for this, we realize that even though we did the best that we could with the information at our disposal, the future may provide different interpretations. If such changes should occur, we would welcome them because they would be proof of expanded scholarship and knowledge.

Like all such efforts, this work is the product of many people, all of whom deserve our special thanks for their help, counsel, and tolerance. Unfortunately, space precludes listing all of them here. However, without them, this volume would never have been completed.

We owe a special debt to Thomas E. Griess, not only for his granting us the opportunity to prepare these studies, but also for his guidance, insights, and scholarly criticism, and for his careful, painstaking editing of our efforts. With the publication of this volume, the creation of a series of textbooks on the History of the Military Art is at last complete. Although General Griess would be reluctant to admit it, his efforts over the last 20 years constitute a contribution that exceeds even those of his distinguished predecessors.

Others, also, are deserving of special mention. For our historical training, we are indebted to many distinguished scholars, including Michael Howard of Oxford University, Theodore Ropp and I.B. Holley of Duke University, Russell Weigley and Andrew Hess of Temple University, and Allen Whiting and Ernest Young of the University of Michigan—to name but a few. The fine artwork in this volume is a tribute to the craftsmanship of Mr. Edward Krasnoborski and Mr. George Giddings. Their maps and sketches speak far more eloquently of their talent than could our words. The administrative staff of the Department of History also deserves our special appreciation. In particular, we thank Mrs. Sally French, for her cheerful supervision of our ofttimes awkward requirements; Mrs. Sharen Pacenza, Mrs. Kara Canfield, and Mrs. Mary Arseneault, for typing both proofs and final editions; and Mrs. Mary Monahan O'Mara, for just being there.

Finally, we extend our gratitude to our colleagues in the Department of History, both past and present, for the intellectual ferment that their agile minds provoked. The kind interest and assistance of all these people made this volume possible. However, any errors in fact or interpretation are solely ours.

Roy K. Flint
Peter W. Kozumplik
Thomas J. Waraksa

West Point, New York

Foreword

For over a century, cadets at the United States Military Academy have studied military campaigns and institutions in a course entitled History of the Military Art. Beginning in 1938, that study of history was supported by texts and maps that were prepared by faculty members under the direction of T. Dodson Stamps, who was then head of the Department of Military Art and Engineering. That process has continued to the present time.

Periodically, as new wars have erupted and significant peacetime military developments have occurred, directors of the Military Art course have found it necessary to modify the content of the course in order to include coverage of more recent events. Indeed, judgments regarding the scope of coverage of the numerous military campaigns and developments over the span of history have been among the most difficult decisions made by course directors. That statement is particularly applicable to this text. Through the use of monographs, the Korean War was taught to cadets beginning in 1957, but it was not until 1978 that the cadets began to study the various Arab-Israeli wars. The present text, *The Arab-Israeli Wars, The Chinese Civil War, and The Korean War,* includes treatments of these two military experiences, and provides an account of the Chinese Civil War.

Thus, the text covers some of the armed conflicts that occurred in the quarter of a century following the Second World War. The conflicts, or wars, were selected to illustrate meaningful points in the evolution of warfare. The selection was also based on the conflicts' impact on a changing world. An important omission is an analysis of the American involvement in Vietnam. That clash was not included because the necessary research could not be completed by the time of the publication of this work. Moreover, it is probably desirable to devote a separate text to the war in Vietnam.

The Department of History is indebted to the faculty members who shared in the writing of the text. They per-formed detailed research, designed new supporting maps and modified existing ones, and wrote the narrative.

After a brief explanation of the historical setting, Thomas J. Waraksa examines the series of clashes that has occurred between Arab and Jew since 1945. Waraksa notes those military and political factors that have influenced Israel's fight for statehood, and describes the precarious teetering between war and peace in the Middle East. In an initial editing of the chapter, Stephen D. Wesbrook provided additional insights to the conflict. In the section on the Chinese Civil War, Peter W. Kozumplik shows how, in the fight for control of China, the application of military force could not bring success without an understanding of and attention to the political problem and closely related socioeconomic conditions. In the last two chapters, Roy K. Flint surveys the Korean War and skillfully demonstrates the difficulty Americans experienced in fighting a limited war. At the same time, he provides perceptive insights on generalship and civil-military relationships. As a group, the authors succeed in illustrating how military power, by necessity, has been used differently since 1945 than it was during the earlier part of the twentieth century.

The present edition of *The Arab-Israeli Wars, The Chinese Civil War, and The Korean War* is essentially the text that was printed for use at the Military Academy in 1981. As editor, I have attempted to clarify certain passages for the general reader, amplify purely military terminology, and improve the evenness of the narrative. The editor is grateful for the advice and suggestions that were tendered by Rudy Shur and Joanne Abrams of Avery Publishing Group, Inc. Ms. Abrams immeasurably improved the narrative through her painstaking editing, corrections of lapses in syntax, and penetrating questions related to clarity of expression.

Thomas E. Griess
Series Editor

Introduction

With the end of the Second World War in 1945, the peace for which millions longed did not come to all parts of the world. In some countries, nationalism, which had been excited in the caldron of war, sparked unrest and revolt against old and often tired regimes. In others, factions that had cooperated during the war reverted to sparring with one another for control of the nation, restating old arguments and fostering long-nurtured ambitions in the process. The Cold War, too, had considerable impact upon governments and peoples, contributing to unrest and occasionally leading to the establishment of proxy regimes that could wage war. The Chinese Civil War, the several Arab-Israeli wars, and the Korean War are representative of the type of armed conflict that thrived in the post-World War II setting just described

Although each of the accounts contained in this book deals with the application of military force, the three wars have no direct connection with one another. There are, however, some common themes. One of them is the influence of the Second World War. In Palestine and China, that war provided future contestants with both a training ground and time for the gathering of strength. In Korea, an unsettled issue attributable to the war left the country divided, with each side desiring unification on its own terms. Finally, World War II brought unequal pressures to bear on the two protagonists who would later duel for the control of China, leaving one in a more advantageous position. Another theme is the influence of atomic weapons on these wars, particularly in the Middle East and Korea. At all times, leaders were cognizant of the danger that existed should the restraint upon the application of force be lifted. A third common theme is that each of the wars discussed was either a civil war or contained several elements peculiar to a civil war.

After 1945, nonmilitary elements were of considerable importance in the origin and conduct of regional wars. Political, social, and economic factors reassumed an important place in the fabric of warfare. Although this was partially due to the conditions cited above, it was more a result of the new military and international environment that had been created with the unleashing of the awesome force of the atomic weapon. It was no longer realistic to think of the application of unlimited force—if, indeed, that doctrine had ever been acceptable. Out of this new environment emerged a controlled form of warfare that is largely the subject of this text.

In the following chapters, the wars are not treated in minute detail. The emphasis is on the interrelationship of politics, strategy, and technology. For the Israelis, superior technology formed a three-legged stool along with a highly efficient intelligence system and inspired leadership. Technology was also important to the United States in the Korean War, where it helped counter superior Communist manpower. The idea that the application of force can be tailored to suit political goals is another point that is evident in the following accounts, although it is sometimes muted by emotional judgments. Finally, these accounts demonstrate the strength of the Superpowers. Lurking in the background, but always a potential influencing force, these two powers played a role whose importance has not declined with the passage of time. An understanding of these changes in the military environment is important to an appreciation of how warfare changed after 1945.

The Arab-Israeli Wars

Recurrent Conflict and Elusive Peace: The Arab-Israeli Wars

Since its founding in 1948, the modern State of Israel has been involved almost continuously in war with its Arab neighbors. Despite both a population that is only one-fortieth the size of that of its potential enemies and a vulnerable geographic position (*see Atlas Map No. 1*), Israel has survived in a hostile environment as a result of a remarkable degree of national cohesion, perseverance, and sacrifice, as well as an exceptional record of victory on the battlefield. Military success, however, has not brought Israel a lasting peace. For a variety of complex social, political, and economic reasons, turmoil has been the norm in the Middle East since the end of the Second World War.

The ancient Jewish nation of Israel was conquered by Rome in 63 B.C. and incorporated into the Empire as the province of Palestine. In A.D. 70, the Jewish population revolted against Roman rule. When the revolt was suppressed by Rome's legions, most of the Jewish population was dispersed. Following centuries of exile, during which the Jewish people could only dream of the re-establishment of a homeland in the Middle East, the Jews moved a step toward the realization of that goal when Hirsh Kalishcher financed a Jewish agricultural colony in Palestine in 1869. Other groups followed. By the turn of the century, the World Zionist Congresses had begun sending to Palestine settlers who were eager to escape oppression in Eastern Europe and to help lay the foundation for a future Jewish state.

These initial immigrants attracted little military opposition other than a few raids mounted by Bedouin bands.[1] As Jewish immigration increased after the 1905 "October Revolution" and subsequent pogroms in Russia, however, the number of incidents fomented by Arabs who were angered by Jewish claims to the land also increased. Accordingly, in 1909 the Jews in Palestine formed a local defense force, the *Hashomer* (watchmen), to guard fields and villages.[2] The formation of this organization was the first attempt by the Jews to provide for their own security. (*See Annex A.*)

While the Jews were beginning an organized migration to Palestine, the British were developing a strong interest in the Middle East because of the Suez Canal, which was an important link in the route to their Indian and Far Eastern colonies. In 1882, Great Britain secured controlling interest in the canal, and thereafter its security became a prime concern of British foreign policy. When the Great War began in 1914, the British declared a protectorate over Egypt, essentially to guarantee that security. After the Ottoman Empire entered the war, the British undertook operations against those Turkish troops who occupied Palestine and the Sinai Peninsula. Both Arabs and Jews saw the war as an opportunity to end Turkish rule, and both skirmished with the Turks in Palestine throughout the war. In addition, the legendary T.E. Lawrence organized Arab resistance to support British operations in the region, and many Jews sought service in the British Army's Jewish Brigade. Following the Allied victory over the Central Powers in 1918, the League of Nations granted Great Britain a mandate to rule most of Palestine and the Sinai.[3] France was to administer Syria and Lebanon.

During the war, the British had aroused conflicting hopes in Arabs and Jews. To gain the support of the Arabs, who viewed all of the Middle East as their rightful domain, Great Britain and France agreed to Arab independence, but did not clearly define what that independence entailed or which specific region the Arab nation would occupy. Subsequently, in 1917, Arthur Balfour, the British Foreign Minister, issued the Balfour Declaration, which promised British aid to the Jews in the creation of a "national home" in Palestine, if this could be accomplished without prejudicing the civil and religious rights of the non-Jewish communities in Palestine. Since both Arabs and Jews had supported Great Britain during the war, both quite understandably expected the British to honor their promises upon its end.[4] Herein lay the seed of discontent that would grow into increasingly violent discord between Arab and Jew in later years. This discord hastened the previously slow evolution of a Jewish state and army.

Discontent in Palestine

Troubles began at the close of the First World War, as soon as the British took control of Palestine. There, the early 1920s were marked by riots, terrorism, and reprisals, as Zionism, with its demand for increased Jewish immigration, clashed with a burgeoning Arab nationalism. The two things the Arabs and Jews had in common were a claim to Palestine and a distrust of the British, who were either unable or unwilling to interpose themselves between the warring factions.[5] The *Hashomer,* which totaled about 100 men, was ineffective against Arab militants. Accordingly, in 1920, the Jewish community in Palestine established the *Haganah* (defense), a military organization created to protect settlements against Arab terrorism. (*See Annex A.*) The *Haganah* was a national force under central control. The Jews now had a unified defense force.[6]

Because the British were unable to maintain peace in the region, the *Haganah* proved invaluable to the Jews. Nevertheless, the Arab riots during the 1920s and late 1930s forced the British to provide limited security assistance to the Jews. In the latter period, the British organized the

Jewish Settlement Police (JSP) to protect the Jewish community. The JSP was armed and paid by the British, and many *Haganah* members served in it on a rotating basis, thus gaining valuable military experience.[7] During the riots, the Jews also increased the size and scope of their many local forces. (*See Annex A.*) With England's publication of the pro-Arab White Paper of May 1939, however, British-Jewish cooperation ceased, and the JSP was eliminated. The White Paper—which, in anticipation of the coming war, attempted to align the Arabs with the British—froze the size of the Jewish establishment in Palestine and envisaged the eventual creation of an independent State of Palestine with an Arab majority. Thus, it imposed severe restrictions on Jewish immigration and land purchases in an effort to maintain the now precarious religious and political balance in Palestine. From the Jewish perspective, the timing of these restrictions could not have been worse. A few months later, when the Second World War began in Europe, Hitler's persecution of the Jews increased, intensifying the need for a national refuge.[8]

The defense capability of the Jewish community in Palestine improved substantially during the late 1930s. The most important development was the creation of an embryonic general staff and general headquarters. Staffed by full-time officers and financed by the labor parties, the general headquarters controlled the development and deployment of *Haganah* forces. The *Haganah* grew into a more organized force, but it lacked adequate weapons, manpower, and experienced leadership. Although individual soldiers were adequately trained, large-scale exercises could not be held because of British opposition. Moreover, the *Haganah* could not control the various splinter groups that were conducting a terrorist campaign against the British.[9] (*See Annex A.*)

David Ben-Gurion set the tone for Palestinian Jewish participation in the Second World War when he said: "We will fight the 'white paper' as if there was no Germany and we will fight Germans as if there was no 'white paper'."[10] The Jews were divided on the extent of their commitment, however. If too many men joined the British, few would be left to defend the settlements. On the other hand, active Jewish support of Great Britain would result in large numbers of Jews receiving military training, and would make the British indebted to the Jewish community after the war. During the conflict, Palestine provided the British with over 30,000 Jewish troops.[11]

Erwin Rommel's early successes in North Africa, and the threat he posed to Egypt and Palestine, forced the British to cooperate officially with the *Haganah*. That cooperation continued until Rommel was forced to retreat

Early Members of the *Hashomer*

An Attempt to Restrict Movement in Jerusalem, 1947-1949

from Egypt in 1942. The threat of a German invasion of Palestine also forced the Jews to begin to convert their guerrilla-oriented force into a more conventional organization, and to plan for the defense of Palestine.[12]

The support the Jews gave the British in Palestine during World War II ended when the Germans surrendered. At that time, the *Haganah* and its splinter groups —the *Irgun Zvai Leumi* (IZL) and the Stern gang— began to harass and attack British troops and installations and to prepare for an eventual clash with either the Arabs or the British.[13] In 1946, the British again severely restricted immigration and rushed almost 100,000 soldiers to Palestine to restore order. Unable to control either Jewish acts of terrorism committed against British troops or the fighting between Palestinian Arabs and Jews, the British Government requested that the United Nations remove the British mandate and divide Palestine between Arabs and Jews. Inevitably, the two groups began to prepare for war.

In 1947, the *Haganah* contained almost 50,000 men; however, its full-time strike force numbered only 3,000. Anticipating a prompt termination of the mandate and recognizing that guerrilla organization and tactics would no longer suffice, the Jews began to create a more conventionally organized and professional army.[14]

The armies of the Arab States encircling Palestine were in a poor state of readiness. Egypt had a large army, but it lacked combat experience, had obsolete equipment, and was poorly led. Moreover, in any clash with the Jews it would be forced to fight at the end of a long and vulnerable line of communication that extended across the Sinai. Syria and Lebanon had just gained their independence from France and were still in the process of upgrading

their colonial police forces into armies. The Arab League's Arab Liberation Army* was not much more than an unorganized guerrilla band. The Jordanian Arab Legion, which numbered about 7,400 men and was partly commanded by British officers, was the only Arab force prepared for combat. The Legion was an elite force with a long history of success.[15]

1948—The War of Independence

Israel's War of Independence began with the signing of the United Nations resolution on Palestine and continued for over a year, until the belligerents signed armistices. This war, the longest of the four major conflicts between the

*The Arab League, composed of Egypt, Iraq, Lebanon, Syria, Transjordan, Saudi Arabia, and Yemen, formed an irregular force to oppose the Jews. The formation of this force—the Arab Liberation Army—was the main unified action of the Arab League.

David Ben-Gurion Proclaims the Rebirth of Israel, May 14, 1948

Arabs and the Jews, can be broken into four phases. The first phase, which began on November 30, 1947 when Great Britain began to withdraw its military forces, consisted of Arab attacks on isolated Jewish communities in the eastern part of Palestine and Jewish attacks on Arab districts in the coastal areas. The Jews were at a disadvantage during this phase because the British, who controlled the coastal ports and dominated the Mediterranean Sea, would not allow any immigrants or arms into the country. The Palestinian Arabs, on the other hand, received arms from their Arab neighbors across the lightly defended land borders. While the guerrillas and small bands were active, the neighboring Arab armies prepared for the onslaught that would be triggered when Israel declared its independence on May 14, 1948.[16]

The invasions of Israel by Jordan, Iraq, Syria, Lebanon, and the Arab Liberation Army marked the beginning of phase two. (*See Atlas Map No. 2.*) The Arabs felt that their regular armies could easily destroy Israel. Because they no longer faced fragmented Jewish defense groups, however, they were destined to be surprised. With the birth of Israel and the formal establishment of the Israeli Defense Force (IDF) on May 26, the various splinter groups joined the IDF and, like the *Haganah* forces, began to lose their old identities as uniforms, ranks, and other accouterments of a regular army were introduced. As the formative

After a United Nations-Imposed Cease-Fire Brings an End to the War of Independence, Moshe Dayan *(with eye patch)* **and Abdullah Tell** *(with back to camera)* **Set the Cease-Fire Lines**

days of the IDF drew to a close, the small forces that defended the settlements completed their evolution during a war to which there was "no alternative."[17]

During this second phase, the IDF organized itself into 12 mobile brigades and reacted to all major threats. The settlements provided strongpoints that effectively delayed many of the Arab advances and permitted the Israelis to make good use of their central position by shifting IDF mobile brigades to stop all the major attacks.[18] The Israelis generally made night attacks in order to offset their lack of firepower and to exploit the Arabs' lack of night-fighting experience. Neither side achieved any major victories. Exhausted and in need of time to reorganize and resupply, Arabs and Jews accepted the United Nations 30-day cease-fire on June 11.[19] The second phase had lasted only 27 days, but the Israelis had been severely tested. They were close to defeat when the cease-fire became effective.

During the cease-fire, both sides made preparations to continue the war. The Arabs emphasized the acquisition of additional weapons and manpower, hoping to launch another offensive and push the Israelis into the Mediterranean.[20] The Israelis, no longer under British restriction, intensified their efforts to bring arms and immigrants into the country. They also were able to strengthen the IDF's organization by eliminating the IZL and Stern gang completely.[21] After analyzing the IDF's activities during the first two phases, the General Staff decided to capitalize on Israel's central position by quickly shifting rearmed and better trained troops to those areas from which offensives could most effectively be launched. No longer would the Israelis rely principally upon the defense. They now realized that they would have to attack in order to consolidate the threatened Jewish settlements.

Capitalizing on their experience in night operations, the Israelis planned a midnight offensive at the end of the cease-fire in order to pre-empt the Arab attack that was expected at dawn. The night attacks of July 11 opened the third phase of the fighting and caused the Arab armies to fall back in confusion. The Israelis were successful on all fronts, gaining substantial territory and almost capturing Jerusalem. (*Actions not shown on maps.*) The Arabs, suffering a serious setback, were embarrassed, but not beaten. Agreeing to a second United Nations cease-fire, they quickly commenced extensive guerrilla operations.

The fourth and final phase of fighting began in October and continued until armistices were signed among the belligerents. The Israeli goal during the October battles was to connect the various Jewish enclaves and consolidate the territory that had been allocated to Israel when the British mandate ended. (*See Atlas Map No. 3.*) Although Jerusalem remained divided, the Israeli attacks were generally successful.[22] The IDF continued to gain experience and gradually developed the capability to plan more sophisticated operations. One of the most successful was Operation AYIN,* which was conducted from December 22, 1948 to January 7, 1949. (*See Atlas Map No. 4.*) The objective of AYIN was to clear the Gaza Strip † by penetrating between the Egyptian forces guarding the roads, thus isolating the strip so that it could be attacked from the rear. The Israelis planned to use the same Roman road that Sir Edmund Allenby had used in his attack on Gaza in 1917. The IDF launched a secondary attack toward the Gaza-Rafah road after an air and artillery preparation, fixing the Egyptians. Meanwhile, the main force of light mobile units moved down the old Roman way and cut the Bir Asluj-Auja road. The mobile force then overran a series of strongholds, blocked the Rafah-Auja road, captured Abu Ageila, and moved to El Arish, where the force was halted when the British threatened intervention. The IDF withdrew from Sinai, but its success increased the pressure on the Egyptians and forced them to ask for an armistice.[23]

At the end of hostilities, over 750,000 Arab refugees were scattered throughout the Middle East. These refugees were unable or unwilling to return to their Palestinian homeland. Thus the Israeli military victory helped to create a political problem that would prove to be one of the greatest threats to the new nation's long-term security.

A New Nation Builds an Army

In the aftermath of the war, there was little euphoria in Israel. The fighting had been hard, and the business of building a nation and army was about to begin. General Yigal Yadin, the Chief of Staff from 1949 to 1952, faced serious problems as he tried to maintain a viable military force during the early 1950s. His first constraint was budgetary. Israel's population doubled between 1949 and 1952, placing a severe burden on the weak economy. There was little money for military salaries, research, weapons, and spare parts. Manpower was not a problem, since universal military conscription for men and women had been adopted in 1949. The quality of the conscripts and the training, however, was low. Many of the immigrants drafted into the IDF barely knew Hebrew, and few had any military experience. Moreover, many of the more capable officers, who otherwise could have trained these recruits, had left the Army and were involved in building the State of Israel or in private business.[24]

Recognizing these limitations, David Ben-Gurion, who served as both Prime Minister and Defense Minister, approved the IDF's plan for an in-depth reserve system organized along Swiss lines. This plan merged the ideas of the Israeli defensive organization and the Swiss-style local reserve system. The IDF would have a small standing army of regular formations composed of career officers, career non commissioned officers, and conscripts. The remainder of the IDF would be composed of reservists organized into units that could be ready for combat within 72 hours. All reservists would first serve a term in the standing army, and thereafter maintain their proficiency through frequent active duty tours with their reserve units.

The IDF initially concentrated on training, and paid little attention to the numerous raids that the Arabs made across the borders. Coping with these raids was a function of the police; moreover, Jewish settlements had been fortified to safeguard the border against the raids. Despite these measures, Arab raids increased after 1949 and were the direct cause of the death of over 100 Israeli citizens each year.[25] As the Arab governments gave greater support to the Palestinian guerrilla groups, the frontier settlements and the small border guards became less able to deal with these raids. With better weapons and equipment, these guerrillas began to increase not only the strength and frequency of their raids, but also the effectiveness. As a consequence, the IDF commenced reprisal raids against the *Fedayeen* (self-sacrificers). The inability of the Israelis to deal with this type of threat, however, became apparent in unsuccessful raids against Arab police stations and training centers just across the border. Israeli units frequently became lost in the dark, and some refused to close with the enemy. When the Israelis lost 27 soldiers in an attempt to dislodge a small group of Syrians holding a hill near Tel Mutilla in May 1951, it became obvious that a change was required.[26]

Reform began with a directive to Brigadier General Ariel Sharon to form an elite force of soldiers to act as a special strike group. Sharon's "Unit 101," which was later reorganized as the 202nd Paratroop Brigade, revived the traditional *Haganah* skill of night fighting, stressed aggressiveness, and carried out numerous successful operations across the borders. Despite the success of "Unit 101," the IDF was still in poor shape when General Moshe Dayan was appointed Chief of Staff in December 1953 and given a mandate to make sweeping reforms. Dayan replaced many young British-trained officers with older officers and soldiers with whom he had served personally.

---

*Some analysts refer to this Israeli attack as Operation HOREV.

†The Gaza Strip is the name given to the narrow section of land that lies between Gaza and Rafah in one direction, and between the sea and the Israeli-Egyptian border in the other direction. In 1948, the Gaza Strip was under Egyptian control.

Yadin had emphasized "spit and polish" and outward appearances; Dayan's emphasis was on training for combat. The infantry focused on aggressive assault techniques while the small armored corps devised its own set of tactics. Techniques were improved during large-scale maneuvers, and training was reinforced by large retaliatory raids against Palestinian guerrilla camps and other Arab military installations. Despite these improvements, the raids became stereotyped. An Israeli reprisal raid against the Jordanian Kalkilia police fortress in 1956 resulted in 60 Israeli casualties when the IDF assault force was surrounded and the relieving force ambushed. This failure focused the attention of both the public and the military leadership on the shortcomings of night reprisal raids. The public deplored the high casualty rates associated with the raids. Military leaders realized that the raids produced uncertain benefits and, because of their repetitive tactics, were being anticipated by the Arabs.[27]

Meanwhile, the overall situation in the Middle East had become increasingly unstable. Russia, using Czechoslovakia as an agent, pumped arms into Syria and Egypt. Late in 1955, Egypt closed the Strait of Tiran to Israel-bound shipping; in September 1956, it declared a state of war against Israel. In Syria, the nationalist Ba'athists took control of the government in a coup and stepped up raids on Israel from the Golan Heights. With Syria and Egypt becoming better armed each day, Israel felt that it had to act quickly before developments got out of control and could no longer be influenced in Israel's favor.[28]

1956—Seven Days in Sinai

In 1956, Egypt nationalized and seized the Suez Canal, thus provoking the British and French to use military force to recover it. Through the French, Dayan learned of a planned Anglo-French attack on Egypt and offered Israeli assistance. In return, the French furnished the IDF with desperately needed weapons and equipment. With war materiel on the way, Dayan planned a seven-to-ten-day conquest of Sinai that he believed would succeed if he could reduce the number of troops normally deployed on the Syrian and Jordanian borders. An elaborate cover plan was devised to complement the impending joint attack on Egypt. Dayan called up reservists for a "massive raid" against Jordan. Initial mobilization was thus completed without alerting the Egyptians to Israeli intentions; total mobilization, therefore, could be delayed until the last possible minute. A small raid, which drew a sharp

warning from the United States,* was in fact carried out against Jordan to further mislead the Arabs as to Israeli intentions.[29]

The IDF invasion plan consisted of three phases. In the first phase, the Israelis intended to use airborne troops to block the Mitla Pass while simultaneously attacking toward Kusseima, Kuntilla, and Nakeb to divert attention from the routes across northern Sinai. (*See Atlas Map No. 5.*) These assaults were designed to appear to be raids, in the hope that they would delay a massive reaction by the Egyptians. If the Anglo-French force failed to attack the Suez Canal on schedule, the Israelis could withdraw and claim the attacks were, in fact, only raids. The second phase involved the capture of Sharm el Sheikh and the isolation of the Gaza Strip by an armored force attacking along the Kusseima-Abu Ageila-El Arish axis; mobile units would then rapidly advance and form a defensive line along the Suez Canal. The final phase would involve defeating the strong Egyptian forces in the Gaza Strip. The plan worked almost to perfection.

The Sinai Campaign began on October 29 with the drop of a battalion of Sharon's 202nd Paratroop Brigade at the eastern end of the Mitla Pass. Simultaneously, the 4th Infantry Brigade, the remainder of the 202nd Paratroop

---

*Israel's mobilization was known to the United States, and, like the Egyptians, President Dwight D. Eisenhower believed that the calling up of reservists was in preparation for an Israeli attack on Jordan. Since 1950, it had been United States policy to support a peaceful and moderate approach in an attempt to secure the territorial integrity of the states of the Middle East. In his warning note, therefore, the President made it clear that the United States was opposed to any military action on the part of Israel, that he wanted mobilization stopped, and that an Israeli use of force could endanger the growing friendship between the two countries.

Debris in the Mitla Pass, 1956

Brigade, and elements of the 9th Infantry Brigade launched successful attacks against the phase one objectives. (*See Atlas Map No. 5.*) The success of the attack on Kusseima caused the commander of Southern Command to launch the 7th Armored Brigade and 10th Infantry Brigade into their phase two attacks a day early. Although Dayan was infuriated, he allowed these units to continue forward, commenting that he would rather "be engaged in restraining the noble stallion than in prodding the reluctant mule." The remainder of Sharon's paratroops linked up with the airhead on October 30. By dusk on that same date, the Israeli 7th Armored had taken Umm Gataf, turned Abu Ageila (which surrendered the next day), and was preparing to race to the passes. Meanwhile, the Anglo-French invasion force had not yet made its airdrop or landings near the canal. The Israelis prepared to take Sinai alone.

During the remainder of the campaign, Israeli forces raced toward the Suez Canal. (*See Atlas Map. No. 6.*) After the 1st Infantry Brigade and elements of the 27th Mechanized Brigade took Rafah on October 1, the 27th Mechanized Brigade advanced along the northern route toward El Arish and then to the canal. After the 7th Armored Brigade took Abu Ageila, it turned west and attacked along the road to Ismailia. The paratroops, disobeying orders to remain east of the Mitla Pass, assailed the pass; heavy casualties were sustained from Egyptian air attacks and a well-laid ambush. Finally breaking through on November 1, they moved southwest, first toward Ras Sudar and later toward Sharm el Sheikh, which the 9th Infantry Brigade was also approaching from the northeast. The Israeli capture of the city on November 5 coincided with the Anglo-French airborne drop and ended the Israeli part of the campaign. The British amphibious assault on November 6, followed by an advance to Quantara, brought the Sinai Campaign to a close.

The Israeli tactical victory that resulted from the speed, audacity, and mobility of the IDF was largely negated by a strategic political error. The Israelis misjudged the mood of the United States, which joined Russia in demanding that Israel, Great Britain, and France evacuate Egyptian territory. Reluctantly, the three complied, and a UN force was established to patrol the border between Egypt and Israel. Although the Egyptian Army had been soundly defeated, Egyptian President Gamal Abdul Nasser was able to claim a political victory. The war, in short, accomplished nothing for the Israelis, who had the military strength to achieve their goals, but not the political support to retain them. All the fundamental causes of the war remained; both Arabs and Israelis knew that another fight was inevitable.

Lessons and Policy: Israel Prepares for War

The Israeli General Staff reviewed the Sinai Campaign, which is often called the "100 Hour War," in a way that might have led uninformed observers to believe that the IDF had been defeated. They not only critiqued military problems, but also began to develop a new military-political doctrine.

A number of important problem areas were identified by the General Staff's exhaustive study of the Sinai Campaign. First, the rapid mobilization of the reserves had been handled poorly. Efficient use of the reserves demanded major changes in notification schedules and the location of equipment stockpiles. Second, Israel found that its allies had not acted as planned after the opening of hostilities. In the future, the small country would have to be prepared to plan and implement military operations without the support of other powers. Third, weapons and other military supplies would have to be stockpiled in Israel before the war, since external events might prevent or delay their delivery. Fourth, the ground support and air superiority roles required an all-fighter air force. The Israeli Air Force (IAF) claimed that it could defend the cities against air attack, and would do even better if equipped with proper aircraft. Fifth, although infantry units were favored for economic reasons, the armored thrusts had achieved spectacular successes and resulted in fewer casualties and a shorter campaign. The IDF therefore decided to increase its tactical emphasis on the use of armored formations. Sixth, the tactical supply system had been shown to be of critical importance in the support of the unexpectedly rapid movements. If the ground elements were to become more mechanized and armored, it would be necessary to move supplies forward more rapidly. A more effective military utilization of civilian vehicles during mobilization would alleviate some of the troubles, and the vehicles would have to be properly maintained to meet mobilization requirements. Seventh, problems in command and control had surfaced. Under Israeli doctrine, commanders had great flexibility in accomplishing their specific missions and authority to continue to advance and attack if success was possible without excessive losses. In Sinai, however, commanders had not been prepared to control troops over vast distances. Radio contact between combat units and support units had often been impossible, even though FM frequencies had not been jammed by the Egyptians. Radios and radio procedures required improvement to facilitate effective command. Finally, it had been made abundantly clear that both an efficient gathering of intelligence and the use of radar systems to obtain early warning of pending events were necessary to permit adequate time for mobilization.[30]

To a nation already financially strained, the cost of these changes was great. Two examples illustrate how Israel used various techniques to economize on its military budget. The Israeli Air Force had made an excellent case for purchasing new aircraft. Tanks could be rebuilt, but there was no way to convert a propeller-driven aircraft into a jet that could handle the MiGs that Russia was sending to Egypt. Although expensive, high-performance aircraft were needed, the air force leaders were prepared to make concessions. They felt that bombers were not necessary due to the lack of strategic targets, and that the number of transports could be kept to a minimum. For armament, the Israelis chose guns instead of missiles. Gun ammunition was less expensive and more readily available. Moreover, "gun fights" generally took place at slower speeds, giving Israeli pilots a tremendous advantage over their opponents because of their country's superior pilot-selection and training procedures. Finally, the Israelis equipped their new aircraft with electronic countermeasure devices ("black boxes"), which could emit signals that would mislead the Soviet missiles that they expected to face.

A second example of Israel's efforts to economize involves the armored corps, which quickly saw that it would rank behind the Air Force in procurement priority. Be-

cause of an inability to obtain new tanks, the tankers bought and completely rebuilt old tanks. Old World War II Shermans were converted to "Super Shermans" with the addition of a low-velocity French 105-mm gun and a modern diesel engine designed for desert warfare. Pattons, Centurions, and captured Soviet tanks also were modified to accommodate desert conditions. In this way, the Israelis were able to produce three or four excellent combat tanks for the cost of one new tank.[31]

The Israeli defense policy that evolved after the Sinai Campaign was adapted to Israel's precarious political and geographic position and its limited resources.[32] The policy can be viewed in four parts. First, peace was desired, but not if it would leave Israel defenseless. Security was Israel's primary concern. Second, in the event of war, Israel had to be prepared to win without outside aid, even in a situation in which it was fighting all its enemies simultaneously. Third, because of its geopolitical position, Israel could not afford to lose a single major battle; such a defeat could mean the loss of a war and the demise of the country. Fourth, although prepared to fight alone, Israel would seek the support or sympathy of the United States to neutralize opposing major powers.[33]

Another tenet of Israeli policy was to emphasize the credibility of the military threat to potential enemies and thereby hopefully prevent war. The defense force that Israel hoped would cow the Arabs was dependent upon the guarantee of sufficient time for full mobilization. To secure that time, the Israelis had to have early warning of a developing threat; an air force to defend the populated areas and to carry the war to the enemy; and a standing force of sufficient strength to gain time by attacking, not trading space.[34] To lend further credibility to their willingness to use force, the Israelis developed and announced certain *casus belli* after which they would consider launching an offensive against a potential opponent. The first and most obvious concern was a threatening massive buildup of Arab forces on one or more of Israel's vulnerable borders. Second was the closing of the Strait of Tiran, the entrance to the Gulf of Aqaba and the Israeli port city of Elath. The third cause, and a reason for many of the Israeli punitive raids, was a high level of guerrilla activity that could not be eliminated by passive defense or selective reprisals. Israel held the host country responsible for raids launched by Palestinian guerrillas from within its borders. Fourth was the preparation for or an air attack on either IAF bases or Israel's scientific or nuclear installations. Fifth was the entry of Jordan into a military pact that permitted the massing of Arab forces on the strategically important West Bank, or an Arab attempt to take over the governments of Lebanon or Jordan, with whom Israel had

An Israeli 155-mm Howitzer Made From a Sherman Chassis and an Imported Gun Assembly

acceptable relations. Sixth was an unbalanced supply of arms to the Arabs. This, in fact, had been a major cause of the 1956 Sinai Campaign. The Israelis were very careful to state, however, that there was no established threshold before which Israel would not strike.[35]

The key element of Israeli military policy was the maintenance of Israel's territorial integrity. If the Israelis felt endangered, they were determined to launch a strategic pre-emptive strike.* They maintained such an offensive orientation for several reasons. First, Israel's geo-strategic situation demanded that the war be fought on enemy territory. Moreover, because of the international situation, the Israelis believed that they would have to defeat the enemy military forces on the enemy's own soil quickly and before the Superpowers could intervene through the UN and establish new boundaries. This, in turn, meant maintaining the initiative and dictating the terms of battle. They planned to fight on all fronts simultaneously while concentrating upon eliminating the strongest opponent first. In summary, the goal was to maintain a strong and intimidating system of defense that would deter, if not prevent, Arab military initiatives of any great significance.[36]

The Road to War

Israel's military-political doctrine had a major influence on the events that led to the 1967 Arab-Israeli War. The first incident of significance began with an Israeli plan to destroy a guerrilla command post in the Jordanian town of Es Samu. The raid resulted in the death of 72 Jordanians in November 1966. Consequently, the Syrians, who had trained, paid, and equipped the guerrillas, began to increase the shelling and harassing of Israeli settlements in upper Galilee. After a period of inaction, the Israeli Government responded with an air attack of Syrian artillery positions on April 7, 1967. The IAF pilots downed six of the MiG-21s sent to oppose them.[37]

Events escalated rapidly after the April 7 dogfight. On May 14, Nasser warned Syria that Israel had initiated a partial mobilization; by May 27, all the Arab nations had pledged support for any member attacked by Israel. Although the Arabs appeared unified and prepared, problems existed within the coalition. The Syrian Army, more a political than a military force, was not ready to resist or make a serious attack. The well-supplied Egyptian Army was busy in Yemen, and relationships between the Egyp-

tians, Syrians, and Jordanians were less than cordial.[38] Each country tried to become the leader against Israel, but Egypt had the combat power.

On May 16, the Egyptians asked the United Nations Emergency Force in Sinai to withdraw from certain border areas, and after much discussion the entire peace-keeping force was withdrawn on May 23. As it departed, the Egyptian forces at Sharm el Sheikh closed the Strait of Tiran. Two days later, the Egyptian Foreign Minister announced that the entry of an Israeli ship into Egyptian territorial waters would be considered an act of aggression. Israel and Egypt began partial mobilization on May 21.[39] Nasser's brinkmanship policy continued as he led the aroused Arab people along a now precarious path. As the coming war would dramatically demonstrate, the Egyptian President had failed to assess Israel's military power accurately.

A week after the closing of the strait, other serious events developed. Seven Egyptian divisions, two of them armored, were moved into advanced defensive positions in the Sinai. (*See Atlas Map No. 7.*) The Israelis, however, were more concerned about a meeting that was held between King Hussein of Jordan and President Nasser. Despite personal misgivings, Hussein signed a military pact with Nasser that put Jordanian troops under Egyptian command. By June 4, Iraq had joined the pact, and Iraqi and Egyptian troops were on Jordanian soil.[40] Israel's concern was heightened by the shelling of Israeli settlements from the Golan Heights and Gaza and by increased Egyptian air activity in Sinai.

After much discussion, increased mobilization, and the formation of a government of national unity, which included Moshe Dayan as Defense Minister, Israel decided to attack. The economic and political costs of the two-week mobilization were high, but demobilization, it was feared, would be viewed as a sign of weakness. The Arabs were getting stronger and more aggressive every day; the Israelis would strike.[41]

1967—The Six Day War

The war started at 7:45 a.m. on June 5 when Israeli aircraft, flying at low altitude across the Mediterranean to avoid detection by radar, caught 11 Egyptian airfields unprepared minutes after the end of the Egyptian dawn alert. Within the next few hours, the Israeli planes destroyed the Egyptian Air Force on the ground, demonstrating such high efficiency that Nasser claimed the IAF was being aided by American and British aircraft.[42] Although

---

*A strategic pre-emptive strike is an aggressive military attack made so as to secure an advantage in the face of an enemy buildup of strength and a likely strike.

warned, the Jordanian, Syrian, and Iraqi Air Forces suffered the same fate later in the day. With the fear of air attack on Israeli cities and troop concentrations eliminated, Brigadier General Mordechai Hod could now divert his fighters to support the IDF's armored thrusts. The IAF's stunning achievements in the first few hours of the campaign had greatly increased Israel's chance of ultimate success.

In the second phase of the war, Israel hoped to defeat the Egyptian, Jordanian, and Syrian armies in turn, using its central position* much as Frederick the Great had used his during the Seven Years' War, when he faced the Russians, Austrians, and French. Major General Yitzhak Rabin planned to initially deploy minimum forces opposite the Syrians and Jordanians and concentrate most of his 220,000-man force against the Egyptians in Sinai. Hoping to defeat the Egyptians rapidly and then turn to whatever threat developed on the other fronts, he massed three armored divisions and two brigades for the attack in Sinai. Rabin intended to slash through the strong Egyptian fortifications near the border and then rush to the Rumani-Bir Gifgafa-Bir Gidy-Mitla Pass line. Here, the IDF would destroy the Egyptian forces as they withdrew along the roads to the passes. Finally, Rabin would secure the canal. (*See Atlas Map No. 7.*) If the Jordanians and Syrians remained on the defensive, this bold plan could succeed.

The ground war would be a test of Israel's newly developed tactical doctrine. That doctrine provided only guidelines for tactical operations, thus leaving field commanders great flexibility. The emphasis was on initiative at all levels and on the accomplishment of the mission. Consequently, strong leadership was required at the middle and lower levels of command. The most important principle of the doctrine was that losses and casualties must be minimized in any possible way without endangering victory; usually, this would be achieved through surprise, speed, and superior firepower.

Brigadier General Yeshayahu Gavish had the task of rupturing Egypt's hardened defensive line, destroying the 7 divisions and 900 tanks positioned there, and then reaching and holding a line at the Suez Canal. He had about 50,000 men and 800 tanks to use in accomplishing this mission. Gavish's plan was to first make two penetrations and then rush armored columns through to the passes and the canal. He massed his divisions for the strike in the north and positioned an independent brigade in the Negev, near Kuntilla, assigning it the mission of misleading the

The Resupply of Rapidly Advancing Israeli Columns

Egyptian 6th Infantry and Shazali Armored Divisions into believing that an attack would come from that area.

Brigadier General Israel Tal's division, composed of armored school instructors and their students, was ordered to attack along the northern route across Sinai. He faced two entrenched divisions supported by strong armored forces. (*See Atlas Map No. 7.*) Tal opened his attack on June 5 by slashing to the coast at Khan Yunis and isolating the Egyptian 20th Infantry Division in the Gaza Strip. He then turned west and attacked and captured Rafah. Rushing through the hedgehog† defenses at Jerardi, Tal was at the outskirts of El Arish by nightfall. During the night, one of Tal's platoons slipped through El Arish and turned the position, which surrendered the next morning after a short and bloody battle. From El Arish, Tal sent a brigade west on the northern route and moved the rest of his division south to Jebel Libni. He then moved west to secure the Bir Gifgafa Pass, which he reached after winning several tank battles. (*See Atlas Map No. 8.*) Tal's division finally arrived at the canal opposite Ismailia on the evening of June 8.

Forty miles to the south of Tal's force, Brigadier General Sharon's armored division had the task of breaking through at Abu Ageila, which was guarded by the Umm Gataf hedgehog—the strongest in Sinai. (*See Atlas Map*

*A force or a nation occupies a central position relative to *several* enemy forces or nations when it is located at the center of an approximate circle while the opposing forces or nations lie at great distances from one another, along the perimeter of the circle.

†A hedgehog position is one that can be defended in all directions. Its trace is thus circular in nature. Egyptian hedgehogs had numerous concrete emplacements, minefields, and reinforced bunkers. The hedgehog at Jerardi was six miles deep and was supposedly unflankable.

No. 7.) In spite of Rabin's reservations, Sharon decided to make a night attack, using four converging forces and a helicopter-borne force to surround the hedgehog. The attack began early on June 6, and by 4:00 a.m. the bulk of Sharon's force was in the vicinity of Abu Ageila. His gamble had paid off. Gavish, who was on the spot, then directed Sharon's division to move south to Nakhl. (*See Atlas Map No. 8.*) Arriving there ahead of the Egyptians after a movement over difficult terrain, Sharon set up a divisional ambush that, with the help of the Independent Brigade and the IAF, virtually destroyed a 20-mile-long Egyptian column that stretched from Nakhl toward Thamad.

Brigadier General Avraham Yoffe's division initially had a reserve role. After Sharon cleared Umm Gataf, Yoffe was ordered to take Jebel Libni, which he cleared prior to the arrival of Tal's division. (*See Atlas Map No. 7.*) Gavish then sent Tal west and Yoffe southwest to take the Bir Gidy and Mitla Passes, thereby sealing off all withdrawal routes. (*See Atlas Map No. 8.*) The withdrawing Egyptians fought well, using minefields skillfully and delaying stubbornly, but Yoffe, despite a lack of fuel, kept pushing his dangerously dispersed columns onward. Because the IAF alone could not close the passes, they had to be taken by ground forces. When darkness came on June 7, Lieutenant Colonel Avraham Bar-Am, the commander of the lead battalion, had only a 105-mm artillery battery, some infantry, and nine Centurion tanks—four of which were being towed. His small force fell in with the retreating Egyptians. As this group approached the defile, Bar-Am pulled his men off to a position called "Custer Ring," where they were able to block the Mitla Pass despite numerous Egyptian counterattacks. On June 8, Yoffe had both passes secured, and forces positioned at the canal. Tal's forces, too, were at the canal. The Egyptian army in Sinai was now cut off. The capture of Sharm el Sheikh by naval forces on June 7 was anticlimactic. As mopping up operations began in Sinai, the IDF used its central position to shift forces to the north.

Brigadier General Uzi Narkis, commanding the Central Command, was unhappy with his role. (*See Atlas Map No. 9.*) Jordan was expected to do little more than make a face-saving effort; the real fighting would be in Sinai. Even the Northern Command would probably see more action against Syria than Narkis would against Jordan—at least that was what intelligence agencies expected. They were wrong. King Hussein intended to honor his agreements, and Narkis would have his fight.

Before noon on June 5, Jordan entered the fray. To seize the initiative, Narkis immediately counterattacked in Jerusalem itself, and ordered Colonel Uri Ben-Ari, hero of Abu Ageila in 1956, to move his brigade of armor forward

from an assembly area near Tel Aviv. He told Ben-Ari to be astride the key terrain north of Jerusalem by next dawn. Ben-Ari knew the ground; as a captain in 1948, he had attacked in the same place. Working in darkness, he moved his Centurions and Shermans over enemy-held terrain that was supposedly impassable to tanks. As the sun rose, Ben-Ari stood on the Jerusalem-Ramallah road and looked down at the West Bank below him. In the meantime, an armored unit from the Northern Command overran Jenin and halted the artillery fire that had been harassing the airbase at Megiddo. By sunset of the second day of fighting, Israel had gained control of Jerusalem and the key ground on both shoulders of King Hussein's salient west of the Jordan River. On June 7, Narkis closed armored pincers at Nablus, seized the bridges over the River Jordan, raced south from Jerusalem to Hebron, and in the process completed the defeat of Jordan's army, the old Arab Legion. On that day, the flag of Israel was raised over the Strait of Tiran, the western defiles in Sinai were occupied, the walls of Jericho were breached to the accompaniment of blaring trumpets, and Narkis prayed at the Wailing Wall in Jewish-occupied Jerusalem. It had been less than three

Generals Narkis, Dayan, and Rabin in Jerusalem, June 1967

Looking Down Into Israel From the Golan Heights

days since Mordechai Hod's IAF had caught Egypt's Air Force on the ground.

After the defeat of Egypt and Jordan, the Israelis moved against Syria, the most outspoken and antagonistic of Israel's neighbors. From the beginning of hostilities, the farmland below the dominant Golan Heights had suffered from Syrian artillery shelling and raids, but no major Syrian attack had been launched. This failure to take the offensive would soon haunt Syria, whose inactivity had allowed Brigadier General David Elazar to shift a brigade south to help cut off the West Bank. Now Rabin was able to send Elazar reinforcements from the Sinai and West Bank. On June 8, the IAF joined artillery units in pummeling the reinforced concrete emplacements, underground installations, and tunnels composing the Maginot-style* fortresses on the steep Golan Heights. (*See Atlas Map No. 10.*) The Israeli offensive began before noon on June 9 with an assault on the fortress of Tel Fahar. Making the attack were two infantry brigades augmented by bulldozers, which were used to clear a path up the heights. The terrain forced the units to move virtually in single file under intense enemy fire. As one battalion became ineffective, another moved forward. Finally, the fort fell. Additional attacks were launched at Godot and Harab.

On June 10, Israeli forces pushed on to Quneitra (Syrian Army Headquarters) and Rafid. When the Syrian Government announced the fall of Quneitra at 8:45 a.m. on June 10, resistance crumbled all along the front and a cease-fire was declared.

The third war between the Arabs and the Jews had ended in less than six days.

The costs of the Six Day War were great. Israeli losses amounted to 5,000 men killed, wounded, or missing on all fronts; almost 400 tanks; and about 40 aircraft. The

*The comparison refers to France's Maginot Line, which the French had hoped would contain a German invasion in the 1930s.

Egyptians lost about 18,000 men, 700 tanks, and close to 400 aircraft. The Syrians lost about 2,000 men, almost 100 tanks, and 55 aircraft. The Jordanians, who inflicted approximately half of the Israeli casualties, lost over 3,000 men, almost 200 tanks, and 18 aircraft.

Territorially, the war ended on an advantageous note for Israel. Her new borders encompassed three times the old area. Not only were Israel's newly seized borders on defensible terrain at the Golan Heights, along the Jordan River, and along the Suez Canal, but the length of her defensive frontier had actually been shortened. The possibility of surprise air attacks on Israeli cities was now reduced, and the cities were out of artillery range.[43] However, political problems associated with maintaining forces on the newly conquered land, coupled with the fact that Israel had initiated the war with its pre-emptive strike, resulted in Israel's isolation from a portion of the world community. Moreover, although the Arab States had been defeated, they were determined to fight again.

The War of Attrition, 1968–1970

Despite Israel's overwhelming victory in the Six Day War, a peace treaty was not concluded, and the Arabs and Israelis began preparing for a fourth round. The six years before the 1973 War can be divided into three overlapping phases. The first phase was one of adjustment, during which both sides reflected on lessons learned in battle, made changes, and began rearming for future hostilities. The second phase involved an unofficial War of Attrition along the borders with Egypt and Syria. During this period, also, the Palestinians launched a massive guerrilla and international terrorist campaign to focus world attention on the plight of the refugees in the Middle East. The third phase was marked by preparations for a coordinated Arab assault.

The Israelis and Arabs approached phase one in vastly different ways. After its rapid conquest, Israel did not feel the need to study the 1967 War in the way it had examined the 1956 Sinai Campaign. Instead of searching for errors, the Israelis looked for reasons to explain their successes.[44] Confident in their assessment that the tank-plane team was the key to victory in the desert, they depreciated the role of combined arms operations. The Israelis also failed to adjust their doctrine to account for the new precision antitank missiles that were being developed by the Superpowers and would most certainly appear on the battlefields of the next war. Holding defensible borders, they thought that the possibility of a successful Arab attack was remote. On the other hand, the Arabs, and especially the Egyptians, were recoiling from a disaster. Hence, they looked for weaknesses both in their own military system and in that of Israel. Their study was intensive and produced a great deal of information. Well-led Egyptian units had fought effectively on both the offense and defense, but the soldiers seemed to be most successful in defensive operations. Egyptian units had not performed well when cut off or when under air and armored attack. They had not been trained for mobile war. Soviet doctrine would have to be modified before it could be applied by the Egyptian Army. The combined arms concept required more emphasis, and more time needed to be devoted to antitank and antiaircraft training.[45]

While absorbing these and other lessons, the Egyptians began a War of Attrition along the Suez Canal that served as a major irritant to the Israelis. The raids and exchanges of artillery fire that constituted this war also served to sustain anti-Israel fulminations while downgrading Egypt's domestic problems.[46] This phase may have begun as early as July 1, 1967, when two Egyptian platoons and an Israeli armored force clashed near the Port Fuad causeway on the eastern side of the canal, opposite Port Said. Tension increased until October 21, 1967, when the Israeli destroyer *Elat* was sunk by a Styx missile fired by an Egyptian warship from within its home harbor at Port Said. The Israelis retaliated by shelling the oil refineries at Suez. An 11-month period of watchfulness followed.[47]

In October 1968, the War of Attrition began in earnest when the Egyptians unleashed the first of many artillery barrages along a 60-mile front of the canal, causing a large number of Israeli casualties. An important part of Egypt's strategy was the launching of frequent and intensive attacks designed to prevent the consolidation of the cease-fire line into a permanent border. The Israelis countered by launching deep commando and air force raids. A successful commando raid after the October barrage against the Maj Hammadi power transformer quieted the Egyptian guns until March 1969. Nevertheless, the barrages forced the Israelis to build fortified observation positions on the east bank of the canal to protect their personnel. (*See Atlas Map No. 12a.*) Known as the Bar Lev Line, this system of observation posts was not a first line of defense; the strength to defend the Line was provided by armored battalions, which were stationed behind the strongpoints and beyond the range of the Egyptian artillery.[48]

The turning point in this unofficial war came later in 1969. The Egyptians stepped up their attacks by concentrating on the Israeli supply routes that ran from the strongpoints to the depots in their rear. The Israelis responded with an ineffective shelling of the oil refineries at Ismailia and Suez. Then, recognizing the limitations of their artillery, Israel called on the air force and also launched commando attacks. Two Egyptian torpedo boats were sunk at Ras Sadat by commandos; an Israeli armored raid, in which captured T-54 and T-55 tanks were used, crossed the canal and disrupted Egyptian activities. Finally, in one of the most daring commando raids of the war, the Israelis managed to capture a sophisticated Soviet radar installation from the Egyptians at Ras Gharib.[49]

The Israelis gained an added advantage when they acquired technologically advanced American F-4 Phantoms, which could reach targets deep in the Nile Valley. Attacks on these targets provoked the Russians to send air defense missile batteries and Soviet-piloted MiG-21 squadrons to Egypt. Wary of the consequences, the Israelis stopped their deep penetrations in return for a tacit agreement that air defense systems would remain in position away from the canal. The Egyptians, however, did not comply, and moved air defense units forward, causing the IAF increased losses over the canal. Soviet airmen, also, tried to engage Israeli fighters, but the Israelis refused engagements until July 30, 1970, when the Soviets lost four aircraft.[50]

On August 7, 1970, an American-sponsored cease-fire went into effect, ending the unofficial War of Attrition. Egypt then moved air defense systems farther forward—up to the line of the canal. In retrospect, the Egyptians were probably forced into the cease-fire agreement by unacceptable materiel losses. The same was probably true of the Israelis, who lost more men during this period than during the 1967 War. The War of Attrition was a stalemate. A stalemate, however, may mean a victory for each side—a victory that the Egyptians very much needed.[51]

Egyptian Preparations

Shortly after the 1967 defeat, the Egyptian High Command had begun preparing for the next major battle with the Israeli armed forces. Egyptian leaders explained the 1967 defeat to their people as being the result of international support for Israel. Nevertheless, the high command objectively analyzed the weaknesses of Egypt's forces and overall defense policy.[52]

Perhaps the most important lesson Egypt had learned from the 1967 War was that it must strike first. To do so, however, required a first-rate Air Force, and that would not be available until the mid-1970s. Egyptian leaders also realized that the Army was not capable of conducting mobile warfare in the Israeli manner. The Egyptians would have to organize a continuous line and train their men to respond to Israeli tactics that depended upon units' penetrating the line and bypassing strongpoints by attacking such units in flank and rear. They also had to convince their soldiers to continue fighting—even when they found themselves isolated.

Egyptian leaders worked hard to improve the quality of the common soldier. The Army ceased recruiting exclusively from the lower classes, in part because the massive amounts of recently arrived Soviet equipment required a better educated soldier. College graduates were drafted and sent to officer schools; everyone was told why he would be fighting. Training by Russian and Egyptian officers became more rigorous and repetitive in order to eliminate careless errors. Morale improved, and Egyptian officers took a more active role in the training. Attention was given to the often neglected areas of maintenance and logistics. Maneuvers and raids were conducted, and limitations on combat capabilities noted.[53] The increasingly well-trained and well-equipped Egyptian soldier caused some concern to the Israelis, who could not be sure of the extent of his improvement. Egyptian leaders grew confident that their new army could conduct successful limited offensives, but did not believe that their command system was yet sophisticated enough to direct fluid battles of maneuver.[54]

President Anwar Sadat and Field Marshal Ahmed Ismail developed a plan that was ingenious both in its simplicity and in its exploitation of Egypt's strongpoints. They envisioned a massive attack on a broad front to seize limited objectives. The keys to the success of such an offensive were secrecy, a real unity of command among the Arabs, and a two-front war that would lessen Israel's advantage of central position.[55] The advance would be preceded by a massive artillery, missile, and air bombardment of Israeli positions along the canal and on the Golan Heights, after which the Egyptians would cross the waterway while the Syrians attacked the heights. For the first time, Israel would have to respond to a fully coordinated Arab offensive.

The Arabs believed that surprise could be achieved because they periodically conducted large maneuvers along the borders and then withdrew. Coincidentally, Israeli intelligence sources felt that the Arabs were incapable of launching a massive attack until 1975, when they believed Egypt might achieve air parity and possibly air superiority. The Israeli intelligence analysts, however, failed to assess Arab intentions accurately. Not until early October 1973 did Israeli intelligence reveal that an attack might be launched as soon as October 6. This lack of hard intelligence created a dilemma for Israel. Total mobilization re-

quired from two to three days, and would be both expensive and disruptive if prolonged during a peacetime situation. At the same time, the Prime Minister had apparently decided that Israel could not politically afford again being the aggressor. Thus, Chief of Staff David Elazar's October 6 early-morning request for authority to launch a pre-emptive air strike was disapproved. Although a large-scale mobilization was ordered in mid-morning, it would not be complete before the battle opened. The Arabs attacked that afternoon.[56]

1973—The War of Many Names

The Arab plan for initial operations was well coordinated and very simple. First, the Egyptians would cross the Suez Canal with infantry divisions and set up a strong defensive position five to six miles east of the canal and within the umbrella of their air defense system. *(See map on page 17.)* There, the troops would dig in and await the expected armored and air force counterattacks with hand-carried antiaircraft and antitank weapons. If the Egyptians were successful in stopping these attacks, they would begin to move to the passes under the second phase of the plan. To the east, the Syrians would seek to recapture the Golan Heights and to cut Israel in two in the north by pushing to the sea. Three infantry divisions, with tanks in front, would lead the attack on the mountain heights. Two armored divisions would be held in reserve for exploitation. By using helicopter-borne forces, the Syrians hoped to surprise and capture the key Israeli position atop Mount Hermon.[57] Israel would thus be forced to defend against simultaneous attacks on two fronts.

In the north, the Golan Heights provided Israel with a dominant defensive line that gave the occupying troops an excellent view of the Damascus plain. (*See Atlas Map No. 11a.*) Along this 30-mile border, the Israelis had built 17 platoon-sized fortifications designed to cause attacking forces to deploy. The forts were supported by two armored brigades with a total of 170 tanks and 10 artillery batteries. Across from the Israeli positions, the Syrians had about 1,500 tanks and 1,100 guns available for the attack. The Israeli 7th Brigade had positioned its battalions along the northern portion of the heights, while the 188th (Barak) Brigade, reinforced by an armored battalion from the 7th Brigade, positioned itself opposite the approach from Rafid. The 188th Brigade had about 100 tanks, and the 7th Brigade about 60.

Golan Heights

The war on the northern front began at 2:05 p.m. with a massive Syrian artillery and air bombardment. The two

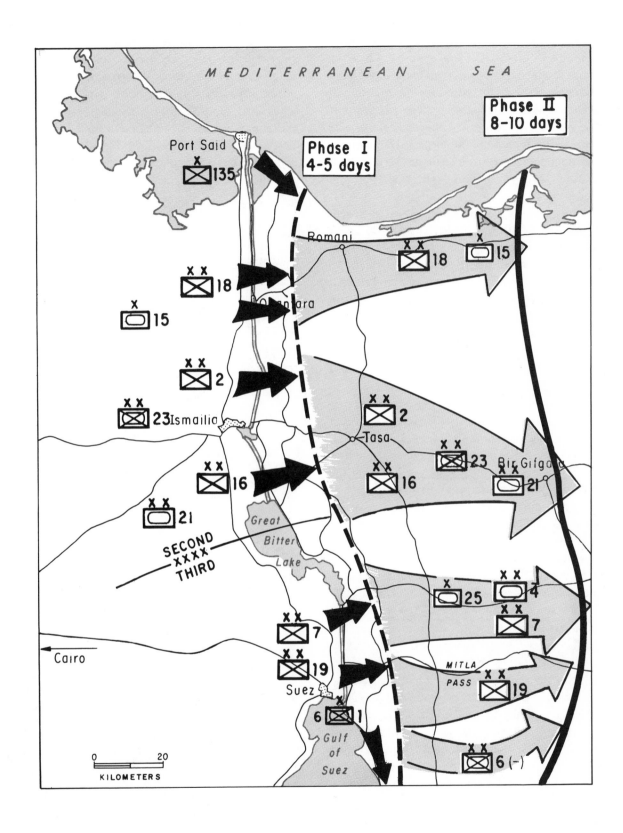

The Egyptian Plan for the October 1973 Offensive

Israeli brigades on the Golan Heights were hard pressed by troops making the ensuing attack. After a series of tank battles, the Israelis were pushed back from the 1967 cease-fire line (the Purple Line). (*See Atlas Map No. 11a.*) The 188th Brigade fought against 6 to 1 odds in the Rafid Gap, and was almost totally destroyed during the first day of fighting. The brigade's intelligence officer was the only senior officer left on October 7, and only seven tanks were still operational. That night, Major General Dan Laner, a reserve division commander, directed newly mobilized squads, platoons, and even single tanks to critical points as they arrived at the front.[58]

Laner's actions, plus the 7th Brigade's use of a well-prepared killing zone,* slowed the Syrian attack. Laner's piecemeal reinforcement also probably saved Major General Rafael Eytan's Northern Headquarters, which the Syrians were assaulting. As the Syrians entered the headquarters compound from the east, Eytan left and continued to direct the battle. By October 9, the 7th Brigade had only seven tanks. Then, however, a battalion commander, rushing back from his honeymoon, arrived with fifteen battlefield-repaired tanks, linked up with the brigade's survivors, and led a counterattack that was the key to stabilizing the sector. By the end of the day, Major General Moshe Peled's reserve division had arrived in the southern sector, and Laner's division had recaptured Eytan's headquarters compound.[59] The deliberate withdrawal and limited successes during the first three days of war on the Golan Heights allowed the Israelis to concentrate their mobilized forces against Syria. This was the critical sector, since there was little room for withdrawal in northern Israel, but considerable ground to trade in Sinai if necessary. By October 10, the Israelis had finally driven the Syrians back beyond the 1967 cease-fire line. The battle had been fierce, and losses were heavy. Every Israeli tank on the line on October 6 was hit, and the Syrians lost over 800 tanks within Israeli territory.[60]

An Israeli counteroffensive toward Sasa began on October 11, with Laner's division attacking east from Quneitra and Eytan's division moving north and then east to attack the flank of the Syrians. (*See Atlas Map No. 11b.*) Peled held the line in the south. The Israelis made good progress. Late on October 12, Laner spotted a large column moving in the south and inquired if Peled had broken through. After being informed that the Iraqis had arrived with an armored division, Laner diverted troops who set up an ambush that destroyed most of the lead Iraqi brigade early the next morning.[61] A reinforcing Iraqi brigade, as well as the Jordanian 40th and 92nd Armored Brigades, then arrived and joined the fight. The line became fairly stable by October 14, and no major shifts occurred despite numerous brigade-sized attacks by both sides. Farther north, the Israelis retook the Mount Hermon position on October 21. Helicopters landed an airborne brigade about nine miles north of the position, which was captured during the night. With the Syrian threat greatly reduced by October 12 and the line stabilized by the fourteenth, the Israeli High Command began to shift reserve forces to the Sinai. There, Israel had received a severe shock when the Egyptians attacked on October 6.[62]

Return to Sinai

Concurrent with the Syrian attack of the Golan Heights, the Egyptians began their attack 250 miles to the southwest, using 240 aircraft against Israeli airfields and headquarters, and 2,000 guns and a brigade of FROG missiles against the Bar Lev Line. As the barrage on the Line began to shift, Egyptian infantrymen and tankers moved up the ramps of the sand castles (or mud forts) that overlooked the Line and began to fire sagger missiles and antitank guns at the forts. This fire kept the Israelis largely neutralized while helicopter-borne commandos and tank-hunter teams crossed the Suez Canal. During the barrage, 8,000 men in rubber rafts crossed the canal, landed between the forts and bypassed them, and moved three to six miles farther east to set up a defensive line. (*See Atlas Map No. 12a.*) The capture of the forts was left to the second and third waves.

Egyptian Engineers Use High-Power Water Hoses to Breach an Israeli Sand Rampart

---

*A killing zone is an area in which firepower is concentrated, making it nearly impossible for the enemy to cross the area in significant strength.

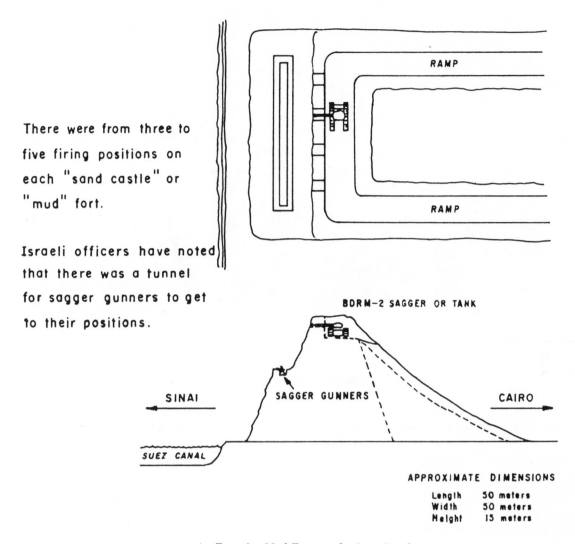

There were from three to five firing positions on each "sand castle" or "mud" fort.

Israeli officers have noted that there was a tunnel for sagger gunners to get to their positions.

An Egyptian Mud Fort on the Suez Canal

Within eight hours, Egyptian engineers, using high-pressure water pumps, cut 60 crossing sites in the high sand banks on the Israeli side of the canal and had bridges and rafts operational. Thousands of troops crossed and strengthened the first wave's defensive position. The second phase of the operation, which was designed as an advance to the Mitla and Bir Gidy Passes followed by a northward turn and drive to the Mediterranean Sea, could not be executed until the Egyptians had secured their initial gains and defeated the expected Israeli counterattack. Therefore, the Egyptians planned to remain within their integrated air defense umbrella and prepare for the expected Israeli armored and air assault.[63] If successful in defeating that effort, they would reorganize and begin the second advance. If they encountered difficulty, they would have Russia request a cease-fire through the UN Security Council.

Technological Surprise

By the evening of October 7, most of the Israeli forts had been captured and the local Israeli counterattacks beaten back. (*See Atlas Map No. 12a.*) The next day, the Egyptians crossed the remainder of the tanks organic to the infantry divisions and defeated the major Israeli counterattacks. The defensive line of saggers, rocket-propelled grenades (RPG7s), antitank guns, and tanks decimated the Israeli armored units, which were advancing without infantry or artillery support.* The Israelis had to quickly relearn how to employ combined arms to fight in the Sinai.

*The armored brigades that attacked had only a mechanized infantry company instead of a battalion. Thus, pure armored attacks were the only action that could be undertaken. This was largely a result of the "lessons" of the 1967 War—the Israelis had more faith in armored operations than in combined arms operations.

Egyptian Soldiers Transport Heavy Weapons Across the Suez Canal

The IAF had encountered two major surprises at the outbreak of hostilities. The first was the size and density of the Egyptian air defense barrier, which the Egyptians had been building since 1970. By October 1973, the air defense belt was 20 miles wide and over 100 miles long. It created a lethal zone from the ground up to 50,000 feet. The barrier contained a complex mixture of mutually supporting high-, medium-, and low-altitude missiles, reinforced with anti-aircraft artillery. Over 130 SAM-2 and SAM-3 sites gave high-altitude protection, while 40 mobile SAM-6 batteries covered the medium altitudes at which Israeli aircraft had operated so effectively in the past. Groups of 12 SAM-7s (short-range, shoulder-launched missiles similar to the United States Army "Redeye") were installed on vehicles and fired in salvoes of four or eight missiles against low-flying aircraft. Conventional heavy-caliber antiaircraft artillery was supplemented by the self-propelled ZSU-23, which was capable of firing four thousand 23-mm rounds per minute. A similar zone had been developed by the Syrians in the Golan Heights area.

The second major surprise was the effectiveness of the SAM-6 missile system, which proved to be extremely accurate against targets at altitudes up to 20,000 feet. The existing IAF electronic countermeasures were incapable of coping with it, and the mobility of the missile batteries made them very elusive targets. While attempting to avoid this system, Israeli aircraft were forced into the low-alti-

tude zone covered by the lethal ZSU-23s and SAM-7s.[64] On the first afternoon of the war, the Israelis lost 30 A-4 Sky-hawks and 10 E-4 Phantoms. During the first week, they lost 80 aircraft—approximately 24 percent of their front-line force.[65] The air defense effort was an important factor in the initial Arab successes, negating the effectiveness of Israeli close air support and providing protection for the attacking Arab ground forces.

Israeli Counteroffensive

By October 10, the Sinai front appeared to have stabilized, and in response to Syrian calls for aid, the Egyptians began to plan the breakout to increase the pressure on the Israelis.[66] Also on October 10, General Sharon received reports from his patrols that the crossing site he had prepared near the Bitter Lakes three years earlier was unguarded and was also at the boundary between the two Egyptian armies. Sharon wanted to act immediately and launch Operation GAZELLE, an attack across the canal. Elazar, however, wanted to wait until more Egyptian armor crossed over the canal. Thus, when the Egyptians began to cross more tanks for the breakout, they played into the Israelis' hands. (*See Atlas Map No. 12b.*) Approximately 1,500 tanks crossed the canal and launched multiple brigade- and division-sized assaults on October 14. These were beaten back with a loss of over 200 tanks, as Egyptian tanks advanced beyond the air defense umbrella and were badly mauled by Israeli tanks and aircraft.[67]

After the battle had been decided on October 14, Elazar issued the orders to begin Operation GAZELLE. (*See Atlas Map No. 13a.*) Sharon's division was to clear a corridor and secure the crossing site. His force, led by a parachute brigade, advanced against little opposition toward high ground known as the "Chinese Farm." As the lead brigade commander approached this area, he sent a company of tanks to the north to secure a crossroads. The unit was promptly destroyed by strong Egyptian forces. Nevertheless, the brigade continued to advance and began to cross the Suez Canal using rafts and bridging sections. As the crossing began, an armored force was sent north to secure the crossing area. This force blundered into the headquarters of two Egyptian divisions that had been bypassed on the way to the canal. A tremendous battle ensued, and the crossing area was not secured until the following night. The Egyptians, realizing that the IDF was attempting a crossing, massed elements of two divisions to attack from the north and directed the 25th Armored Brigade to attack from the south. The brigade was ambushed and lost 26 tanks; the divisional forces in the north failed to dislodge the Israelis defending the crossing corridor.[68] Despite a lack of orders, Sharon's units crossed the canal and began to fan out and destroy or capture air defense sites. For the first time in the 1973 War, a dent had been created in the Egyptian air defense system. Although new air tactics and improved electronic countermeasures were introduced during the conflict, the final answer to the antiaircraft missile threat proved to be the use of ground forces to penetrate the missile belts and destroy the launching sites.

An Israeli Bridge Across the Suez Canal

With air support assured and a bridge completed, Sharon threatened Ismailia on October 17 while the divisions of Major General Avraham Adan and Brigadier General Kalman Magen began to cut off the Egyptian Third Army Headquarters in Suez City. Other Israeli forces pressured Third Army forces on the east bank. (*See Atlas Map No. 13b.*) One Israeli force nearly cut off an entire army, but failed to do so because it could not be rapidly reinforced. If the Egyptians had launched a massive attack against Sharon on the west bank as soon as they learned that he was across the canal, they probably could have destroyed his weak force. Believing Sharon's force to be very small, however, they felt it could be dealt with after the eastern bank was stabilized.[69] This was a fortunate occurrence for Israel, because its military forces were having other troubles.

Israeli Problems

Israeli operations in Sinai were not conducted with the smoothness or efficiency that had previously characterized IDF activities. The chain of command was frequently violated, and unity of command often seemed nonexistent. There was a great deal of arguing between Defense Minister Dayan and Chief of Staff Elazar over who would make decisions. On the battlefield, Dayan had a former chief of staff, Chaim Bar-Lev, at Southern Headquarters observing and reporting on Major General Schmuel Gonen, the front commander, thus detracting from Gonen's status. The chain of command was ineffective on many occasions because commanders disobeyed or disregarded orders. Sharon was a major offender, and on several occasions bypassed Gonen and communicated directly with Dayan. The canal crossing caused a great controversy. From the first day of the Egyptian attack, Sharon wanted to cross the Suez. Elazar wanted Dayan to make the decision, but Sharon did not want to wait. Elazar agreed to the crossing only after the Egyptian attack on October 14 was stopped. When Sharon was unleashed, he crossed the canal, but then disobeyed his orders to delay until a bridge was completed and the bridgehead secured. Thus, Gonen was forced to cross his other divisions more quickly than had been anticipated.[70]

A change that had taken place in the IDF structure after the 1967 War also plagued the Israelis during the first few days of the 1973 War. Based upon the experience of the earlier war, the IDF had formed many pure tank units and neglected combined arms training.[71] Moreover, in 1973, Israeli tanks carried few of the antipersonnel rounds needed to neutralize the Egyptian infantry and their antitank weapons. Without infantry for close support and artillery for preparatory fires,* the IDF tanks were very vulnerable to the Egyptian soldier, who put up a stiff fight. Under the pressure of actual combat, the Israelis realized the need for resurrecting the combined arms team. The use of artillery and close infantry support permitted the tanks to work more effectively.[72]

Although the IDF almost completed the investment of the Egyptian Third Army, it could not subdue the Second Army. (*See Atlas Map. No. 13b.*) A cease-fire went into effect on October 24, despite violations on each side by units seeking a final advantage.† At that time, the Israelis and Egyptians were on each other's bank of the canal; both forces were exhausted.

A Critique

Everyone claimed victory after the cease-fire. The Israelis asserted that they could have gone to Cairo; but, in fact, they had suffered heavy casualties, were at the end of a tenuous supply line, and still faced two undefeated Egyptian armies. The Syrians had lost some territory, but had given Israel a severe scare at the start of the war before successfully withdrawing to the Sasa line and holding off the Israelis. The Iraqi forces continued to have trouble, but the Jordanian performance was up to par.[73] The strong

*Preparatory fires are supporting fires that prepare, or soften, an area by disrupting the enemy unit's tactical integrity, thus impairing the enemy's ability to operate effectively.

†The cease-fire was proposed by Russia when it became clear that the Egyptian Third Army was in danger of being surrounded by Israeli forces. The United States agreed, insisting that the cease-fire be linked to peace talks. The Superpowers first agreed on the wording of the resolution to be submitted to the UN Security Council and then obtained the agreement of Egypt and Israel. Originally intended to be effective on October 22, the cease-fire did not become firm until October 24, following violations of the first agreement by both Egypt and Israel and a threat of armed intervention by Russia.

performance of the Egyptians was the big surprise of the war. Israeli tank crews had to be continuously on the alert for antitank missile crews, which seemed to spring up everywhere, and IAF pilots had similar problems with antiaircraft missile and gun crews. The Egyptian command system at higher levels showed distinct improvement, and the direct cooperation and timing between Egypt and Syria was especially evident. The Israelis were forced to develop a healthy respect for the Egyptians, whom they had ridiculed for three decades.

The losses incurred by the opposing countries in the 1973 War are not accurately known. Authorities disagree in their estimates. The tabulation below is based upon several sources and represents approximate figures.

The 1973 War opened with offensives for limited objectives and ended with cease-fires, not peace treaties. Nevertheless, it changed the situation in the Middle East drastically. The Israelis lost the aura of invincibility; the Arabs regained a great deal of pride and unity, as well as a foothold in Sinai. The use of an oil embargo by the Arab members of the Organization of Petroleum Exporting Countries (OPEC) against Israel's allies forced nations to consider carefully the potential costs of supporting Israel. The initial Arab successes produced a fear in the international community that Israel would be forced to use the nuclear weapons that many believed it possessed. For the first time, both Superpowers assumed a position of readiness because each felt that the other might intervene militarily, even if only to enforce a cease-fire.

Assessing the military aspects of the war, the Superpowers had cause for concern. The ammunition expenditures and armored vehicle losses seemed astronomically high for such a short war. Sophisticated weapons for air defense and antitank use were shown to be chillingly effective. The substantial losses inflicted on high-performance aircraft by missile air defense systems caused some military ana-

Nation	Committed Forces	Killed	Wounded	Captured/ Missing	Total
Egypt	315,000	5,000**	12,000**	8,031	25,031
Syria	140,000	3,100	6,000	500	9,600
Jordan	5,000	28	49	—	77
Iraq	20,000	218	600	20	838
Other Arab States	25,000	100	300	—	400
Total Arabs	505,000	8,446	18,949	8,551	35,946
Israel	310,000	2,600*	8,000†	508	11,108

*Postwar deaths from wounds not included. Soviets estimate about 8,000 killed in action.

†Wounded not evacuated from field medical facilities not included. Soviets estimate about 20,000 wounded in action.

**U.S. estimate about 13,000 killed in action and 11,000 wounded in action.

Forces and Losses for the 1973 War

lysts to doubt the viability of close air support in the future. The effectiveness of inexpensive precision antitank missiles against very complex, expensive armored vehicles also raised questions about the utility and survivability of armor on modern, high-intensity battlefields. Massive resupply efforts had to be launched to maintain client states. The United States drew upon its NATO stocks of weapons to keep Israel supplied, while the Soviet Union shipped large amounts of equipment to the Arabs by sea and air. The war continued only because the Superpowers provided the materiel needed; otherwise, fighting would have ended on October 15 for lack of supplies.

After the war, the Superpowers resupplied their clients with arsenals greater than the pre-1973 levels. Given these arms and the tensions of the region, the potential for another war is always present. With OPEC's control of oil and its support of the Palestinian movement, Israel may find itself isolated from outside support in another war. Accordingly, Israel has attempted to become militarily self-sufficient. The 1979 peace accords with Egypt solved some of Israel's problems, but Egypt cannot completely isolate itself from the other Arab countries. Israel still cannot relax while Syria remains hostile and the Palestinian question remains unsolved. The treaty with Egypt does not guarantee peace for Israel, but it does offer hope for the future—a hope that the continuing war might end, and the elusive peace be secured.

A Perspective

The Israeli military experience provides an excellent modern example of how an outnumbered nation can fight and win. Because of the continual danger of national extinction, the Israelis have organized as a nation in arms. Without maintaining a large regular force or permitting excessive military influence in the government, they have responded to their peculiar strategic challenge in a way that has allowed them to dominate their region militarily. Universal conscription, a responsive reserve system, central position, and a highly competent, mobile regular force have allowed the Israelis to successfully counter each perceived or real military threat. At the tactical level, their operations have been marked by audacity, courage, and decentralized control. In a very short time, the Israeli armed forces have established a tradition of excellence and a worldwide reputation for professionalism.

Critics of Israel, however, have argued that the Israelis have relied too heavily on the application of military force, that the essence of the Clausewitzian relationship between war and politics, military force and political ends, has somehow eluded Israel's leaders. Because of political failures in 1956, military victory did little to guarantee Israel's security. After the 1967 military victory, the Iraelis felt that a solution to their security problem had been found in the strategic depth provided by the occupied lands. Yet the occupation of this new territory severely strained their military and economic resources, further isolated them from the world community, and damaged the world's perception of the legitimacy of their cause. Ironically, it was the success of Arab arms in 1973 and the temporary Israeli military setback that created a political environment which, for the first time, allowed the Israelis to conclude peace accords with their most formidable enemy. However, the Israeli military response to Palestinian guerrilla operations, coupled with their treatment of the Arab population in Israeli-occupied lands, has eroded international support for Israel, strengthened the Arab political position, and increased the willingness of the Palestinians to resist Israeli domination.

The Arab nations have mitigated the effects of their military disasters with political resolve and skill. Moreover, the Egyptians in particular have demonstrated that a defeated military force can quickly reform itself and perform creditably in the next conflict. After 1967, the Egyptians looked to the future and initiated changes. They modified the composition of their military forces by drawing soldiers from the most educated segments of their society, developed a simple plan to minimize command and control problems, and vigorously rehearsed planned operations to achieve a high level of performance. Moreover, they mastered necessary technological skills and successfully deployed new antitank and antiaircraft missiles to counter the traditional strength of Israeli armored and air forces. Finally, Egyptian President Sadat limited his national objectives, realizing that even a limited military victory would have enormous political effects.

Both Superpowers have used the Middle East as a testing ground for technological innovations. Because they have provided their clients with some of their most sophisticated weapons, military analysts have looked to the Arab-Israeli conflicts to test theories regarding the future high-intensity battlefield. Analysts have frequently commented on the similarities in doctrine and tactical skill between the Israelis in 1967 and the Germans in 1939 and 1940. But the Israeli "blitzkrieg" may have been the last—the end of an era. In 1973, the two weapons systems around which "blitzkrieg" was devised—the high performance airplane and the tank—were seriously challenged by the proliferation of relatively inexpensive precision-guided missiles. Pronouncements that the tank and fighter-bomber were obsolete were not widely accepted, but most analysts agreed that warfare had changed significantly. Many nations, including the United States, modified doctrine as a result of this war.

Although the Arab-Israeli wars were fought in the nuclear age, they were marked by the same types of political, geographic, and military limitations that have characterized other periods of limited war. Wars were frequent, yet destruction was minimized; major population centers were rarely touched. Battles were characterized by maneuver and were fought in sparsely populated areas. When one side gained tactical dominance, major powers stepped in to limit the extent of victory or defeat. The nation that maintained military dominance before the cease-fire gained bargaining chips for subsequent political negotiations. So far, Israel has garnered most of the chips. Nevertheless, it has failed to gain the lasting peace that is essential for its security.

Notes

¹Edward Luttwak and Dan Horowitz, *The Israeli Army* (New York, 1975), pp. 4–5; Yigal Allon, *The Making of Israel's Army* (New York, 1970), p. 4; J. Brower Bell, *The Long War: Israel and the Arabs Since 1946* (Englewood Cliffs, NJ, 1969), p. 5.

²Allon, *The Making of Israel's Army,* p. 4; Dan Kurzman, *Genesis 1948: The First Arab-Israeli War* (New York, 1970), p. 133. Luttwak and Horowitz, *The Israeli Army,* p. 6; Zeev Schiff, *A History of the Israeli Army (1870-1974),* trans. and ed. by Raphael Fothstein (San Francisco, 1974). pp. 3–5, 9.

³Yigal Allon, "The Making of Israel's Army: The Development of Military Conceptions of Liberation and Defense," in *The Theory and Practice of War,* ed. by Michael Howard (New York, 1965), p. 338; Luttwak and Horowitz, *The Israeli Army,* pp. 6–7.

⁴Allon, "The Making of Israel's Army," p. 338; Dana Adams Schmidt, *Armageddon in the Middle East* (New York, 1974), pp. 43–44; Bell, *The Long War,* pp. 6–8; R.R. Palmer, *A History of the Modern World,* 2nd ed., revised with the collaboration of Joel Colton (New York, 1964), pp. 678, 698; Walter Laquer (ed.), *The Israel-Arab Reader* (New York, Bantam edition, 3rd printing, 1971), pp. 12–18.

⁵Allon, *The Making of Israel's Army,* pp. 5–6; Schmidt, *Armageddon in the Middle East,* pp. 108–113.

⁶Luttwak and Horowitz, *The Israeli Army,* pp. 6–8; Allon, *The Making of Israel's Army,* pp. 6–7; Allon, "The Making of Israel's Army," pp. 339–340; Schiff, *A History of the Israeli Army,* pp. 8–10.

⁷Allon, *The Making of Israel's Army,* pp. 8–11; Luttwak and Horowitz, *The Israeli Army,* pp. 12–16; Schiff, *A History of the Israeli Army,* pp. 17–19.

⁸Luttwak and Horowitz, *The Israeli Army,* p. 16; Allon, *The Making of Israel's Army,* pp. 7, 11–12.

⁹Luttwak and Horowitz, *The Israeli Army,* pp. 16–19; Allon, *The Making of Israel's Army,* pp. 14–16.

¹⁰Allon, *The Making of Israel's Army,* p. 15.

¹¹*Ibid.,* p. 16; Luttwak and Horowitz, *The Israeli Army,* p. 24, states that Palestine provided 27,000 Jewish troops during World War II; Schiff, *A History of the Israeli Army,* p. 22, cites 32,000.

¹²Luttwak and Horowitz, *The Israeli Army,* p. 19; Allon, *The Making of Israel's Army,* pp. 16, 18.

¹³Schiff, *A History of the Israeli Army,* pp. 25, 28; Schmidt, *Armageddon in the Middle East,* p. 123; Luttwak and Horowitz, *The Israeli Army,* pp. 23–24.

¹⁴Schiff, *A History of the Israeli Army,* pp. 25, 28; Schmidt, *Armageddon in the Middle East,* p. 123; Luttwak and Horowitz, *The Israeli Army,* pp. 23–24.

¹⁵Luttwak and Horowitz, *The Israeli Army,* pp. 28–29; Schiff, *A History of the Israeli Army,* pp. 28–29; Bell, *The Long War,* pp. 127–130; Schmidt, *Armageddon in the Middle East,* pp. 122–123.

¹⁶Luttwak and Horowitz, *The Israeli Army,* pp. 27–33; Allon, *The Making of Israel's Army,* pp. 30–34.

¹⁷Trevor N. Dupuy, *Elusive Victory* (New York, 1978), pp. 7–10, 19; Luttwak and Horowitz, *The Israeli Army,* pp. 22–27, 37–39; Schiff, *A History of the Israeli Army,* pp. 35–37.

¹⁸Allon, *The Making of Israel's Army,* pp. 30–34; Luttwak and Horowitz, *The Israeli Army,* pp. 33–34, 36.

¹⁹Luttwak and Horowitz, *The Israeli Army,* p. 37; Allon, *The Making of Israel's Army,* pp. 34–37; Israel Tal, "Israel's Defense Doctrine: Background and Dynamics," *Military Review,* 58 (March 1978), 26.

²⁰Luttwak and Horowitz, *The Israeli Army,* pp. 41–42; Allon, *The Making of Israel's Army,* pp. 37–38; Schiff, *A History of the Israeli Army,* pp. 45–46; Bell, *The Long War,* pp. 156, 161, 165–167.

²¹Bell, *The Long War,* pp. 123–124; Allon, *The Making of Israel's Army,* pp. 34–35; Luttwak and Horowitz, *The Israeli Army,* pp. 37, 39, 41.

²²Bell, *The Long War,* pp. 201–208; Luttwak and Horowitz, *The Israeli Army,* pp. 47–48; Kurzman, *Genesis 1948,* pp. 647–677; Allon, "The Making of Israel's Army," pp. 403–405.

²³Allon, "The Making of Israel's Army," pp. 406–411; Luttwak and Horowitz, *The Israeli Army,* pp. 48–52, 64; Bell, *The Long War,* pp. 218–225.

²⁴Luttwak and Horowitz, *The Israeli Army,* pp. 71–75, 98–102; Schiff, *A History of the Israeli Army,* pp. 53–59; Michael I. Handel, *Israel's Political-Military Doctrine,* Occasional Papers in International Affairs, No. 30 (Cambridge: Harvard University Center for International Affairs, 1973), pp. 16–20; Allon, *The Making of Israel's Army,* pp. 47–48.

²⁵Luttwak and Horowitz, *The Israeli Army,* pp. 105, 108.

²⁶*Ibid.,* pp. 106–107; Schiff, *A History of the Israeli Army,* p. 57.

²⁷Luttwak and Horowitz, *The Israeli Army,* pp. 139–140.

²⁸Ernest Stock, *Israel on the Road to Sinai, 1949–1956; With a Sequel on the Six Day War, 1967* (Ithaca, NY, 1967), pp. 183, 192; Schiff, *A History of the Israeli Army,* pp. 63–67; Luttwak and Horowitz, *The Israeli Army,* p. 141; Schmidt, *Armageddon in the Middle East,* p. 128; Allon, *The Making of Israel's Army,* pp. 56–57.

²⁹Moshe Dayan, *Diary of the Sinai Campaign* (New York, 1966), pp. 60–63, 71–74; Luttwak and Horowitz, *The Israeli Army,* pp. 148–150; S.L.A. Marshall, *Sinai Victory: Command Decisions in History's Shortest War, Israel's Hundred-Hour Conquest of Egypt East of Suez, Autumn, 1956* (New York, 1958), pp. 24–26; Dupuy, *Elusive Victory,* pp. 142–143. Dave Richard Palmer, "The Arab-Israeli Wars, 1948–1967," in the Department of Military Art and Engineering, *Readings in Current Military History* (West Point, 1969) contains an excellent, though brief, account of the 1956 Sinai Campaign, pp. 163–171; the following account of the 1956 War is based upon this source, unless otherwise noted.

³⁰Luttwak and Horowitz, *The Israeli Army,* p. 164; Handel, *Israel's Political-Military Doctrine,* pp. 37–40.

³¹Handel, *Israel's Political-Military Doctrine,* pp. 42–43.

³²Luttwak and Horowitz, *The Israeli Army,* pp. 202–205; Allon, *The Making of Israel's Army,* p. 63.

³³Allon, *The Making of Israel's Army,* p. 63; Handel, *Israel's Political-Military Doctrine,* p. 64.

³⁴Allon, *The Making of Israel's Army,* pp. 61–63; Handel, *Israel's Political-Military Doctrine,* p. 67.

³⁵Handel, *Israel's Political-Military Doctrine,* p. 65; Allon, *The Making of Israel's Army,* pp. 70–71.

³⁶Allon, *The Making of Israel's Army,* pp. 64–65; Handel,

Israel's Political-Military Doctrine, pp. 66–67.

[37]Michael Howard and Robert Hunter, *Israel and the Arab World: The Crisis of 1967*, Adelphi Papers No. 41 (London: Institute for Strategic Studies, 1967), p. 13; Luttwak and Horowitz, *The Israeli Army*, p. 210.

[38]Luttwak and Horowitz, *The Israeli Army*, pp. 221–223; Allon, *The Making of Israel's Army*, pp. 76–79; Howard and Hunter, *Israel and the Arab World*, pp. 15–19.

[39]Allon, *The Making of Israel's Army*, p. 78; Bell, *The Long War*, p. 408.

[40]Howard and Hunter, *Israel and the Arab World*, pp. 24–26; Schmidt, *Armageddon in the Middle East*, pp. 142–143.

[41]Luttwak and Horowitz, *The Israeli Army*, pp. 221, 223.

[42]Howard and Hunter, *Israel and the Arab World*, p. 30; Luttwak and Horowitz, *The Israeli Army*, pp. 233–259, gives a detailed account of the Sinai fighting. Palmer, "The Arab-Israeli Wars, 1948–1967," pp. 172–184, gives a good summary of the entire 1967 War; the following account of the 1967 War is based upon this source, unless otherwise noted.

[43]Luttwak and Horowitz, *The Israeli Army*, pp. 282–283, 299–301; Howard and Hunter, *Israel and the Arab World*, p. 39; Handel, *Israel's Political-Military Doctrine*, pp. 51–52; Jerusalem Carta, *Secure and Recognized Boundaries; Israel's Right to Live in Peace Within Defensible Frontiers—Elements in the Consideration of Israel's Position on the Question of Boundaries* (Jerusalem, 1971), pp. 34–35; Dupuy, *Elusive Victory*, p. 333.

[44]Tal, "Israel's Defense Doctrine," p. 29; Elizabeth Monroe and A.H. Farrah-Hockley, *The Arab-Israeli War, October 1973: Background and Events*, Adelphi Paper No. 111, Winter 1974/75 (London, 1974), pp. 2–3, 10; Edgar O'Ballance, *No Victor, No Vanquished* (San Rafael, CA, 1978), pp. 49, 51; Chaim Herzog, *The War of Atonement: October, 1973* (Boston, 1975), pp. 2, 28.

[45]D.K. Palit, *Return to Sinai: The Arab Offensive, October 1973* (New Delhi, 1974), pp. 40–41; Herzog, *The War of Atonement*, p. 31; O'Ballance, *No Victor*, pp. 28, 74; Shimon Shamir, "Arab Military Lessons from the October War," in *International Symposium on the Military Aspects of the Israeli-Arab Conflict*, ed. by Louis Williams (Tel Aviv, 1975), p. 172; Interview and Lecture, "The Egyptian Crossing of the Suez Canal during the 1973 Arab-Israeli Conflict," with Major General Abu Gazzala, Egyptian Defense Atache to the United States, West Point, New York, March 9, 1978.

[46]Herzog, *The War of Atonement*, pp. 8–10; Palit, *Return to Sinai*, pp. 24–28; Monroe and Farrah-Hockley, *The Arab-Israeli War*, p. 14; Luttwak and Horowitz, *The Israeli Army*, pp. 314, 322, 323; Hassan El Badi, Taha El Magdoub; and Mohammed Dia El Din Zohdy, *The Ramadan War, 1973* (Dunn Loring, VA, 1978), p. 10. *The Ramadan War* divides this period into the Egyptian Phases of Defiance, June 1967–August 1968; Active Defense, September 1968–February 1969; the War of Attrition, March 1969–August 1970; and No War, No Peace, August 1970–October 1973.

[47]Luttwak and Horowitz, *The Israeli Army*, pp. 315–316; Dupuy, *Elusive Victory*, pp. 348–349.

[48]Herzog, *War of Atonement*, pp. 4–6, 11; Luttwak and Horowitz, *The Israeli Army*, pp. 314–317; Dupuy, *Elusive Victory*, 316–362.

[49]Dupuy, *Elusive Victory*, pp. 363–364; Luttwak and Horowitz, *The Israeli Army*, pp. 318–321; Herzog, *War of Atonement*,

pp. 8–9.

[50]Luttwak and Horowitz, *The Israeli Army*, pp. 322–326; Herzog, *War of Atonement*, pp. 9–11; Dupuy, *Elusive Victory*, pp. 364–367.

[51]O'Ballance, *No Victor*, pp. 2–3; Dupuy, *Elusive Victory*, p. 369; Luttwak and Horowitz, *The Israeli Army*, pp. 326–327; Herzog, *War of Atonement*, pp. 9–11.

[52]J. Bowyer Bell, "National Character and Military Strategy: The Egyptian Experience, October 1973," *Parameters*, 5 (Spring 1975), 14; Palit, *Return to Sinai*, pp. 21–22; U.S. Army Command and General Staff College, *Selected Readings in Tactics: The 1973 Middle East War*, RB100-2 (Fort Leavenworth, 1976), Vol. 1, pp. 1–4 to 1–5.

[53]Bell, "National Character and Military Strategy," p. 13; Shamir, "Arab Military Lessons," p. 173.

[54]Palit, *Return to Sinai*, pp. 31–32, 39; U.S. Army CGSC, *Selected Readings*, p. 4–8; Monroe, *The Arab-Israeli War*, p. 16; Bell, "National Character and Military Strategy," p. 173.

[55]Palit, *Return to Sinai*, pp. 44–46; Chaim Herzog, "The Middle East War, 1973," Royal United Services Institute, *Journal* (March 1975), 4; O'Ballance, *No Victor*, pp. 34, 39, 43, 45; Herzog, *War of Atonement*, pp. 32, 33, 36, 38, 39.

[56]U.S. Army CGSC, *Selected Readings*, p. 4–5; Luttwak and Horowitz, *The Israeli Army*, pp. 342–343; Insight Team of the London *Sunday Times*, *The Yom Kippur War* (New York, 1974), pp. 120–121.

[57]Herzog, *War of Atonement*, pp. 72–73, 75; Palit, *Return to Sinai*, p. 94; Luttwak and Horowitz, *The Israeli Army*, pp. 373, 378, 390; O'Ballance, *No Victor*, pp. 124–129.

[58]Herzog, *War of Atonement*, pp. 61–62; O'Ballance, *No Victor*, pp. 122, 131–135; U.S. Army CGSC, *Selected Readings*, pp. 3–4, 3–7 to 3–8.

[59]U.S. Army CGSC, *Selected Readings*, p. 3–8; O'Ballance, *No Victor*, pp. 134–136; Herzog, "The Middle East War," p. 9.

[60]Herzog, "The Middle East War," p. 9; Herzog, *War of Atonement*, pp. 112–115.

[61]Herzog, *War of Atonement*, p. 138; Luttwak and Horowitz, *The Israeli Army*, p. 391; O'Ballance, *No Victor*, pp. 203, 216; Insight Team, *Yom Kippur War*, p. 315; Palit, *Return to Sinai*, p. 112.

[62]Palit, *Return to Sinai*, p. 104; O'Ballance, *No Victor*, p. 216; U.S. Army CGSC, *Selected Readings*, p. 3–10; Shamir, "Arab Military Lessons," p. 188.

[63]O'Ballance, *No Victor*, pp. 69–84; Palit, *Return to Sinai*, pp. 64–68; Schmidt, *Armageddon in the Middle East*, p. 205; Insight Team, *Yom Kippur War*, pp. 133–147, 169, 224–226; U.S. Army CGSC, *Selected Readings*, pp. 4–5 to 4–9.

[64]U.S. Army CGSC, *Selected Readings*, pp. 5–1 to 5–3.

[65]Christopher Chaut et al., *The Encyclopedia of Air Warfare* (New York, 1977), p. 239.

[66]O'Ballance, *No Victor*, pp. 94, 96, 102–103, 105–106, 115, 155; Dupuy, *Elusive Victory*, pp. 465, 485–487.

[67]U.S. Army CGSC, *Selected Readings*, pp. 4–10 to 4–13; Herzog, *War of Atonement*, pp. 155–204 gives a detailed account favoring the Israelis; O'Ballance, *No Victor*, pp. 93–117, 147–167 tries to give a more accurate and balanced account.

[68]O'Ballance, *No Victor*, pp. 221–234; U.S. Army CGSC, *Selected Readings*, pp. 4–12 to 4–14; Herzog, *War of Atonement*, pp. 208–222, 226–228; Insight Team, *Yom Kippur War*, pp. 326–341.

[69]Insight Team, *Yom Kippur War,* pp. 337–341, 343–346; Herzog, *War of Atonement,* pp. 220–225, 229–246; O'Ballance, *No Victor,* pp. 228–249; U.S. Army CGSC, *Selected Readings,* pp. 4–13 to 4–16.

[70]O'Ballance, *No Victor,* pp. 229–230, 237–238, 246–247, 350–351; Luttwak and Horowitz, *The Israeli Army,* pp. 378–379, 381, 383; Insight Team, *Yom Kippur War,* pp. 236–237, 243–245.

[71]Insight Team, *Yom Kippur War,* p. 234; Luttwak and Horowitz, *The Israeli Army,* p. 363; O'Ballance, *No Victor,* pp. 54, 57; Herzog, *War of Atonement,* p. 270.

[72]Herzog, *War of Atonement,* pp. 270–271; Insight Team, *Yom Kippur War,* pp. 384–398; U.S. Army CGSC, *Selected Readings,* pp. 4–11 to 4–12, 4–15 to 4–17.

[73]U.S. Army CGSC, *Selected Readings,* p. 5–19; Palit, *Return to Sinai,* p. 110; O'Ballance, *No Victor,* p. 198.

Annex A
The Origins of the Israeli Army, 1909–1948

DATE	ORGANIZATION	MEMBERSHIP/ STRENGTH	LEADERSHIP	MISSION/TRAINING/ DOCTRINE/OPERATIONS	REMARKS
1909	*Hashomer* ("watchmen").	Less than 100 members at its peak.		Organized to protect Jewish villages and fields against robbery, murder, and rape. Also attempted to carry out small re- prisals against Arabs who tried to harm Jews.	
World War I	"Zion" Battalion, Judean Battalion (British Army).	Jewish volunteers.		Fought first at Gallipoli, and later in Palestine.	Proposed to British by Josef Trumpeldor and Ze'er Jabotinsky.
Post- World War I	Overt regional defense units.	A few hundred volunteers.		Organized strictly for self-defense.	
1920	*Haganah.*	Small group of unpaid activists.	No organized leader- ship; local branches run by volunteers.	Organized to protect Jewish populace from Arab violence; little systematic training; passive defense.	Formed from local defense groups; an illegal, clandestine organization.
1929	*Haganah.*	Small group of unpaid activists.	5-man committee of Jewish Agency assumes responsi- bility for supervision of *Haganah.*	Poorly trained and equipped; training standards varied from place to place.	Illegal, clandestine organization.
1931	*Irgun Zvai Leumi* (national military organization popu- larly known as *"Haganah B"*).	Small group of unpaid activists.		Even less training than the *Haganah.*	Splinter group of *Haganah.*
1936	*Nodedet* ("patrol").	Young volunteers from Jerusalem *Haganah.*	Yitzhak Sadeh.	Aggressive defense; used to track down and ambush Arab guerrillas.	Brief experiment; not supported by *Haganah.*
1936	Jewish Settlement Police (JSP).	22,000 members at peak in 1939.		Provided small guard units for isolated settlements.	Raised, trained, armed, and paid by British; gave the *Ha- ganah* a legal cover.

DATE	ORGANIZATION	MEMBERSHIP/ STRENGTH	LEADERSHIP	MISSION/TRAINING/ DOCTRINE/OPERATIONS	REMARKS
1937	*FOSH* (field forces).	Volunteers from JSP and other guards (*notrim*); 1,000 members by 1938.	Yitzhak Sadeh.	Well-trained, mobile, offensive tactics; *FOSH* tactics were later adopted by *Haganah*.	*Haganah* authorized Sadeh to form *FOSH*.
1937	*Irgun Zvai Leumi* (IZL).	5,000 members at peak.	Menachem Begin.	Organized as party militia by Revisionists.	Operated in the Jerusalem area.
1938	Special Night Squads (SNS).	Mixed unit of British and *Haganah* soldiers.	Captain Orde Wingate.	Cooperated with *Haganah* units on clandestine basis; active defense, commando raids.	
1940	*Hish.*	Unpaid volunteers.		Permanent, but not full-time mobile force; weekend, summer-camp training.	Formed after disbanding of *FOSH*.
1940	*Haganah.*	Volunteers.	G.H.Q., general staff; Ya'acov Dori, first Chief of Staff.	Trained small groups of guerrillas in *kibbutzim*.	
World War II	*Lehi* (Stern gang).	A few hundred activists.	Avraham Yai Stern.	Aggressive terrorist organization; sabotage, assassination.	
1941	*Palmach.*	Core of former *FOSH*, SNS men; 1,000 men, 300 women, 400 reservists (on call) in 1944.	Yitzhak Sadeh, then Yigal Allon (1945).	Mobile defense force; intensive training conducted primarily at squad level; high standards of individual skill and group morale.	Only full-time force in *Haganah*.
World War II	Jews in British Army.				Provided many senior IDF commanders.
1944	*Irgun Zvai Leumi* (IZL).	A few hundred members.	Menachem Begin.	Used for terrorist attacks against British police and military installations.	
1947	*Haganah.*	43,000 members, of which 32,000 belonged to *Him* (Home Guard).		Internal security; ill-equipped, poorly trained; major operations were smuggling refugees.	Still an illegal organization.
1947	*Hish.*	6 brigades, 3,000 to 4,000 men each.	Put under control of *Haganah's* G.H.Q.		Manned on full-time basis.
1947	*Palmach.*	Recalled reservists regrouped into 3 brigades.			Integral part of *Haganah*, yet maintained distinctive political attitudes.

The Chinese Civil War

The Protracted War 2

On Saturday, October 1, 1949, Mao Tse-tung* stood atop Tien An-min Gate in the city of Peking and formally proclaimed the establishment of a People's Republic of China. In doing so, he brought to a close some 37 years of civil warfare and established the first reasonably secure regime in China since the fall of the last imperial dynasty in 1912. Already, his opponents—Chiang Kai-shek and his Nationalist Party—were re-establishing their regime on the island of Taiwan. By the end of the year, they would be completely ejected from the Chinese mainland. But protected by American naval power, they would continue to provide a threat and a challenge to Mao's new regime, providing a source of tension and instability throughout East Asia that remains today.

The story of how it was possible for Mao and his group to topple Chiang and his Nationalists, despite Chiang's American advice and assistance, is one that is particularly relevant to students of military affairs. The civil war that continued in varying degrees from 1912 to 1949 spawned important new strategies of revolutionary and people's wars. The Communist success in China also demonstrates the very close integration of China's military affairs with its social, economic, and political contexts—a relationship that is always present in a nation, but rarely as obvious as it is in this story. Finally, this account illustrates the danger of failing to understand cultures that are different from Western ones in terms of aspirations, moral values, and socioeconomic organization. Had Americans understood the Chinese, they would have realized by 1945 that Mao

would probably win the contest for China, and that the assistance they provided—or could have provided—would not change the outcome.

Historical Background

Chinese civilization stretches back in an unbroken course for some 3,000 years. It was based on a labor-intensive agrarian sector that always employed about 75 percent of the total population. These peasants farmed very small plots of land on a family basis and lived very close to the subsistence level in order to support the remaining 25 percent of the population, which lived in the cities and towns. Indeed, the average family plot was only 1.7 acres, the minimum amount of land upon which an average family could subsist.[1] However, frequent natural disasters often dropped these farmers below the subsistence level. Thus, throughout Chinese history, the peasants rarely had enough to eat. Mere survival was a full-time occupation—increasingly so in the twentieth century.

Although Chinese agriculture was labor-intensive, most of this labor was required only during the planting and harvesting seasons. For this reason, only about 35 percent of the peasants normally worked full time in the fields.[2] During the growing seasons, the excess laborers were available for cottage industries, military service, forced labor, or—when times were bad—banditry.

The heavy labor requirements for planting and harvesting combined with the small plots of land to make agriculture a communal activity. Although the land was privately owned or rented, everybody in the village worked together, sharing tools and animals. Indeed, the water control systems required cooperation to insure both maintenance and equitable water usage. Unlike the American farmer, who relied on himself for success and thus prized his individual-

*Since the Chinese language is written in characters, several systems have been devised to phonetically render it in Western script. The system developed by the People's Republic of China and seen in contemporary newspapers is called the Pin-yin system. However, as most scholarly works still utilize the older Wade-Giles system, this has been used throughout this chapter. In Pin-yin, Mao's name would be written Mao Zedong, and Peking would be Beijing. Also note that the Chinese surname always comes first. Further details and pronunciation guide are contained in Annex B on page 65.

ity, the Chinese farmer always depended on his group. Thus, it is not surprising that the traditional Confucian ethical system stressed the subordination of the individual to the group—be it the family, the village, or the state—and condemned individualism as being selfish.

This economic basis was reflected in the traditional Chinese political organization. Instead of seeking power and wealth, the basic purpose of the Chinese Government was to provide for the welfare of the people. In support of this principle, the Government maintained reserve grain stocks to compensate for periodic famine. It directly operated major water control projects, such as the dikes that kept the Yellow River in its channel and the 1,100–mile Grand Canal that linked north China with south China. It also controlled the prices of critical commodities such as grain, salt, and iron. Private trade was regarded with suspicion, as the merchant hurt both producers and customers in making his profit. Similarly, during the founding years of most of China's major dynasties (each of which ruled for about 300 years), the new government would nationalize all land and equitably redistribute it among the peasants. However, despite these early attempts at state socialism, the basic theory was that the best government was that which governed least. Thus, the Government dominated a tiny portion of the gross national product—less than 2 percent during the mid-nineteenth century.[3]

This complacent and stable society was rudely shaken in the nineteenth century by the interjection of Western ideas and influences. Spurred by their Industrial Revolution, enticed by a vast Chinese market, and convinced of the superiority of their own civilization, the westerners demanded trading privileges and backed these demands with force. Easily beaten in a series of minor wars from 1839 to 1895, the Chinese were forced to sign a series of treaties that imposed heavy indemnities, allowed the westerners to administer large regions on behalf of the Chinese Government, and permitted the westerners to defend these regions with their own troops. By 1900, France and Japan dominated much of the coastal region in south China, the British controlled the Shantung Peninsula, and the Russians and Japanese vied for control of Manchuria. (*See Atlas Map No. 15.*) The treaties were demeaning to the Chinese. Not surprisingly, therefore, the elimination of foreign influence became a major objective, and remained so until the westerners were finally expelled in 1949.

The increasing Western pressure greatly weakened the traditional Chinese sociopolitical order. The Chinese Government tried to develop industries that would provide a sufficient industrial base to make the aid from the Westerners unnecessary, but it lacked the resources to do so. To fund this vain effort, the Government compounded its

problems by negotiating massive foreign loans at a high rate of interest. Even as late as 1935, fully a quarter of Chiang Kai-shek's governmental budget was committed to paying the interest on loans that the last dynasty had arranged.[4] The political balance of power within China was also disrupted. New military technology acquired to respond to the Western threat gave the Chinese armed forces a greater capability to intervene in domestic politics than they had ever possessed. However, because of the Government's poverty, those forces were regionally recruited, commanded, and funded. Thus, the Government lacked any control mechanism over either the forces or the regions in which they operated. Pre-eminent among these regional forces in the early twentieth century was the Pei-yang Army—a German-trained modern force of six divisions under Yüan Shih-k'ai, who was the local civil governor. The Pei-yang Army enjoyed such independence that, during the Boxer Rebellion of 1899–1901, when the Government rashly declared war on eight major foreign powers, Yüan was able to declare his neutrality and successfully remain aloof from all fighting.

The Western impact also caused fundamental social changes. The new armies were staffed with a new type of professional soldier—one who discarded many of the traditional ways of life, but did not fully adopt Western ways. In the treaty ports, the influx of industry, small as it was, also created an entirely new class: the urban proletariat. At the same time, despite the inferior status accorded to merchants in the traditional social order, a new merchant class arose in the treaty ports. Many members of the *compradore* class—so-called because it was largely comprised of entrepreneurs who had gotten their start by serving as Chinese contracting agents for Western firms—became quite wealthy by 1900. However, because they generally adopted Christianity as well as Western styles of dress and living, they were condemned by conservatives and radicals alike as traitors to their cultural heritage—the ''running dogs of imperialism,'' as a contemporary phrase put it. In sum, particularly in the urban coastal regions, a society that had been stable and unchanged for millennia suddenly experienced more change in decades than the Europeans had in centuries. This was naturally very disruptive, and was made more so by the fact that in the inland regions, the rate of change was much slower—when there was any change at all. The society began to lose cohesiveness and to fragment. Illiterate and generally unaware of the changes going on in the world about them, the peasants were largely unaffected by these events, except to the extent that their lot was worsened by new industrial products that wiped out the traditional cottage industries.

Finally, the arrival of the Westerners with their superior

science and technology caused major changes in Chinese thinking as the social and ethical systems were called into question. In spite of a natural reluctance to abandon ideas that had been accepted for over 3,000 years, some of the intellectuals uncritically accepted Western ways. However, most of them tried to determine exactly what formed the foundation for Western success in financial, technological, and military areas, and to adopt the bare minimum necessary from Western practices. These intellectuals began to translate Western theoretical works, and thus, for the first time, to expose themselves to ideas such as democracy, liberty, individualism, liberalism, capitalism, and socialism. This caused serious problems, because ideas that had taken generations to be developed and refined circulated in China simultaneously, making it extremely difficult to resolve their contradictions. This difficulty was increased by the problem of translating these new concepts and their definitions into a language not equipped to deal with them. "In a culture where the closest definition of liberty was 'running wild without a bridle,' concepts of free elections and delegated responsibility tended to be vague."[5] Overall, the impact was very unsettling—as if in American society the entire Judeo-Christian and Greco-Roman ethical values were discredited, and no one could decide which values should be abandoned or how they could best be replaced. There was an "ideological vacuum: the ancient Confucian ethical sanctions and . . . imperial rule had lost their potency, while modern beliefs and institutions of popular government, either parties in competition or party dictatorships, had not been established."[6]

The Revolution Begins

Given these profound changes, by 1900 the stage was set for the fall of the imperial system. It came in the city of Wuhan* in central China on October 9, 1911, when units of the new army mutinied, seized the city, and proclaimed the fall of the dynasty. Their rebellion was spontaneously joined by all who were dissatisfied with the old regime—particularly with its inability to keep the westerners at bay. Although there was virtually no fighting, by the end of December 1911, the dynasty ruled little more than the imperial palace in Peking. However, since the revolution occurred almost by accident, there was little coordination or cohesion between the regional groups that had independently thrown off imperial rule. Chaos reigned, and into

*Wuhan actually consisted of three contiguous cities on the Yangtze River—Wuchang, Hankow, and Hanyang.

Sun Yat-sen

this confusion stepped two men, neither of whom had been directly involved with the outbreak of the revolution.

The first of these men was Sun Yat-sen, one of the world's first professional revolutionaries. Intensely nationalistic, Sun had launched his first abortive *putsch* in Canton in 1894,[7] aiming first to overthrow the dynasty and then to expel the westerners. By 1905, he had amalgamated several revolutionary groups to form an organization that later evolved into the Kuomintang, or Nationalist Party. He rapidly gained support by proclaiming his famous Three Principles of the People—nationalism, democracy, and people's livelihood. However, except for nationalism, his definitions of these principles were vague. Continuing his struggle against the dynasty, Sun launched his tenth *putsch* in Canton during March of 1911 but, once again, he was unsuccessful. However, without his knowledge, his followers rebelled in Wuhan six months later. Sun was then in the United States, but he returned to China, arriving in Shanghai in December 1911. There, on January 1, 1912, he was proclaimed President of the Chinese Republic.

The other man who sought and gained political power was Yüan Shih-k'ai. It was to Yüan that the dynasty turned for salvation as it rapidly lost support in the final months of 1911. In his Pei-yang Army of 40,000 men,[8] he had the finest and most cohesive body of troops within China. A master politician, Yüan played the revolutionaries and the imperialists off against each other. By the end of January 1912, he had maneuvered the imperial court into abdicating in return for a generous settlement.[9] He also demanded that Sun resign so that Yüan could take his place.

After less than one month in office, Sun's government was already faltering because, while he was an inspiring leader, he was an inept administrator and was directing inexperienced people. To all involved, only Yüan seemed to be capable of creating a new political order, so Sun resigned in his favor in February 1912, and a traditional authoritarian government was set up under the facade of a representative government. However, while he possessed the ability to outmaneuver both the dynasty and Sun and to secure international recognition for his regime, Yüan lacked sufficient legitimacy and military power to overcome the provincial groups that had seized power during the revolution. "Without the moral sanction of the emperors and lacking the troops to effectively police the vast nation, Yüan . . . recognized any [provincial] authority, legitimate or not, that could enforce order and remit [some] revenues to Peking."[10] While Yüan lived, the unity of his Pei-yang Army lent credibility to what claimed to be a national government. Unfortunately, this unity was due only to personal loyalty; when he died in 1916, the national polity fell apart as the generals began to maneuver among themselves to assume his mantle.

After Yüan's death, China entered the Warlord Period—a period that, despite a nominal unity imposed by Chiang Kai-shek, really only ended with Mao's victory in 1949. Although the facade of a national government continued to be maintained, China was actually divided and ruled by a varying number of competing warlords who maneuvered politically by using military force. There was no commonly understood or accepted set of moral or political values to replace the traditional ethics that had been discredited with the fall of the dynasty. Thus, the political process inevitably descended to the use of force; as Mao later said, "politics come from the barrel of a gun."

An understanding of the Warlord Period is important to the comprehension of later events. The boundaries and leaders varied over time (*see Atlas Map No. 16*), and each area governed and financed itself from the traditional land tax and such foreign loans as it could obtain. Though nominally military men, the warlords were basically politicians who used force because no other recognized medium of political expression existed. There was fighting throughout the period, but results were as often determined by negotiation as by fighting.* When two forces

met for battle, the weaker leader usually tried to achieve the best terms possible. The stronger was equally keen to reach an agreement because the losses that he would incur in battle would leave him vulnerable to a third party. Moreover, if he negotiated, he could co-opt his rival's forces into his own and be that much stronger. The fighting that did occur took place along critical lines of communication and, although large numbers in all armies lacked firearms,* casualties were high because of the lack of medical services. Nonetheless, there was no shortage of soldiers; a total of some 2 million men were under arms through 1925.[11] However, soldiers joined armies not out of motivation for a cause, but rather to insure being fed at reliable intervals. If fed, they cared little about whom they served; if at all possible, however, they preferred not to fight at all.

During the Warlord Period, little direct damage was done to the economy except for the diversion of scarce capital that could have been funneled into economic development. The modern sector of the economy in the treaty ports† was not damaged, although it was slowed by disruptions. In the agricultural sector, crops were destroyed or taken as the poorly disciplined armies supported themselves by pillaging from the hapless peasants. Even though no lasting direct damage was done in the agricultural sector, the Warlord Period did cause significant indirect damage. Due to instability in the countryside, many of the leading families, which had always furnished rural leadership, fled to the protection of the treaty ports, leaving a leadership vacuum. Moreover, it was not uncommon for a victorious army to demand the annual land tax from an area after that area had already paid its annual land taxes to the losing army. Because this drove many peasants to sell their land, during the 1920s and 1930s land increasingly became concentrated in the hands of a relatively small group of wealthy owners. In sum, overall conditions in the countryside worsened. Already at the subsistence level, many of the peasants began to slip beneath it.[12]

During the early part of this period, Sun Yat-sen and his Kuomintang (the KMT, or Nationalist Party) tried three times to establish a government in south China at Canton. Each time, he failed to obtain the Western financial aid that might have enabled him to succeed, and each time he was chased out by the local warlord coalition. After the failure of his third attempt in 1921, he went to Shanghai,

---

*In part, this practice was common because from the time of Sun Tzu, traditional Chinese military theory emphasized that, when possible, it is better to achieve the objectives of war through negotiation or bribery.

*Through 1949, all Chinese armies—Warlord, Nationalist, and Communist—had one-half to two-thirds as many rifles as men. The remaining troops served without arms in rear echelon assignments, or were expected to equip themselves on the battlefield.

†A treaty port is a port that must be kept open for foreign trade according to the terms of a treaty.

the focal point of Chinese intellectual activity during this period.

During the Warlord Period, also, a new sense of Chinese nationalism arose in the treaty ports—a nationalism directed against the westerners and the Japanese, who seemed to be encouraging the fragmentation of China. To a degree, this nationalism was precipitated by the First World War, which greatly benefited the modern sector of the Chinese economy by forcing European industry to concentrate on the war effort, allowing indigenous Chinese industry to thrive, unhampered by competition. Concomitantly, the Japanese joined the Allied Powers in August 1914 and seized the German concessions in the Shantung Peninsula in north China. Despite the fact that Chinese nationalists felt that these concessions should revert to China, the Japanese kept them. Furthermore, in 1915, when Yüan Shih-k'ai could not obtain funds from Western bankers, the Japanese agreed to a favorable loan. However, they simultaneously presented the infamous Twenty-One Demands, and thus attempted to turn China into a virtual Japanese colony.[13] While Allied pressure prevented implementation of the worst of these demands, the Japanese greatly strengthened their position in China. In response, during August of 1917, China, also, joined the Allied Powers, with the objective of obtaining a seat at the peace conference in order to forestall the Japanese. This appeared logical, since American President Woodrow Wilson's principle of national self-determination seemed to preclude the old spheres of influence. The Japanese, however, had already made secret agreements with the other powers that confirmed their possession of the Shantung concession, thereby frustrating the Chinese. When the results of the Versailles Conference became known in China, the urban intellectuals protested vigorously, and there were massive strikes and boycotts against Japanese goods in the treaty ports.

The overall result of China's experience in the First World War was the discrediting of the Western example among many of the intellectual and commercial elite. Chinese entrepreneurs of the *compradore* class saw how much more successful they could be without Western competition, while leading thinkers saw the wide discrepancies that existed between the idealistic foundation of Wilson's Fourteen Points and the cynical reality of politics as it was really practiced. The Chinese had difficulty understanding this dichotomy, because throughout their history the deed had always remained close to the word. Disillusioned and bitter, these men saw Western aspirations and the ideals of democracy and liberalism as shams. There was also the image of a war that had almost destroyed Western civilization before it ended, leading many Chinese to argue that it

probably would be better not to follow the Western example. After all, immersed as it was in civil war, the Chinese civilization did not need lessons in self-destruction.

During this period of disenchantment with Western ideals, the militant Marxism of the Soviet Union was particularly attractive because it offered an alternative means of dealing with the great powers in the international arena. If a country could not obtain equal treatment within the existing international system, it could withdraw from the system, as the Soviet Union had done, repudiate the obligations of the previous regime, and nationalize foreign holdings. The Soviet model also offered a mechanism for solving China's internal difficulties—for unifying the country and expelling the westerners. Marxism provided a plausible, if incomplete, explanation of history, an ideal for social organization, and a detailed strategy for mobilizing, organizing, and bringing these changes about. It seemed to be a badly needed primer on nation building.* The Soviet Union cleverly maximized the impact of its example; too weak and torn by civil wars to enforce old treaties, it unilaterally renounced all of them and any rights in China. In this atmosphere, a group of men, which included some of China's most distinguished intellectuals, met to form a Chinese Communist Party (CCP) in July 1921. At that time only 27 years old, Mao Tse-tung was a provincial delegate representing his home province of Hunan.† At this same time, in Shanghai, after the failure of his third attempt to establish the KMT in south China, Sun Yat-sen sought two things: aid in organizing the diverse groups that followed him into a cohesive and dynamic party, and financial support. Unable to satisfy these needs by other means, he allied the KMT with the Communist International (Comintern)** in January 1923.[14] The price of that alliance was that the members of the small but dynamic CCP joined his KMT but retained their CCP membership.

The KMT-Comintern alliance was important. The KMT was reorganized along the lines of the Soviet Communist Party and, although not itself Communist, it sent delegates to the annual Comintern congresses in Moscow. In

---

*This is one of Marxism's biggest advantages. It provides a blueprint for nation building that, despite great costs, obviously works, based on the example of the Soviet Union rising to Superpower status. While Americans understand what a democratic society should look like in its sum, they seem unable to explain it *systematically* and to integrate its components in a way that is meaningful to a person who has not had American values inculcated within him from birth.

†Mao was born on December 26, 1893. While only 27 years of age by Western style of counting, since the Chinese have always counted the time spent in the womb as one year, he was 28 by their reckoning.

**The Communist International—also called Comintern and the Third International—was organized by the Bolsheviks in 1919 to direct the activities of Communist movements throughout the world.

February of 1923, Sun Yat-sen and the KMT returned to Canton once again to establish a new government. This time, his government was to last, even though the Western nations rejected his final plea for financial assistance. At the same time, Sun's thinking became increasingly leftist. His principle of people's livelihood became defined in socialistic rather than capitalistic terms—not surprising, given the traditional Confucian emphasis on socialism. As he now saw it, his revolution would take place in three stages. First, there would be a military phase to accomplish the reunification of the country under martial law. This would be followed by a period of political tutelage under a party dictatorship, while the people were politically awakened and educated. Finally, once the people were ready for it, the third stage of true democracy would begin. It was to be the KMT's tragedy that it got caught between the authoritarian first and second stages of the

revolution, and never progressed further until it retreated to Taiwan. During these years, the CCP played a decisive role in KMT activities—a role far out of proportion to its small membership.[15]

Rise of the Kuomintang

Only in tenuous control of the Canton vicinity, Sun realized that the formation of an army was essential if his political party were to compete in the absence of a political system. To create a military academy upon which a party army could be built, Sun selected Chiang Kai-shek, a 36-year-old professional soldier who had graduated from both Yüan Shih-k'ai's old Paoting Military Academy and the Japanese Military Academy.[16] First, however, Sun sent him to the Soviet Union in 1923 to study the latest concepts in Soviet doctrine and organization. Although he admired the efficiency and discipline of the Soviet Army, and particularly its system of political commissars, Chiang concluded that Soviet communism was just czarist imperialism under another name.[17] Upon his return to China, the Whampoa Military Academy opened its doors to its first class of 499 cadets in June 1924.[18] Eventually, it was to graduate a total of 7,399 officers, each after six months of study. Many of these were to rise high in China's armed forces; even four top Communist field commanders, including Lin Piao, were Whampoa graduates. Training at the academy was conducted with the assistance of Soviet military advisers, and the course emphasized political indoctrination rather than purely military training. The appointment of a 26-year-old general, Chou En-lai,* to the key position of deputy head of the political department underlines the importance of the Communist role in the KMT structure. In October 1924, the first Russian arms were received by the KMT,[19] and by the end of that year two regiments of what was to become the National Revolutionary Army (NRA) were formed. A division-sized force was created by April 1925, and Chiang was named commander-in-chief of the NRA while remaining superintendent of Whampoa.[20] However, he was still far from being important in the KMT's councils.

While the military arm of the KMT was gaining strength, the political arm remained disorganized. Despite the Soviet-style reorganization, the party was still a loose amalgamation of individuals and interests whose sole unifying ethics were nationalism and loyalty to Sun Yat-sen.

Chou En-lai

*Chou was born of a well-to-do family in Kiangsu Province in 1898. He was later educated at Nankai University. It was in France that he embraced communism.

The various groups on the left wing of the party, largely composed of the urban intellectual elite, desired not only to accomplish national reunification, but also to simultaneously implement a social revolution throughout the country. The CCP was a minor element of this wing of the party. The right wing of the party, composed largely of members of the *compradore* class and of the urban commercial elite, also wanted to accomplish the national reunification—but without disrupting the existing social status quo. The left wing of the party had the advantage of possessing a political program; while the right wing controlled the party's access to funds. In the center of the political spectrum was Chiang and the NRA that he increasingly dominated. When Sun suddenly died in March of 1925, the left wing of the KMT, under his heir, Wang Ching-wei, seemed to be dominant in the party. After Chiang staged a coup in March 1926, however, it was obvious that he really had the upper hand, even though the left wing still nominally held power.[21] Chiang was torn between two courses of action: he wished to retain Soviet support and improve conditions in the countryside, but he also wanted to accomplish orderly reform without disrupting the status quo and the right wing of the party. Thus, he did not seek a decisive confrontation. Despite his ambivalent centrist position, the Western press habitually referred to Chiang as the "red" or "bolshevik" general, partly due to the revolutionary slogans in his speeches and his habit of ending them with a raised clenched fist and the phrase "long live the world revolution."[22]

Chiang's *de facto* leadership of the party was confirmed in July of 1926, when he launched his Northern Expedition to unify all of China under KMT rule. This had long been Sun Yat-sen's cherished ambition, and by launching it on his own, Chiang assumed Sun's mantle—even though Wang Ching-wei was still the official leader of the KMT. Now numbering some 85,000 troops and 6,000 Whampoa cadets, the NRA was organized into six armies. However, only one of these armies was actually composed of party troops.[23] The remainder consisted of various warlord contingents that had been absorbed into the NRA when their leaders "simply joined the Kuomintang and continued in their old commands but under a revolutionary designation."[24]

Striking first at the Yangtze River basin, the expedition was organized into two columns. (*See Atlas Map No. 17.*) The western column, consisting of three armies, was expected to defeat a warlord coalition of 250,000 men[25] and capture Wuhan. It was under the command of General Li Tsung-jen, an ex-warlord. Under Chiang's personal command, the eastern column had as its mission the capture of Nanchang and the defeat of another 250,000 men under a second warlord coalition. Overall, the campaign was expected to last all summer. Then, operating from bases at Wuhan and Nanchang, the NRA would consolidate its position in central China and push on to Peking.

The western column moved quickly, arriving at Wuhan in September 1926. Delayed by more stubborn resistance, however, Chiang did not capture Nanchang until November 1926. Despite frequently harsh fighting, the NRA's

Chiang Kai-shek and Wang Ching-wei in Canton, November 1925

rapid advance of some 600 miles along a front of approximately 400 miles was due to its superior motivation, training, and equipment, as well as to extensive popular mobilization done by the KMT's left wing in advance of the armies. Moreover, continuing the warlord pattern of warfare described earlier, many of the minor warlord commanders preferred to switch sides and retain their commands and stature rather than fight and lose everything. Thus, some 34 district warlord contingents joined the NRA during this first phase of the Northern Expedition.[26] As planned, during the winter of 1926–1927, the NRA proceeded to consolidate its position by mopping up much of central China.

By the time that the NRA reached central China, it had become obvious to all that the Northern Expedition was going to be successful, at least initially. However, without a strategy that specified what course to pursue after reunification was achieved, the debate greatly intensified among the KMT factions over which direction the revolution should take. The need for immediate action further heated the debate because, as the army had moved north, members of the KMT's left wing and of the CCP had moved with it into the countryside, appropriating and redistributing the land, mobilizing the peasants, and building mass movements that threatened to get out of control. In doing this, they were only responding to the dissatisfaction voiced by the peasants over taxes, usury, and land tenure—problems that were developing spontaneously as a result of the political vacuum left by the departing warlord troops. As Mao Tse-tung, who then headed the KMT's Peasant Institute, later said concerning this period: "We organized the peasant movement, we didn't create it."[27] These actions in the countryside irked the right wing of the party, which saw the loss of its possessions, and caused uneasiness within the army because much of its officer corps came from well-to-do landowning families.[28]

The situation in Shanghai gave Chiang further reason to favor the right wing of the party. Chiang and the KMT leadership had originally intended to bypass Shanghai and press on to Peking; then, when they moved against the international community in Shanghai, they would do so with a united China at their backs. They miscalculated, however.

> Shanghai refused to wait. The [25,000 or so] foreign residents had reacted with panic at the epic surge from Canton. They saw the victorious army of liberation in only one color—red. For hadn't the Soviet Union armed and supplied it? Bloody revolution was approaching and it could have only one meaning— the looting of Shanghai's wealth and the massacre of its foreign population.[29]

Following calls for assistance, some 30,000 foreign troops were rapidly deployed in Shanghai.[30] Fearful that these troops might intervene to the detriment of the reunification movement, Chiang changed his mind and pressed the KMT government, now at Wuhan, to authorize the immediate capture and pacification of Shanghai. The Wuhan leadership, however, insisted on retaining Peking as the next objective, and, after further argument, it stripped Chiang of his political posts. Although Chiang was retained as military commander-in-chief, the rebuff drove him closer to the right wing of the party.[31]

Matters reached a climax in February and March of 1927 when the leftist-inspired Shanghai General Labor Union called general strikes that seemed certain to provoke Western interference. Thoroughly alarmed by what seemed to be the capping blow to a series of leftist excesses that appeared likely to further fragment China, Chiang quickly and decisively joined forces with the right wing of the party. Beginning on April 12, 1927, he expelled his Soviet advisers, moved his troops into Shanghai after insuring Western neutrality, and proceeded to exterminate several thousand Communists and leftist KMT agitators. Similar blows simultaneously struck by the NRA in Canton and Nanking scattered the CCP to the countryside. The Wuhan Government responded to this unilateral move by dismissing Chiang from his position as commander-in-chief of the NRA and by ejecting him from the KMT. Then Chiang demonstrated where the real power lay when he proclaimed his own rival KMT government at Nanking on April 18, 1927. By the end of July 1927, the Wuhan faction had capitulated and joined Chiang's government.[32] From this point until his death in 1976, Chiang was to remain the central figure in the KMT.

Surprised by the speed of Chiang's coup and still trying to follow orthodox doctrine, which dictated that the revolution would be led by the urban proletariat, the CCP leaders responded with a series of countercoups throughout the rest of 1927 and 1928. Their plan was to first use those NRA units loyal to their cause to capture key cities, and then inspire the urban workers to rise in rebellion. Thus, with 20,000 men they struck at Nanchang on August, 1, 1927,[33] a date that would be celebrated as the birthday of the Red Army. Their success in capturing the city was due in part to the fact that the NRA commander, General Chu Teh, a German-educated ex-warlord, was secretly a Communist.[34] However, the expected proletarian uprising never materialized; within five days, the city was recaptured by an overwhelming NRA force, and the poorly trained Communist troops were dispersed. The CCP made similar attempts with other troops against Wuhan and Changsha during the Autumn Harvest Uprisings in September 1927, but these were even less successful.

Mao, meanwhile, argued strongly against the CCP stress on the urban proletariat. Acutely aware of the unrest in the countryside, he stressed that the peasants should be the vanguard of the revolution. He also argued that the movement must depend upon a highly motivated, well-trained, regular military force for success rather than on worker uprisings, which might or might not take place. For these heresies, he was condemned by the CCP's Central Executive Committee as a "rightist military opportunist," and was suspended from his position as an alternate member of the party's politburo.[35] The existing policies of the CCP continued to be pursued. However, thoroughly fragmented, lacking regular contact with their advisers in the Comintern in Moscow, and dispersed throughout the countryside, the CCP seemed to offer little threat to anybody.

Chiang has been criticized for not eliminating the CCP in 1927. However, given the appalling conditions in the countryside, even if the Communists had been exterminated, other leaders would have risen to exploit peasant unrest. After all, that had happened less than a century earlier, when similar conditions existed during the T'ai-p'ing Rebellion. Also, given the similarity between the Communist programs that were developed later and the Confucian traditions of authoritarian social welfare, any programs promulgated by such replacement leaders would not have been too different from those of the CCP. Possessing a rural background himself, albeit an elite one, Chiang was very likely aware of this. However, if he had successfully reunited the country, he would have had the opportunity to moderate the situation by accomplishing measured reform in an orderly manner. It was his misfortune that he never had this opportunity because he never managed to reunify the country.

After forcing the Communists into the countryside, Chiang proceeded with the second phase of his Northern Expedition—the march on Peking to eliminate China's legitimate government. This second phase of the Northern Expedition differed radically from the first. The first phase, the march to the Yangtze River basin in 1926, had been a genuine revolutionary march. The NRA's success stimulated the growth of mass movements that, in turn, facilitated its progress. Countryside social relationships that had been virtually unchanged for millennia began to be altered. However, the second phase, the march from central China, was a war "very similar to the other warlord wars of the era."[36] Facing disunited opposition led by Feng Yü-hsiang in the northwest, Yen Hsi-shan in Shansi Province, and Chang Tso-lin in northern China and Manchuria, Chiang negotiated prior to marching. With a tri-umphant NRA that was stronger than each of the independent warlord forces, he negotiated from a position of strength. He secured Feng's and Yen's support by promising them virtual autonomy in their regions after the campaign was over, and he recognized Chiang as supreme in Manchuria if he would vacate north China.[37] The campaign was decided before it was begun.

Initiating the second phase of the Northern Expedition, four columns simultaneously converged on Peking. (*See Atlas Map No. 17.*) Feng and Yen each led their own troops, now flying the KMT banner, in separate columns, while Li Tsung-jen advanced up the Peking-Hankow Railway from Wuhan and Chiang moved through the eastern provinces from Nanking.[38] Beginning in April 1928, all movements proceeded smoothly, encountering only token resistance until Chiang's column met well-equipped Japanese forces, which were deployed in Shantung Province to protect their substantial commercial interests. There were bloodly clashes between the NRA and the Japanese before Chiang was able to disengage, apologize to the Japanese, and continue his march on Peking. All of this took time, and Li Tsung-jen and Feng Yü-hsiang arrived first in June 1928. As they moved into the city, Chang Tso-lin retired to Manchuria without fighting.[39]

With the Northern Expedition complete, Chiang established his capital at Nanking* and prepared to enter the second of Sun Yat-sen's three stages of revolution—political tutelage under a party dictatorship. However, although his regime was now recognized abroad as China's central government, the means by which Chiang had executed the Northern Expedition, allying himself with and absorbing self-sufficient warlord commanders still in command of their own troops, meant that he never truly unified the country. After the Northern Expedition was complete, there were several major military factions. Even though all flew the KMT banner and were nominally part of the NRA, each controlled its own army of several hundred thousand men and governed its own territory.[40] (*See Atlas Map No. 18.*) Thus, Chiang and his NRA—now numbering some 420,000 troops[41] and by far the strongest single contingent—directly ruled only some four or five provinces in the lower Yangtze River basin. Despite Chiang's efforts to accomplish further reunification, the warlords allied with him would neither give up their regional autonomy nor allow a reduction of their forces; to do so would have weakened their political power in a political system that still lacked accepted rules.

This lack of unity was reflected in further fighting. In

---

*The former capital, Peking, called "northern capital," was renamed Peiping, or "northern peace," and its metropolitan province, Chihli Province, was renamed Hopeh Province.

mid-1929, Li Tsung-jen and his faction tried to expand into central China. Chiang managed to block this move, but Feng Yü-hsiang took advantage of his preoccupation to try to expand into Shantung. In a campaign that involved hundreds of thousands of troops, Chiang moved troops north and managed to defeat Feng by November 1929.[42]

A much more significant threat occurred in the summer of 1930. Fearing that Chiang's rule was in danger of moving from a party dictatorship to a personal dictatorship, Wang Ching-wei and his faction within the KMT allied themselves with Feng and Yen Hsi-shan in the northwest and set up their own national government in Peking in June 1930. This time, the fighting was fierce—the bloodiest fighting since the dynasty had been overthrown in 1912. Chiang won only after receiving assistance from Chang Tsolin's son, Chang Hsueh-liang of Manchuria. Although minor clashes continued to occur throughout the 1930s, this was to be the last large-scale warlord conflict. The situation devolved into an uneasy state of mutual tolerance that was made formal by a KMT decision in 1933. It was agreed that the warlords would give nominal allegiance and some revenues to Nanking while the party would no longer try to unify the country by force. Instead, it would consolidate the few provinces under its direct control and then gradually try to extend its influence to other regions.[43] New threats, however, were to abort even this effort to achieve unification.

The Nationalist Decade

Based at Nanking in 1928, Chiang's Nationalist Government was a party dictatorship of the KMT that aimed to carry out the second stage of political tutelage in accordance with Sun Yat-sen's three-stage revolution. However, as it was established, the Government had a schizoid character. "Neither democratic nor totalitarian, neither socialist nor capitalist, the regime looked both to the modern West and to the Chinese past as though stuck in between."[44] In the best Soviet tradition, party and government completely overlapped; indeed, many of the party ministries simultaneously functioned as governmental ministries. But unlike the Soviet model, the KMT was never a cohesive or disciplined party. Instead, even apart from the warlords, it was an amalgamation of competing factions based only on a nationalism whose initial objective had already been achieved. Thus, Chiang ruled by playing these factions off against one another and by shifting his policies in order to keep in tune with shifts in the

power bases. In the civil sector, he presided rather than governed. This, of course, did not lead to the stable, well-conceived, long-term policy planning and implementation that was necessary for economic and social development. In political terms, while some slow progress was achieved toward centralization and a reduction of Western privileges, warlords still effectively controlled most of China, and Western gunboats still cruised the Yangtze River at will.*

Two other aspects of the Nanking Government's political situation played an important role in the outcome of the civil war. The first of these was the agreement with the warlords that prevented it from seeking popular support in most of China. The KMT was based almost entirely on the urban sector of the population, which was only 27 percent of the total population even in the small area that it did govern.[45] Within this sector of the population, the KMT was very successful in mobilizing support, and most of the urban proletariat was won back from its earlier CCP affiliation. However, it never made a real effort to mobilize the peasants in the countryside; virtually nobody in either the KMT or the CCP during those years ever expected the illiterate peasants to be concerned about the nature of government. Thus, the KMT's base of support was very narrow. Much of it came from the *compradore* class, giving the CCP an easy target upon which to focus discontent.

The other distracting aspect of the Government's political situation was that the party army was completely independent of civil authority and subordinate only to Chiang. This is not surprising, since Chiang's power within the KMT was directly based on his control of the army. Nor should it be surprising that, from 1932 onwards, Chiang turned those regions recovered from the warlords and from the Communists over to the army for administration, instead of placing them under civil government.[46] Over time, the army developed a vast bureaucracy that paralleled and competed with the civil structure at almost all levels. In the final analysis, instead of a government with a subordinate army to implement its policies, the NRA had a subordinate government to implement its wishes. The tail was wagging the dog.

Another basic problem was that the Government's agreement with the warlords prevented it from tapping the resources of most of the provinces. Indeed, 15 of the 27 provinces managed to appropriate *all* of their provincial revenues. Thus, the central government barred itself from access to the 65 percent of the total gross national product

---

*The USS *Panay* was making such a patrol in December 1937 when it was accidentally sunk by Japanese aircraft.

that the agricultural sector represented. Because there was no income tax, the largest source of government revenue came from maritime customs. In disbursing this revenue, even prior to the war with Japan, an annual average of 40.3 percent was allotted to pay military costs, while another 25 to 37 percent serviced the debt. This left very little for other uses such as industrial promotion or agricultural development, particularly when one considers the fact that total central government expenses averaged only 3.5 percent of the total gross national product during this period. It also left very little to pay the salaries of the civil servants, a situation that encouraged the growth of corruption. Even so, only 80 percent of the total government expenditures were ever covered by revenue receipts.[47] The government made ends meet by occasionally withholding payment or supplies from the troops, by borrowing additional money at rates of up to 40 percent annually,[48] and by increasing the amount of currency in circulation. As a consequence of this last measure, the face value of the notes in circulation rose from 350 million Chinese dollars in 1929 to 868 million Chinese dollars in 1935,[49] without any increase in financial reserves. The result was spiraling inflation.

To Chiang's great disadvantage, conditions in the countryside remained virtually unchanged. Between 60 and 90 percent of the farmers were still tenants or semi-tenants, and they still had to pay the land taxes and surtaxes that could be as high as 350 percent of the basic tax.* The interest on agricultural loans was still as high as 30 percent per year.[50] The KMT, however, did promulgate a land law aimed at reducing rents to only 37 percent of the annual crops and reducing interest to only 15 percent per year.[51] But even in the areas where the party directly governed, every attempt to implement these provisions evoked such a howl of protest from the landowning and moneylending interests that the government was forced to back off.[52] The law remained on the books, but only as a reminder of something promised and not granted. Given its very narrow base of popular and financial support, it was:

> small wonder that . . . [the KMT] could not implement its professed social and economic programs. In fact, a general feeling prevailed over many complacent KMT personnel that since the peasants had suffered for ages, it mattered little if they were asked to wait a little longer—until the government had solved the far more pressing problems of domestic insurrection and foreign aggression.[53]

*These surtaxes were often highest in those areas directly administered by the Nanking Government.

Had the peasants been left alone, this assumption might have been valid. However, they were not.

Communist Revival

Ironically, Chiang did the Communist movement a favor when he dispersed it into the countryside during 1927 and 1928. Before that time, the CCP leaders had competed with the KMT in trying to mobilize the tiny urban sector of the population. When driven from the cities and towns with prices on their heads as bandits, however, they had no option but to reluctantly follow Mao Tse-tung's heretical advice and turn to the peasantry as a means of supporting their movement. In the countryside, the survivors of the 1927 and 1928 setbacks established themselves along the provincial borders and in the zones where competing warlord or KMT jurisdictions met. These border areas minimized the danger of attack, because the warlords or governors controlling adjacent provinces were reluctant to make any move against the CCP that their neighbors might interpret as an act of hostility.[54] In these reasonably secure regions (*see Atlas Map No. 19*), away from the major lines of communication, Communist survivors proceeded to develop their bases. The largest of these was centered in the city of Juichin in Kiangsi Province, and was under Mao's rule. Here, in April 1928, Mao and his fellow survivors of Changsha linked up with Chu Teh and the survivors of Nanchang. With a combined strength of only about 2,000 men, Mao and Chu Teh used a process of trial and error to slowly develop the integrated politico-military strategy that was to result in overwhelming success 21 years later.[55]

The first requirement for a base area was that it be a secure, self-sufficient region from which tax collectors could be expelled and in which the CCP could implement its own reforms and extract its own revenues. The means used to achieve this security involved more than a mere military defensive perimeter, for the CCP aimed not just at controlling revenue, as did the warlords and the KMT. The CCP sought to influence and mobilize the entire population.[56] Thus, the movement had to establish deep roots based on committed peasant support that was obtained not by subversion but by responding to peasant needs and aspirations.[57] To achieve this end, the CCP used the famous Mass Line Strategy—a strategy of integrated sociopolitical and military mobilization that was related to economic conditions. Although it did not originate with Mao, he adopted it very early, and became its most avid propagandist.[58] In fact, notwithstanding Western military analyts' emphasis on the Communist use of superficial guerrilla tactics, it was the Mass Line Strategy that was the key to Mao's eventual success.

In a typical implementation of this strategy, the first step involved sending CCP political teams and regular units of the Red Army into an area not yet controlled by the CCP. Inherently conservative, the peasants were suspicious of the troops. Ultimately, however, the people were impressed by the good behavior and discipline of the Red Army, since it not only refrained from looting, but also worked with them during the critical planting and harvesting seasons. Moreover, the Army showed unusual generosity in dividing and sharing captured arms and ammunition with the village militia organizations.[59]

The first job of the political teams was to investigate the manifold peasant grievances in order to determine which were most deeply felt so that they could be emphasized for maximum effect.[60] Realizing that an individual's courage increases when he is in a group, the CCP held village meetings at which the people could air their grievances and discuss solutions for them.[61] Whenever possible, the political cadre members attempted to encourage self-generated solutions. This phase of open meetings was conducted simultaneously with selective terror aimed both at disorienting and cowing the opposition and at showing the peasants that they could take action into their own hands to improve their lot.[62] At the same time, the political teams organized the entire population into various groups—village militias, Red Guards, youth leagues, and women's organizations—with the objective of eventually tying everybody into at least one group. This facilitated population control, the recruitment of future cadre, and the dissemination of information.[63] Eventually, township governments were formed to coordinate these groups and implement the Communist programs.[64]

The basic Communist program that was set up within a liberated area depended upon a system of land redistribution that was virtually impossible to resist. Rather than working to confiscate all private land, this system appropriated only that land which belonged to those whom the CCP termed to be militarists, landlords, or rich peasants. Unless these targets resisted, not all of their land was taken; they were usually left with enough land to qualify as middle peasants—which, of course, defused much of the resistance that might otherwise have occurred.[65] All confiscated land was equitably distributed among the poor peasants, while confiscated money and material goods went into the party coffers.[66] Even so, there was not enough land to provide everybody with an amount sufficient for subsistence, so the CCP augmented the redistribution program with reductions of rents and interest rates along the lines of the KMT's own Land Law of 1930. The CCP also implemented a progressive taxation system that spread the tax burden more equitably.[67] While the result was short of a utopia, these programs vastly improved the average peasant's condition, thereby inspiring unusual motivation and commitment to the party. The peasants knew that if the Communists were ejected, the original living conditions would return. For the first time, the peasants had a reason for making a commitment to a system; they had something worth fighting for.

It must be emphasized that the Mass Line Strategy was never rigid. This was so partly because of internal dissensions within the CCP that caused shifts in the methods of its implementation, and partly because Mao and his followers emphasized flexibility. The CCP never did more than the masses would directly support.[68] Thus, at any given moment, the degree to which these programs were actually in effect varied widely from region to region. As Mao wrote at the time: "We must go among the masses; arouse them to activity, concern ourselves with their weal and woe; and work earnestly and sincerely in their interests . . . . If we do so, the broad masses will certainly give up support and regard the revolution as their very life. . . ."[69] He constantly cautioned against moving faster than the peasants were willing to go.

This strategy of revolution involved far more than just troops and guerrilla tactics. The Red Army's role in the strategy was two-fold: first, to help the peasants revolt and seize the land; then, to protect them. Because neither the KMT nor the warlords had their locus of power in the countryside, by the time their troops could be mobilized and deployed, the CCP had frequently already consolidated its territory.[70]

It is not surprising that the CCP's results were most spectacular in the Kiangsi region. Beginning with some 2,000 men in April 1928, Mao and Chu Teh had 22,000 men in their segment of the Red Army (the Fourth Red Army) by the end of 1929. Political development proceeded in tandem with this military growth, and the autonomous Kiangsi Soviet was proclaimed in February 1930. In November of 1931, Mao formally announced the region's secession from the Nanking Government when he established the Soviet Republic of China. At that time, the Kiangsi region totaled over 19,000 square miles—about the size of Switzerland—and contained some 3 million people. In addition, there were another 6 million people[71] scattered in five other major soviets that "had attained some permanence and stability as independent political entities."[72] (*See Atlas Map No. 19.*)

This spectacular Communist growth was not without its problems. In 1927, when Chiang purged the Communists from the KMT, the CCP's Central Committee went into hiding in the International Community in Shanghai, where Chiang could not reach them.[73] There, its leadership continued efforts to mobilize the urban proletariat, still believing that any revolutionary impetus would have to come from the industrial workers. Virtually all agreed that the role of the peasants—if they had one at all—was at most auxiliary. Then, in June of 1929, Li Li-san was selected by the Comintern to lead the CCP. Impressed with the spectacular successes that the Communist soviets were achieving and encouraged by the warlord risings against the KMT in 1929 and 1930, Li decided that the KMT's fragile coalition was falling apart and that the time was ripe for a major push out of the soviets and back into the cities. As he saw it, Chiang had made the task even easier by withdrawing most of the better NRA troops from central China to fight in the north.[74]

In accordance with Li's strategy, Red Army units were to move out of the soviets, capture major cities such as Wuhan, Changsha, and Nanchang, and then be reinforced by spontaneous workers' uprisings in the cities. In implementation, however, with the sole exception of Changsha, the Red Army failed to take the cities. In all cases, the proletariat failed to rise, and NRA counterstrokes once again dispersed the Red Army. In disgrace, Li Li-san was dismissed and recalled to Moscow. However, the damage had been done; the campaign had forcefully drawn Chiang's attention to the fact that the CCP was far from being impotent. He decided to deal with this resurgent menace as soon as he finished with his current campaigns in the north.[75]

A New Type of Civil War

After Chiang suppressed the Wang-Yen-Feng coalition, he turned against the Communist soviets. He would spend the next six years unsuccessfully trying to eliminate this threat. Between October 1930 and October 1934, he launched a total of five extermination campaigns against the soviets. Due to factors largely beyond his immediate control, none of these campaigns was successful. In the first two campaigns, fought between October 1930 and June 1931, Chiang concentrated against the Kiangsi Soviet and Chu Teh's Fourth Red Army. However, underestimating the Communist power, he used provincial warlord troops against them in an effort to eliminate the Communist threat and weaken his warlord adversaries at the same time. In each campaign, the NRA made a single thrust, and in each case Chu Teh's troops conducted a strategic

withdrawal, exploiting the Clausewitzian law of the diminishing force of the offensive and encouraging the warlord troops to disperse in pursuit. Then, mustering militia and guerrilla reinforcements as he retired, Chu Teh would suddenly concentrate his forces and destroy major NRA formations. The extermination campaign then collapsed, because the warlords naturally disliked losing their troops and thereby their influence in KMT politics.[76]

Although the NRA forces were far superior to those of the Red Army in numbers, arms, ammunition, and heavy equipment, the Red Army had other advantages. Its troops were more motivated; indeed, most of the warlord soldiers captured during the campaigns were eventually recruited into the Red Army. The Communist troops were also more disciplined and more flexible in response to the tactical situation.[*] With their light equipment and rates of march that compared very favorably to Stonewall Jackson's famous American Civil War "foot cavalry," they had an excellent mobile warfare capability.[†] Furthermore, since the Red Army was operating in familiar terrain inhabited by people sympathetic to its cause, it had superb intelligence. Thus, Chu Teh's tactics took maximum advantage of both his own strengths and his enemy's weaknesses. In short, he implemented his defensive strategy with guerrilla tactics—tactics that, as early as 1928, he summed up in this poem:

> When the enemy advances, we retreat.
> When the enemy halts and encamps, we harass him.
> When the enemy seeks to avoid battle, we attack.
> When the enemy retreats, we pursue.[77]

Realizing the extent of the Communist threat after the failures of 1930 and 1931, Chiang launched a Third Extermination Campaign under his won command in July 1931. This time, Chiang stiffened the army with elite units of his own Central Forces and devised a more complex strategy. Instead of the single thrust used in prior campaigns, he planned a dozen simultaneously striking columns. Moreover, in addition to the Kiangsi Soviet, he aimed at mopping up the various minor soviets. He was successful in eliminating two of the outlying soviets in Hupeh Province; but, once again, the drive to crush the Kiangsi Soviet halted as Chu Teh slipped his regulars between Chiang's

---

[*]This favorable attribute was largely due to the fact that commanders at all levels in the Red Army were encouraged to use their initiative.

[†]In 1935, during the Long March, Lin Piao's I Corps covered 125 miles in 3 days. (See William Morwood, *Duel for the Middle Kingdom,* New York, 1980, p. 201). Also during the Long March, a Red Army regiment was alleged to have covered 80 miles in 24 hours during the maneuvering at the Lu-ting Bridge. (See Dick Wilson, *The Long March, 1935,* New York, 1973, p. 200).

columns to mount converging attacks in their rear.[78] Before Chiang could respond, the Japanese absorption of Manchuria in September 1931 required his attention.

Japan's involvement in China was intimately connected with domestic Chinese events, and played a key role in facilitating Mao's eventual success. The Japanese had long controlled the Manchurian economy, and they regarded that region both as essential to their economy and as a geopolitical bulwark against Russia. During the Warlord Period, they had supported Chang Tso-lin and his son, Chang Hsueh-liang, in Manchuria. In the summer of 1931, when it appeared to all outside observers that Chiang was on the verge of crushing the Communists and creating a more unified China, the staff of the Japanese army in Manchuria, the Kwangtung Army, predicted that Chiang's next step would be a new alliance with the Soviet Union and a joint assault on Manchuria. To preclude this, on September 18, 1931, the Kwangtung Army began to absorb Manchuria without governmental authority, achieving total control of the region and forcing Chang Hsueh-liang into northern China by early 1932. This forced Chiang Kai-shek to abandon his campaign and move north to watch both the Japanese and Chang Hsueh-liang. In the treaty ports, and particularly in Shanghai, anti-Japanese sentiment was quite fierce. However, despite the intensity of anti-Japanese sentiment, Chiang believed that the primary problem facing China was not the threat of external aggression posed by Japan, but rather the threat of renewed internal dissension posed by the CCP. Concentrating his own efforts on the domestic threat and hoping that the Leauge of Nations would deal with Japan, he negotiated a truce on May 5, 1932 that left the Japanese in control of Manchuria.[79] This decision was realistic in military terms, since China was in no condition to fight Japan. However, it cost Chiang much support among the intelligentsia, the students, the urban elite, and even the warlords—all of whom wanted to expel the Japanese. Moreover, Chiang's most powerful warlord competitor, Chang Hsueh-liang, was now within China proper with his army intact and hoping to recover Manchuria. Finally, the truce gave a new weapon to the CCP. Far removed from the Japanese in southern China, Mao's new Soviet Republic of China declared war on Japan in April 1932.[80]

In December 1932, the accommodation with the Japanese completed, Chiang turned back to deal with a CCP that had been granted a 15-month respite. On both sides, much had occurred during the interval. Convinced that the future of its revolution lay with the rural soviets, the CCP Central Committee had moved down to the Kiangsi Soviet in late 1932, pushed Mao aside, and condemned him for being overly conservative. Then, firmly in control, the

Central Committee had pushed for radical redistribution programs. It had 200,000 troops in all of the soviets combined, and over 100,000 in the Kiangsi Soviet, the latter now organized as the First Front Army. The Central Committee had also abandoned the Mao-Chu Teh guerrilla tactics in favor of static positional tactics, seeking to deny all liberated territory to the KMT.[81] Thus, in the final analysis, the respite had weakened the CCP's ability to defend itself. On the KMT side, the foundations for a strengthened NRA had been laid by an increasing number of German military advisers. Beginning as early as 1927, when Chiang expelled his Soviet military advisers, a German military mission had served with the NRA's Central Forces. During its tenure in China, which ended in 1942,[82] this mission introduced German staff methodology, organization, and equipment to the Central Forces. The concepts that these experts introduced, however, were those that had been thoroughly learned during the First World War—static, positional tactics and the rectangular division organized and equipped to fight in trench warfare.* They were quite unsuited to a war of mobility.

It was in the context of these changes that the Fourth Extermination Campaign began in December 1932 when 400,000 NRA troops assaulted all of the Communist soviets. Again, the planning envisioned multiple thrusts into the center of the CCP territories. This time, fighting in line under the new CCP policy that required all territory to be defended, Chu Teh began to lose ground. Once again, however, Chiang's expected success caused uneasiness in the Japanese Kwangtung Army. In March 1933, again without governmental approval, it struck south of the Great Wall in an effort to create a buffer zone between the KMT and Manchuria. As in 1931, Chiang had to suspend operations in the south and focus his attention on the north, allowing Chu Teh's counteroffensive to sweep the NRA from its newly gained territories.[83] In accordance with his earlier priorities, Chiang again reached a truce with the Japanese in May 1933, allowing them to garrison troops in Chahar and Jehol Provinces and creating a demilitarized zone in the eastern part of Hopeh Province.† This new truce further increased Chinese discontent with his regime, and further angered Chang Hsueh-liang.

Although the Fourth Extermination Campaign did not make lasting gains within the Kiangsi Soviet, it did eliminate several of the outlying Communist soviets located on

---

*The rectangular division was built around four regiments of infantry, which were organized into two brigades. It was considerably larger than the more flexible World War II triangular division, which was organized around three regiments of infantry, and was designed to be more mobile.

† This truce is known as the T'ang-ku Truce. It also limited the number of troops that each side could garrison in the Peiping district.

its flanks. With these bastions gone, the way was clear for Chiang to pursue a new strategy in his Fifth Extermination Campaign—a strategy of encircling the main soviet, cordoning it off with concentric circles of mutually supporting blockhouses and pillboxes, and then gradually compressing it until the CCP was crushed. Concomitantly, following his own oft-quoted statement that suppression of the CCP was 30 percent a military problem and 70 percent a political problem, Chiang planned to reorganize the liberated population to resist future CCP actions.

The Fifth Extermination Campaign was launched in October 1933. With 750,000 men, Chiang struck the Kiangsi Soviet, while thousands of other troops moved against the last remaining minor soviets. In accordance with the new strategy, the NRA troops completed their encirclement and established the first of their cordons. Fully committed to the CCP's new policy of static, positional defense, Chu Teh dispersed his 100,000 troops to defend his entire perimeter. In doing so, he sacrificed the initiative, forfeited the inherent advantages of his troops, and played to the strengths of the NRA. His troops fought well, but with a total of only 60,000 rifles, no artillery, and five aircraft without fuel, they lost heavily as the NRA steadily pushed the cordon inward with short, powerful drives from all sides.[84]

In April of 1934, the CCP's Central Committee realized that the Kiangsi Soviet could no longer be held, and so began planning a massive breakout. The survivors of the remaining soviets were directed to disengage from their opponents, and advance detachments of the First Front Army broke out of the Kiangsi Soviet in the early autumn of 1934. Some 15,000 soldiers and 20,000 to 30,000 political cadre members were detailed to remain behind* in order to carry on the movement in the south, while the bulk of the First Front Army broke out of the cordon to the southwest during late October 1934. Consisting of some 91,000 personnel, it took advantage of the NRA's lack of flexibility, mobility, and internal communications to break through four successive cordons. In doing so, however, the First Front Army was gradually reduced in strength. At the end of November 1934, when it completed the breakout and began the Long March, the First Front numbered only 35,000.[85]

The Long March of the CCP was an epic achievement by anybody's accounting. Mao's group moved first to the west and then north and northeast to the town of Yenan in Shensi Province. (*See Atlas Map No. 19.*) It marched a

*One of those left behind was Mao's brother, Mao Tse-tan, the commander of the Red Army's 5th Independent Division. He was killed as the NRA mopped up the area. Also left behind were Mao's two infant children by his third wife, Ho Tzu-chen. They completely disappeared.

The Long March

total of 6,600 miles in 235 days—averaging 17 miles per day for the entire year, or 26 miles per day if the rest periods are not counted. These were not easy miles, for the CCP troops and party cadre had to cross 18 mountain ranges and 24 major rivers; they traversed 11 of China's provinces, while fighting or skirmishing virtually all the way. In all, the Long March was very much a time of testing and proving. Only the fittest and most committed survived. It is difficult to determine precisely how many people completed the march, as different commands began moving at different locations and at different times, and they arrived in Shensi Province at different times. Furthermore, many of the troops and party members who finished the march had been recruited enroute, while others deserted or were dropped off along the way in order to accomplish party work. However, as near as can be determined, only about 5,000 men survived the entire march. As Mao himself arrived in Shensi Province with about 8,000 men, some 7,000 men arrived before him, and about

30,000 arrived after him, the CCP totaled about 45,000 party members and soldiers at the end of the journey.[86]

The Long March decided the future leadership and strategies of the CCP. When the First Front Army left Kiangsi, Mao was at the nadir of his career, not only without power in the party, but also with a party membership that had been reduced to probationary status by the Central Committee in July 1934.[87] However, after disengaging from the main NRA forces in the Kiangsi region, the Red Army captured the town of Tsunyi in Kweichow Province in January 1935. (*See Atlas Map No. 19.*) There, the columns halted to rest while the party leadership held a conference to determine what had gone wrong and what was to be done next. At this Tsunyi conference, Mao violently attacked the Central Committee's leadership and policies, emphasizing that the radical land policies had detracted from the party's support. He also argued that the emphasis on defending all territory with static, positional tactics had been disastrous. As he was not alone in this condemnation, and as his own previous strategies had worked, the Central Committee reluctantly delegated all substantive power to a new Revolutionary Military Council under Mao's chairmanship.[88] It was also at this conference, again at Mao's insistence, that the tiny soviet near Yenan in northwest China's Shensi Province was selected as the CCP's destination. Mao also shrewdly used the march to further CCP ends. He turned it into a crusade, arguing that the CCP was moving north to build a base from which to fight the Japanese. [89] Furthermore, as he pointed out at the time: "The Long March is also an agitation corps. It declares to approximately 200 million of eleven provinces that only the road of the Red Army leads to their liberation. . . ."[90] From this point on, Mao was the dominant character in the party's decisionmaking process. Yet, still not the official leader of the party nor its undisputed *de facto* leader, he "should probably be thought of as first among equals in a collective leadership. . . ."[91]

Chiang tried to halt the CCP's march, but lack of communications in western China prevented his formations from moving at the Red Army's speed. Making use of his interior lines of communication, he attempted to insert blocking forces ahead of the Red Army's wheeling movement. However, he was hampered by the fact that the Communist forces were marching on different routes (*See Atlas Map No. 19.*) Chiang also misjudged the ultimate destination of the CCP forces. During the first part of the Long March, he aimed at preventing a union of the CCP forces. After that union was accomplished in June 1935, he not unreasonably assumed that the CCP was headed due north to Sinkiang Province or to Outer Mongolia— there to link up with the Soviet Union and receive direct

assistance.[92] Instead, the Red Army turned northeast toward Shensi Province, inside Chiang's blocking forces. Finally, even when Chiang did manage to correctly position blocking forces, he was frustrated by the Red Army's speed, because its vanguard frequently punched through his barriers before sufficient NRA troops could converge to halt it.

Once established in the Yenan region, Mao again implemented the Mass Line Strategy to mobilize the population and expand both his territory and his forces. However, new elements were integrated into this sociopolitical strategy. Aware that the literacy rate was only about one percent in this particularly poor and backward area, Mao introduced an extensive education program that concentrated on practical rather than theoretical or political education; in so doing, the party made extensive use of films, opera, and dance troupes to convey its message.[93] Other subtle elements were introduced to gain popular support. For example, even though in Yenan they controlled a 40,000-inhabitant county seat, the CCP leadership, rather than living in the town, stayed in caves carved out of the nearby hillsides. This, naturally, was meant to illustrate the party's egalitarian attitude.* In the same vein, as the CCP rapidly grew in size and the complexity of government increased, Mao launched a rectification movement to insure that both the party and the Government remained in touch with and responsive to the people.† Although not entirely successful, "at least the Communists tried to deal with the problems of bureaucratization . . . in contrast to the Nationalists . . ." who did very little along these lines.[94] While not completely successful in party purification, by 1944, Mao was the undisputed leader of the CCP. He insisted that the party lead by subtle guidance rather than overt coercion.** Thus, although authoritarian in nature, the party's rule was benevolent by Chinese standards, bringing it as closely in line with the traditional ethic of government as the Communist ethic of individual subordination to group welfare was to the traditional Con-

---

*These cave dwellings are very common in northwest China, as they are warm in the very harsh winters and cool in the very hot summers. Thus, in their romantic and egalitarian "caves of Yenan," Mao and his colleagues probably lived far more comfortably than they would have in the town.

†This rectification movement of the early 1940s was the direct ancestor of Mao's "100 Flowers Campaign" of the 1950s and his "Great Proletarian Cultural Revolution" of the 1960s—both of which also aimed at destroying party elitism.

**An example of this technique was Mao's campaign against the foot binding of females, a practice stemming from the ancient custom of binding baby girls' feet to insure that they stayed tiny. While beautiful to Chinese men, the girls grew up to be virtual cripples. Finding that his exhortations and laws were being ignored, he simply created jobs for nimble-footed girls. This had an immediate effect. Mao never hesitated to use the indirect approach when he felt it necessary to minimize opposition.

fucian ethic. By its actions, the CCP proved that it aimed to enhance the welfare of the common man, who was, of course, a peasant. It is not surprising that, once again, support for the CCP grew by leaps and bounds.

Immediately after the Communists arrived in Shensi Province at what became the Yenan Soviet, Chiang launched an improvised attack. When it failed, he began to prepare a Sixth Extermination Campaign, which was to be conducted by 300,000 troops, mostly drawn from Chang Hsueh-liang's Northeast Army.[95] However, Chang, increasingly bitter at the loss of his territory in Manchuria and north China to the Japanese, was becoming more responsive to the popular outcry that the Chinese should be killing the Japanese instead of other Chinese. Thus, while sending back reports that he was still preparing to move against Yenan, he actually reached an informal truce with the CCP in the summer of 1936.[96]

In October of 1936, Chiang flew to Sian and obtained a promise from Chang that he would move immediately against Yenan. However, Chang not only ignored this promise, but actually allowed a separate supporting attack to be routed by the Red Army.[97] When Chang continued to procrastinate, Chiang flew to Sian again on December 7,

Chiang Kai-shek at the Time of the Japanese Invasion of China

1936 and threatened Chang with retaliatory action. This time, Chang moved. While Chiang Kai-shek was resting at a spa near Sian, Chang's troops attacked his villa just before dawn on December 12, 1936, forcing Chiang to flee up the hillside while his bodyguard was killed.[98] Within hours, he was captured and brought before Chang. There, Chang demanded that he reverse his policies regarding the Japanese. CCP and KMT histories disagree on precisely what happened next, but Chiang was released on December 25, 1936 through the joint intervention of his wife and Chou En-lai of the CCP. Within weeks, a United Front, which joined the KMT, the CCP, and all other minor parties against Japan, was proclaimed. This was not a coalition government, but rather an informal alliance of all factions throughout China, designed to counter the common enemy. Nonetheless, Chou En-lai led a Communist delegation to Nanking. This uneasy alliance—and, indeed, the entire situation in China—was profoundly affected by an incident that occurred near Peking six months later.

An Interruption: Japanese Expansion in China and World War II

On July 7, 1937, an unpremeditated incident took place at the Marco Polo Bridge, in the demilitarized zone near Peking. There, during night maneuvers conducted by the Japanese garrison in the tiny treaty port of Tientsin, a Japanese soldier disappeared.* At once, the Japanese commander demanded Chinese help in finding him. By dawn, fighting had broken out between the garrison troops and the NRA's Twenty-Ninth Army.[99] The local commanders tried to negotiate, but the higher echelons on both sides were unwilling to compromise. The Japanese High Command again saw the dangers of a united China allied with the Soviet Union—and, as it turned out, this was a very real danger. From July 1937 to June 1941, the Soviet Union provided almost half of all foreign aid received by the KMT, as well as some 500 pilots and military advisers† and about 1,000 aircraft.[100] In 1938 and 1939,

_____

*The lost soldier is alleged to have turned up a few weeks later as a deserter.

†As a good-will measure, this Russian effort far exceeded that of the unofficial United States "Flying Tigers" effort. In terms of quality, however, the American assistance probably compared much more favorably. The Flying Tigers, organized in 1941, consisted of about 100 American aviators—former United States Army, Navy, and Marine officers—and maintenance personnel who volunteered to serve as mercenaries in China. They were under the command of Claire L. Chennault, a colonel in the Chinese Air Force who was a retired United States Army Air Force captain.

Japanese fears were further fueled by serious clashes between the Soviet Far Eastern Army and the Kwangtung Army along the northern Manchurian border.

Knowing that popular opinion would not condone another truce with the Japanese, Chiang made an aggressive speech on July 17, 1937 and moved NRA troops into the demilitarized zone. The Japanese responded by announcing a deadline for the withdrawal of these troops. They attacked before the deadline expired,[101] however, and with this act of aggression, Japan's China Incident began. It was to have a tremendous impact on the outcome of the duel between Chiang and Mao.

With the onset of war, the Chinese implemented the United Front and, in August 1937, the Red Army was formally incorporated into the NRA as the Eighth Route Army* under Chu Teh. "The units remained Communist but adopted Nationalist uniforms and standards . . . and received weapons and supplies . . ." in the amount of some 500,000 Chinese dollars per month through 1940. Later, in

---

* The Eighth Route Army was later redesignated the 18th Army Group, but the former designation is used throughout this text because the force was best known by that name.

October 1937, Chiang's headquarters authorized the formation of a second Communist NRA organization, the New Fourth Army, which was to amalgamate those Red Army units still operating in southern China.[102] This United Front would work reasonably well as long as Japan exerted pressure; but when that pressure lessened, the United Front collapsed in all but name and aspiration.

The Japanese were unprepared for the conflict. When war broke out, the Kwangtung Army was in the throes of reorganizing from rectangular to triangular divisions, and Japan did not mobilize its economy for war until March 1938.[103] The initial Japanese strategy envisioned a general southward drive from north China and Manchuria, simply attacking the NRA frontally until Chiang was forced to the negotiating table. In line with this strategy, the Japanese cleared the Peking vicinity of NRA troops during August of 1937. In September, the main drive to the south began;[104] but already the focus of action had shifted even farther to the south.

Hoping to gain Western support to defeat the Japanese, on August 8, 1937 Chiang directed that an attack be made on the Japanese position in the International Settlement in

The International Settlement in Shanghai, 1937

Shanghai. Chiang's intention was to provoke a Japanese response that would involve the substantial Western contingents there.* However, the Western troops remained strictly neutral and, on August 13, 1937, the Japanese began to deploy forces in the Shanghai vicinity that totaled over 200,000 men by November 1937. In response, Chiang committed more and more of his best troops, and eventually had over 1 million men engaged on the Shanghai front. Harsh and bloody fighting leading to 50 percent casualties on both sides continued until December, when the Japanese finally made a wheeling movement that outflanked the Chinese defenses and cleared the road to Nanking.[105] Abandoning that city to a Japanese sack that lasted two weeks and killed between 40,000 and 100,000 civilians,[106] the KMT government withdrew to Wuhan, still vainly trying to gain Western assistance. This failing, Chiang commenced to plan a further withdrawal up the Yangtze River to Chungking in Szechwan Province. His idea was that "retreat to the hinterland was the better part of valor until the international situation blew up and propelled allies his way."[107] Furthermore, he correctly anticipated that withdrawal before each enemy advance would cause the Japanese to overextend themselves and thereby make their eventual defeat that much easier. While they did overextend themselves, the result was far from what Chiang intended.

After the capture of Nanking, the Japanese paused to recoup their losses. In the summer of 1938, with their reserve forces mobilized, they began a slow push up the Yangtze River from Nanking. Despite minimal NRA resistance, they did not take Wuhan until October 1938,[108] and this gave the KMT enough time to evacuate the government as well as much of the industry between the central Yangtze basin and Szechwan Province. However, this gain for the KMT was more than offset by a simultaneous Japanese amphibious push down the south Chinese coast that captured all of the port cities, including Canton, by October 1938.[109] With Chiang's major channels of outside support severed, the Japanese had realistic expectations of forcing his capitulation by destroying his capability to wage war.

In north China, meanwhile, the Japanese were making overall gains, if occasionally suffering a setback. In late September 1937, Lin Piao, commander of the Eighth Route Army's 115th Division, gave a foretaste of things to come when he ambushed two Japanese divisions in Pinghsin Pass in Shensi Province. The Japanese suffered 6,400 casualties at a cost of only 300 of Lin's forces, but this

victory was not enough to stem the Japanese tide.[110] In the spring of 1938, they launched a new offensive aiming at the Yellow River. It was the eastern column of this drive, consisting of some 80,000 men, that Li Tsung-jen attacked with some 400,000 NRA troops on April 1, 1938 at Taierchuang. Personally advised by General von Falkenhausen, the chief of the German Military Advisory Group, Li's army inflicted heavy losses on two Japanese divisions[111] in what was to be China's only major victory in eight years of war with Japan. Nevertheless, despite the fact that the NRA broke the dikes of the Yellow River, killing hundreds of thousands of Chinese civilians, the Japanese reached their objectives by June 1938, when they captured the city of Kaifeng in Honan Province. Thus, by the end of 1938, Chiang's forces had been pushed out of north and central China, had sustained some 800,000 casualties, and had lost most of their best troops and equipment.[112] (*See Atlas Map No. 20.*) From this point until 1944, the war in China developed into a desultory stalemate between the Japanese, the KMT, and the CCP.

Whereas the Japanese originally had expected to force Chiang to the negotiating table within three months, by the end of 1938 they had deployed 1,500,000 troops to China and sustained over 300,000 casualties. Japan wanted to end the war, but neither Chiang nor Mao was ever willing to accept the proffered terms. Most of Japan's troops in China were subsequently deployed either in Manchuria—to watch the primary enemy, the Soviet Union—or on the southwestern front, to watch Chiang and the remnants of the NRA. The few remaining troops, about 250,000 men of the North China Army, were sparsely deployed in garrison and railway-patrol duties.[113] Without sufficient men to control the countryside, the Japanese were confined to the cities, the towns, and the railway lines between them. In effect, although they had driven the KMT out of north China, the Japanese had failed to replace Chiang's leadership. Consequently, from 1938 onward, the Japanese strategy in China was passive; capable of doing little more than awaiting the anticipated but never realized Chinese surrender, Japanese troops mounted no major offensives until 1944.

When the Japanese pressure slackened, the United Front began to crumble. Although still providing financial support to the Eighth Route Army, in mid-1939 the KMT deployed 200,000 troops (the number was later increased to over 500,000) to blockade the Yenan Soviet. At the same time, the NRA attacked to recover parts of Shensi Province from the CCP, and moved to eliminate CCP cells throughout those parts of southern and western China that it still controlled.[114] Some semblance of cooperation continued, however, until January 1941, when the NRA

*In addition to the Japanese garrison, there were a British brigade, a French brigade, a U.S. Marine regiment, and minor Dutch and Italian contingents in the Shanghai International Settlement at the time.

turned on the New Fourth Army and wiped out its headquarters.[115] Although joint cooperation between the two
factions ended then, the Communist forces continued to
be listed in NRA tables of organization, and their troops
still wore NRA uniforms. Furthermore, the two sides still
negotiated, and the CCP continued to maintain a liaison
office in Chungking.

Secure behind the mountains of the upper Yangtze Valley, Chiang settled down in Chungking to await allies and
assistance. At the same time, he planned to rebuild his
economy and to train new armies, first with German and
Soviet aid and later with American help. The basis for this
reconstruction had been laid during the withdrawal from
the lower Yangtze basin when defense-oriented industries
were taken apart and carried to Szechwan. Although
about 70 percent of these industrial plants were successfully re-established, they were to prove of little worth. The
Japanese seizure of the coast isolated the KMT from the
outside world, and the loss of the maritime customs revenue exacerbated already critical raw material and transportation shortages. Saddled with a massive bureaucracy
and rampant corruption, the faltering Government
proved totally inadequate to deal with problems that
would have taxed even the most efficient of governments.
Given critical scarcities of food, housing, and raw materials, the officials controlling these assets found it most
profitable to withhold them to drive the prices up; as a
consequence, very little was produced.[116] Even with American aid after 1941, the reduced KMT revenue base was
unable to meet the ever-increasing war expenses and, with
expenses five times as great as its revenues, the Government could only resume its prewar practice of printing
more money to pay its debts. The result was staggering
inflation. In 1937, 3 Chinese dollars equaled 1 American
dollar; by 1945, an American dollar was worth 120 Chinese dollars.[117]

The KMT's armies were a reflection of the ineffective
and often corrupt Government. Officers of depleted formations drew pay and supplies for full-strength units, and
then withheld rice from their troops to sell on the black
market. Thus, although Chiang's armies totaled over 5.7
million men, he:

> ...had few men of any quality left.... The Kuomin-
> tang armies were rotting away in idleness, eroded by
> desertions and disease. New recruits were con-
> scripted by press gangs paid by the head for the men
> they brought in. Only peasants too poor to afford
> the immunity were caught. Roped together, they
> were marched to induction centers where beatings
> and starvation diets began. Conditions were so bad
> that only 56 percent of the inductees reached their

assigned units, the rest deserting or dying on the way.
Of the 1,670,000 men drafted in 1943, 735,000 simply disappeared, either as fugitives or corpses.[118]

In this situation, American aid, which totaled some $1.54
billion from 1941 to 1945,* was inadequate. "Coming late
to a hard-pressed government, [it] served more as a crutch
to lean on than as a means to cure its ailments."[119]

By way of contrast, in Yenan, Mao established a solid,
self-sufficient base with extensive popular support. Both
inflation and bureaucracy were under control, and his
army increased daily in size and effectiveness. Indeed, the
American Dixie Mission that was sent to Yenan in 1944
reported that "...the Communists' area [was] 'a different
country' and Yenan [was] 'the most modern place in
China.'"[120]

Although the Yenan region was even more isolated than
Chiang's Szechwan, its population and resources were successfully mobilized through application of the Mass Line
Strategy. Unhampered by the requirements of positional
warfare (e.g., regularized battle traces and lines of communication), Mao slipped small regular units of the Eighth
Route Army behind Japanese lines, where they further
pursued the Mass Line Strategy. Their task was facilitated
by the fact that the Japanese had destroyed the traditional
leadership structure without replacing it. Indeed, since
many of the wealthy collaborated with the Japanese, the
CCP political cadres were easily able to create the impres-
sion that nationalism and socialism were but two sides of
the same coin. By the summer of 1939, Red Army units
were dispersed behind Japanese lines throughout north
China, creating and defending bases, mobilizing irregular
guerrilla units and militia, and turning the Japanese rear
areas into the frontline.[121]

This strategy of using guerrilla military tactics to support political development, however, proved frustrating to
many of the commanders of the Eighth Route Army. Encouraged by the United Front concept, they wanted to
fight a conventional war. To curb their desires, Mao detailed the military component of his strategy in a 1938
pamphlet entitled *Problems of Strategy in Guerrilla War
Against Japan.* "As a final carrot for his commanders, ...
[he] promised that guerrilla warfare would be expanded
into a more aggressive form that he called 'mobile' warfare and, as a last step, transformed into 'regular' warfare
when the time came to take the offensive and drive the
Japanese out of China."[122] This is the genesis of Mao's
famous Three Stages of People's War. It is ironic that it

*This amounted to only about 3 percent of the total amount of lend-lease
aid the United States doled out to all recipients in World War II.

was initially formulated as a response to the conventional desires of the soldiers, and that it was never implemented in its original context. By 1940, when the Eighth Route Army had some 400,000 regular troops under arms[123]—a figure almost ten times its authorized strength—its commanders were even more keen to fight conventionally. Eventually, Mao authorized the Hundred Regiments Offensive, which began on August 20, 1940 with some 150,000 soldiers. This offensive was aimed at doing maximum damage to the enemy by attacking industrial sites and lines of communication and then smashing the Japanese as they responded. Even though accorded very little publicity at the time, it was the largest Chinese offensive of the war, and cost the Japanese and their puppet troops some 38,000 casualties.[124] Although successful in the short run, this semi-conventional offensive proved to be premature, as the CCP did not have the political bases in the occupied zone to consolidate its success. Accordingly, after December 1940, the CCP's basic strategy reverted to the political mobilization of Mao's Mass Line concept.[125]

The Hundred Regiments Offensive served to awaken the Japanese to the Communist threat, and Japan's North China Army responded with a drive to expel the Red Army from the occupied zone. At first, this drive involved raids to search out and destroy the Communist troops, but these raids rarely managed to uncover CCP military activity. The Japanese then escalated their efforts, cordoning off villages, expropriating the grain to starve the CCP (and the inhabitants), and summarily executing all within each village whose families had not lived there for generations.[126] While this policy achieved some success, it failed to make serious inroads on CCP development; usually, the cadres were alerted by sympathetic peasants, and were able to evacuate themselves and much of the grain before the Japanese troops arrived.

Despairing of the ineffectiveness of these measures, the Japanese further escalated their efforts in the fall of 1941 with the *Sanko Seisako,* or Three Alls Campaign—kill all, burn all, and destroy all. In this campaign to exterminate the CCP, the north China "villages became slaughterhouses in the course of looting and raping; then funeral pyres as the torch was applied. The sack of Nanking was daily repeated in miniature everywhere in the land,"[127] and the population of this region of north China declined from some 44 million people to about 25 million people. However, as with the London blitz or the Allied bombing of Germany in the concurrent European war, this use of terrorism served to stiffen the will of the people to resist. The peasants could not ignore the Japanese even if they so wanted. They had no option but to fight back, and the CCP provided them with the necessary weapons, organi-

zation, training, and leadership. Thus, the CCP reaped the benefit of the backlash against the Japanese atrocities. Even if not attracted by socialism or nationalism, the desire for mere survival made the people join the Communist movement, because the CCP was the only faction fighting the Japanese behind their lines.

In response to the horrors of the Three Alls Campaign, the CCP decreased its overt military activity, fighting Japanese detachments only when necessary to secure arms or supplies. This, in turn, resulted in decreased Japanese military activity. For the rest of the war, the CCP devoted 70 percent of its effort to sociopolitical organization, 20 percent to countering KMT attempts to frustrate the Communist movement, and only 10 percent to fighting the Japanese.[128] However, unlike the idle NRA, of which it was technically a part, the Red Army was busily engaged in organizing and helping the peasants in the countryside. The result was that by 1945, the CCP had some 860,000 regulars under arms, and actually controlled much of the territory in north China that was nominally occupied by the Japanese.[129] (*See Atlas Map No. 21.*) Long before the war with Japan was over, the CCP had built the extensive base that was to prove decisive in supporting its eventual victory over the KMT.

The three-way stalemate continued until 1944, with both the CCP and the KMT waiting for the United States to defeat Japan while preparing for the eventual showdown that each wished to avoid but regarded as inevitable. American leaders during this time urged Chiang and the KMT to go on the offensive against the Japanese. After all, over half of Japan's overseas troops were in China even though the front was relatively stable and quiet.[130] It was correctly assumed that a reawakening of the front would force the Japanese to devote even more effort to China, and thus shorten the war. The mission given General Joseph Stilwell was to open the Burma Road and increase the supplies reaching Chiang's Szechwan base, to reorganize and streamline the NRA, and to launch the offensive against the Japanese. To enhance the NRA's efficiency, Stilwell planned both to reduce its organization from 300 to 100 divisions and to replace inefficient generals with competent officers (e.g., Li Tsung-jen, Chiang's most threatening political rival).[131]

Focusing only on the military aspects of his mission, Stilwell ignored the political realities of Chiang's delicate balance of power with the semi-independent warlords. Chiang, however, saw no reason to waste his slender and carefully-husbanded strength when all in China knew that the Americans would easily beat the Japanese, regardless of what the Chinese did. On the other hand, he did not wish to abruptly refuse the Americans and thus risk losing their aid. Chiang therefore took advantage of a dispute between Stilwell and his nominal subordinate, Major General Claire Chennault, who commanded the Fourteenth U.S. Air Force. An infantryman, Stilwell claimed that victory could only be won on the ground. A disciple of Douhet and Mitchell, Chennault argued that, once he built up his base infrastructure in south China, he could bomb the Japanese islands into submission. By supporting Chennault, Chiang found a tailormade excuse to do nothing.[132] As the ancient Chinese strategic text, the *Sun Tzu,* said: " 'To win a hundred victories in a hundred battles is not the acme of skill; rather it is to subdue the enemy without fighting at all.' And that is exactly what Chiang had done. He had kept himself on the side of victory without contributing his strength to it."[133]

Japan radically changed the situation in May 1944 by invading the rest of central and southern China. This operation was meant both to destroy Chennault's airbases and to establish a direct land link between Manchuria and Indochina—a link that had been made necessary by the destruction of most of the Japanese merchant marine forces. (*See Atlas Map No. 21.*) In this largest Japanese offensive since 1938, Japan not only accomplished its objectives, but also proved that the NRA was powerless to resist its troops in the field.

Following the Japanese capture of Chennault's advance airbases, American policymakers tried to induce cooperation between the CCP and the KMT. They hoped that a workable coalition could be created and brought to bear against the Japanese. Although both Chinese factions were far more concerned with the shape of China after the war than they were in temporary expedients to expel the Japanese, they agreed to talk. But neither side trusted the other, and with good reason. The CCP demanded a full coalition government, intending to complete the bourgeois revolution and then begin the socialist

General George C. Marshall *(second from left)* **and Mao Tse-tung** *(far right)* **During Marshall's Visit to China, 1946**

revolution years later; the KMT demanded that the Red Army be disbanded. Both realized that the CCP could and eventually would try to subvert a coalition government, and that with the Red Army disbanded, the KMT could and would try to exterminate the CCP. Nevertheless, the talking continued when World War II ended with meetings between the leaders of both parties—both Chiang and Mao participated—taking place from August 28, 1945 to October 10, 1945.[134] Conducted at the KMT's wartime capital of Chungking, these meetings resulted in several promising agreements: cooperation in developing a new constitution that would complete the transition to democratic government in accordance with Sun Yat-sen's three-stage revolution; a plan to implement phased, parallel reductions in force that would maintain the KMT's 5 to 1 numerical troop superiority; and the establishment of tripartite truce teams, consisting of equal numbers of U.S., KMT, and CCP personnel, to mediate truce violations.[135]

Promising as these agreements were, both sides balked at implementing them. When this became obvious in November 1945, President Harry Truman sent General George C. Marshall to China. Marshall managed to resurrect the negotiations, and in January 1946 he actually achieved agreement by both sides concerning the structure of a coalition government. But the two factions were actually stalling for time. Having no intention of allowing an armed CCP to participate in a coalition government, Chiang wanted to move his troops into position in the former Japanese-occupied territory in north China and Manchuria. For their part, the Communists wanted to expand their liberated areas and to mobilize popular urban support for a new government, which they intended to dominate.[136] As a result, Marshall's efforts came to naught.

Maneuvering for Position

In its initial moves, the KMT planned to reoccupy north China and Manchuria as quickly as possible. To this end, the United States deployed 113,000 troops and moved some 500,000 NRA troops by air and sea into north China's cities to accept the Japanese surrender.[137] Despite this American assistance, inadequate planning made the KMT effort less than successful. As it evacuated its Szechwan base, the KMT neglected the industries so laboriously moved there in 1938. Then, as it moved into the north China's cities, it treated the recovered factories as war booty and the residents as collaborators—whether justified or not. One particularly unwise measure required in-

habitants to exchange their occupation currency for Chinese dollars at an unfavorable rate of exchange that wiped out their savings. This especially affected the small but vocal urban middle class, and left very little capital available for private economic development. Furthermore, government factories received preferential treatment in financing and in the allocation of raw materials. To many capitalists, the choice was essentially between inefficient and corrupt socialism imposed by the KMT or efficient socialism imposed by the CCP. Finally, and all too understandably, KMT bureaucratic corruption increased as officials sought to compensate themselves for the deprivations they had suffered during the war years.[138]

During this initial postwar period, the CCP was not idle. Beginning in March 1945, just before the war with Japan was over, the Red Army had launched a series of offensives that were intended to establish a CCP barrier between China and Manchuria, thus improving its position on the ground.[139] At the end of the war, Chu Teh immediately sent his troops forward to accept the Japanese surrender, but General Douglas MacArthur's headquarters directed the Japanese to surrender only to the Soviet Union in Manchuria and to the KMT in that area from the Manchurian border through North Vietnam. As a result, the CCP disarmed only some 30,000 Japanese troops in north China, while the NRA took custody of some 1,250,000 Japanese troops and re-equipped itself with their arms.[140] But even considering American assistance to the KMT, the CCP had a tremendous advantage in north China for reasons already recounted but little understood at the time. The CCP already controlled the north Chinese countryside and the railway lines between the cities. Thus, the post-VJ Day race for north China had been won before it was begun.

The situation in Manchuria, however, was another story. Because neither the KMT nor the CCP had any base there, Manchuria was the big prize as both parties attempted to control what Japan had developed into China's most advanced region. Pursuant to the Yalta agreement between all of the Allied Powers except China—the one most involved—Soviet troops invaded Manchuria on August 9, 1945, just prior to the Japanese surrender, and then proceeded to disarm the Kwangtung Army. Although the Soviet Union might have been expected to support the CCP, it actually played a very equivocal and contradictory role. As the Americans airlifted KMT troops and officials into the Manchurian cities and Lin Piao led some 100,000 Red Army regulars into the Manchurian countryside, the Soviet Union's most significant effort was to appropriate and ship industrial equipment valued at over $858 million back to Russia.[141] Apart from this, the Soviets recognized

KMT sovereignty in Manchuria and helped install KMT officials in the cities. Although the Soviet Union had the ability to insure CCP control of Manchuria, it failed to do so. Perhaps this was because the CCP was by then confident in its own form of Marxist doctrine, and, not willing to become a Soviet satellite, shunned further Soviet assistance. Perhaps, also, the Soviet Union feared a new war with the Americans, or assumed that the KMT would win an ensuing struggle. At any rate, the Russians worked with the Americans to bring the CCP and the KMT together, and gave the CCP little direct aid. Nevertheless, when the Soviet troops departed, some 300,000 rifles and 50,000 machineguns that had belonged to the Kwangtung Army were turned over to Lin Piao's forces, which then proceeded to occupy the major Manchurian cities.[142]

Once negotiations with the KMT became deadlocked in late 1945, the CCP abandoned its hopes to achieve socialism via the bourgeois revolution and confidently began to seek total victory through further fighting. However, even though the CCP had a more committed popular base of support, better control of its economy, better motivated troops, less corrupt bureaucrats, and a comprehensive and successful strategy, it commanded only 600,000 to 800,000 regulars and some 2 million militiamen to counter a KMT that could muster over 5 million regular troops.[143] Accordingly, the CCP's strategy continued to be tactically defensive but strategically offensive—aimed at expanding territorial control while reducing the KMT forces to numerical parity. Key aspects of this strategy involved continuing the land reform, fighting only when the Red Army had a minimum local superiority of 3 to 1, refusing to defend specific territory unless such a defense had a probability of success, and recruiting ex-puppet troops and NRA prisoners of war. This last aspect of the strategy proved most efficient as over 800,000 ex-NRA troops were integrated into the CCP formations between 1945 and 1949. Chiang bore the cost of their training and equipment while Mao reaped the benefits of their service.[144] Furthermore, since the Red Army did not deliberately commit itself to battle unless it stood an excellent chance of winning, it generally *did* win. This gave its troops tremendous confidence in their ability.

Chiang's strategy of attempting to achieve a military solution and then working on political, economic, and social reconstruction ironically complemented Mao's plans. To implement his military strategy, Chiang intended to position about 5 million troops on a massive arc stretching from Harbin to Lanchow—an arc that would extend from Boston to St. Louis to Tulsa in the United States. (*See Atlas Map No. 22.*) He would then launch two converging attacks from the arc with the 1,330,000 men that constituted his effective field strength.[145] An ambitious strategy

under any circumstances, in Chiang's case it was particularly ambitious, given the worsening economic conditions and the general disenchantment with the KMT as it moved back into the cities. In 1946, prices rose 700 percent in the areas of China that the KMT controlled, and the KMT's currency steadily depreciated until it was worthless. While an American dollar had been worth 120 Chinese dollars in 1945, it was worth 11 million Chinese dollars in August of 1948.[146]

General Marshall warned "that further military efforts would only exacerbate Chinese economic and political conditions, since the Communists were too strong to be destroyed militarily. . . ."[147] But Chiang discounted this warning. He did not believe that inflation would bring about economic disaster "because the agrarian economy of China was governed by forces different from those of industrial western states."[148] Since the rural subsistence-level economy was largely a self-sufficient barter economy, Chiang was correct in his basic analysis, and his advisers were wrong. In his calculations, however, he overlooked the fact that the CCP-controlled rural economy of north China was little affected by the inflation, while his own base of support, which had always been in the cities, was badly damaged by it. Basically, Chiang gambled on a quick military solution—on winning within six months, before the whole structure came tumbling down.[149]

In contrast, the CCP continued to expand its Mass Line Strategy in order to fight a long war. Its leaders confidently expected that the KMT's political and economic problems would pull it down over time, especially if prodded by judicious military action. As a direct result of the land reform programs, some 1,600,000 poor peasants joined the Red Army during the final stages of this long civil war. Mao and his colleagues were so confident that they proclaimed in June 1946 that they would win no later than June 1951; soon afterwards, in August 1946, they publicly published a detailed strategic analysis that accurately forecast precisely how and why the KMT would lose.[150]

The Civil War Resumes

Sustained open warfare broke out in June 1946, when the NRA commenced the clearing of the central and northern Chinese cities and lines of communication, and drove Lin Piao's forces out of the Manchurian cities that they had occupied since the Soviet withdrawal two months earlier. Instead of retreating to the southwest to rejoin the main elements of the Red Army, Lin withdrew due north to a position from which he could threaten the right flank of

Chiang's great cordon.[151] By October 1946, the cordon was completed as the NRA captured the pivotal Manchurian city of Kalgan. As a result of these KMT moves, the negotiations between the CCP and the KMT finally ended on November 19, 1946, and Marshall departed China for the last time on January 8, 1947. During the initial phases of its great campaign, the NRA was most successful. But Chiang's gains, however impressive, did not insure ultimate victory.

> . . . it seemed that Chiang Kai-shek was triumphant everywhere. He held all the major cities of Manchuria and North China and seemed capable of taking as many more as he chose with little effort. Few understood the real situation—that outside the cities, in the vast and decisive countryside, the Communists were dominant, fighting a shrewd war of attrition calculated to whittle the Nationalists down to size.[152]

Indeed, Mao's war of attrition was most effective. By 1947, some 400,000 of the NRA's regulars had been killed or captured, while the strength of the CCP forces—now renamed the People's Liberation Army (PLA)—had grown to 1,950,000 regulars and guerrillas, in addition to the militia.[153]

Even though his cordon was in place, Chiang's grand offensive was delayed by inflation, starvation, and the lack of money to pay his troops. However, it finally commenced in March 1947, when 230,000 men began a drive north from Sian to Yenan. This force was intended to link up with a comparable drive to the west from Kalgan, the two movements constituting a giant pincers operation. (*See Atlas Map No. 22.*) Pursuant to the CCP strategy already outlined, Mao refused to defend Yenan, and the CCP leadership retired to the northwest. Thus, although the CCP capital of Yenan was captured, the result was an empty victory, much like the British capture of Philadelphia in 1777 during the American War for Independence. Furthermore, as Mao retreated from Yenan, PLA regulars ambushed and halted the drive from Kalgan while simultaneously cutting the lines of communication of the forces making the Sian drive, forcing them to fall back on Sian with over 100,000 men killed, wounded, or captured.[154]

Chiang's grand strategy was ruined. He had gambled and lost, and his American military advisers now urged him to withdraw south of the Great Wall. Although a withdrawal would possibly have been a militarily wise solution, Chiang refused to do this because it would have entailed abandoning Manchuria to the CCP and accepting a *de facto* partition between north and south China.[155] This was politically unacceptable, because it would have undoubtedly toppled his faction from its insecure control of the

KMT. No regime that had fought the Japanese primarily for the control of Manchuria could afford to abandon it so quickly. To Chiang, abandoning Manchuria was tantamount to abandoning his struggle for the control of China.

Realizing that the KMT rear areas and lines of communication were weak and overextended, the CCP began limited counteroffensives in the summer of 1947. With much of the NRA's strength still in Manchuria and north China, the PLA struck at central China, particularly at the railways that ran through the region. By November 1947, it had cut the Peking-Hankow (Wuhan) Railway, the critical link between north and central China. No longer using guerrilla tactics, but rather the tactics of mobile war, the PLA still sought to overextend and sap the strength of the NRA instead of win territory; its military action was still complemented by political and social mobilization.[156] The lack of flexibility within the NRA's structure made it difficult to respond to these PLA initiatives. Moreover, even if the NRA had been as technically proficient as the German or American armies, China's lack of a decent rail or highway net would have precluded its ability to transfer sufficient reserves and defeat these widely separated and irritat-

Mao Tse-tung With His Army, 1947

ing PLA thrusts, particularly since the PLA merely retired when it met stiff opposition.

In December 1947, while the NRA's attention was diverted to central China, Lin Piao's 4th Field Army* began to move south in Manchuria against KMT forces that had been sitting idle in their city garrisons. Reinforced by a massive recruiting of peasants and ex-puppet troops, Lin's forces far outnumbered the NRA garrison forces. Striking quickly, the 4th Field Army inflicted some 150,000 casualties on the NRA, pressed the remaining 300,000 troops into the Changchun-Mukden area, and cut the NRA's land communication with north China. From this point on, the KMT had to resupply its Manchurian garrisons by air, using Chinchow on the south Manchurian coast as a base.[157]

By the summer of 1948, the CCP had achieved its initial objective of reducing the enemy to military parity. At that time, the PLA had 3,000,000 regulars to oppose only 2,900,000 in the NRA ranks.[158] The KMT was on the defensive with some 300,000 troops still in Manchuria, another 100,000 in Shantung Province, 500,000 more in the rest of north China (centered in Peking), and the remaining troops in central and southern China. Moreover, the PLA was supported by a massive militia to handle its auxiliary, rear area, and garrison duties, as well as to provide a pool of semi-trained replacements. By contrast, the NRA's reserves were depleted, and there was political unrest in the cities due to the ever worsening economic conditions.[159] Emboldened by this new position of parity, the PLA captured the Manchurian supply base at Chinchow in August 1948, sealing the fate of the remaining NRA forces in Manchuria. Then, the next month, an all-out CCP offensive began, with the PLA operating for the first time in large tactical formations which were supported by captured tanks and artillery.[160]

In four quick and brilliant campaigns that were conducted almost simultaneously and on a geographic scale surpassing any military action in European history, the PLA smashed the NRA, ejected it from north China and Manchuria, and crushed its ability and will to resist. The first of these campaigns involved the final conquest of Manchuria, an area roughly the size of modern France. In October 1948, Lin Piao's 4th Field Army, 600,000 men strong, attacked the 300,000 men in the encircled and starving NRA garrisons at Changchun and Mukden. (*See Atlas Map No. 23.*) Changchun was captured by the PLA on October 20, 1948, after the NRA's Sixtieth Army revolted and turned on the other defending troops. Mukden fell on November 2, 1948. The Manchurian Campaign

*PLA field armies were the equivalent of army groups.

cost the KMT some 470,000 of its best trained and equipped troops.[161]

While Lin Piao's 4th Field Army was completing the conquest of Manchuria, General Ch'en Yi's 3rd Field Army drove east to conduct the Liaohsi-Shenyang Campaign in Shantung Province (*See Atlas Map No. 23.*) Lasting from September 12 through November 2, 1948, this campaign completed the conquest of the Shantung region, an area the size of the Low Countries in Europe. The NRA lost another 100,000 men and 50,000 rifles to the PLA.[162]

For the next campaign, Ch'en Yi's 3rd Field Army was joined by the PLA's 2nd Field Army under General Liu Po-Ch'eng directly after the conquest of Shantung. Together totaling between 550,000 and 600,000 men, Ch'en's and Liu's forces quickly wheeled and turned south. (*See Atlas Map No. 24.*) To counter this thrust, Chiang decided to defend a line along the Huai River—the traditional boundary between north and south China. Centering on Hsuchow, he deployed some 550,000 to 600,000 men. The PLA opened the offensive on November 6, 1948, only four days after Ch'en Yi had closed the Liaohsi-Shenyang Campaign. Almost immediately, four NRA divisions in the center of Chiang's long defensive line switched sides and joined the PLA. The PLA then drove into the gap, splitting the NRA forces. This was followed by drives down the seacoast and in the west to cut the NRA units off from reinforcement or supply by sea. When these three PLA columns met in the south, they created two massive encirclements within which virtually all of the defending forces were contained. Once the encirclements were completed, the PLA began to mop up the NRA formations, unit by unit.[163]

Chiang immediately tried to break through to his encircled forces with a drive from the south spearheaded by his armored corps, but extensive PLA antitank ditches, the adverse weather of mid-winter, and logistical difficulties involving NRA tank movements halted the relief effort before it could break the encirclements. Failing to effect the relief of the trapped forces and losing his elite armored corps in the process, Chiang then ordered his air forces to bomb his troops' own positions and thus prevent their equipment from being captured by the PLA. This "proof that their supreme commander thought more of hardware than of the lives of his own men [virtually] ended resistance,"[164] and the last trapped NRA units surrendered on January 10, 1949. Following this surrender, the PLA's 2nd and 3rd Field Armies immediately pushed south to the Yangtze River.

In the words of Peter Young, a distinguished British military historian, this 65-day battle, the Huai-hai Battle, was "one of the great battles of modern history."[165] By the time it was over, the NRA had suffered 175,000 more casualties, and an additional 325,000 men had been captured by the PLA.[166] Furthermore, since the PLA's 1st Field Army was still in the northwest, the Huai-hai Battle completed the encirclement of the remaining 500,000 NRA troops in north China. These troops became the objective of the PLA's fourth great campaign, the Peking-Tientsin Campaign. Even before the Huai-hai Battle was over, Lin Piao's 4th Field Army moved south from Manchuria in December 1948 and joined General Nieh Jung-chen's North China Field Army* to advance on the NRA garrisons in Peking and Tientsin. (*See Atlas Map No. 24.*) These were overwhelmed by the end of January 1949.

The Peking-Tientsin Campaign completed the PLA's great offensive. As a result of this *blitzkrieg,* in the space of only three months, Chiang lost a total of 1,400,000 men and their equipment. This amounted to about half of his nominal strength, but a much greater percentage of his actual combat power since his remaining formations were generally second echelon units. Although Chiang had held supreme command throughout one of the worst disasters in world military history, it must be remembered that his uncertain control of China's inadequate rail network made it impossible for him to move troops rapidly enough to counter PLA initiatives. Even a tactical genius would have had difficulty under these conditions. Nevertheless, the NRA's problems should not dim the accomplishments of the PLA's commanders. Even given the superiority of their troops and tactical intelligence, the PLA commanders faced precisely the same obstacles to effective communication and coordination. Thus, the precise integration of rapid and massive troop movements over an area as large as all of Western Europe qualifies Chu Teh and his army group commanders for inclusion in the ranks of accomplished commanders. At the conclusion of these brilliant campaigns, China was effectively partitioned at the Yangtze River into a Communist north and a Nationalist south. The Nationalist south, however, was defended by an army whose will and capacity to resist had been broken.

The remainder of the civil war was somewhat anticlimactic. It was obvious to all that only a miracle could save the KMT. While the Huai-hai Battle and Peking-Tientsin Campaign were still drawing to a close, Chiang attempted to negotiate peace terms. Mao contemptuously rejected them. Chiang also appealed desperately to the West for aid in salvaging the KMT's position, but there too he was rejected.[167] Then, on January 21, 1949, he resigned the

Presidency of the Republic of China, and a new government under Li Tsung-jen took charge. While the PLA was regrouping and reorganizing, Li sent a delegation to the CCP headquarters in Peking to negotiate a peace settlement. Although the delegation accomplished its mission, the settlement gave all real power to the CCP; thus, Li's government rejected it on April 20, 1949. Meanwhile, Chiang began planning a withdrawal to Taiwan. In the months following his resignation, he began to move 500,000 of those men whose commanders were still loyal to him as well as the remainder of the government's financial reserves† and much of its archives and art treasures to Taiwan.[168] (*See Atlas Map No. 25.*) This, of course, left Li with few resources with which to establish his government or conduct a viable defense of south China.

On April 21, 1949, the day after Li's government rejected the peace settlement that its representatives had negotiated in Peking, the rested PLA 2nd and 3rd Field Armies crossed the Yangtze River on a 300-mile front—a major achievement of military engineering because the Yangtze River was several miles wide and, in that area, deep enough to accommodate major ships. They then swept through Nanking, Nanchang, and the southeast China countryside. At the same time, Lin Piao's 4th Field Army moved on their western flank, capturing Wuhan on May 17, 1949. Lin's forces then took Changsha. Finally, on October 14, 1949, two weeks after Mao had proclaimed the formation of the People's Republic of China, Lin captured Li Tsung-jen's last capital at Canton.[169] (*See Atlas Map No. 25.*) Throughout the areas of China that the PLA had bypassed, warlords and KMT administrators struggled to obtain the best possible terms from the CCP. With the capitulation of Szechwan Province in December 1949, 37 years of civil war came to an end.[170] However, the beginning of a new era had already been signaled in April of 1949, when the British sent four warships up the Yangtze River to protect foreign investments. Firing on them, the PLA captured one ship and chased the other three out of the river. Thus, 107 years of foreign intervention came to an end, achieving what had been the major underlying purpose of the revolution in the beginning.[171]

A Perspective

An explanation of how the Communist victory took place is important not only to an understanding of China today

---

*The North China Field Army is sometimes referred to as the 5th Field Army, but it was never formally so designated.

†The financial reserves consisted of approximately $300 million. About 2,000,000 persons fled the mainland with Chiang's forces.

but also to a comprehension of precisely what Mao's form of revolutionary war, or people's war, really involves. The military aspects of the war reveal very little that was new; guerrilla tactics were used successfully in the American Revolution and in the Spanish War for Independence, from which the term "guerrilla" derives. However, the military dimensions of Mao's type of war mean nothing without the underlying political, social, and economic dimensions. In the 1920s, the political game in China was a closed game, with competition restricted to the warlords, who jockeyed for political power by using force. By expanding the participation in the game through involvement of the urban elite, the 25 percent of the population that was aware of contemporary events, the KMT proved able to gain a precarious dominance over the warlords. By further expanding the game through mobilization of the previously quiescent peasants, who comprised 75 percent of the population, the CCP proved able to control the game completely, notwithstanding KMT efforts.

Once the CCP was forced to mobilize the last 75 percent of the population, and once it was allowed to do so without hindrance, the KMT could never have won with its narrow base of support. When the CCP moved into the countryside, implementing its drastic but necessary program of social reform, the KMT's only chance for success would have been to move in a parallel manner. It would have had to implement its own reforms and adopt a strategy similar to the CCP's Mass Line, carefully integrating military aspects into the socioeconomic aspects of a coordinated and mutually supportive political strategy. Had it done so, it probably would have been successful, since it succeeded when it competed with the CCP for the support of the small urban proletariat. It is ironic that once he was confined to Taiwan Province and freed from vested interests, Chiang quickly adopted draconian land reform programs and built a viable and dynamic regime upon them. Had he been able to do so on the mainland 20 years earlier, the CCP might have had its support co-opted before it became a major threat. Obsessed with military solutions to the social and economic problems that the CCP represented, and both distracted and weakened by the war with Japan, the KMT never had a chance to do so.

After the 1927 coups, when Chiang moved politically to the right and made that wing of the KMT dominant, the party stood for capitalism and individualism. These were Western concepts that were alien to traditional Chinese ethics and, indeed, actually condemned and despised by them. Since they were concepts borrowed from the hated westerners, they also represented a betrayal of the initial objective of the revolution—the expulsion of foreign influence. This was in direct contrast to the CCP's programs

of socialism, group endeavor, and individual subordination, concepts highly prized by traditional Chinese ethics. The CCP's close association with the traditional ethic became more pronounced in 1927 when it was forced by the KMT to deviate from Marxist doctrine and concentrate on the peasants instead of the proletariat. Thus, the KMT accidentally converted a rather innocuous rival with little chance for success into a major contender whose success was very likely. Furthermore, after 1927, the KMT ceased to be a revolutionary party in all but name. Instead, it aimed at preserving the status quo that had been achieved. This would have been a viable objective had existing conditions been to the satisfaction of the majority of the population and provided for everybody's minimum expectations from life. After the CCP awakened the peasants and proved to them that they could demand and get a more equitable division of China's resources, however, conditions needed further modification, and the KMT failed to provide it. Thus, the KMT aborted its own very promising revolution before it was completed.

A key problem that hampered KMT success was the fact that it was never a cohesive and unified party. This disunity precluded stable, integrated long-term planning, and also precluded the actions necessary to develop a viable and effective government. The inability to reduce military expenditures and produce a balanced budget represents but one example of this problem. Furthermore, the lack of cohesion precluded gaining adequate party control over the countryside. If the CCP hadn't existed, or the KMT had worked in relative harmony with the CCP, Chiang could have been successful in the long run. However, the CCP did exist, and Chiang refused to co-opt or otherwise use it after 1927.

By 1945, the KMT's only real chance to dominate China eventually would have been to compromise and establish a coalition government, working either to bring the CCP into its own movement or to win the CCP's support. Had it done so, the KMT might have been able to emulate the Western Europeans and forestall the CCP's plans to bring about a socialist revolution after the bourgeois revolution had been completed. A key problem here was the KMT's perception of the CCP as a tool of Russian communism. This perception was totally mistaken. In actuality, the CCP was a nationalistic expression aiming at reform that was basically compatible with the Chinese tradition. During its early, formative years, it was heavily dependent on the Comintern for advice and direction. After the failure of the Li Li-san Line in 1930, however, and particularly after Mao's rise to ascendency, the CCP rejected Russian guidance and boldly implemented its own radically different programs. While certainly Communist, the CCP was, and is, a manifestation of Chinese nationalism, not Russian imperialism.

Other factors—such as inept generalship, lack of control and standardization, and poor motivation within the NRA—certainly contributed to the KMT's debacle. While these shortcomings hastened the KMT's defeat, they were only symptoms of the underlying fault in Chiang's regime. The KMT fell because of its attempt to impose a military solution on a political problem without dealing with the fundamental socioeconomic conditions that had caused the political problem in the first place. This effort was doomed to failure.

Notes

[1]Figures taken from James Harrison, *The Long March to Power* (New York, 1974), p. 9. Ever since the first census, that of A.D. 2, the average Chinese family contained five persons. During the author's 1978 travels through the People's Republic of China, he found that the figure of five persons per family was still being used for planning purposes. Today (1987), in an effort to control the birthrate, the Chinese Government penalizes families that contain more than three persons.

[2]Albert Feuerwerker, *The Chinese Economy, 1912–1949* Ann Arbor, MI: University of Michigan Center for Chinese Studies, 1968), p. 33.

[3]Dwight Perkins, "Government as an Obstacle to Industrialization: The Case of Nineteenth Century China," in *The Journal of Economic History,* Vol. XXVII, No. 4 (December 1967), p. 487.

[4]Feuerwerker, *Chinese Economy,* p. 53.

[5]William Morwood, *Duel for the Middle Kingdom* (New York, 1980), pp. 32–33.

[6]John Fairbank, Edwin Reischauer, and Albert Craig, *East Asia: The Modern Transformation* (Boston, 1964), p. 649.

[7]Morwood, *Duel,* p. 30.

[8]*Ibid.,* p. 53.

[9]*Ibid.,* pp. 52–53.

[10]*Ibid.,* p. 68.

[11]Harrison, *Long March,* p. 43.

[12]This paragraph is based on arguments in Feuerwerker, *Chinese Economy,* pp. 22, 28, 32.

[13]Morwood, *Duel,* p. 66.

[14]Harrison, *Long March,* p. 51.

[15]Harrison, *Long March,* pp. 76–77.

[16]Morwood, *Duel,* p. 34.

[17]*Ibid.,* p. 96.

[18]Hy Pu-yu, *A Brief History of the Chinese National Revolutionary Forces* (Taipei, 1973), p. 5. Of the Whampoa Military Academy's entering class of 499 cadets, some 80 were affiliated with the CCP and its youth organization (Harrison, *Long March,* p. 56).

[19]Fairbank et al., *East Asia,* p. 682.

[20]Hu, *Revolutionary Forces,* pp. 14–15.

[21]James Sheridan, *China in Disintegration* (New York, 1975), p. 161.

[22]Morwood, *Duel,* p. 113.

[23]Fairbank et al., *East Asia,* p. 687.

[24]Sheridan, *China,* p. 168.

[25]Harrison, *Long March,* p. 83.

[26]Fairbank et al., *East Asia,* p. 687.

[27]Harrison, *Long March,* p. 84.

[28]Sheridan, *China,* p. 170.

[29]Morwood, *Duel,* p. 117.

[30]Harrison, *Long March,* p. 93.

[31]*Ibid.,* pp. 88–90.

[32]*Ibid.,* p. 96.

[33]*Ibid.,* p. 122.

[34]Morwood, *Duel,* pp. 152–153.

[35]Harrison, *Long March,* p. 130.

[36]This quotation and the analysis that precedes it is from Sheridan, *China,* p. 179.

[37]Morwood, *Duel,* p. 157.

[38]Fairbank et al., *East Asia,* p. 696.

[39]Morwood, *Duel,* pp. 157–158.

[40]Harrison, *Long March,* p. 152.

[41]Harrison, *Long March,* p. 152.

[42]Sheridan, *China,* pp. 184–185.

[43]*Ibid.,* p. 186.

[44]Fairbank et al., *East Asia,* pp. 691–692.

[45]Feuerwerker, *Chinese Economy,* p. 7.

[46]Fairbank et al., *East Asia,* p. 697.

[47]Feuerwerker, *Chinese Economy,* pp. 48–53; Immanuel Hsu, *The Rise of Modern China* (New York, 1975), p. 688.

[48]Fairbank et al., *East Asia,* p. 700.

[49]Feuerwerker, *Chinese Economy,* p. 53.

[50]Harrison, *Long March,* p. 211.

[51]*Ibid.,* p. 318.

[52]Morwood, *Duel,* p. 215.

[53]Hsu, *Rise,* p. 687.

[54]Scott Boorman, *The Protracted Game: A Wei-ch'i Interpretation of Maoist Revolutionary Strategy* London, 1969), p. 73.

[55]Harrison, *Long March,* p. 143.

[56]Boorman, *Protracted Game,* p. 62.

[57]Sheridan, *China,* p. 248.

[58]Harrison, *Long March,* p. 346.

[59]Morwood, *Duel,* p. 150.

[60]Harrison, *Long March,* p. 205.

[61]Morwood, *Duel,* p. 150.

[62]Harrison, *Long March,* p. 207.

[63]*Ibid.,* p. 145.

[64]*Ibid.,* p. 207.

[65]Morwood, *Duel,* p. 168.

[66]Harrison, *Long March,* p. 207.

[67]*Ibid.,* p. 146.

[68]*Ibid.,* 210.

[69]Harrison, *Long March,* p. 209.

[70]Boorman, *Protracted Game,* p. 70.

[71]Harrison, *Long March,* pp. 164, 199; Morwood, *Duel,* pp. 168, 178; Hsu, *Rise,* p. 672.

[72]Sheridan, *China,* p. 249.

[73]Hsu, *Rise,* p. 666.

[74]Harrison, *Long March,* p. 176.

[75]Morwood, *Duel,* p. 170.

[76]This account of the First and Second Extermination Campaigns is based on Harrison, *Long March,* p. 192, and H.H. Collier and Paul Chin-chih Lai, *Organizational Changes in the Chinese Army, 1895–1950* (Taipei, 1969), p. 159.

[77]Sheridan, *China,* p. 247.

[78]Collier and Lai, *Chinese Army,* p. 159; Morwood, *Duel,* p. 171; Harrison, *Long March,* p. 191.

[79]Hsu, *Rise,* p. 664.

[80]Harrison, *Long March,* p. 191.

[81]Hsu, *Rise,* pp. 672–673; Harrison, *Long March,* pp. 200–201.

[82]Peter Young, *A Dictionary of Battles, 1816–1976* (New York, 1978), p. 198.

[83]Hsu, *Rise,* pp. 665, 672.

[84]Harrison, *Long March,* pp. 192, 239, 246; Collier and Lai,

Chinese Army, pp. 185–186.

[85]Harrison, *Long March,* pp. 234, 242–244.

[86]Harrison, *Long March,* pp. 238–239; Sheridan, *China,* p. 252; Hsu, *Rise,* p. 675.

[87]Hsu, *Rise,* p. 674.

[88]Morwood, *Duel,* pp. 197–198.

[89]*Ibid.,* p. 199.

[90]Harrison, *Long March,* p. 238.

[91]Harrison, *Long March,* p. 246; Morwood, *Duel,* pp. 198–199, and Sheridan, *China,* p. 252.

[92]Morwood, *Duel,* pp. 199–211.

[93]Harrison, *Long March,* p. 320.

[94]*Ibid.,* p. 317.

[95]Morwood, *Duel,* p. 225.

[96]Harrison, *Long March,* p. 267.

[97]*Ibid.*

[98]Morwood, *Duel,* pp. 231–232. See also Harrison, *Long March,* pp. 268–269, and Hsu, *Rise,* p. 678.

[99]Hsu, *Rise,* p. 701; Lincoln Li, *The Japanese Army in North China, 1937–1945* (Tokyo, 1975), p. 34; Marius Jansen, *Japan and China: From War to Peace, 1894–1972* (Chicago, 1975), pp. 393–394.

[100]Hsu, *Rise,* p. 724; Harrison, *Long March,* p. 278.

[101]Jansen, *Japan and China,* p. 394.

[102]Harrison, *Long March,* p. 269.

[103]Peter Duus, *The Rise of Modern Japan* (Boston, 1976), p. 220.

[104]Harrison, *Long March,* p. 276.

[105]Morwood, *Duel,* p. 258.

[106]Morwood, *Duel,* p. 258 gives the figure of two weeks for the sack of Nanking. Hsu, *Rise,* p. 703 claims that there were 100,000 civilian casualties, while Young, *Dictionary,* p. 104, puts the figure at only 40,000.

[107]Morwood, *Duel,* p. 262.

[108]Harrison, *Long March,* p. 277.

[109]Young, *Dictionary,* p. 164.

[110]Harrison, *Long March,* pp. 276, 296; Morwood, *Duel,* p. 260.

[111]*Ibid.,* p. 261.

[112]Young, *Dictionary,* pp. 164–165; Jansen, *Japan and China,* p. 395.

[113]Li, *Japanese Army,* p. 9.

[114]Harrison, *Long March,* pp. 280, 350.

[115]*Ibid.,* p. 280.

[116]Feuerwerker, *Chinese Economy,* pp. 22, 24.

[117]Morwood, *Duel,* p. 130.

[118]*Ibid.,* p. 300.

[119]Fairbank et al., *East Asia,* p. 717.

[120]Hsu, *Rise,* p. 722.

[121]Morwood, *Duel,* p. 274.

[122]*Ibid.,* pp. 270–271.

[123]Harrison, *Long March,* p. 269.

[124]Morwood, *Duel,* pp. 280–281; Harrison, *Long March,* pp. 300, 316.

[125]Harrison, *Long March,* p. 316.

[126]Morwood, *Duel,* pp. 282–283.

[127]*Ibid.,* p. 384; Harrison, *Long March,* pp. 300, 316.

[128]Morwood, *Duel,* p. 321.

[129]Harrison, *Long March,* p. 294.

[130]Hsu, *Rise,* p. 736.

[131]Morwood, *Duel,* p. 292.

[132]Morwood, *Duel,* pp. 292–312; Barbara Tuchman, *Stilwell and the American Experience in China, 1911–1945* (New York, 1972), pp. 454–463.

[133]Morwood, *Duel,* p. 305.

[134]Morwood, *Duel,* p. 5.

[135]Harrison, *Long March,* pp. 377–378, 386.

[136]Morwood, *Duel,* pp. 314, 337; Harrison, *Long March,* p. 375.

[137]Harrison, *Long March,* pp. 371, 386.

[138]Feuerwerker, *Chinese Economy,* pp. 24–25; Harrison, *Long March,* p. 382; Morwood, *Duel,* p. 355; Hsu, *Rise,* p. 771.

[139]John Gittings, *The Role of the Chinese Army* (London, 1967), p. 2.

[140]Harrison, *Long March,* p. 371.

[141]Gittings, *Role,* p. 2; Harrison, *Long March,* p. 379.

[142]Gittings, *Role,* p. 14; Harrison, *Long March,* pp. 379, 390; Morwood, *Duel,* p. 339.

[143]*Ibid.,* pp. 371–372.

[144]Morwood, *Duel,* pp. 342, 349–350; Gittings, *Role,* p. 6.

[145]Morwood, *Duel,* pp. 340–342.

[146]Harrison, *Long March,* p. 391; Morwood, *Duel,* pp. 356–357.

[147]Harrison, *Long March,* p. 391.

[148]Hsu, *Rise,* p. 756.

[149]Gittings, *Role,* p. 10.

[150]Harrison, *Long March,* p. 390; Gittings, *Role,* p. 10.

[151]Gittings, *Role,* p. 6; Harrison, *Long March,* p. 390.

[152]Morwood, *Duel,* p. 350.

[153]Harrison, *Long March,* p. 396.

[154]Morwood, *Duel,* pp. 350–354.

[155]Gittings, *Role,* p. 4; Morwood, *Duel,* p. 354.

[156]Gittings, *Role,* pp. 6–7.

[157]Gittings, *Role,* p. 7; Hsu, *Rise,* p. 759; Harrison, *Long March,* p. 373.

[158]Gittings, *Role,* p. 18.

[159]Gittings, *Role,* p. 7.

[160]*Ibid.,* p. 8; F.F. Liu, "Defeat by Military Default," in *The Kuomintang Debacle of 1949: Conquest or Collapse?* (Boston, 1966), p. 9.

[161]Harrison, *Long March,* p. 424; Liu, "Defeat," p. 11; Hsu, *Rise,* p. 416.

[162]Harrison, *Long March,* p. 423; Gittings, *Role,* p. 8.

[163]Morwood, *Duel,* pp. 369–370; Hsu, *Rise,* p. 760; Gittings, *Role,* p. 8.

[164]Morwood, *Duel,* p. 369.

[165]Young, *Dictionary,* p. 172.

[166]Harrison, *Long March,* p. 424; Morwood, *Duel,* p. 369.

[167]Gittings, *Role,* p. 8.

[168]Harrison, *Long March,* pp. 425–426; Morwood, *Duel,* p. 374.

[169]Harrison, *Long March,* pp. 425–426; Gittings, *Role,* p. 9.

[170]Gittings, *Role,* p. 9.

[171]Harrison, *Long March,* p. 426.

Annex B
Wade-Giles/Pin-Yin Conversion and Pronunciation Guide

This guide covers the principal Chinese names contained in the text. The column on the left shows the Wade-Giles spelling as used in the text, while the Pin-yin spelling is given in the center column. The phonetic rendition given in the right column, sounded as in English, provides the correct pronunciation. Each group of letters—e.g., "Youahn" or "Jiahng"—should be pronounced as one syllable.

WADE-GILES	PIN-YIN	PHONETIC
Names		
Chang Hsueh-liang	Zhang Xueliang	Jahng Shway-leeahng
Chang Tso-lin	Zhang Zuolin	Jahng So-lin
Chen Yi	Chen Yi	Jen Yee
Chiang Kai-shek	Chiang Kai-shek	Jiahng Kai-shek
Chou En-lai	Zhou Enlai	Joe En-lie
Chu Teh	Zhu De	Jew Duh
Feng Yü-hsiang	Feng Yuziang	Fung You-Shiang
Li Tsung-jen	Li Zongren	Lee Soong-ren
Lin Piao	Lin Biao	Lin Beow
Liu Po-ch'eng	Liu Bocheng	Lew Bo-cheng
Mao Tse-tung	Mao Zedong	Mao Zuh-doong
P'eng Teh-huai	Peng Dehuai	Pung Duh-why
Sun Yat-sen	Sun Yat-sen	Soon Yaht-sen
Wang Ching-wei	Wang Jingwei	Wahng Jing-way
Yen Hsi-shan	Yan Xishan	Yen She-shan
Yüan Shih-k'ai	Yuan Shikai	Youahn Sher-kai
Places		
Changchun	Zhangzhun	Jahng-jun
Changsha	Changsha	Jahng-shah
Chinchow	Jinzhou	Jin-joe
Chungking	Chongqing	Jung-king
Huai-hai	Huai-hai	Hwhy-hi
Kiangsi	Jiangxi	Jiang-see
Nanchang	Nanjang	Nahn-jahng
Nanking	Nanjing	Nahn-jing
Peking	Beijing	Bay-jing
Shanghai	Shanghai	Shahng-hi
Sian	Xian	See-ahn
Tsunyi	Zunyi	Soon-yee
Yangtze	Yangze	Yahng-zuh
Yenan	Yanan	Yon-ahn

The Korean War

Korea: From Victim to Victor   3

Muffled by the persistent rains of the early summer monsoon, the artillery of the North Korean People's Army opened fire on troops of the Army of the Republic of Korea as they stood watch south of the 38th Parallel. The first rounds fell at approximately 4:00 a.m. on June 25, 1950. Unlike border incursions in the recent past, they continued to fall until well after daybreak.* The first South Korean troops to suffer the full impact were dug in on the Ongjin peninsula and in the Kaesong area, both of which lie on the western side of Korea.† (*See map on page 70.*) About 30 minutes after the preparatory fires began, the North Korean 1st and 6th Infantry Divisions, the 3rd Constabulary Brigade, and one regiment of the 105th Armored Brigade crossed the border to fix the South Korean defenders in place while troops of the main effort prepared to strike. An hour later, at 5:30 a.m., the clanking of North Korean T-34 tanks signaled the advance of the units making the main attack. They moved just north of Uijongbu, astride the shortest route between the 38th Parallel and Seoul, the capital of the Republic of Korea. Here, the rest of the 105th Armored Brigade spearheaded the North Korean 3rd and 4th Infantry Divisions in a drive to capture Seoul. Farther to the east, in the mountains of central Korea, two more infantry divisions, the 2nd and the 7th, struck the South Koreans. The fourth prong of the attack was aimed down the east coast of Korea. There, the 5th Infantry Division, a motorcycle regiment, and an independent infantry unit, all supported by previously infiltrated guerrillas, crossed the 38th Parallel heading for Samch'ok. At 6:00 a.m., motorized junks and sampans landed amphibious assault troops on the coast, north and south of Samch'ok.[1] Thus began the military confrontation between forces of the Communist bloc and the United States and its allies.

In response to this attack, President Harry S. Truman ordered the armed forces of the United States to intervene on behalf of the Republic of Korea against the invading army of North Korea. In subsequent months, General of the Army Douglas A. MacArthur led the fight to save the South Koreans from being overrun, first defending at Pusan and later counterattacking decisively at Inchon. Concurrently, the United States undertook the leadership of the Western Allies against what were perceived to be the hostile intentions of the Soviet Union. Early in October, MacArthur's United Nations Command crossed the 38th Parallel in pursuit of both the remnants of the North Korean Army and the unification of Korea. Instead of victory, however, MacArthur found his men fighting a new enemy, the Chinese Communists. By the end of November, the United Nations Command had suffered defeat at the hands of the Chinese. Thereafter, both sides fought for tactical advantage near the 38th Parallel in a war of attrition. Meanwhile, the Chinese and North Koreans waged a propaganda campaign, and, through negotiation, the United Nations sought a way to disengage.

The Allies' military defeat in Korea deserves far more attention than soldiers have given it in the past, for it had a profound effect on future military policy and command relationships. Most military commentators have emphasized the victories at Pusan and Inchon. Gaining satisfaction from these examples of tactical and strategic mobility, they have explained the subsequent American defeat by charging civilian leaders with unwarranted interference in

*The precise time that the North Koreans opened fire varied as much as an hour from one end of the frontier to the other. Korean time is 13 hours in advance of eastern daylight time; therefore, 4:00 a.m., June 25, was 3:00 p.m., June 24 in Washington, D.C. Each time used in this chapter is the local time at the place where the action being described occurred.

†Spelling of place names is taken from maps, Korea, 1:50000, AMS L524, produced by the Army Map Service, United States Army Corps of Engineers, 1950. The single exception to this policy is the use of the anglicized spelling of Inchon. This spelling was chosen because of its common and frequent usage throughout this text.

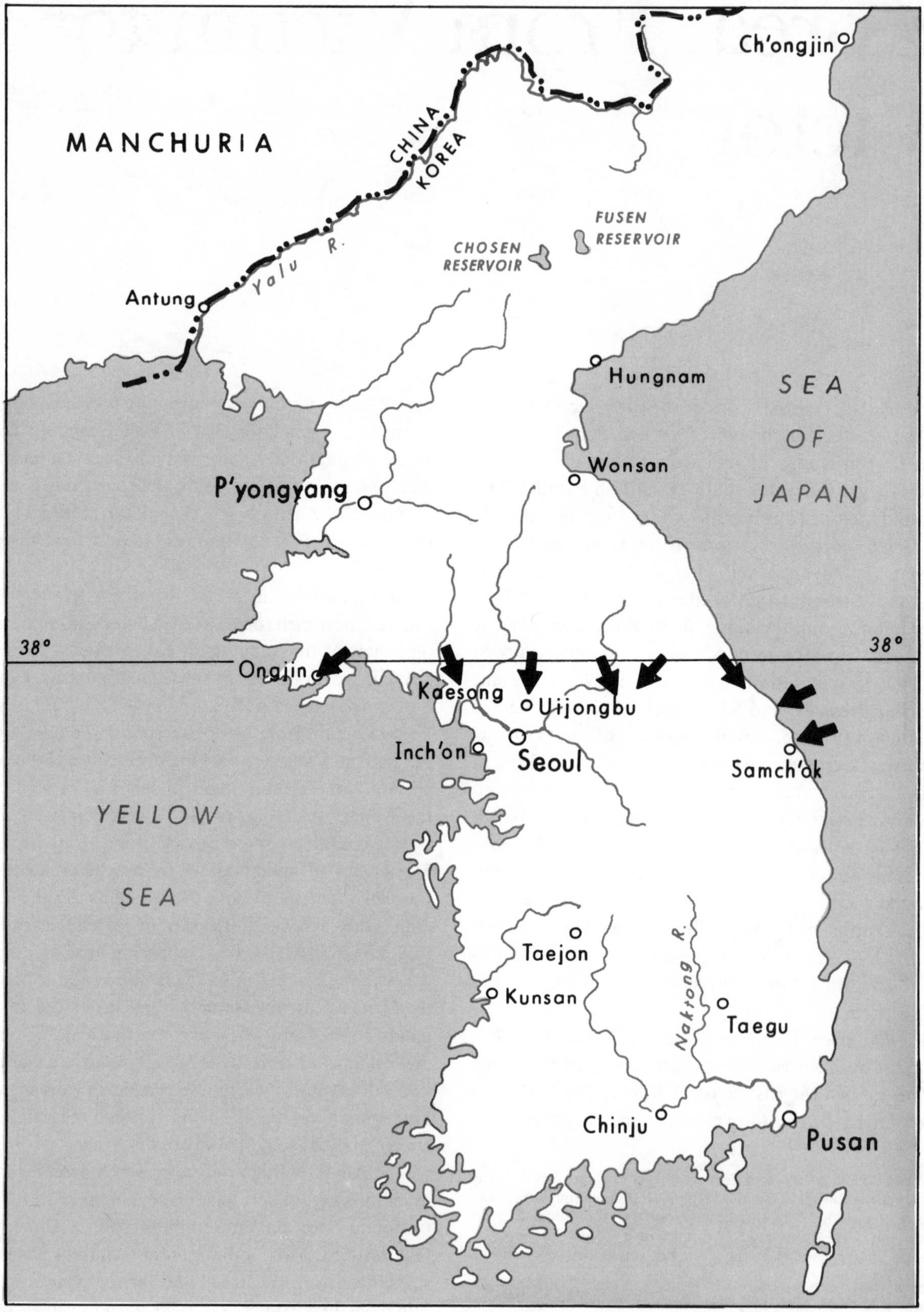

The North Korean Invasion, June 25, 1950

military affairs or by decrying the lamentable state of American preparedness. While there are elements of truth in these arguments, they avoid the main issue. The search for an explanation demands that we ask how MacArthur's United Nations Command managed to maneuver itself into such a vulnerable position in the first place. With a limited kind of victory in hand along the 38th Parallel at the end of September 1950, what happened to bring on defeat in November and to force the United States to seek a negotiated peace in the ensuing years of the war?

The International Background

When the guns of World War II fell silent in 1945, and Americans overwhelmingly demanded the role of world leadership, President Truman led the United States into a close peacetime bond with Europe.[2] A solid majority in each region of the country embraced internationalism in some form—either by membership in the United Nations (UN) or by participation in some type of postwar alliance or international policy system.[3] Whether through cause or effect, American internationalism flowered at the same time that hostility between the United States and her former ally, the Soviet Union, was mounting.

In the years that followed, the Cold War erupted and intensified as the United States and the Soviet Union clashed over their conflicting interests. Soviet actions in the eastern Mediterranean, Czechoslovakia, and Berlin made the United States determined to contain the spread of Soviet influence. The political position of the United States was reflected in a series of commitments and policies: the Marshall Plan, which offered postwar aid to those war-ravaged countries of Europe; the Truman Doctrine, under which the United States assisted Greece and Turkey in the fight against communism; the policy of containment, a corollary of the Marshall Plan that sought to prevent Soviet expansion; and membership in the North Atlantic Treaty Organization (NATO). Once again, the United States had cast her lot with her traditional allies in Western Europe. By 1949, the structure, if not the substance, of the central alliance system of World War II had been re-established. The enemy had changed, and the issue was now containment of the Soviet Union, but most of the old friendships and the ground over which the allies might fight were the same. Meanwhile, the war and its aftermath also entangled the United States with Asian allies.

Though far less consciously contrived than the Western alliance, links of various strengths had been forged between the United States and Japan, Taiwan (formerly

President Harry S. Truman

called Formosa), and Korea. (*See Atlas Map No. 26.*) Stationing her strongest occupation force in Japan immediately after the war, the United States governed through General MacArthur, who acted as the Supreme Commander for the Allied Powers as well as senior American military commander in the Far East. Under the vigorous leadership of that old hero of the Pacific war, the United States formed close political and economic bonds with Japan as the years passed. In a speech delivered in January 1950, Secretary of State Dean Acheson demonstrated the strategic importance of Japan by including her within the American defense perimeter of the Pacific. Acheson described a line that ran from the Aleutian Islands to the Philippines and included Japan and Okinawa. By excluding Taiwan and Korea, he reaffirmed the accepted policy of the administration, one proposed by the Joint Chiefs of Staff (JCS) as early as 1947 and publicly endorsed by MacArthur in 1949.[4] In 1950, therefore, approved emergency plans for the Far East did not provide for the defense of either Taiwan or Korea.[5]

Following World War II, Chiang Kai-shek's struggle with the Chinese Communists had frustrated the hopes of the Truman administration for China. Well before Mao Tse-tung and his forces drove the Chinese Nationalists

General of the Army Douglas MacArthur

from the mainland to Taiwan in the fall of 1949, Washington had anticipated Chiang's ultimate defeat. Although the administration did not want to wash its hands of Chiang, the cost of defending Taiwan was simply too high.[6] By 1950, America's commitment to China was at its lowest ebb.

In contrast to its relationship with Chiang Kai-shek's government on Taiwan, the United States had assumed responsibility for setting up and protecting the South Korean Government.[7] When the war against Japan came to its sudden end in 1945, the United States found itself unexpectedly in charge of the southern half of the Korean peninsula. (*See Atlas Map No. 26.*) With Russian troops advancing on Korea from the north and American forces on Okinawa preparing to land in South Korea, the JCS proposed that the Russians accept the surrender of Japanese forces north of the 38th Parallel and that the United States take the surrender in the south. Accordingly, Russian troops moved into Korea on August 8, 1945, and United States forces entered the country on September 8. At that time, the 38th Parallel had no great political significance. It simply served to divide Korea in such a way as to give the United States a port in the north (Inchon) and one in the south (Pusan) to facilitate the repatriation of Japanese troops.[8]

The United States and the Soviet Union then established a joint commission to form a provisional Korean government. But the Soviets and the Americans disagreed

on the credentials of various Korean political groups that sought to govern the land, and mutual suspicion mounted as the Soviets condemned the United States as a colonial power. By May 1947, discussions had reached a complete stalemate on all major issues inherent in Korean unification. Ominously, the 38th Parallel hardened into an international boundary between the Communist Democratic Republic of Korea in the north and Syngman Rhee's Republic of Korea in the south. Increasing tension along this boundary led to frequent military clashes between North and South Koreans throughout 1949 and into 1950. In August 1949, North Korea launched a large-scale invasion of the Ongjin peninsula. After heavy fighting, the assault was repulsed, only to be renewed in October. Guerrillas, who reportedly were subject to general orders from the North, waged a campaign of terror over large areas of South Korea.[9] By June 1950, even though the Korean peninsula was outside of the defense perimeter described six months earlier by Acheson, South Korea was potentially an important part of the American postwar system that had been erected to contain Soviet influence.

Strategic Issues

When the JCS contemplated the strategic problem faced by the United States in the Cold War milieu, they agreed that the abstract concept of containment of the Soviet Union and its Communist ideology had to be given shape and substance. At the close of World War II, the United States had accepted obligations that were to become military requirements in the years ahead. She agreed to occupy Germany, Austria, Trieste, Korea, and Japan, both to help guard against the revival of fascism and to begin political reconstruction. Commitments to support the United Nations and to occupy and govern the defeated territories required the stationing of conventional military forces both in the United States and overseas. Quite naturally, however, the American people and their elected leaders demanded a demobilization of the wartime force. Even before the war ended, the United States had begun to reduce her armed strength to a postwar level of about 1.5 million men. In six months, demobilization was halfway complete. During that time, the Army discharged 4 million men; it would discharge over 2 million more in the next six months. Matching cutbacks in the Army, the Air Force dropped from 218 groups to 109. The Navy boasted that its demobilization was over halfway complete by January 1, 1946.

As the political breach between the Soviet Union and the Western Allies widened, Soviet military strength quickly replaced resurgent fascism as the main military threat to the interests of the United States. If the Soviets resorted to war, they would be able to employ overwhelming land forces almost immediately against the nations of Western Europe and the occupation forces of the United States. The great distance between the Soviet European heartland and the Far East limited possible Soviet operations in that area and reduced the threat accordingly. Although lacking long-range aircraft, the Soviets could support ground operations with powerful tactical air forces. At sea, the Soviet surface navy was a negligible threat, but the Soviet submarine force was growing. The Soviet Union had potentially abundant resources and, as time passed, could develop an industrial capacity far exceeding its achievements in World War II.[10] At least initially, the Joint Chiefs believed that Soviet capabilities restricted operations to Europe and the land masses adjacent to the Soviet Union. But weapons the Soviets could develop in the future would pose a genuine threat to the continental United States. Civilian and military analysts alike estimated that the Soviets could develop long-range strategic bombers, nuclear weapons, and missile delivery systems. Soviet potential, in the long run, was seen to be virtually unlimited. The critical unknown was the length of time it would take them to deploy the new air-nuclear weapons system.

Until the Soviet Union developed a nuclear capability, the Joint Chiefs knew that the possession of nuclear weapons gave the United States an important military advantage. The new technology suggested new parameters for military power. Jet propulsion assured increased range, speed, and striking power, causing many strategists to accord greater importance to airpower than to seapower.[11] Moreover, beyond the contemporary manned aircraft, one could reasonably anticipate the use of rockets and guided missiles as nuclear delivery systems. Civil defense had been of questionable value even in World War II; now, the quantum jump in offensive striking power raised serious questions about the ability of *any* defense system— even one using modern radar and propulsion techniques—to affect the survival of a nation and its ground forces under nuclear attack. Since Hiroshima, many observers had realized that the strategic threat posed by nuclear weapons relegated all tactical and strategic doctrine, so painfully developed during the war, to the status of theories that once again had to be thoroughly studied.[12]

With the passage of time, military strategists tried to detach themselves from their experience in World War II. The Army staff, including at that time the Army Air Force

staff,* studied the nature of the strategic problem and concluded that the United States could no longer defend itself as an island, isolated from the rest of the world. In an age dominated by airpower, warfare would be truly global, and distance alone would provide the cushion of time in which to react to attack. Never again would there be time to mobilize while allies absorbed the shock of aggression, as had been the case in 1914 and 1939. Convinced that the traditional battlefield would all but disappear, the staff believed that the only effective defense was to be found in a worldwide network in which offensive forces would be constantly alert and prepared to engage an aggressor.[13] The implications of the new warfare demanded a peacetime command system patterned after the successful organization that had brought victory in World War II.

Army and Army Air Force leaders advocated a merger of the services under a single cabinet officer and a chief of staff. The Navy, on the other hand, opposed merger, instead supporting a federal system of cooperation and coordination.[14] After a series of abortive attempts to gain passage of a satisfactory bill, a compromise finally emerged in the form of the National Security Act of 1947. The new organization—essentially following the Navy proposal—federated the Army, the Navy, and the new Air Force in a National Military Establishment.† The legislation recognized the Joint Chiefs of Staff as a permanent agency and provided them with a small 100-man coordinating staff. The law authorized the JCS to prepare strategic and logistical plans and to give strategic direction to the armed forces. To accomplish these tasks, JCS committees assisted the small joint staff. One of the most important of these, the Joint Strategic Plans Committee, prepared current and future strategic plans, studies, and policies.[15]

By the spring of 1950, the Joint Chiefs had developed a strategic plan for study by the National Security Council (NSC) and its supporting agencies.[16] The new emergency war plan contemplated a strategic defensive in Asia and a strategic offensive in Europe against the Soviet Union. The mid-range objective was to retain a foothold in Western Europe that would serve as a base of operations for the offensive once ample forces had been assembled. To do this, the United States had to be prepared to deploy a strategic reserve rapidly. The first task of this reserve was to defend the United Kingdom and to hold a line that protected Western Europe, preferably no farther west than

---

*The comment here refers to a time frame before 1947. With the passage of the National Security Act of 1947, the United States Air Force came into being as a coequal of the Army and the Navy.

†After the act was amended in 1949, the National Military Establishment was known as the Department of Defense.

the Rhine River. The United States would also have to secure a bridgehead in northwest Africa to maintain control of the western Mediterranean Sea. In addition, the Joint Chief's considered the Cairo-Suez area critical; they demanded continued control of that area and a secure line of communication extending from it to Gibraltar. In the Far East, the primary task was to defend Japan, Okinawa, and the Philippines. Taiwan was to be denied to the Soviets as a base of operations.[17] To make all of this possible, the United States had to defend the Western Hemisphere against all forms of attack, particularly from the air. This was to be accomplished by maintaining an around-the-clock readiness to deliver an atomic attack against the Soviet Union and by controlling essential lines of communication.

Agreeing on a strategy was far simpler than creating the forces necessary to implement it. In a period of fiscal austerity, the plan failed to resolve really hard issues pertaining to traditional service roles and missions. In a battle of the budget between 1948 and 1950, the Air Force was clearly the victor, and air-nuclear deterrence of the Soviet Union came to be viewed as the predominant solution to the nation's strategic problem.

The Air Force emphasized its primary responsibility for air-nuclear retaliation by concentrating its share of the budget on the creation of a strong strategic air force—to consist of intercontinental-range B-36 bombers—at the expense of tactical support for ground forces. The other

services were somewhat neglected in the rush to build an effective air-nuclear deterrent. Naval officers complained of generally unsatisfactory readiness caused by a continuous turnover of personnel, a shortage of experienced crews, and a reduction in the number of combatant ships. Major combatant ships operated with only 67 percent of their wartime strength, and the two Marine Corps divisions numbered less than 40 percent of their authorized wartime strength.

In regard to being capable of dealing with the situation it was about to face, the Army ended up in the worst shape of all. Of the ten Army divisions and separate regiments on active duty when the Korean War broke out, four infantry divisions (the 7th, 24th 25th, and 1st Cavalry Divisions) were in Japan on occupation duty. The 5th Regimental Combat Team was in Hawaii, and the 29th Infantry Regiment was in Okinawa. In addition, one infantry division, two infantry regiments, and a constabulary force roughly equal to a division were in Europe, and two infantry regiments were in the Caribbean. The remainder, constituting the general reserve, was concentrated in the United States. All of the divisions, except the one in Europe, were understrength in each of their three regiments. All four of the divisions in Japan were below their authorized peacetime strength of 12,500, a figure that was itself only 66 percent of the wartime strength. Available manpower had been consolidated so that each regiment had only two instead of the normal three battalions, none of the regiments had its

The Joint Chiefs of Staff, 1950: *(Left to right)* Admiral Forrest P. Sherman, General Omar N. Bradley, General Hoyt S. Vandenberg, and General J. Lawton Collins

authorized tank companies, and artillery units were operating at reduced strength and with only two-thirds of their units.[18] To make matters worse, troops assigned to Europe and Japan were young and inexperienced, and they had grown soft from the relatively easy life of an occupation army.[19]

Although the Army maintained its authorized ten-division structure, it did so at the expense of combat readiness, not only by reducing the strength of individual units but also by eliminating units that were part of the mobilization base.[20] During the pre-Korean War years, the goal of the Army was minimum reduction of combat units and maximum elimination of "fat." Thus, although in the Army, as in the other services, the percentage of combat forces increased, there was also a dangerous reduction in the support units—the "fat"—so essential for sustained combat. Moreover, the Army's budget was used largely for maintenance, pay, and allowances, at the expense of equipment modernization. The only bright spot for the future was the maintenance of the machinery for selective service. Otherwise, the Army was a hollow shell.

Although the flaws in America's strategic plan were not initially perceived by the Joint Chiefs, these deficiencies became all too apparent at the outbreak of the Korean War. As events would show, the major weakness of the air-nuclear strategy was that it was based on erroneous assumptions about the effect of nuclear deterrence. While the defense system might influence an industrial power like the Soviet Union, how was the United States to cope with enemies elsewhere in the world, where the theory of strategic air warfare had less application—or, perhaps, no application at all? How was she to deter an agrarian foe, lacking the vulnerable industrial plants upon which Western societies depended? How was she to fight against an anti-mechanistic strategy based on overwhelming manpower in the hands of governments unintimidated by nuclear weapons, and confident that they would not be used in any event? This was precisely the dilemma created by the North Korean attack.

Decision to Intervene in Korea

As officials in the Department of State worked to fashion a fitting response to the North Korean attack, they were totally unaware of the ultimate intentions of the North Koreans, or even the extent of the invasion. Information was still confined to sketchy reports provided by the American Ambassador and the Korean Military Advisory Group (KMAG). General MacArthur's headquarters in Tokyo was no better informed. From the very first notification, however, decisionmakers and their advisers assumed that there was a major crisis, and therefore an urgent need to take action. As they surveyed their options, the quickest, safest, and most attractive choice was to act through the United Nations; no alternative was seriously considered. Ambassador at Large Philip C. Jessup summed up the feelings of the moment: "We've got to do something, and whatever we do, we've got to do it through the United Nations."[21]

After studying initial reports of the North Korean invasion, the United States Government called for an emergency session of the United Nations Security Council on June 25. When the details of the situation had been confirmed and it had been determined that the North Korean attack was a breach of the peace, the Security Council called upon the North Korean Government to cease hostilities. The resolution further requested ". . . all members to render every assistance to the United Nations in the execution of this resolution and to refrain from giving assistance to the North Korean authorities."[22] By June 27 it was clear that the North Koreans intended to disregard the resolution, so the Security Council met again. The American delegate reviewed the deteriorating situation in Korea and proposed a new resolution. After a considerable debate over a less strident proposal offered by the Yugoslav delegation—Ambassador Jacob Malik of the Soviet Union was not present to veto the American proposal—the Security Council recommended that ". . . the members of the United Nations furnish such assistance to the Republic of Korea as may be necessary to repel the armed attack and to restore international peace and security in the area."[23] With this act, the UN laid the legal groundwork for the second important decision, one that had already been made by the United States Government—the decision to provide military aid to the Republic of Korea.

As soon as they received word of the attack, the Joint Chiefs began to study the implications of American aid. In a series of conferences with President Truman and his top-level advisers that began on June 25, they concluded that while the combat readiness of MacArthur's forces suffered from the economy drive that had been in effect for the past five years, the Soviets—if, indeed, they were responsible for the North Korean invasion—had picked the one area in the world where American military forces of all arms were well positioned to intervene.[24] Still, American involvement only increased slowly during the week that followed. At first, United States air and naval forces were directed only to protect Korean ports and the evacuation of American noncombatants from Korea, and to provide supplies to the Republic of Korea (ROK) Army. Later, on

June 26, the President instructed MacArthur to provide air cover to the ROK Army south of the 38th Parallel. On the twenty-ninth, the President decided to let MacArthur employ his air forces against military targets in North Korea when such support would directly benefit ROK operations. Army logistical and signal troops were to be sent to Korea to perform essential service and communications tasks. Further, the President permitted MacArthur to use Army combat troops to secure the port and an airfield at Pusan, on the southeastern tip of Korea. These combat troops were specifically restricted from assisting the ROK defense farther to the north.

On the night of June 29, the last act of American intervention unfolded when General J. Lawton Collins, the Army Chief of Staff, received MacArthur's somber report: the South Korean forces were in confusion, had not fought seriously, and lacked leadership; they were incapable of gaining the initiative. The only remaining hope was to introduce United States ground forces. Reluctantly, the President approved MacArthur's request.[25] He and his advisers had proceeded cautiously during the week, for they genuinely wanted to avert war. In particular, the Joint Chiefs wanted to avoid a commitment that might divert strategic weapons from Europe and the Soviet Union and tie up scarce ground forces in Korea. The irony of the situation was all too clear to them: the world's greatest air-nuclear power was about to engage in a conventional land war against the soldiery of Asia. It is hard to imagine a more asymmetrical situation. But the decision to intervene in Korea was political, not military. President Truman and Secretary of State Dean Acheson were convinced that the North Korean—and Soviet—challenge had to be met with something more than UN resolutions if the credibility of the United States as the leader of the "free world" was to be maintained. As a result, leaders of the administration coped with the crisis in a series of discussions, wavering between political determination and military caution. Determination finally prevailed over caution, and the nation committed its meager conventional forces to a local war in Asia.

By nightfall on July 1, a small advance force of two reinforced rifle companies of the 1st Battalion of the 21st Infantry Regiment, 24th Infantry Division landed at Pusan. Their arrival signaled the beginning of an unprecedented problem of time and distance in which North Korean forces, by now well south of the 38th Parallel, would race MacArthur's forces for the port of Pusan. Meanwhile, 5,000 miles away, the United States began to mobilize her military power. Somehow, the Joint Chiefs of Staff had to equalize those distances.

Command Organization

When the United Nations and the United States decided to cast their lot with the Republic of Korea, the situation could not have been much worse. American intelligence estimated that the advance elements of the 24th Division and the weakened South Koreans were facing nine North Korean divisions numbering 80,000 men and capable of threatening the port of Pusan within two weeks.[26] In light of this estimate, the UN Security Council resolution of June 27, which aimed at restoring peace and security in the area, seemed overly ambitious. Nevertheless, on June 30, the Joint Chiefs directed MacArthur to employ his ground forces in addition to the air and naval forces already committed.[27]

But for what purpose were these forces to be committed, and how were they to know when they had accomplished their mission? General Omar N. Bradley, Chairman of the Joint Chiefs of Staff, later stated that MacArthur's military objective was to repel the attack and drive the North Koreans back, north of the 38th Parallel.[28] There was no formal directive to MacArthur giving a concrete objective, for a commander at his level of responsibility was normally given mission-type orders, devoid of detail and qualification. In the early days of the war, the goal of restoring the *status quo ante* gave MacArthur all of the direction he needed while confining the war to the Korean peninsula. In terms of political effects, such an objective had universal appeal, as it established an appropriate penalty for North Korea's act of international outlawry while avoiding direct confrontation with the Soviet Union. For the time being, it was an objective that could be supported by all right-minded men—and it was, perhaps, even more than MacArthur could accomplish on the battlefield.

For the first two weeks of the war, the armed forces of the Allies operated under MacArthur by dint of the resolution of June 27 and by the cooperation of individual governments, rather than as part of a unified military command. UN Secretary General Trygve Lie and President Truman moved quickly to link the UN to the battlefield. A resolution passed on July 7 requested all member states wishing to provide military forces and assistance to South Korea to make such forces and assistance available to a combined command operating under the Government of the United States. Further, the Security Council requested that the United States designate the commander of the force. By this act, the United States Government became the Executive Agent for the UN for all matters affecting the war in Korea, and MacArthur became the Commander-in-Chief, United Nations Command. There was no provision for close supervision of operations by the UN; the resolution asked only that the United States Government report to the Security Council on the course of action taken by the unified command in Korea.[29] In effect, then, the United States Government controlled the Allied war effort in Korea.

Within the Department of Defense, the chain of command from the Joint Chiefs to MacArthur was clear, and day-to-day direction of the war came from the JCS. Because the Korean War was essentially a land war, the Army dominated the operation. General Collins, the Army Chief of Staff, was the Joint Chiefs' Executive Agent for the Far East, and as such initiated many recommendations for study and decision. Moreover, although MacArthur was a unified commander, subordinate to the Joint Chiefs and exercising operational command over all land, sea, and air forces in the Far East Command, he never really changed the style of command that had served him so well during World War II. MacArthur ran an Army headquarters in which the handful of assigned Air Force and Navy staff officers played relatively minor roles. Naval and air planning went on in the naval and air component headquarters, much as it had during the last war.[30]

Until the North Korean invasion, the Eighth Army, commanded by Lieutenant General Walton H. Walker, had been on occupation duty in Japan. When war broke out, its divisions quickly deployed to Korea. Once a senior headquarters of the United States had been established to command the ground action, Syngman Rhee, President of the Republic of Korea, instructed his Chief of Staff to place himself and the ROK Army under American command. Later in the war, contingents from other UN member nations also joined Eighth Army under Walker's command.

Almost wholly dependent upon the existing American chain of command, the efforts of the defenders accomplished about as much as could be expected. The Joint Chiefs scoured military posts and bases in search of reinforcements for MacArthur. The General Reserve was devastated as half of its 140,000 men and much of its equipment went to MacArthur during the summer of 1950.[31] Congress gave strong support by reviving the dormant Selective Service System, permitting the President to order units and personnel of the Reserves and National Guard to active duty, raising the statutory strength ceiling of the armed forces, and authorizing the President to place members of the armed forces on active duty for a year. But most of this was long-term support, while MacArthur's immediate problem was salvaging the tactical situation in Korea.

Delay and Withdraw

MacArthur's sole hope of saving the South Koreans was to hold the port of Pusan until help arrived. Pusan was the only port left in UN hands that could accommodate the entry of modern military forces in large enough quantities to affect the outcome of the war. It possessed enough piers and cargo handling facilities to berth 23 deep-water ships and 14 Landing Ships Tank (LSTs). In 1950, it could only discharge 14,000 tons per day, however, because shortages of skilled labor, cargo handling cranes, railroad cars, and good highways prevented full utilization of the port. Thus, a race was underway, with North Korean forces—a mere 200 miles to the north—and American forces in Japan struggling to reach and secure this decisive objective. The outcome of the race would depend upon MacArthur's ability to marshal and move enough combat troops to delay the North Koreans, while the Joint Chiefs rushed reinforcements from the United States, 16 sailing days away. MacArthur's first problem, then, was to slow the advance of the enemy.

Capitalizing on the surprise their invasion had achieved, North Korean troops pressed their successful main attack toward Seoul. (*See Atlas Map No. 27.*) North Korean infantry crossed the Han River on June 30, and suddenly ran into bitter resistance. For three days, their

Lieutenant General Walton H. Walker *(left)* and Major General William F. Dean at the Front, July 8, 1950

advance was markedly slowed. Finally, after concentrating a tank force on the south side of the river, the North Koreans once again broke loose. On July 4, they rolled into Suwon in the west and into Yoju and Wonju in the center. On the east coast, a ground column linked up with the amphibious force at Samch'ok.

After their landing on July 1, the first two rifle companies of the American 24th Division moved immediately to positions near Osan. On July 5, the rifle companies, known as Task Force Smith, made their first contact with six North Korean tanks and an undetermined number of infantry just north of Osan.[32] With the arrival of American troops, the enemy offensive slowed somewhat, but overall it continued to move southward along each of the three axes of advance.[33] Clearly, regardless of the local effect of a handful of American troops, the success of the delaying action depended upon resistance by the South Korean Army.

After the initial surprise, the performance of the South Korean Army improved markedly. It was, however, limited by the lack of materiel. In 1949, when the American military forces finally withdrew from Korea, they left enough supplies to support a land army of 65,000, a civil police force of 3,500, and a coast guard of 4,000. The equipment for this force consisted of 91 light artillery pieces, 19 armored cars, 11 half-track armored vehicles, and 20 liaison-type aircraft. Army units could count on nothing heavier than rifles, carbines, and mortars. Their equipment was divisional in nature and intended to support a force designed only to prevent border raids and to preserve internal security.[34] Armed as they were, the South Koreans might fight valiantly, but their effectiveness against modern armored columns was marginal.

After committing Task Force Smith to battle near Osan, MacArthur pushed the remainder of the 24th Division into Korea, completing the move by July 6. In Japan, the 25th Infantry Division and the 1st Cavalry Division prepared to follow. The 24th Division rushed north to confront the enemy on what appeared to be the axis of the main attack leading from Seoul to Taejon and Pusan. (*See Atlas Map No. 27.*) On July 8, 24th Division troops engaged the enemy at P'yongt'aek and Ch'onan. On the eleventh, further engagements took place at Choch'iwon. Then, between July 13 and 15, the 24th Division fell back to take advantage of the natural obstacle of the Kum River. Meanwhile, on July 8, the 25th Division began to move from Japan to Korea, and then advanced north to join the 24th Division.[35]

As early as June, when he had reconnoitered the Han River line, MacArthur had conceived of a counterstroke. In his plan, a marine brigade and the 1st Cavalry Division

would land at Inchon while the 24th and 25th Divisions drove the enemy back against the Han River. But after the 24th Division had been driven from its positions around Choch'iwon on July 12, the situation became so desperate that the Commander-in-Chief had to scrap his plans for mounting an early counteroffensive.[36] Further, between July 18 and 22, the 1st Cavalry Division landed on the east coast at Pohang and deployed inland to block the enemy drives down the east coast and in the center.[37] Thus, by late July, all of MacArthur's resources, less the 7th Infantry Division, were engaged in battle.

Lieutenant General Walker, commanding the Eighth Army, took a good, hard look at the developing situation. Although they would be of no help in mounting a counteroffensive, reinforcements were on the way. The 5th Regimental Combat Team (RCT) was enroute from Hawaii, and the 2nd Infantry Division and 1st Provisional Marine Brigade had sailed from the United States. After collecting all available data on the status of troops in Korea, the progress of those enroute and scheduled to arrive in the next 10 days, the organization of the port of Pusan, and the ammunition and supply levels, Walker developed a plan to delay the enemy. His idea was to use the 24th and 25th Divisions and the South Koreans to gain maximum possible delay west and north of a line that ran north from the southernmost coast along the Naktong River, and then turned east and ran to the coast at Yongdok. *(See map on page 79.)* If forced to fall back, he would defend Pusan with all available forces from behind the Naktong River line until reinforcements arrived and the Eighth Army could undertake a counteroffensive.[38]

A .30-Caliber Browning Light Machinegun in Position South of Taejon, July 1950

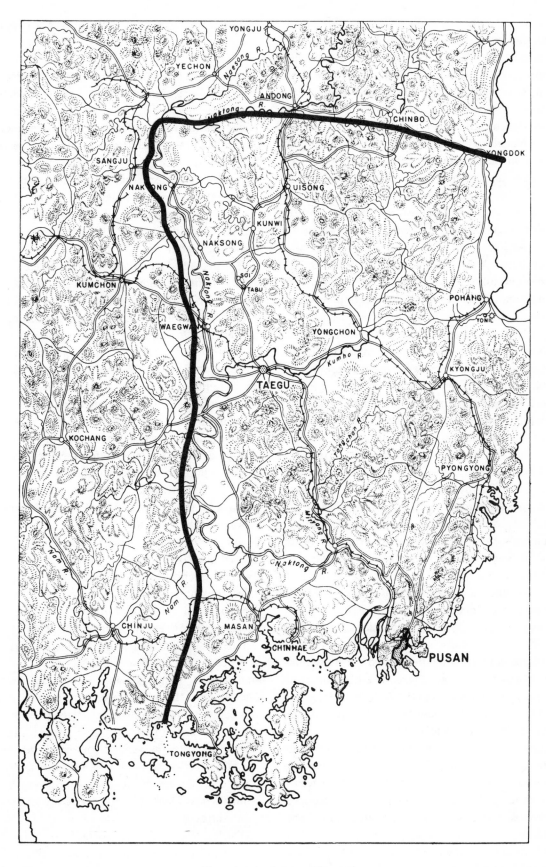

Trace of the Naktong River Line

If this concept were to succeed, Walker needed a delay of two full days at Taejon. (*See Atlas Map No. 27.*) The task fell to the battered 24th Division. In a fierce battle costing many casualties, including Major General William F. Dean, its Commanding General, the 24th gave Walker the two days he needed.[39] Still, enemy pressure continued to increase, forcing the Allies to shrink their line even further. For his part, General Walker was disappointed by the failure of his divisions to stop the enemy, particularly between Taejon and Taegu late in July. Once again, MacArthur diverted forces earmarked for the counteroffensive by ordering the 1st Provisional Marine Brigade and the 2nd Division, then enroute to Japan, to sail directly for Pusan.[40]

Suddenly a new development threatened Pusan and the UN lifeline. On July 23, aerial reconnaissance detected two North Korean units, the 4th Division and the 6th Division, moving down the west coast of the peninsula. Making a deep turning movement, they appeared to be heading toward Kwangju and then east to Masan and Pusan. (*See Atlas Map No. 27.*) While there was no way to prevent the enemy from outflanking the Eighth Army, MacArthur believed that if the Eighth Army held the main attack in the center on the Taejon-Taegu axis, the enemy would be stopped. In fact, he told the Joint Chiefs that the situation was developing just as he had anticipated. Nevertheless, the Joint Chiefs were apprehensive, and began to consider a seaward withdrawal of MacArthur's forces should they become compressed into an indefensible bridgehead.[41]

At the front, there were no discussions of withdrawal. MacArthur publicly proclaimed that there would be no "Dunkirk" in Korea. Walker voiced similar sentiments to the commanders and staffs of the 1st Cavalry and 25th Divisions following withdrawals in those units.[42] In effect, Walker ordered the Eighth Army to hold fast.

Stopping the enemy, however, was easier to order than to accomplish. The pressure in the central regions and in Masan and Pusan to the south threatened the entire position. The North Korean 6th Division, advancing from Kwangju to Masan, encountered the 24th Division, which was trying to hold a 65-mile-long line with only two regiments. Walker sent two recently arrived battalions of the 29th Infantry Regiment to assist the battered 24th. These two battalions, nothing more than raw recruits, went into combat without training, without test firing their weapons, and without time to ready their equipment. In desperation, untrained Koreans were also ordered into the fight, 100 to each American rifle company. After fierce fighting in front of Masan, the enemy drive came to a halt—but only after Walker had committed the 27th Infantry Regiment, his last reserve.

Defense of the Pusan Perimeter

Weighing the overall situation, Walker decided that he had to reduce the length of his front in order to defend against further enemy penetrations. He could no longer afford the luxury of delay and withdrawal; the defenders had run out of space. At the same time, he had to preserve sufficient depth in his position to permit the maneuver of reserves against penetrations that might successfully breach the line. Walker therefore ordered the Eighth Army to withdraw behind the Naktong River line, effective August 1. There it would establish what came to be known as the Pusan perimeter.[43]

A three-sided front, the Pusan perimeter was 150 miles long, running from Masan in the southwest, north to the village of Naktong, and then east to Yongdok on the coast. (*See map on page 79.*) American troops defended the western side, while South Korean units held the northern one. Within the perimeter, a railroad loop connected the port of Pusan with Taegu and Kyongju, enabling supplies to reach the defending forces. The Naktong River line was never a continuous, coordinated defensive position, enjoying overlapping and interlocking fires. On the contrary, because manpower was at a premium, the line consisted of scattered strongpoints and a few local reserves.[44] It was an area too large to defend with the forces at hand, but too small to permit further enemy advance. It survived only because of the timely arrival of reinforcements rushed to Korea by the Joint Chiefs of Staff.

As infantry, artillery, and armored units arrived, they moved quickly to the front, where every man was needed. When the perimeter battle began, MacArthur's forces totaled four understrength American divisions; five South Korean divisions, reorganized from the survivors of the invasion; the 5th Regimental Combat Team; the 1st Provisional Marine Brigade; and all the tactical aircraft that the Air Force, the Navy, and the Marines could muster. By mid-August, reinforcements of over 500 medium tanks had changed the odds to 5 to 1 in favor of American armored units. Naval gunfire supported friendly units on the sea flanks of the perimeter, and the blockade of enemy seaports and sea movement continued. As the battle for the perimeter raged in an area far more constricted than had been the case during the withdrawal, the Air Force found it possible to give effective close air support to the ground troops.

During this period, a favorable air situation and the arrival of reinforcements enabled Walker to mount his first counterattack. He chose to direct it against enemy forces closest to Pusan, in front of Masan. (*See Atlas Map*

Infantrymen Direct 75-mm Recoilless Rifle Fire Against Enemy Positions During the Defense of the Pusan Perimeter

No. 28a.) Walker first instructed the 25th Division to assume responsibility for the southern half of the 24th Division's overextended sector. On August 7, after attaching the 5th RCT and the marine brigade to the 25th Division, he unleashed this force against the enemy in Chinju. Because the operation had been hastily organized, the performance of the task force suffered from poor coordination. The attack was stalemated, and after five days of seesaw battle, Walker called it off in order to cope with new problems farther to the north.[45]

The North Koreans had readied 10 divisions for an assault on the Naktong River line. Beginning on August 5, they launched two attacks—one against the South Korean forces north of Taegu and the other against the American forces that held the western line of the river. (*See Atlas Map No. 28a.*) In sizing up the threat to Pusan after stabilizing the situation in front of Masan, Walker decided to give first priority to that sector of the Naktong River line south of Taegu—an area known as the Naktong Bulge. An enemy penetration in this region would have cut the railroad line from Pusan to Taegu and placed the defenders in mortal danger, whereas enemy success north of Taegu would have merely pushed the defenders back along their lines of communication, without disrupting the flow of supplies. Fortunately for the UN forces, the North Koreans failed to coordinate the two blows to achieve simultaneous impact. This played into the hands of Walker, an experienced commander of armored forces who was predisposed to employ mobile warfare. Walker had to defend his extended fronts with understrength units in scattered strongpoints, blocking the likely avenues of approach. By American standards, Walker's artillery support was weak; no more than three batteries could mass their fires at any one point on the line.[46] To compensate for his deficiencies, Walker attached his reserve, the 1st Provisional Marine Brigade, to the 24th Division. The 24th counterattacked on August 17, and by the next night the bulge was clear, freeing the reserve to move to counter a new threat. On the Taegu front, held by the South Korean II Corps, the North Koreans forced a crossing of the Naktong River between August 4 and 9. Drawing up in front of the South Koreans and the 1st Cavalry Division, these forces attacked toward Taegu, forcing the South Korean Government to evacuate that city and withdraw to Pusan. Again, Walker relieved the pressure by rushing his reserves to the north, this time stopping the enemy in a battle fought between August 18 and 25. On the east coast, the South Korean I Corps slowed and finally stopped a North Korean drive aimed at Pusan. Walker sent only a small American task force, consisting of an infantry battalion with artillery and armor, to support the South Koreans.

By the end of August, the defenders had thrown back all the enemy units that had assailed the Eighth Army and South Korean positions in the uncoordinated offensive. But Eighth Army had little time to enjoy its respite. The next onslaught began the night of August 31, and this time it was well coordinated.

The September offensive had the same objectives as those designated for the August attack, but differed in that the blows fell simultaneously and more savagely. By September 10, Eighth Army was again under heavy pressure. (*See Atlas Map No. 28b.*) In the east, the North Koreans captured Pohang on the coast and severed the Pohang-Taegu lateral road. In the center, they forced the 1st Cavalry Division back to within 15 miles of Taegu. Further, they drove the 2nd Division almost to Yongsan in the Naktong Bulge sector, and then resumed their drive on Masan after making gains in the 25th Division sector. Once again, the invaders neared Pusan and threatened to cut the lifeline running north from the port.

Reacting in such a way as to cover Pusan and at the same time reinforce the most threatened sectors, Walker again employed a mobile defense, shifting and committing reserve units at the critical moment. He attached the marines to the 2nd Division and ordered it to clear the

The Naktong Bulge, Pusan Perimeter, August 18, 1950

Naktong Bulge. He then positioned 24th Division head-quarters and one of the division's regiments where it could move to the aid of the 25th Division, the 2nd Division, or the ROK defenders to the north. The battle raged, but by September 12, the North Korean offensive had spent itself on all fronts. By then, virtually all enemy combat units were concentrated against Pusan. Their long line of supply, under constant air bombardment, presented an inviting target for a turning movement. The time for a counter-offensive had arrived.

The Inchon Landing

MacArthur had been planning a counterstroke against the waist of the Korean peninsula since the first week of the war, but North Korean successes had forced him to postpone any action until September. On July 23, MacArthur had first informed the Joint Chiefs of his concept for a two-division landing at Inchon. Once Walker withdrew inside the Pusan perimeter, MacArthur felt sure that the Eighth Army could hold its position. Thus, he began to build an invasion force by diverting forces to Japan that had been intended for Korea.[47] The Joint Chiefs disliked

the plan. But MacArthur was ruthless; he committed just enough force to impede the North Korean attack on Pusan, while husbanding men and materiel to mount the counterattack. His reliance on an instinctive sense of how much to send and how much to withhold was both his greatest gamble and his most striking professional accomplishment.

Inchon was the worst sort of amphibious objective. The hydrographic conditions there were so bad that even though Inchon was the capital port, and the second largest port in South Korea, its development had been inhibited by the nature of its harbor.[48] The tides in Inchon harbor averaged 29 feet, and ran as high as 36 feet. The many small islands standing offshore funneled the tides into the harbor at high speed and then acted as buffers to the receding water. Therefore, over the centuries, great mud flats extending out from shore as far as 6,000 yards had developed, forming a vast swamp at low tide. LSTs could approach only at flood tide, and would settle in the mud as soon as the tide turned. The LSTs required 30-foot tides to float, and such conditions occurred only three or four days a month. Low tides were common from May to August, and beginning in October, rough waters made the approach through the narrow Flying Fish Channel extremely dangerous. Hydrographic records indicated that September 15 was the ideal time for a landing at Inchon; after that, the next available date was October 11.[49] MacArthur favored the September date, as it would allow him to gain an additional month of campaigning before the onset of winter.

LSTs Left High and Dry at Low Tide in Inchon Harbor

Wolmi-Do and the Harbor of Inchon

The Inchon objective area presented almost as many tactical problems as it did ones caused by the hydrographic conditions. The tides, the current, and the treacherous, twisting, narrow channel required a daylight approach with an assault landing in the afternoon. There would be little time for consolidation of an objective before dark. Furthermore, the approach to Inchon had to be made by a route dominated by Wolmi-do Island, which, if fortified and manned, could complicate the landing. Wolmi-do had to be seized first, on an early tide; the landing at Inchon would have to await the next high tide. Tactical surprise would therefore be lost.

The objective of the landing force, the city of Inchon, was in character with the rest of the area. The city had a population of about 250,000—comparable in size to Omaha, Nebraska—and had to be approached directly from the sea. There were no beaches. Assault troops would have to storm over the 12-foot-high seawall that protected the town from the tides.[50] An alert enemy would presumably know the hydrographic conditions and be prepared to defend Wolmi-do, concentrating his fire on the confining approach route during periods of greatest vulnerability. Should the landing force make it to the seawall and gain a foothold ashore, the task of fighting house-to-house through Inchon would present a formidable challenge.

From the first, MacArthur maintained an unwavering faith that the strategic opportunity that would result from

a seizure of the Inchon-Seoul area would far outweigh the technical difficulties of landing in Inchon harbor. He believed that the North Koreans, concentrated far to the south against Pusan, would be vulnerable to a turning movement aimed at the thinly held zone between the 38th and 37th Parallels. To arguments that he should land closer to the Eighth Army, MacArthur countered that while a landing farther south might cut the enemy's communications, it would not destroy his army. The real vulnerability of the enemy was his long, exposed supply line; cut it, and the Allies could seal off the peninsula and gain a complete victory.[51] But there were many doubters, some of whom were in MacArthur's own command. Rear Admiral James H. Doyle and Major General Oliver P. Smith, Commanding General of the 1st Marine Division, were his chief opponents. Both had been amphibious commanders in World War II, and both were disenchanted with Inchon as a landing site. There were doubts at other levels as well. The Joint Chiefs worried about the strategic consequences of failure, and their skepticism originated in part from the fears shared by the Navy and Marines. This does not mean that the Joint Chiefs opposed a counteroffensive; on the contrary, they realized that regaining the initiative by offensive action was the next logical step. The question was where and when. The Joint Chiefs had to consider the problem of rescuing MacArthur if his plan misfired. They hesitated to strip the General Reserve bare and then "risk all on one daring throw of the dice. . . ."[52] In spite of

Marines Head for the Beach at Inchon, September 15, 1950

opposition, MacArthur's eloquent defense of his scheme resulted in reluctant concurrence by the JCS.*

Briefly, the plan was as follows. Beginning early in September, naval air elements from the carriers of the Seventh Fleet were to strike targets on the west coast of Korea, gradually converging on Inchon. Air Force aircraft were to provide general air support to the whole theater by isolating the objective area. In addition, the Air Force was to support the Eighth Army in the Pusan perimeter and be prepared to drop the 187th Airborne Regimental Combat Team into an objective area on order. ROK marines were to feint at Kunsan, threatening the enemy forces concentrated around Pusan. The landing force—two regiments of the 1st Marine Division under the command of the newly formed X Corps—was to land in Inchon on September 15, D-Day, under the cover of naval gunfire and close air support provided by the 1st Marine Air Wing. (*See map on page 85.*) After the capture of Inchon, X Corps was to press on to Kimpo Airfield and the south bank of the Han River by D+2. The marines were then to cross the Han River, capture Seoul, and seize the dominant high ground north of the capital. Meanwhile, the 7th Infantry Division was to land in Inchon and advance on the right, or south, flank of the marines to secure the south bank of the Han River and the high ground north of Suwon. Thereafter, the X Corps was to be the anvil on which the Eighth Army

would deliver a hammer blow to destroy the North Koreans. The Eighth Army's attack was to begin on D+1 and follow the Taegu-Taejon-Suwon axis until linkup with X Corps was complete.[54]

On September 12, the 5th Marines, formerly the 1st Provisional Marine Brigade, sailed from Pusan for Inchon and a rendezvous with the rest of the 1st Marine Division. Following a brief but intense gunfire and air preparation at dawn on the fifteenth, the regiment's 3rd Battalion went ashore at Green Beach on Wolmi-do. (*See map on page 85.*) After an easily won skirmish lasting only 45 minutes, the island fell. That evening, the 1st and 2nd Battalions of the 5th Marines landed at Red Beach. Using ladders to scale the seawall, LSTs to ram breaches in the wall, and explosives to blow holes in it, the marines stormed into the city. At Blue Beach, the 1st Marines came ashore. By nightfall, both regiments had dug in and were ready for the expected counterattack. It never came; MacArthur had been right.

Early the next day, the marines attacked Kimpo Airfield, securing it before nightfall. (*See Atlas Map No. 29.*) On D+2, the 7th Infantry Division landed unopposed at Inchon and sped inland to sever the main escape routes of the North Korean Army, then concentrated around Pusan. Without stopping, the marines swept into Seoul, where they met bitter resistance from its defenders. MacArthur announced its capture on the twenty-fifth, although on that date there were still a number of North Koreans fiercely defending part of the city. It wasn't until September 28 that fighting finally subsided and the capital was secure. By October 1, the marines held a line well to the north, controlling the main approaches to the city and the port. (*See Atlas Map No. 29.*)

---

*Army Chief of Staff, General J. Lawton Collins, later stated that at all times the JCS were in complete agreement with assaulting Inchon. However, the evidence indicates that Collins must have been using the word "Inchon" interchangeably with "counteroffensive," for he certainly objected to Inchon as a landing site. The dominant opinion in Washington was that amphibious operations were obsolete. MacArthur specifically ascribes this view to General Omar Bradley, chairman of the Joint Chiefs of Staff. Bradley, MacArthur claims, believed there would never be another successful amphibious movement.[53]

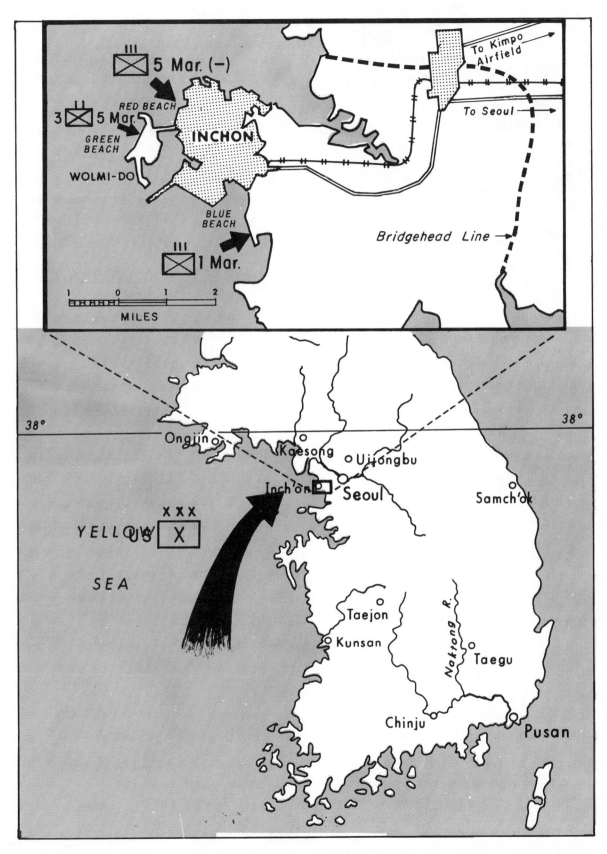

General Concept for the Inchon Invasion

A Marine Fires on the Enemy in Seoul

Far to the south, the Eighth Army experienced great difficulty breaking out of its perimeter on D+1. The troops were worn and exhausted after months of sustained combat, and ammunition was in short supply.[55] Moreover, the units lacked the proper equipment to cross the Naktong River. There were only two bridges available for the entire army, and armor in particular had great difficulty getting across the river. The greatest obstacle, however, was the enemy. Despite constant bombardment by psychological warfare leaflets and broadcasts, the enemy gave no sign whatsoever that he was even aware of the Inchon landing. The air offensive that was supposed to weaken him seemed to have fazed him not at all. Finally, on September 22, the North Koreans showed the first signs of collapse. The next day, they began a general withdrawal, and Walker ordered the Eighth Army to pursue. (*See Atlas Map No. 29.*) Suddenly the front fell apart, and columns of Eighth Army and South Korean units streamed north, taking the surrender of thousands of enemy soldiers. Late on September 26, a task force from the 1st Cavalry Division linked up with the 7th Infantry Division near Osan. Thereafter, the United Nations forces' only task was the policing of defeated North Korean troops.

Until this point, the war had been waged with marked success. The American Government had been aggressive in meeting the crisis, Congress had been cooperative, and the Joint Chiefs' dispatch of reinforcements had equaled the task, winning the race for Pusan. MacArthur and Walker had met the challenge of the North Korean invasion, had effectively patched together a coalition field

command, and had saved the South Koreans by pushing back the enemy. MacArthur's brilliant generalship, particularly at Inchon, had provided the edge. Perhaps most remarkable of all, the delay, withdrawal, defense, and counteroffensive had been supported logistically with little or no unnecessary hardship to the fighting men. Relations among the Allies were smooth as the American effort was slowly transformed into a United Nations operation. But the euphoria that followed the victory at Inchon obscured the indications of approaching disaster. The United Nations' warmaking machinery had performed spectacularly during a period of adversity, but it was destined to flounder in its search for an option that gave promise of victory.

Crossing the 38th Parallel

The turning point in the Korean War came when the United States Government decided to cross the 38th Parallel and enter North Korea. The decision to enter North Korea was not an impetuous one. As early as July 11, officers on the Army staff had wondered what would happen when UN forces reached the parallel.[56] Members of the Joint Chiefs speculated about it in discussions with MacArthur during conferences held on July 12 to 14.[57] On July 13, Syngman Rhee publicly asserted that the Koreans would not stop at any boundary. Questions about crossing the parallel arose in the Department of State, and by July 17 the matter had reached the National Security Council, where President Truman asked the NSC staff to study the matter.[58]

On September 1, the NSC staff sent its study to the Departments of State and Defense. While admitting that there was sound legal basis for the movement of UN forces into North Korea, the NSC staff concluded that crossing the 38th Parallel was not a necessary ingredient of victory, that the war would ultimately stabilize along that parallel, and that the probability of Soviet or Chinese intervention in the event of such a crossing was dangerously high. The staff also outlined restraints on military operations should the President decide to move north. No UN troops should enter Manchuria or the USSR; only South Korean troops should operate along the Manchurian and Soviet borders; and if the Soviets or Chinese intervened before crossing, the operation should be canceled.[59]

The Joint Chiefs objected to much of the NSC study. Future combat operations limited by the 38th Parallel would solve nothing; contemporary doctrine demanded the destruction of the North Korean Army to prevent a renewal of the aggression. MacArthur would, therefore,

have to pursue the enemy into North Korea. They disagreed that UN units were likely to fight Soviet and Chinese forces; the South Koreans would in all probability
simply mop up the remnants of the North Korean Army,
while other UN forces would withdraw quickly and confine their activities to South Korea. In this debate, the JCS
adhered to the traditional view that no prior restrictions
should be placed on MacArthur if crossing the 38th Parallel were necessary to accomplish his mission.[60] Sound as
their arguments may have seemed, they contained some
surprising inconsistencies.

On September 7—the same day that the Joint Chiefs
forwarded their opinions on crossing the 38th Parallel to
the Secretary of Defense, and only a week before D-Day at
Inchon—the JCS also sent a message to MacArthur, reo-
pening the question of the Inchon invasion. Pointing out
that virtually all of the nation's ground power had been
allocated to Korea and that there would be no new reinforcements available until 1951, they expressed concern
that if the operation failed, the capability of the United
States to influence actions elsewhere would be crippled.
One can sympathize with the Joint Chiefs' caution and
applaud their careful consideration of all the issues. What
is difficult to understand, however, is how they could simultaneously consider crossing the 38th Parallel. An advance into North Korea was dependent upon a successful
landing at Inchon, a matter of considerable risk according
to the Joint Chiefs. Certainly, then, a plan to continue the
offensive into North Korea—without reinforcements,
over increasingly mountainous terrain, and into the expanded northern half of the peninsula—should have elic-
ited at least equal caution. The arguments marshaled
against MacArthur's Inchon plan were equally applicable
to the question of crossing the 38th Parallel. In addition, a
new factor had to be considered: the possibility of intervention by Chinese Communist Forces (CCF). Full-scale
intervention by the CCF was a continuing threat, even
though the Central Intelligence Agency (CIA) concluded
that such intervention was unlikely in 1950, barring a Soviet decision for global war.[61] Regardless of the weaknesses
in the Joint Chiefs' argument, the National Security
Council adopted their position, and on September 11—
four days before D-Day at Inchon—the President approved the new policy. MacArthur was to begin planning
for an advance into North Korea.

Not surprisingly, MacArthur's success at Inchon al-
layed most of the earlier fears of the Joint Chiefs. Confidence in the old hero soared, and the JCS felt free to turn
their attention to matters that assumed higher priority during the crucial month of September. More and more, the
planning of military operations in Korea was left to Mac-

Arthur, while the JSC attended to the details of supple-
mentary appropriations for rearmament of the United
States and her allies, oversaw the mobilization of the nation's military and industrial power, directed a wide variety of other wartime projects, and increasingly became
involved in negotiations affecting the reinforcement of
NATO against the worldwide Communist threat. On September 8, the President publicly committed the United
States to reinforcing NATO with four to six divisions.[62]
Thereafter, the Joint Chiefs were to press their search for
troops to send to Europe. As the situation seemed to improve in Korea, they began to count on MacArthur's arranging the early transfer of one or two of his divisions. So
they approved their commander's concept for crossing the
38th Parallel without receiving the full details of the plan.
Too quick to give the general his head, the Chiefs had cause
for concern.

MacArthur's plan for crossing the 38th Parallel was
flawed in several ways. Under it, the United Nations Command was to attack north of the 38th Parallel in order to
complete the destruction of the North Korean Army as an
organized fighting force. *(See map on page 88.)* Destruction of the enemy was to be accomplished by air and naval
action as well as an amphibious-ground campaign. Walker's Eighth Army was to conduct the main effort in a
ground offensive along the Kaesong-Sariwon-P'yongyang
axis in conjunction with an amphibious landing by the X
Corps at Wonsan. Once ashore, the X Corps was to advance across the peninsula to P'yongyang against the rear
of the enemy forces opposing the main effort. To avoid
alarming the Chinese, only South Korean forces were to
pursue the enemy north of the Chongju-Kunu-ri-
Yongwon-Hamhung-Hungnam line. The 3rd Infantry Division and an airborne regimental combat team were to
remain in reserve initially.[63] In order to be ready for the
amphibious operation, MacArthur ordered Major General Edward M. Almond, commander of the X Corps, to
turn over the Seoul area to Walker by October 7. Almond
was then to move the 1st Marine Division to Inchon for
embarkation on the ships that had brought it to Korea. To
avoid intolerable congestion in the port, the 7th Infantry
Division was to move by road and rail to Pusan, and embark there. The corps was to load and sail in time to land at
Wonsan on October 20. Eighth Army was to plan the main
attack for October 19.[64]

MacArthur's decision to send the Eighth Army overland in the main attack from Seoul to P'yongyang and to
withdraw X Corps from the Seoul area to carry out an
amphibious secondary attack at Wonsan is questionable.
First, contemporary doctrine for pursuit and exploitation
called for the employment of direct pressure and encircling

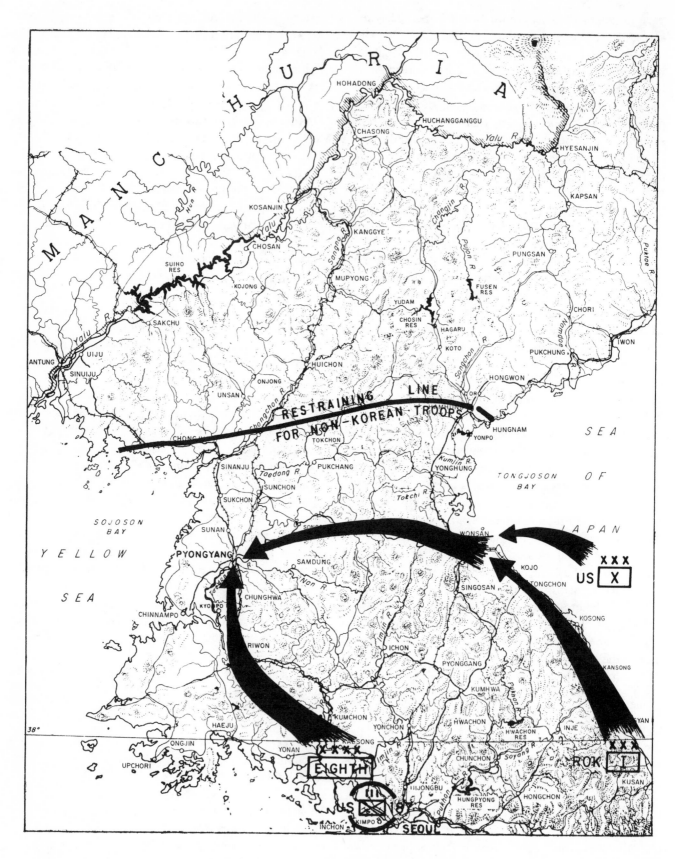

MacArthur's Concept for Crossing the 38th Parallel

Supplies Are Unloaded at Inchon

forces against a retreating enemy. According to that doctrine, the key to a successful pursuit and exploitation was the speedy resumption of the offensive, either to prevent the enemy from reconstituting an integrated defense or to conduct an effective delay. The October 19 date chosen for the main attack was simply too late to trap the survivors of the Inchon reversal. Second, MacArthur made a fundamental error by adopting a plan in which the secondary attack took priority over almost every aspect of the main attack. When the Seoul campaign ended, the Eighth Army was strung out from the Naktong River to Seoul; some kind of reorganization was imperative before Walker's

men could take part in the pursuit. On the other hand, the X Corps was generally disposed to the north of the Eighth Army. Moreover, it was well provisioned from ships still unloading at Inchon, and relatively fresh when compared with the units of the Eighth Army. In short, the X Corps was in position to attack north over the 38th Parallel in any direction MacArthur wanted. Yet, instead of exploiting the speedy resumption of the attack that these dispositions afforded, MacArthur chose to withdraw the X Corps to the rear, while the exhausted Eighth Army moved north to mount the main attack. Third, MacArthur created a serious logistical problem for the Eighth Army. By ordering the X Corps to embark the 1st Marine Division at Inchon, he blocked the inbound movement of supplies at a time when the Eighth Army was desperately in need of replenishment after its 200-mile march from the Naktong River. With only a trickle of supplies moving between Pusan and Seoul, and with replenishment from Inchon denied, the Eighth Army had to rely on approximately 1,000 tons of supplies, including ammunition, airlifted daily to the Seoul area to conduct the main effort.[65]

These disadvantages were apparent to many in MacArthur's own command and to a few in Washington, yet no one protested vigorously. Major General George L. Eberle, MacArthur's G-4,* favored placing the X Corps under Eighth Army, and moving the whole force overland, perhaps from Seoul, through Ch'orwon, to Wonsan. He believed that such an organization would be easier to supply until Wonsan was captured and opened to shipping. Major General Edwin K. Wright, MacArthur's chief planner, also preferred placing the X Corps under Eighth Army after Inchon, and did not approve of the inclusion of the amphibious operation at Wonsan. Major General Doyle Hickey, MacArthur's Chief of Staff, was reportedly in agreement with Eberle and Wright.[66] Vice Admiral C. Turner Joy, Commander of Naval Forces, Far East, also objected to the amphibious movement of the X Corps. Along with many other naval officers, he believed that the embarkation of the X Corps at Inchon would interfere with the logistical buildup of the Eighth Army. He was concerned that the concentration of shipping and landing craft in an amphibious operation would reduce overall combat replenishment. He also feared encountering the mines that had been reported in Wonsan harbor. Joy felt sure that the ROK I Corps, advancing rapidly along the east coast road, could capture Wonsan before October 20, thus making an administrative unloading of the marines likely. Joy and his subordinates were convinced that the X Corps could march overland to Wonsan in a much shorter time and with much less effort than it could move by sea.[67]

General Walker wanted to exploit the favorable location of the X Corps and to continue the attack quickly in order to complete the entrapment of the retreating North Koreans. If that corps were to be placed under the Eighth Army commander, Walker reasoned that the force could advance rapidly overland to both P'yongyang and Wonsan. He thought it was a mistake not to press the advantage so dearly won at Inchon and Seoul. Like Joy, Walker also believed that the ROK I Corps would capture Wonsan and

that the Eighth Army would capture P'yongyang before the amphibious force could even reach Wonsan. Walker was supported by his own logistician, who believed that the whole force could be supported from Inchon and Pusan and by air until Wonsan was captured.[68]

For whatever reason—the attraction of another amphibious operation, a failure to consult with his staff, a poor appreciation of his logistical situation, or simply a personal determination to lead intuitively—MacArthur stuck to his decision and never admitted that he was aware of the objections of his own staff or his naval advisers. When Joy tried to take his objections directly to MacArthur, Hickey, although sympathetic, told Joy that the general had made up his mind about the landing; there was no use trying to talk him out of it.

MacArthur then compounded the planning errors by making the difficult logistical situation even worse. From the time of the plan's conception, the X Corps had made its logistical arrangements with Japan Logistical Command. But in the midst of loading the X Corps, MacArthur suddenly shifted responsibility for logistical support of all UN forces in Korea to the Eighth Army. This included the X Corps. Thus, Walker became responsible for coordinating the logistical support of the corps without having any control over its operations.[69] Why MacArthur did this is not clear. He may have wanted to free the corps staff to supervise the loading of the two divisions at Inchon and Pusan in order to meet the tight time schedule. He may have felt that the army logistical staff had a greater capability than the corps staff. Or MacArthur may have planned on Walker's assuming operational control of the X Corps after the landing at Wonsan. If the latter were true, MacArthur may have reasoned that the Wonsan operation would be of short duration and that, therefore, Walker's responsibility would be continuous following the landing.

Although the Eighth Army worked hard to assist the X Corps in its embarkation, difficulties still arose when unloading began in the objective area. Rations arrived on large ships, bulk loaded, requiring the complete unloading of ships before they could be assembled for issue. The distribution of signal supplies was delayed because all signal items had been loaded aboard one ship and unloaded at a single location, even though required at three different beaches. Because the request for petroleum, oil, and lubricants (POL) for the 7th Division was canceled erroneously, these materials were never loaded by Japan Logistical Command. This necessitated an emergency shipment of POL from Japan to meet the requirements of the division. Colonel Aubrey D. Smith, G-4 of the X Corps, claimed that these and other problems resulted from the change of

---

*Since World War I, the staffs of American units commanded by general officers have been made up of G-sections. A G-4 is the staff officer responsible for planning for supply and services.

command channels at a time when staffs were over-worked, facilities were overcommitted, and the need for close and continuous coordination was never greater.[70] In any case, MacArthur's action further complicated Walker's primary task of commanding the main attack across the 38th Parallel.

Nevertheless, Walker was impatient to start north. By the end of the first week in October, the ROK I Corps had crossed the 38th Parallel on the road to Wonsan along the east coast, and the UN General Assembly had passed a resolution that cleared the way for the movement of UN troops into North Korea. If Walker waited until Inchon was once again open, following the departure of the marines, he would surely lose contact with the enemy. On the other hand, should his logistical support break down completely, he could conceivably fail to catch the fleeing North Koreans. Walker finally decided that his most urgent task was to maintain the pressure on the enemy. Ready or not, on October 7 the 1st Cavalry Division sent patrols across the 38th Parallel. On the next day, more patrols followed, and on October 9, the rest of the American 1st Cavalry Division and the ROK II Corps also crossed the border. Now the Allies were advancing in both the east and the west. (*See Atlas Map No. 30.*)

MacArthur's faulty campaign plan triggered other tactical decisions that, although understandable, were integral parts of the unfolding tragedy. At first, resistance crumbled quickly as the full weight of the Eighth Army was directed toward P'yongyang. By nightfall of October

Cleaning Out an Enemy Emplacement

19, a South Korean division had captured the center of the North Korean capital. On the east coast, the ROK I Corps advanced even more rapidly, and by October 11 it had captured Wonsan. But the X Corps had not even left port to rendezvous for the October 20 D-Day. A new problem had arisen in the form of a complex minefield in Wonsan harbor. Naval minesweepers were moved into the area and reinforced by Japanese and Korean vessels, but October 20 came and went without the X Corps going ashore. Ultimately, the 1st Marine Division landed on the twenty-sixth, and the 7th Division landed at Iwon, 178 miles north of Wonsan, where it disembarked under the watchful eyes of the ROK I Corps.

In the end, the rapid advance of the ROK I Corps, the early capture of P'yongyang, and the delayed arrival of the X Corps forced MacArthur to change his plans. The enemy had escaped. By October 20, in all likelihood the North Koreans were already north of the Ch'ongch'on River. North Korean Government installations had moved from P'yongyang on October 12, and by the twentieth they had set up a temporary capital in Kanggye, near the Manchurian border. There was no longer a need either for a westward advance by the X Corps or for further complicating the Eighth Army's supply situation. Having opened the port of Wonsan and having advanced so far north in the east, it would have been better to accept the failure of the encirclement and make the best of the situation.

After returning from a meeting with President Truman at Wake Island, MacArthur canceled the plan to cut and seal the peninsula between Wonsan and P'yongyang. On October 16, he issued an operation order for a parachute assault by the 187 Airborne Regimental Combat Team on October 20 in order to intercept the retreat of the North Koreans from P'yongyang. The next day, MacArthur issued new orders in which he established a boundary between the Eighth Army and the X Corps. The boundary ran along the watershed of the Taebaek Mountains, from the 38th Parallel to the Manchurian border. He ordered his army to advance to a new restraining line located between 50 and 100 miles closer to the Yalu River.[71] The offensive rolled north at a rate of about 10 miles a day, aided by the parachute drops of the 187th at Sukch'on and Sunch'on. A week later, MacArthur lifted all restrictions on the maneuver of ground forces south of the Yalu River. With this act, he disobeyed the instructions he had received from his government prohibiting the movement of non-Asian troops into the territory immediately adjacent to Manchuria and the Soviet Union.[72]

Actually, MacArthur was reacting to the consequences of his earlier decisions. Because of the difficulty of the terrain, he had lost contact with part of the enemy army

President Truman and General MacArthur at Wake Island, October 15, 1950

after Inchon. His subsequent decisions, lacking the inspiration, insights, and careful staff work of his earlier ones, failed to produce success. Realizing that the Wonsan operation would once again fail to trap his foe, MacArthur tried to salvage his only chance for complete victory. He resorted to a rapid overland pursuit to the Yalu River. (*See Atlas Map No. 30.*) Now he could foresee a possibility that the enemy forces would again escape if their destruction were left to the limited quality and quantity of the South Korean army. Given these circumstances, from MacArthur's viewpoint the lifting of restrictions on the use of his forces was a logical and essential step. He needed every available man to destroy the enemy. What MacArthur did not understand was that his crossing of the 38th Parallel had caused the Chinese to set a giant ambush. Thus, his decision to recover victory through direct pressure would

result in the situation that the United States had sought to avoid: the intervention of Chinese forces.

None of this was known to the Joint Chiefs. Their involvement in other matters made them oblivious to MacArthur's errors and to the full extent of his danger. There is no indication that anyone in the administration fully understood MacArthur's dilemma. In the Pentagon, some staff officers realized that MacArthur had lost contact with a portion of the enemy forces; others saw the serious risk to his army should the Chinese intervene; still others understood his supply difficulties. But no one person or agency appears to have understood just how bad his situation really was. Quite the contrary, it was precisely at this time that the Joint Chiefs were planning to dismantle MacArthur's forces in the belief that the war was essentially over.

Notes

[1]Roy E. Appleman, *South to the Naktong, North to the Yalu (June–November 1950), United States Army in the Korean War* (Washington, D.C., 1961), pp. 21–28.

[2]"The Quarter Polls," in *Public Opinion Quarterly,* 9 (Spring 1945), 101.

[3]Frederick W. Williams, "Regional Attitudes on International Cooperation," in *Public Opinion Quarterly,* 9 (Spring 1945), 38–45.

[4]William J. Sebald and Russell Brines, *With MacArthur in Japan: A Personal History of the Occupation* (New York, 1965), p. 179.

[5]Matthew B. Ridgway, *The War in Korea* (Garden City, NY, 1967), pp. 10, 12–13; also see Louis Johnson's testimony in U.S., Congress, Senate, Committee on Armed Services and Committee on Foreign Relations, *Military Situation in the Far East and the Facts Surrounding the Relief of General of the Army Douglas MacArthur from His Assignments in that Area,* pt. 4, 82nd Cong., 1st sess., 1951, p. 2672; hereafter cited as *Military Situation in the Far East.*

[6]Glenn D. Paige, *The Korean Decision (June 24–30, 1950)* (New York, 1968), pp. 62–63.

[7]See the statement by the Secretary of State on extension of economic aid to the Republic of Korea, March 7, 1950, in U.S. Department of State, *American Foreign Policy, 1950–1955: Basic Documents,* Department of State Publication 6446, General Foreign Policy Series 117 (Washington, D.C., 1957), p. 2534.

[8]"Record of the Actions Taken by the Joint Chiefs of Staff Relative to the United Nations Operations in Korea from 25 June 1950 to 11 April 1951," prepared by the Joint Chiefs of Staff for the Senate Armed Forces [sic] and Foreign Relations Committees, April 30, 1951, CCS 013.36 (4-20-51), Bulky Package, National Archives, p. 3. See also Ridgway, *War in Korea,* p. 7, and Dean G. Acheson, *Present at the Creation: My Years in the State Department* (New York, 1970), p. 581.

[9]Memo, Major General Charles Bolte to General Alfred Gruenther, July 28, 1950, subject: "Responsibility for Withdrawing Troops from Korea," in DA File OPS 091 Korea (C), National Archives; Reports, KMAG to DA, KMAG G3 Operations Reports, nos. 38 to 51, March 18 to June 16, 1950 in DA File OPS 091 Korea (S), National Archives; Far Eastern Economic Assistance Act of 1950, *U.S. Code Congressional Service,* Vol. 2: *Legislative History,* 81st Cong., 2nd sess., 1950, pp. 1921–1922.

[10]U.S., Congress, House, Committee on the Armed Services, *Unification and Strategy, a Report of Investigation,* by the Committee on Armed Services. H.R. Doc. 600, 81st Cong., 2nd sess., 1950, p. 16.

[11]U.S., Department of Defense, *First Report of the Secretary of Defense, 1948* (Washington, D.C., 1948), p. 11.

[12]Bernard Brodie, "Implications For Military Policy," in *The Absolute Weapon,* ed. by Bernard Brodie (New York, 1946), pp. 3–4, 17.

[13]U.S., Congress, House, Committee on Appropriations, *Military Establishment Appropriation Bill for 1948, Hearings,* before a subcommittee of the Committee on Appropriations, House of Representatives, 80th Cong., 1st sess., 1947, p. 12.

[14]*Unification and Strategy,* p. 1; James V. Forrestal, *The Forrestal Diaries,* ed. by Walter Millis with the collaboration of E.S. Duffield (New York, 1951), p. 60.

[15]*Unification and Strategy,* p. 1; *First Report of the Secretary of Defense, 1948,* pp. 75–77.

[16]U.S., National Security Resources Board, *A Case Study in Peacetime Mobilization Planning: The National Security Resources Board, 1947–1953* (Washington, D.C., 1953), pp. 103–104.

[17]Memo, Major General Bolte to Secretary of the Army, June 28, 1950, subject: "Situation in the Far East," Annex B, Part II, "Impact of Current Developments on U.S. Strategy," in DA File OPS 091 Korea (TS), National Archives.

[18]Ridgway, *War in Korea,* p. 34; Appleman, *South to the Naktong,* p. 49.

[19]J. Lawton Collins, *War in Peacetime: The History and Lessons of Korea* (Boston, 1969), p. 66; Sebald and Brines, *With MacArthur in Japan,* p. 195.

[20]U.S., Department of the Army, *Semiannual Report of the Secretary of the Army,* July 1 to December 31, 1949 (Washington, D.C., 1950), p. 136.

[21]Paige, *The Korean Decision,* p. 100.

[22]*Military Situation in the Far East,* pt. 5, pp. 3370–3371.

[23]*Ibid.*

[24]Collins, *War in Peacetime,* pp. 4, 12.

[25]"Record of Actions," p. 11.

[26]James F. Schnable, *Policy and Direction: The First Year, United States Army in the Korean War* (Washington, D.C., 1972), p. 105.

[27]Memo, JCS to Secretary of Defense, May 18, 1951, subject: "Directives and Orders to General MacArthur Containing Restrictions on the Conduct of the Korean Campaign," in DA File G3 091 Korea, National Archives.

[28]*Military Situation in the Far East,* pt. 2, p. 954.

[29]*American Foreign Policy, 1950–1955,* p. 2550.

[30]Schnable, *Policy and Direction,* p. 102.

[31]Memo, Major General Bolte to Chief of Staff, July 26, 1950, subject: "Depletion of the Army's General Reserve by Requirements for Korea," in DA File OPS 326 (TS), National Archives.

[32]Message, CX57242, CINCFE to DA for CSGPO July 5, 1950, subject: "Report of First Contact of U.S. Troops with North Korean Forces," in DA File OPS 091 Korea (S), National Archives.

[33]First Report of the United Nation's Command (UNC) to the Security Council, United Nations, on the Course of Military Operations in Korea, July 25, 1950 in *Military Situation in the Far East,* pt. 5, p. 3388.

[34]Memo, G3 to Secretary of the Army, June 26, 1950, subject: "Military Assistance Furnished to Korea," in DA File OPS 091 Korea, National Archives; Memo and fact sheet, Major General Lemnitzer to General Duff, et al., July 7, 1950, subject: "Military Assistance to the Republic of Korea," in DA File OPS 091 Korea, National Archives.

[35]Douglas MacArthur, *Reminiscences* (New York, 1964), p. 345.

[36]Collins, *War in Peacetime,* pp. 115–116; Schnable, *Policy and Direction,* pp. 139–140.

[37]Lieutenant General Edward M. Almond's testimony in U.S., Congress, Senate, Committee on the Judiciary, *Interlocking Subversion in Government Departments. Hearings Before the Subcommittee to Investigate the Administration of the Internal Security Act and Other Internal Security Laws,* 83rd Cong., 2nd sess., 1954, p. 2065.

[38]Appleman, *South to the Naktong,* pp. 149–150.

[39]*Ibid.*

[40]Schnable, *Policy and Direction,* p. 143.

[41]*Ibid.,* p. 113; Memo, Colonel C.R. Kutz, Chief of Joint War Plans, to General Schuyler, July 31, 1950, subject: "Withdrawal from Korea," in DA File OPS 091 Korea (TS), National Archives.

[42]Collins, *War in Peacetime,* p. 93.

[43]*Ibid.,* p. 96; Ridgway, *War in Korea,* p. 28.

[44]Ridgway, *War in Korea,* pp. 29–30.

[45]Collins, *War in Peacetime,* p. 97.

[46]Brigadier General G.B. Barth, "Tropic Lightning and Taro Leaf," an unpublished memoir in S.L.A. Marshall Papers, U.S. Army Military History Research Collection, Carlisle Barracks, Pa., p. 22.

[47]Schnable, *Policy and Direction,* pp. 166–168.

[48]Collins, *War in Peacetime,* p. 115.

[49]*Ibid.,* pp. 118–119; Lynn Montross and N.A. Canzona, *The Inchon-Seoul Operation* (Washington, D.C., 1955), pp. 41–42; James A. Field, *History of United States Naval Operations: Korea* (Washington, D.C., 1962), p. 177; Ridgway, *War in Korea,* p. 38.

[50]Collins, *War in Peacetime,* pp. 118–119; Montross and Canzona, *The Inchon-Seoul Operation,* p. 177; Ridgway, *War in Korea,* p. 38.

[51]MacArthur, *Reminiscences,* pp. 349–350; Collins, *War in Peacetime,* p. 125.

[52]Ridgway, *War in Korea,* p. 39.

[53]*Military Situation in the Far East,* pt. 2, p. 1295; Field, *Naval Operations: Korea,* p. 174; MacArthur, *Reminiscences,* p. 346.

[54]Collins, *War in Peacetime,* p. 123; Field, *Naval Operations: Korea,* p. 123; Schnable, *Policy and Direction,* pp. 146, 152.

[55]Barth, "Tropic Lightning and Taro Leaf," p. 33.

[56]Memo, Lieutenant Colonel Tennesson, G3-PPB, to Major General Boltke, July 11, 1950, subject: "Unresolved Matters Pertaining to the Korean Situation," in DA File OPS 091 Korea (S), National Archives.

[57]Collins, *War in Peacetime,* p. 144.

[58]Acheson, *Present at the Creation,* p. 584; Schnable, *Policy and Direction,* p. 177.

[59]Marshall's testimony in "Transcripts of Hearings Held by the Committee on Armed Services and the Committee on Foreign Relations: Inquiry Into the Military Situation in the Far East and the Facts Surrounding the Relief of General of the Army Douglas MacArthur from his Assignments in that Area," in Records of the Senate Armed Services Committee, Vol. 10, p. 1881. This is the classified version of U.S., Senate, *Military Situation in the Far East.*

[60]Collins, *War in Peacetime,* p. 146.

[61]Acheson's testimony in *Military Situation in the Far East,* pt. 3, p. 1832.

[62]Acheson, *Present at the Creation,* pp. 568–570.

[63]HQ FECOM OPO Z, October 20, 1950, in DA File OPS 091 Korea, National Archives; Collins, *War in Peacetime,* p. 158.

[64]Schnable, *Policy and Direction,* p. 188.

[65]Memo, October 10, 1950, subject: "Field Trip with General Turner, 3 Oct 1950," in "Historical Report: Staff Notes and Substantiating Data, 1 October–31 October, 1950," HQ FEAF Combat Cargo Command (P).

[66]Appleman, *South to the Naktong,* p. 610; Collins, *War in Peacetime,* p. 162; Schnable, *Policy and Direction,* pp. 189–191.

[67]From contemporary interviews with Admiral Joy and Rear Admiral Arleigh A. Burke, Deputy Chief of Staff, HQ USNAVFE, quoted in Malcolm W. Cagle and Frank A. Manson, *The Sea War in Korea* (Annapolis, MD, 1957), p. 119.

[68]Collins, *War in Peacetime,* pp. 160–161; Appleman, *South to the Naktong,* pp. 611–612; Schnable, *Policy and Direction,* p. 189.

[69]Ridgway, *War in Korea,* p. 48; Schnable, *Policy and Direction,* p. 207.

[70]See the letter by Colonel Smith, quoted in Schnable, *Policy and Direction,* pp. 207–208, in which Smith is critical of MacArthur's handling of the logistical arrangements.

[71]Almond's testimony, *Interlocking Subversion,* pp. 2102, 2123; Schnable, *Policy and Direction,* p. 216; Appleman, *South to the Naktong,* p. 612.

[72]"Record of Actions," p. 51.

Korea: "An Entirely New War" 4

While General Douglas MacArthur's forces were consolidating their gains in the Seoul area in late September of 1950, the Department of the Army began to plan for the end of the war. Secretary of the Army Frank Pace directed a review of programs that could be curtailed in the event of an early end to the fighting. Planners turned their attention to diverting supplies then enroute to Korea, returning excess supplies to the United States, and stationing troops who were to be redeployed from the Far East.[1] After President Harry Truman's meeting with General MacArthur at Wake Island on October 15, optimism soared. UN forces were streaming north across the 38th Parallel virtually unopposed. MacArthur confidently promised to send the 2nd Infantry Division to Germany before the end of 1950 and to release the 3rd Infantry Division in the spring of 1951. Thereafter, the Army felt secure in canceling all replacements scheduled to arrive in Korea after November. On October 25, the Joint Chiefs of Staff (JCS) concluded that the services of the French battalion were no longer needed. The next day, the JCS proposed that the Greek Brigade be reduced to a battalion. Even Lieutenant General Walton H. Walker sensed the mood. On October 22, his headquarters requested authority to divert ammunition ships to Japan since the stocks in Korea were ample for the occupation. The next day, the Japan Logistical Command sought to return the ammunition ships to the States and to cancel all outstanding requisitions for ammunition.[2] Current statistical reports of captured and destroyed equipment reinforced the optimism and made credible the predictions of a great victory.[3] By October 26, North Korean resistance seemed to have collapsed.

There was, however, little time to enjoy the successes of late October. Beginning at about noon on the twenty-fifth, the ROK II Corps on the right of the Eighth Army recoiled in surprise from a furious counterattack that increased in tempo as the days passed. (*See Atlas Map No. 30.*) The

ROK 1st Division was particularly hard hit, and a regiment that had reached the Yalu River on the twenty-sixth was cut off—swallowed up, almost without a trace. The climax came on the night of November 1, when the 8th Cavalry Regiment of the 1st Cavalry Division withdrew under attack by an enemy division near Unsan in the center of the line. The 24th Division on the extreme left, driving toward Sinuiju, experienced little difficulty by comparison; but in the east, the X Corps ran into similar problems. First the South Koreans and then the marines encountered a reinvigorated enemy. On November 2, the 7th Marines, while advancing toward the Chosin Reservoir after relieving a Korean regiment, ran into stiff resistance. (*See Atlas Map No. 31.*) The marines immediately engaged in a fierce running fight, inflicting heavy casualties on their foe. While frontline troops fought for their lives, intelligence officers tried to identify the enemy. Gradually, prisoner of war reports from the Eighth Army and the X Corps indicated that elements of several Chinese Communist Forces (CCF) divisions were in contact.[4] By November 2, the senior field commanders had undeniable evidence from across their fronts that the CCF had intervened.

Chinese Intervention

Before the UN Forces' October crossing of the 38th Parallel, Chinese leaders had made an attempt to ward off direct confrontation with the Americans. In late September, using the Government of India as its spokesman, the Chinese Government warned the UN that it would intervene to protect the existence of North Korea. The Chinese followed this general warning with a more specific one on October 3. Chou En-lai called the Indian Ambassador, K.M. Panikkar, to an extraordinary conference, during which Chou warned that if United States Army units crossed the 38th Parallel, China would enter the war. Chou made clear that it was not the South Koreans he feared, only the Americans. Panikkar immediately relayed this information to the United States Government through the British Foreign Office. On the same day, Andre Vishinsky, the Soviet Foreign Minister, called for the withdrawal of all foreign troops, a cease-fire, and a coalition Korean government to rule until elections.[5] Secretary of State Dean Acheson interpreted these events as a combined Sino-Soviet attempt to save the North Korean regime. He interpreted Chou's words, therefore, as a bluff, rather than as a policy statement.[6] A week later, the Chinese repeated their warning in a broadcast over Peking radio.[7]

American intelligence estimates had credited the CCF with the capability of intervening, but most analysts regarded intervention as unlikely.[8] As early as October 4, an intelligence summary from MacArthur's headquarters had estimated that nine CCF divisions may have entered North Korea, and had observed that the increasing frequency of these sitings was ominous. Between October 8 and 14, MacArthur's headquarters concluded that the CCF could mass at multiple crossing sites along the Yalu River in great strength. Still, no one seriously believed that the Chinese intended to intervene decisively.

Chinese Prisoners Captured in North Korea, October 1950

After the Eighth Army crossed the 38th Parallel, the Chinese delivered another warning. On October 11, the Chinese Ministry of Foreign Affairs announced that "Now that the American forces are attempting to cross the thirty-eighth parallel on a large scale, the Chinese people cannot stand idly by with regard to such a serious situation created by the invasion of Korea. . . . "[9] And the Chinese were not idle. Unknown to MacArthur, Washington, or anyone else, the Chinese began sending CCF divisions into North Korea three days later. Between October 14 and November 1, some 180,000 men of the Chinese 4th Field Army crossed the Yalu River. Marching at night and hiding in the forested mountains during the day, the CCF secretly massed in front of the Eighth Army.[10]

Regardless of intelligence indications to the contrary, optimism prevailed following the Wake Island meeting of Truman and MacArthur. Even after the stiffening resistance that began on October 25, Chinese intervention was not accepted at face value.[11] Although Major General Charles A. Willoughby, MacArthur's G-2,* reported that there were CCF units in North Korea, he did not believe that their presence signified serious intervention. On October 28, he asserted that the time was long past for the Chinese to save the North Korean Government.[12] Not surprisingly, then, the presence of Chinese forces brought no change in MacArthur's plans.

The Precarious Position of the Eighth Army

While reports of CCF involvement may not have moved MacArthur, enemy bullets had convinced Walker and his men that it was time to take stock. Walker prudently brought his headlong pursuit to a halt as he tried to fathom the situation to his front. On October 31, he redisposed his army by holding a bridgehead over the Ch'ongch'on River near Anju and withdrawing the rest of his forces south of the river. (*See Atlas Map No. 31.*) Fierce fighting continued until November 6, when the enemy suddenly broke off his attacks and melted into the forests and mountains to the north. In response to MacArthur's demand for an explanation of the halt and redeployment, Walker apprised him of the facts.

Tactically, the situation was dangerous. On October 25, the Eighth Army had begun advancing on a broad front in widely separated columns in pursuit of the defeated North Korean Army. An ambush and surprise attack by fresh enemy units, at least some of which were Chinese, caused a complete collapse and disintegration of the ROK II Corps.

*A G-2 is responsible for planning for intelligence functions.

An American Infantryman Whose Buddy Was Killed in Action Is Comforted by a Comrade

In South Korean units, complacency and overconfidence, encouraged by success against the North Koreans, were immediately replaced by fear of the CCF. Abandoning all that it had gained, the ROK II Corps retreated to Kunu-ri before order could be restored; by that time, the corps was only 50 percent effective.[13] Moreover, the CCF attack on the South Koreans and the 1st Cavalry Division, on the right (east) of the Army, seriously threatened the only road supplying the US I Corps on the west flank. This forced Walker to temporarily withdraw the exposed columns of the American corps and to regroup the entire force south of the Ch'ongch'on River. There, he proposed to build up his meager supplies before resuming the offensive to the border.[14]

Once faced with serious resistance, the Eighth Army's logistical weakness finally took its toll. As Walker well knew, the drive to the north had been a calculated risk, with no possibility of accumulating reserve stocks of supplies. The problem became one of keeping supplies moving forward to sustain the fast moving and dispersed columns. However, the advance was simply too rapid to allow the repair and renovation of transportation facilities to keep pace, and a shortage of trucks was keenly felt. The

construction of a fuel pipeline between Inchon and Kimpo Airfield had allowed the reallocation of some trucks, but it still took 200 trucks daily to transport fuel and food north of Seoul.[15] Railroad trains could proceed only as far north as Munsan-ni, near the mouth of the Imjin River, where supplies had to be unloaded, trucked across the river, and reloaded onto trains on the north bank. (*See Atlas Map No. 31.*) As soon as P'yongyang had fallen, air force elements opened the airfield for the airlift of supplies from Seoul and Japan. As much as 1,000 tons a day from this source, much of which was ammunition, nourished the Eighth Army in its drive to the Yalu River.[16]

Shortages imposed great hardship on the combat units in the forward areas. Some troops had moved into regions where the means of transportation were undeveloped or nonexistent. The distribution of supplies to these units was a real problem. For example, while there was sufficient winter clothing in Korea to equip the men in the forward divisions, many small units had to deploy before issue was complete. Some men were still in summer clothing even after the temperatures plummeted. Equally serious was the shortage of food. The ports were shipping not more than 20,000 rations a day, when 60,000 to 75,000 were needed, and the forward units had no stocks to make up the difference. Small units, moreover, often had to move away from their kitchens. Thus when bad weather impeded the emergency airdrop of rations to remote outposts, the men had serious doubts about the availability of their next meal.[17]

These supply shortages and determined enemy resistance forced Walker to order a halt of the Eighth Army's advance. Operating with as little as one day's supply of ammunition and facing strong CCF concentrations, Walker's army was in greater trouble than anyone in Tokyo or Washington realized. Wisely, Walker concluded that he must open the port of Chinnamp'o and extend the railroad to P'yongyang before he could continue north. (*See Atlas Map No. 31.*) MacArthur had to agree.

In spite of Walker's caution, MacArthur believed the Chinese intervention to be a piecemeal action designed to achieve limited goals, rather than a coordinated effort aimed at decisive action. Nevertheless, he gave them credit for being able to commit up to 29 of their 44 divisions, then disposed along the Yalu River, and to support them with up to 150 aircraft. The picture darkened even more on November 3, when MacArthur's intelligence summary reported 316,000 CCF regulars and another 274,000 irregulars or security forces deployed in Manchuria at crossing sites along the Yalu. Still, MacArthur thought that the Chinese sought only limited objectives.[18] Not convinced, Army planners in the Pentagon reversed the dismantling of forces in Korea as MacArthur suddenly called for more combat strength and requested permission to bomb the bridges over the Yalu to stop the movement of men and materiel over the river.[19] The possibility of having to take direct action against Chinese forces compelled officials in Washington to rethink the whole question of limiting military action.

An American Reassessment

Even in the darkest days before Inchon, administration leaders had believed that restraint in the Korean War was necessary to obtain and preserve the support of America's allies and other members of the United Nations. Above all, they wanted to minimize the threat of retaliation, either in East Asia or Europe. The Joint Chiefs, in particular, had urged a policy of limited involvement in Korea in order to gain the time necessary to mobilize the nation's military and industrial resources. The United States was not yet in a position to risk a showdown with the Soviet Union, and military leaders hoped that the conflict could be kept under control until the United States and her allies had rearmed.[20]

To date, the only limits placed on MacArthur had been geographical. Air and naval forces had been given strict orders to avoid the borders of Manchuria and the Soviet Union, and the ground forces of non-Asian countries were to stop short of the Yalu River. The possibility of using nuclear weapons, however, had first been discussed early in July. Only a small circle of people in the administration, including the military, had access to nuclear data. Even MacArthur knew little of nuclear plans beyond discussions about the possible use of the weapons in his own theater of operations. The fact is that a policy on the use of nuclear weapons had never been clearly stated beyond the general assertion that the United States had no intention of employing them in Korea. Even so, the Army staff was prepared to recommend their use for the most compelling military reasons: to cover and protect the evacuation of a large United Nations force in order to avert a major military disaster—presumably, the capture of significant portions of the Eighth Army of the X Corps.[21]

There were also sound reasons for *not* employing nuclear weapons. America's allies were strongly opposed to initiating nuclear war. The British, in particular, tried to influence American policy in this regard, largely because they feared that the United States would become preoccupied with a nuclear war in Asia and divert weapons from the defense of Europe. Also, American policymakers knew that the United States had too few weapons to permit

their expenditure so far from Europe, the area presenting the major threat to American security. Moreover, the mountainous, compartmentalized terrain in Korea would attenuate nuclear explosions, thus limiting their effects to relatively small valleys. The nuclear weapons of that era were simply not designed for such a battlefield. Staff officers worried that the employment of nuclear weapons at that early date might result in the dropping of a dud, and thus risk the study of the weapons by Soviet observers. It was entirely possible that shortcomings might be revealed that would diminish their deterrent value in Europe.[22] Finally, there was the practical problem of finding and hitting targets. In Korea, the only appropriate targets were troop units; the meager North Korean industrial plant had already been easily destroyed by aircraft armed with conventional weapons. By the time troop targets were identified, the fire mission requested, permission to use nuclear weapons obtained from the President, and the flight from Guam, Hawaii, or the United States completed, the enemy troops would have long since dispersed.[23]

There was, therefore, little chance that the United States would initiate a nuclear war in Korea. The real danger was that some accident might cause the war to spill over its geographical limits. There had already been three separate incidents in which American aircraft, through error, had violated the geographical restrictions and attacked targets in Manchuria and the Soviet Union. Fear of border violations, or the threat of border violations, grew, therefore, as United Nations forces advanced through ever-diminishing North Korean territory to the international boundary. To American leaders, if not the general public, the world situation was explosive. The central problem was the Sino-Soviet Treaty. China was the greatest interest that the Soviets had in East Asia, and the risk of lost prestige alone might force the Soviets to take action on behalf of China. Should this happen, the probability of expanding the war would greatly increase—and to the disadvantage of the United States. The Soviets could reinforce the Chinese with large numbers of aircraft and volunteer crews, eventually outnumbering United States air forces. Already, significant numbers of MiG-15s were in Manchuria. The Soviets might even reinforce the Chinese with Soviet Army units.

What really frightened the administration was the ability of the Soviet Union to launch nuclear war. Intelligence reports credited the Soviets with the capability of attacking the United States with 50 bombs of 60–80 kilotons each by the spring of 1951. Presumably, they had a lesser capability in the winter of 1950. Scenarios prepared for a civil defense study estimated that a Soviet attack could strike anywhere in the United States, with the main attack aimed at the Northeast or the Pacific coastal region. General Bradley summarized the problem: the Soviets had the bomb, how many could only be estimated from intelligence reports; they had the ability to deliver the bombs by aircraft with sufficient range to reach the United States; the United States could not stop all of the aircraft should the Soviets try to attack.[24] This realization, coupled with the acknowledged conventional superiority of Soviet forces in Europe, sobered American decisionmakers as they weighed the consequences of a provocative incident in Manchuria or the Soviet Union.

Ignoring for a moment the implications of a worldwide expansion of the war, American military leaders considered the consequences of widening the war in East Asia. If restrictions were lifted, the United States might have a difficult time protecting Japan. The critical shortfall was American airpower. According to General Hoyt Vandenberg, Air Force Chief of Staff, the United States Air Force was operating on a "shoestring," in view of the nation's global responsibilities. While the Air Force could probably successfully combat the Soviet Air Force, the resulting attrition would cripple American airpower. It would be 1953 before American industry could make up the losses. Practically speaking, the United States could neither "pick at the periphery" nor lay waste to China or the Soviet Union.[25]

Military men also believed that a widening of the war in East Asia, particularly in the air, would work to the tactical disadvantage of UN operations in Korea. The logical targets for an air attack against China were so widely scattered and so numerous that even a much larger air element than that possessed by MacArthur would be relatively ineffective. On the other hand, Chinese retaliation against the highly concentrated UN installations at Inchon, Pusan, and Wonsan would inflict great damage. Furthermore, air attacks against UN ground forces, not yet under attack, could interrupt airfield operations, the movement of supplies, and the mobility of reserves. In short, military leaders in Washington were virtually unanimous in believing that it was better to confine the air war to the Korean peninsula than to endure enemy air attacks.[26]

Late intelligence estimates, circulating among all high-level planning and policy groups, offered scant encouragement. The most recent report, a Central Intelligence Agency (CIA) paper dated November 6, estimated—erroneously as it turned out—CCF strength in North Korea to be between 30,000 and 40,000, with another 350,000 ground troops immediately available as reinforcements. The CIA considered even this underestimated strength sufficient to halt the UN advance, either by piecemeal commitment or by coordinated action. The CIA concluded that at any moment the situation could get out of control. The Chinese had staked their prestige on supporting North Korea, and they knew the risks. They were ready for general war.[27]

Renewal of the UN Advance

Against this ominous background, MacArthur's messages alternated in mood. On November 4, in response to a JCS request for a new estimate in light of CCF involvement, he stated that there was no serious threat, and that it would be illadvised to reach hasty conclusions. But on the sixth, MacArthur requested permission to use 90 B-29s to attack the Yalu River bridge at Sinuiju in order to slow the flow of reinforcements. After the Joint Chiefs' refusal to authorize the bombing, MacArthur warned of the American bloodbath that would occur if he were not permitted to stop the infiltration by striking the bridges or if his freedom of action were further limited. Then, on November 9, he sent the JCS his overall conclusions about the Chinese intervention, this time sounding a contrastingly optimistic note. He urged that there be no weakening of resolution, and that the UN press on to victory.[28]

The President and Joint Chiefs were puzzled by the variations in MacArthur's tone. They were unclear about the tradeoff between MacArthur's proposed tactical measures and the risk of widening the war. Although the Joint Chiefs feared that actions taken to bring about an immediate solution to the problem might create far greater strategic problems in the long run, they chose to support the general because he based his arguments on tactical considerations. They simply could not argue tactics at long range; above all, they feared assuming the responsibility for denying MacArthur the requested authorization when they lacked sufficient information upon which to base such a decision. The Joint Chiefs had either to accept MacArthur's judgment about his problems or to usurp his prerogatives and probably force his relief. The former might be militarily risky, but it also might work; the latter could bring heavy political fire, both from MacArthur's politician friends and from the public, to whom he was a hero of gigantic proportions.

Neither the setback suffered during late October and early November nor the growing caution within the administration deterred MacArthur. He continued to prepare for the renewal of the offensive. By mid-November, his forces were at about 45 percent authorized strength. They were located about 45 miles from the Yalu River, and were widely dispersed. His logistical situation had gradually improved because of both the Eighth Army's success in opening the port of Chinnamp'o near P'yongyang and the Air Force's all-out effort to airlift supplies to P'yongyang. Nevertheless, shortages of certain classes of supply forced MacArthur to postpone his resumption of the offensive until November 24. In a message notifying the Joint Chiefs of the delay, MacArthur seemed optimistic once again, adding that the air attacks on the bridges in the last 10 days had greatly diminished the flow of enemy reinforcements and supplies.[29]

By November 20, efforts to increase the stockage of supplies had begun to produce results. Two days later, General Walker notified MacArthur that he could renew the advance. On the east coast, the X Corps had always been better off logistically than the Eighth Army, receiving ample supplies through the ports of Wonsan, Hungnam, and Iwon. To increase MacArthur's overall firepower, the Joint Chiefs had sent reinforcements of three Marine Corps fighter wings.[30] All was in readiness.

Along the battlefront, the enemy seemed to have disappeared. On November 20, MacArthur reported that enemy forces had broken contact and were apparently withdrawing, although he was unsure of what this signified. American commanders noted a defensive attitude on the part of the North Koreans and the Chinese. The absence of aggressiveness on the part of the enemy was of only minimal comfort to the troops, however; winter had arrived, and the temperature fell to 10° F in the west and -20° F in the east. As Walker prepared to renew the offensive with a closely controlled and coordinated attack, his orders to the corps commanders reflected caution and prudent respect for the enemy. By November 23, the troops of the Eighth Army were in their attack positions preparatory to jumping off the next day.

MacArthur was edgy about the stillness along the front. He was even more concerned about the distance between the flanks of the Eighth Army and the X Corps. He instructed his air arm to patrol the gap with great care, seeking concentrations of enemy troops, weapons, and vehicles. When nothing could be detected from the air, MacArthur once again grew optimistic. In a last-minute message to the Joint Chiefs, MacArthur counted his advantages: the Air Force had sharply curtailed enemy reinforcements and supply; X Corps was prepared to envelop the enemy; and Walker's Eighth Army was in position to complete the compression and close the vice. This, he assured the Joint Chiefs, should end the war.

On November 24, Eighth Army troops moved forward as planned against light to moderate resistance, gaining 12 miles in the first 36 hours. Soon after dark on the twenty-fifth, however, strong formations of the Chinese Communist Forces struck suddenly and with great force against

the center and the east flank. *(See Atlas Map No. 32.)* The ROK II Corps scattered under heavy attack near Tokch'on; in the center, the US IX Corps reeled, held briefly, and then gave ground again, falling back to the south side of the Ch'ongch'on River; and, although under no pressure, the US I Corps on the left withdrew in concert with the rearward movement of the IX Corps. On November 27, Walker notified MacArthur at his headquarters in Tokyo that the CCF were attacking in strength, but that it was still too early to tell if they meant to sustain their counteroffensive. Meanwhile, in the eastern sector, CCF units struck savagely at the X Corps, attempting to cut off its widely separated columns from their line of communication. The next day, Walker estimated that the enemy numbered 200,000. In his mind there was no longer any doubt that the CCF had opened a major offensive against the United Nations forces.

A Devastating Chinese Counterstroke

MacArthur reported the CCF offensive to the Joint Chiefs on November 28. In another abrupt reversal of tone, he now protested that his forces lacked sufficient strength to meet the Chinese threat, and that ". . . consequently we face an entirely new war. . . ." For this reason, his plan for the immediate future was to pass from the offensive to the defensive, making adjustments as required by the situation.[31] On the twenty-ninth, the Joint Chiefs approved MacArthur's plan to assume the defensive, but pointedly asked how he would coordinate operations between Eighth Army and X Corps.[32] The next day, MacArthur replied that in order to reduce the pressure on the Eighth Army he planned to leave the X Corps in northeast Korea as a threat to CCF operations. Even though the Eighth Army had begun reeling south, MacArthur still harbored illusions about his capability for successful and decisive action. Such an appraisal at that stage of the operation was more than the Joint Chiefs could accept, so they ordered MacArthur to extricate the X Corps from its exposed position on the northeastern front and to coordinate the juncture of both forces.[33] By this time, it was clear that the CCF intended to destroy UN forces and seize all of Korea.

In the days that followed, all UN elements withdrew under the blows of the CCF. Falling back to P'yongyang, the Eighth Army abandoned the North Korean capital on December 5. After burning everything of value to the enemy, Walker's command continued its march south, recrossing the 38th Parallel on December 15. In the X Corps' sector in the east, the 1st Marine Division and the 7th Infantry Division fought their way toward the corps base at Hungnam. Fighting gallantly under difficult weather conditions and virtually surrounded by the enemy, the marines finally reached Hamhung on December 10 and completed their withdrawal to Hungnam the next day. Major General Edward Almond's X Corps began to evacuate its two forward beachheads at Wonsan and Hungnam immediately. The 3rd Infantry Division and ROK marines completed their seaborne withdrawal from Wonsan prior to December 15, and at Hungnam the evacuation began on the same date. By the twenty-fourth, the corps had completed the operation; in all, 105,000 American and ROK troops, 17,500 vehicles, and 350,000 tons of cargo were successfully embarked. Among the evacuees were 91,000 North Korean civilians who had elected to move south with the UN troops.[34]

In the midst of the withdrawal, the Eighth Army lost its commander when General Walker died in a jeep accident on December 23. At MacArthur's request, Lieutenant General Matthew B. Ridgway flew immediately to Korea and assumed command. Ridgway had had a distinguished career as a combat commander in World War II. He had been the first commander of the 82nd Airborne Division, and had led the XVIII Airborne Corps during the drive across France and Germany. After the war, he served in key positions on the Army staff. There, he became intimately familiar with the problems of waging a limited war in the nuclear age. Taking over as the Eighth Army streamed south, Ridgway sought to consolidate a position on which he could reorganize his retreating command. (*See Atlas Map No. 33.*) On January 4, 1951, he was forced to abandon Seoul, the South Korean capital, and to fall back once again below Osan and Samch'ok. But with only light enemy patrols following, Ridgway was finally able to establish a line running from P'yongt'aek in the west, to Wonju in the center, to Samch'ok on the east coast. There, the X Corps joined him. Organizing his army with three American corps in the west and center and two ROK corps in the east, Ridgway prepared to regain contact with his enemy and resume the offensive to the north.

Changing War Aims

The war that Ridgway was to fight differed significantly from the one that his predecessor had waged. Weeks earlier, while Walker struggled to keep a foothold in South Korea and MacArthur maneuvered to turn the North Korean flank, the two generals had few doubts about where they were going and what they had to do. The enemy army had to be defeated, its homeland occupied, and the will of

Generals Douglas A. MacArthur and Matthew B. Ridgway

the North Korean Government and its people destroyed. Regardless of the ruminations of the Truman administration, MacArthur had defined victory in traditional terms. But the defeat along the Yalu and Ch'ongch'on Rivers changed all that. In Washington, in the UN, and in the capitals of those nations contributing UN troops and equipment, the victory that MacArthur sought was unacceptable if the price to be paid was a broader and more destructive war.

MacArthur was quick to focus attention on the issue. On December 3, he had told the JCS that the war in Korea now had to be viewed as an entirely new war. The strategic concepts applicable in a war against North Korea were not appropriate for a war against China. To continue withholding resources would result in the steady attrition of UN forces, leading to their final destruction. He called for political decisions and strategic plans adequate to meet the new situation.[35] The Joint Chiefs were deeply concerned, both by the tone of MacArthur's message and by the course of the Eighth Army's headlong withdrawal. They decided, therefore, to send their Army member, General J. Lawton Collins, to Tokyo to confer with MacArthur. On December 6, the JCS announced that the situation in Korea had increased the possibility of general war; American commanders worldwide were directed to increase their readiness.

At the same time, Allied governments also showed their concern for the deteriorating situation. On December 4, the British Prime Minister, Clement Attlee, visited President Truman to discuss the future of UN operations in Korea. He had been disturbed by Truman's public remark that the United States was considering the use of all weapons, including nuclear, to restore a favorable balance in Korea. During their conference, which went far beyond nuclear policy in its scope, the two leaders made a crucial decision that was to change the direction of the UN war effort. Truman and Attlee agreed to abandon the objective of unifying the Korean peninsula and to revert to the original war aim of preserving the Republic of Korea. Hereafter, UN forces were to contain the CCF while negotiating to terminate the conflict.

Simultaneously, in the UN, member nations also sought to initiate peace negotiations. The neutral states, led by India, proposed that a three-member negotiating group seek a cease-fire. To show their support for truce talks, on December 19 the General Assembly adopted a cease-fire resolution. But China's reaction to the UN resolution was consistent with its hostility. China demanded the immediate withdrawal of all Americans and other UN forces, the removal of American protection of Taiwan, and the seating of a delegation of the Chinese Communist Government in the UN. The UN concluded from such a militant response that negotiations with the Chinese were not feasible at this time—whereupon the American delegation began seeking support for a resolution labeling China as an aggressive nation. Even though such a resolution was eventually passed, the consensus in the UN supported the new and moderate limited war aims agreed to by Truman and Attlee.[36]

Collins visited MacArthur on December 4–7, and began the process through which the new war aims were to be converted into a military directive. In the course of their discussions, MacArthur told the Army Chief of Staff that if the UN established an effective blockade of China, initiated aerial bombardment of the Chinese mainland, reinforced the UN Command with 60,000 Nationalist Chinese troops, and permitted Chiang Kai-shek's forces to invade South China, he could continue to hold a favorable position in Korea. Otherwise, the UN Command should evacuate the peninsula. Collins carried MacArthur's views back to the JCS, where they were discussed in the context of the worldwide situation and the new war aims. Finding MacArthur's proposals for retaliation against China to be inconsistent with the political goals of the UN alliance, the JCS directed MacArthur to establish a line in South Korea

that would be tactically advantageous. Further, he was to defend in successive positions, inflicting maximum damage on the enemy. The Joint Chiefs also requested MacArthur's views on evacuation from Korea.[37]

Replying on December 30, MacArthur offered a counterproposal, recommending again the retaliatory measures that he had mentioned earlier to Collins, criticizing the JCS for using only part of America's combat power in Korea, and once more suggesting that unless UN policy was changed, evacuation would be necessary. It was clear that the old general seriously disagreed with the new war aims adopted in Washington and the UN. Because his position was irreconcilable, on January 9 the JCS rejected MacArthur's proposals for retaliation against China. They repeated their instructions to defend Korea in successive positions, subject to MacArthur's primary responsibility for preserving his army and defending Japan. If it was essential to evacuate Korea to save the army, he should evacuate.[38]

MacArthur's next response on January 10 was a turning point in his relations with Washington, and undermined the effectiveness of his position thereafter. He told the Joint Chiefs that morale of his troops was at a low ebb because they had been falsely condemned for their fighting abilities. Reason demanded that they be evacuated; but even though the position in Korea was untenable in view of the restrictions placed upon his command, the army would hold on to a bridgehead for any length of time, up to its complete destruction.[39] As David Rees, a perceptive analyst of the situation, has pointed out, "MacArthur was trying to reverse policy by using the threat of Eighth Army's engulfment as a lever to force Washington to adopt his programme."[40] MacArthur thus employed the most devastating and forceful argument he had: he predicted annihilation of his command while shifting the responsibility for such a disaster onto the policy adopted by his superiors.

Understandably, MacArthur's message was deeply disturbing to the President and to his closest advisers. Out of their deliberations, however, came a reaffirmation of the policy that they had adopted. First, the JCS sent another directive to MacArthur, ordering him to stay in Korea if possible. Second, they prepared a contingency study for the National Security Council, outlining possible courses of action against China should the UN be driven off the peninsula or confined to an enclave around Pusan. This paper included MacArthur's retaliatory proposals for further study. To insure MacArthur's complete understanding of the new policy, President Truman wrote a personal letter, explaining the advantages that would accrue to the United States and her allies if the UN Command could hold on in Korea, and reaffirming his intent to punish the aggressors against South Korea.[41] Not willing to risk misunderstanding by sending messages alone, Truman had both the directive and his personal letter hand-carried to Tokyo by Generals Collins and Vandenberg. Beyond acting as messengers, Collins and Vandenberg had the more important task of determining by personal inspection if Ridgway and the Eighth Army were capable of holding out on the peninsula. From what they saw at the front in the following days, Collins and Vandenberg concluded that the Eighth Army could continue operations in Korea as long as it was in the best interests of the UN to do so. The basis for their conclusion was Ridgway's effect on the Eighth Army—one of the great examples of generalship in the history of American arms.

Ridgway's War

Within two weeks after taking command, Matthew Ridgway turned a retreating army into a deadly offensive weapon. From the time that MacArthur had told him "the Eighth Army is yours, Matt. Do what you think best," Ridgway was determined to attack as soon as he could.[42] Visiting divisional and regimental headquarters across the entire front, the new commanding general sized up his subordinates while listening to their views. He quickly concluded that the army lacked a winning spirit, and then set about forcefully reminding his commanders of "the ancient Army slogan: 'Find them! Fix them! Fight them! Finish them!' "[43] No longer would the Army resort to the "bug out" that had become a routine part of unit planning. The Eighth Army must seize the initiative. Spurning terrain as an objective, Ridgway wanted to destroy enemy manpower, weapons, and equipment. From this point on, the war of containment was to become a war of attrition to force the Chinese to negotiate a cease-fire favorable to the territorial integrity of South Korea. Stressing security, the general insisted that his corps commanders coordinate their operations carefully and inflict maximum punishment on the enemy. After assuring himself that everyone understood what he wanted and consolidating the Eighth Army positions along the P'yongt'aek-Wonju-Samch'ok line, Ridgway ordered all units to reestablish contact with the CCF. Beginning on January 7, 1951, infantry patrols began to probe northward. During the following week, it was found that CCF units were passive in the eastern sector, but were massing for an attack between Osan and Suwon in the west. The time was right for the Eighth Army to move.

Although his staff recommended against offensive action, Ridgway decided to strike the massing enemy force. The reluctance of his staff to attack was an expression of the general attitude afflicting the frontline units when Ridgway took command. "To a man the Eighth Army Staff was against offensive action north and I alone had to make the decision."[44] The attack, mounted by a tank-supported regimental combat team and known as Operation WOLFHOUND, commenced on January 15. (*See Atlas Map No. 33.*) While the attack inflicted some casualties on the enemy, it was most notable as an example of the new offensive spirit instilled by the commanding general. Moreover, the operation was observed by Collins and Vandenberg during their visit to the Far East, and strongly influenced their conclusion that the Eighth Army could hold its own. On January 16, Collins told newsmen that "we are going to stay and fight," and Ridgway asserted that "there is no shadow of doubt in my mind that Eighth Army can take care of itself in the current situation."[45] In an optimistic report to the JCS, Collins observed that the Eighth Army was in good condition and

General Matthew B. Ridgway

was improving daily under the leadership of Ridgway. He found conditions in the ROK Corps less encouraging, but not without hope. His optimism was strongly reinforced by the poor performance of the CCF units. They had usually fled in the face of American firepower, and had made no major move south from the Han River. Most encouraging were the signs of weakness in CCF logistics and the low morale in some Chinese units. Collins concluded, therefore, that evacuation from Korea was a political matter and need not be made for military reasons.

The Army Chief of Staff's optimistic report had a profound effect on American leadership. The credit belonged to Ridgway, who refused to accept defeat. Although he had been under no orders to halt the retreat, and could have continued south without criticism, his combative spirit and generalship were decisive in avoiding an even greater military disaster.[46] He imbued his army with confidence in the face of a numerically superior enemy. Rather than resorting to political peptalks, Ridgway insisted on maintaining a strict barracks-like brand of discipline. His soldiers soon realized that they were fighting neither for abstractions such as democracy nor against communism; they were fighting to seize objectives ordered by the chain of command. From this time on, the Eighth Army became a professional army, concerned with fighting a war of limited objectives, but seemingly undisturbed by the numerical superiority of its enemy. Perhaps more important, Ridgway showed that the situation in Korea was not as desperate as it had been pictured by MacArthur. The result

Infantrymen From the 187th Airborne Regimental Combat Team Fire a 75-mm Recoilless Rifle, February 5, 1951

was that the JCS began to bypass MacArthur with increasing frequency and to deal directly with Ridgway. MacArthur's fall from his pre-eminent position had begun.

Encouraged by the success of Operation WOLFHOUND, Ridgway sought new opportunities for offensive action. Following another successful reconnaissance in force towards Inchon by the IX Corps on January 22, Ridgway ordered the I and IX Corps to mount a two-division drive north of Suwon and Yoju toward the Han River. (*See Atlas Map No. 34.*) The objective of what came to be called Operation THUNDERBOLT was to gain information about enemy dispositions, disrupt enemy concentrations, and inflict maximum destruction. The attack began on January 25 and made steady progress against light resistance. The tactics employed were fairly simple. The operation commenced with a long-range artillery preparation, followed by a heavy barrage from the more accurate 105-mm howitzers firing from short range. Tank guns fired directly at known and suspected fighting positions, and fighter-bombers burned the enemy defensive works with napalm and bombs. Infantrymen, secure in their holes, joined in with rifles, machineguns, recoilless rifles, and mortars. Intense preparatory fires lasted throughout the morning. In the afternoon, as an eyewitness later recalled, "the infantry crept up the slopes of the hills to find out if anyone was left there."[47]

By the end of January, Ridgway had still not located the CCF main line of resistance. However, his forces were four to six miles north of their starting line, and were gaining momentum. By February 10, the I Corps had reached the Han River and neutralized Seoul by capturing Inchon and Kimpo Airfield. This was a promising beginning for the UN drive which, known to its frontline troops as the "meatgrinder," was to continue rolling north for the next three months.

With his left flank anchored on the Han River, Ridgway designed Operation ROUNDUP to employ the X Corps, located in the central sector, in a drive toward Wonju and Hoengsong, supported by the ROK III Corps on its east flank. (*See Atlas Map No. 34.*) As the UN troops advanced north of Wonju during the night of February 11, two CCF armies and a North Korean Corps attacked from north of Hoengsong and broke through three ROK divisions. Moving over the snow-covered mountains and establishing ambushes behind the front in a manner reminiscent of their operations in November and December of 1950, the Chinese forced Ridgway to order a withdrawal to Wonju. The enemy then shifted his attack west to Chip'yong-ni. Ridgway was sure that the enemy attacks would falter if he could hold Chip'yong-ni and Wonju. At Chip'yong-ni, the 23rd Infantry Regiment and the French Battalion de-

Prisoners Are Brought in During Operation KILLER, February 27, 1951

fended valiantly, breaking a ring of three enemy divisions attacking in massed waves against the UN perimeter. For three days, from February 14 to 16, the 23rd fought surrounded and supplied only by air. When it was over, Western firepower had killed thousands of Chinese soldiers in a test of manpower against modern weapons. Farther east, in what veterans called the "Wonju shoot," the Chinese renewed the attack, again employing waves of soldiers—and again suffering heavy casualties. As David Rees noted, "the UN defense had triumphed—and for the remainder of the Korean War it would remain in the ascendant."[48]

After six days, the enemy offensive subsided, exhausted from losses and inadequate logistics. Ridgway seized the initiative. In what was aptly coded Operation KILLER, he sought to secure control of the road between Wonju and Kangnung in the central sectors. (*See Atlas Map No. 34.*) Employing the IX and X Corps, Ridgway directed a closely coordinated movement within and between the two corps with the main purpose of killing all enemy troops to the front. The new offensive was launched on February 21, and the enemy fell back with diminishing resistance. By

the twenty-ninth, the Eighth Army had reached its limit of advance. By March 1, the entire CCF front south of the Han River had collapsed and the UN Command stretched from Kimpo to Kangnung, 30 miles south of the 38th Parallel.

While the February offensives gave the Eighth Army much reason for rejoicing, the troops still faced serious problems. Foremost were heavy rain and thawing snow in the combat zone. Movement of supplies by vehicle became increasingly difficult over boggy roads and damaged bridges, and Ridgway called for more resupply by air. Further, Eighth Army was short of manpower in its combat units. In an attempt to offset the CCF's great numerical superiority, the Commanding General cut his service units drastically and transferred men to the combat divisions. To assist, MacArthur levied service units in Japan and sent urgent requests for reinforcements to the JCS. Still, Ridgways' units remained far below their authorized strength, for the problem was Army-wide, and the stateside mobilization base had not yet caught up with the many demands for trained men. The shortage of manpower also had a serious effect on rear area security. In many parts of South Korea, CCF guerrilla operations made the movement of supply convoys unsafe. ROK troops, most of whom were only partially trained, shouldered the brunt of counter-guerrilla operations; but even though some improvement could be seen, there continued to be a wastage of supplies and a diversion of combat units badly needed in the line.[49]

Consistent with the offensive spirit instilled by Ridgway, the advance resumed on March 7 when the Eighth Army launched Operation RIPPER. The purpose of RIPPER was to destroy all enemy forces below Line IDAHO, a large salient with the town of Ch'unch'on at its apex. *(See map on page 106.)* Although enemy resistance initially restricted the drive to a slow pace, by March 13 Communist strength had begun to diminish. After UN forces crossed the Han River east of Seoul and threatened CCF communications, the Chinese withdrew from the South Korean capital, leaving it largely undefended. Eighth Army troops entered it on March 15. Ch'unch'on, an important supply and communications center, was seized on the twentieth, again without much of a fight. Ridgway then decided to enlarge RIPPER by directing the I Corps to advance in a northwestwardly direction to the Imjin River. The corps would be supported by an airborne landing to be made by the 187th RCT near Munsan-ni. The paratroopers dropped on March 23 and quickly linked up with ground elements, but most of the enemy had already withdrawn; the advance to the Imjin was almost without bloodshed. By the end of the month, as Ridgway's forces

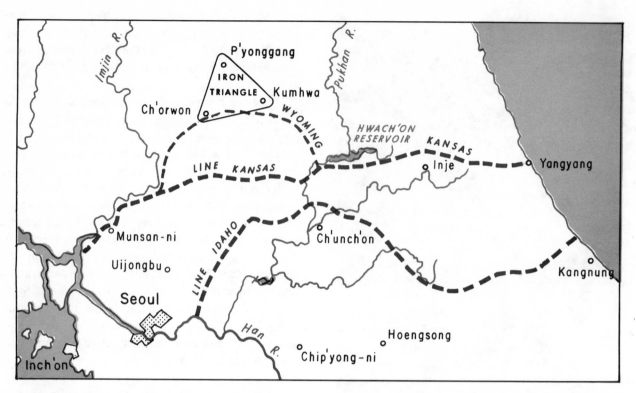

Phase Lines Controlling the Advance of the UN Command in Operations RIPPER and RUGGED, March-April 1951

reached and secured Line IDAHO, it had become clear from recent actions and combat intelligence reports that the CCF was falling back to prepared positions north of the 38th Parallel.

For the second time, the question of crossing the 38th Parallel arose. Without orders to the contrary, MacArthur chose to follow the CCF. "My present intention," he wrote to Ridgway, "is to continue current type of action north of the parallel, but not to proceed further than your logistics would support. . . ."[50] Clearly, MacArthur still did not want such a decision dictated by political considerations. Fortunately, neither the Department of Defense nor the Department of State believed that the 38th Parallel had any special significance any longer, so the President decided to treat the crossing as a purely military problem.[51]

When MacArthur authorized Ridgway to cross the 38th Parallel, the Eighth Army commander was ready. Promptly he issued the order for Operation RUGGED, which was to be another careful advance, made for the purpose of inflicting casualties and retaining the initiative. The operation had as its objective Line KANSAS, which was entirely within North Korea. RUGGED began on April 5. In four days, units in the western two-thirds of the zone reached the objective; in the more rugged terrain to the east, progress was slower. Anxious to keep the enemy off balance and noticing that enemy resistance was stiffening, Ridgway decided to continue the advance to Line WY-

OMING. During the past two weeks, he and MacArthur had become aware that the CCF were building strength in the Iron Triangle—a communication center described by the towns of Ch'orwon, P'yonggang, and Kumhwa at its corners—and were rapidly assembling the men and materiel to mount their own counteroffensive. The purpose of advancing to Line WYOMING and seizing the southern base of the Iron Triangle was to disrupt this assembly and meet it on the most favorable and northerly ground. In anticipation of a strong enemy offensive, Ridgway also issued Plan AUDACIOUS on April 12. Its purpose was to permit an orderly fighting withdrawal through carefully chosen phase lines. He retained sole authority for implementing the plan and emphasized that its purpose was to make an enemy advance prohibitively expensive while maintaining the tactical integrity of the defending corps. This was to be Ridgway's last order as Eighth Army Commander, for he had suddenly been chosen Commander-in-Chief of the Far East and UN Commands. In exasperation, President Truman had relieved MacArthur and called him home.

The Relief of MacArthur

Like the protagonist in a classical tragedy, MacArthur hastened his own ruin as the consequence of a defect in character that was responsible for both his greatness and his downfall. His tragic flaw was arrogance and overbearing pride.

From the beginning of the war, MacArthur had relied upon his reputation and strong personality to achieve his ends. Still the national hero, his hauteur was accepted as a natural trait of a great old soldier. In fact, one could argue that without his arrogant treatment of friends and enemies alike, he would never have been able to accumulate the forces he used so boldly to surprise the North Koreans at Inchon. On a more mundane level, the trait caused nothing but trouble. Even before the intervention of the Chinese, the general and the President had clashed over American policy regarding Taiwan. Early in the war, MacArthur had made an ill-advised visit to Chiang Kai-shek to discuss their mutual interests in East Asia. A public statement issued by Chiang hinted at secret agreements between the two, and cast MacArthur more in the light of an independent sovereign than an American general.[52] Truman was irritated, but inclined to overlook the indiscretion. Later, in a letter to the Veterans of Foreign Wars, MacArthur stressed the strategic importance of Taiwan and called for continued American control over the island. Just as the United States might profitably use Taiwan as a base against China, so too would it be a formidable threat to the United States in the Pacific if controlled by the Chinese.

Because the United States position on Taiwan in Congress and the UN was to deny any territorial ambitions or special relationship with Chiang's domain, Truman directed MacArthur to withdraw the letter before it became public. Although MacArthur protested innocence of any overt attempt to embarrass the administration, Truman was indignant, and considered relieving MacArthur as early as August 26, 1950. Thereafter, MacArthur confined his criticism—primarily concerning restrictions on his use of combat power—to private official channels between himself and the JCS. Nevertheless, he created great concern in Washington and allied capitals when he lifted the restraining line on nonAsian troops in October. Similarly, he startled his superiors when he proposed bombing the Yalu River bridges in November. But these disagreements had been worked out quietly. More serious was MacArthur's erratic fluctuation of moods in response to evidence of Chinese intervention in November; his alternating optimism and pessimism began to undermine confidence in his military judgment. Still, all criticism had been kept private, and it was only after the Chinese intervened that he decided to take his case to the public.

With his historical position threatened by the defeat of the UN Command in North Korea, MacArthur spoke sharply in his own defense. Early in December, he complained to the press that the restrictions placed upon him were "without precedent in military history."[53] President Truman smoldered, as by inference his administration had been blamed for the defeat along the Ch'ongch'on River. For the second time, the President considered relieving MacArthur. More public criticism in the first week of December caused the President to issue an Executive order to his Cabinet chiefs requiring government officials to clear all public statements concerning foreign policy with the Department of State and those concerning military affairs with the Department of Defense.[54] Clearly, the order was aimed at MacArthur. The general once again resorted to official channels to communicate his views about his government's policy. As discussed earlier, he proposed retaliatory measures against China and repeated them frequently, but always properly, through the JCS. Then, on February 13, 1951, he told the press that unless he was permitted to attack the Chinese in their sanctuary, he could not hope to move north of the 38th Parallel in strength. Again, on March 7, he reminded the nation that a new strategy for war against the Chinese—presumably, his— had yet to be formulated. Both of these statements were in violation of the President's Executive order of December 6.

The crisis reached its peak in mid-March. Encouraged by Ridgway's offensive, the administration decided to renew its efforts for negotiation in hopes that the Chinese might now be more receptive to a truce. The President's advisers reasoned that since the CCF and North Koreans had been driven north of the 38th Parallel, the objective of UN operations—that is, the ejection of the aggressors from South Korea—had been achieved. Further, unification of the peninsula should and could be accomplished without further fighting. Placing the prestige of the President behind the proposal, Truman's staff drafted a message to the Chinese Government, offering to negotiate a settlement of the war. On March 20, the JCS forwarded the general contents of the President's message to MacArthur, making it clear that further coordination with allies in the UN was necessary before it could be put in final form. At the same time, they asked him to comment on what latitude he needed in his directive to insure successful operations in North Korea and the continued security of forces. MacArthur replied that the restrictions placed on his forces prevented him from mounting large-scale operations in North Korea leading to occupation, and that, therefore, his current directives were adequate. Then, to the shock of the President and his advisers, on March 24 MacArthur issued his own "ultimatum" to the enemy, kicking the pins from under the President's initiative. Brimming with new-found confidence, the general claimed that the recent success of UN military forces revealed the CCF to be overrated in all aspects of combat power, except numerical strength. Despite the restrictions placed on UN military activities and the advantages accruing to the enemy, the Chinese were incapable of achieving their goal of unifying the peninsula under Communist rule.[55] Ignoring the intention of the President to invite negotiations, MacArthur went on to say, "I stand ready at any time to confer in the field with the Commander-in-Chief of the enemy . . ." to find a way to achieve the goals of the UN without further fighting.[56]

President Truman was furious. Not only had MacArthur pre-empted Presidential prerogatives and once again criticized the policy of the United States, but he had also frightened UN members, who now wondered just who was directing the American war effort. The least of MacArthur's sins was violation of the December 6 directive on public statements. Technically, MacArthur had stayed within his authority as Commander-in-Chief, UN Command. He had not seen the full text of the President's message, and had clearly dealt with military matters only in his own announcement. Nonetheless, he had acted at cross-purposes with both his President and the UN. Truman interpreted this to be a direct challenge to his authority as Commander-in-Chief. He could no longer tolerate what he saw as insubordination.

As it turned out, the chain of events that ultimately led to MacArthur's relief was already underway. On March 20, MacArthur had written to Joseph W. Martin, the minority (Republican) leader of the House of Representatives, expressing his views on American foreign policy. In that letter, which was a response to Martin's request for comments, MacArthur repeated his belief that Asia was as important as Europe, and that the war in Korea should be pressed to victory. On April 5, close on the heels of the negotiations incident, Martin released the contents of MacArthur's letter. The next day, Truman started the process through which MacArthur would be relieved from command on April 11.

From a historical point of view, the drama of this incident obscured crucial problems endemic to the Korean situation in which the President and MacArthur found themselves involved. MacArthur's relief shocked the American people, for he represented traditions and widely held attitudes about the meaning of victory. His disagreement with Truman's policy of seeking a settlement short of enemy capitulation was shared by many Americans. Although short-lived, the clamor on his behalf amounted to a sizable political uprising, enjoyed and encouraged by the President's political opposition. Pressing their advantage, Republican Congressmen forced a senatorial investigation of the facts behind the incident. During May and June, lengthy hearings, which, for the most part, were open to public scrutiny, enabled MacArthur's advocates to vie with administration spokesmen in a political struggle over the history and future of American foreign policy. As the contending arguments were aired, and after the emotionalism surrounding the general's return to the United States died down, a consensus emerged among Americans that generally supported Truman's actions. Thus, in the end, the President won widespread support for his views that America's real interests lay with her European and NATO allies, and that the fighting in Korea should be contained and ended as quickly as possible to avoid a widening of the war. Nevertheless, agreement with Truman's overall view did not imply support for the implementation of his policies. Throughout the last two years of the war, frustrated critics decried the difficult negotiations, and condemned the wasteful and seemingly meaningless war of attrition fought along the line of contact in Korea. Eventually, disenchantment with protracted war became the major political issue in the Presidential election of 1952, and played a large part in the victory of Dwight D. Eisenhower.

Less conspicuous, but perhaps more important to the military profession than the political effects of MacArthur's relief, was the impact on the American system of command. First, the traditional supremacy of civilian authority over military command was affirmed. Even though partisan Republican support for MacArthur grew hysterical at times, few seriously doubted that the facts in the case warranted the relief of a general who challenged a constitutional principle. It is possible to argue, at least in theory, that MacArthur's loyalty was to the Constitution, rather than to the political administration that was temporarily running the government. MacArthur considered it his duty to speak out on issues that he thought were vital to the security of his country. If he was stifled, who then would warn the country of danger? Nevertheless, MacArthur's oath of office demanded that he obey the legal orders of his superiors. This he repeatedly failed to do when he defied the Executive order of December 6 requiring the clearance of public statements by senior government officials.

For failing seriously to consider consolidation short of the border, the nation's senior military leaders must take responsibility. The Department of Defense and the Joint Chiefs of Staff, relatively new organizations trying to localize the first potentially dangerous war in the nuclear age, were at first prudently cautious. Overburdened by their responsibilities, however, they too easily abandoned their wary approach. The Joint Chiefs, conservative in their response to the Inchon plan and then overbold in their assessment of the risks to be incurred by crossing the

38th Parallel, failed to see their inconsistency, and permitted their error to be built into the President's decision to cross. Moreover, after the spectacular success at Inchon they were only too willing to give the victorious MacArthur wide latitude in winding up the whole Korean affair as they concentrated their attention on the rearmament of the United States and the reinforcement of NATO. As a consequence, the Joint Chiefs saw the drive into North Korea through the eyes of MacArthur. Too late, they realized that the military situation was not as he had portrayed it.

But what were they to do? The Joint Chiefs, as well as the President and his top civilian advisers, were grappling with an entirely new experience. Never before had the direction of battle contained such far-reaching implications as it did in Korea in the nuclear age. In World War II, decentralization of authority and responsibility to unified military commanders was found to be the only effective way to direct the efforts of air, sea, and ground forces. Under these conditions, MacArthur and the other theater commanders worked effectively. The Joint Chiefs themselves had been a part of that system and fully endorsed it, for they knew no other way. But once the Soviet Union's possession of the air-delivered nuclear weapon made strategic nuclear attack against United States territory a real possibility, there was an urgent need to coordinate closely the policies of the President, the Joint Chiefs, and the theater commander. Failing this, an ill-advised decision in a local war might easily spark a global conflict. Although the President and his advisers understood this, they had not as yet explored alternative systems for controlling their field commanders, and were unwilling to risk the consequences of tampering with tradition. As Truman said: "You pick your man, you've got to back him up." In the end, it took MacArthur's challenge to the constitutional authority of the President to force a change in the American system of command.

Finally, the greater dilemma involved strategic direction of the war. What had been missing all along was close coordination between battlefield goals and worldwide coalition goals. Having assumed the leadership in both areas, the President and his advisers had allowed the battlefield objective, which was to unify Korea by force, to coexist with the broader strategic goal of avoiding a wider war, a goal that proved to be incompatible with unification. Either MacArthur should have been given the resources to unify Korea regardless of the risks, or he should have been stopped short of the Manchurian border in order to avoid a wider war. After directing MacArthur to cross into North Korea without the resources to defeat both the North Koreans and the Chinese, the administration found itself faced with the worst possible outcome: a divided Korea *and* a war with China. Clearly, the Truman administration was neither conceptually nor organizationally ready to fight a limited war. After the defeat in North Korea, the administration finally subordinated the freedom of action traditionally accorded the local commander to the demands of global strategy. Eventually, this priority led to the dismissal of MacArthur.

Stabilizing the Front

When Ridgway moved to replace MacArthur in Tokyo, Lieutenant General James A. Van Fleet, an experienced corps commander in the European theater during World War II, became the new Commanding General of the Eighth Army. Van Fleet had returned from Greece a year earlier after having directed the American advisory and support effort that had resulted in a Greek victory over Communist insurgents. During the summer of 1950, both he and Ridgway had been seriously considered as Walker's successor should anything happen to the general. Now, Van Fleet found himself in command of a victorious army,

High-Level Conference: Generals James A. Van Fleet and Matthew B. Ridgway

positioned north of the 38th Parallel, and awaiting the expected CCF counteroffensive.

A change in command for a military unit can create disruptions that linger in the unit for a period of time. This was the case when Van Fleet assumed command of the Eighth Army, many of whose personnel had grown to deeply admire and respect Ridgway. Moreover, Ridgway was convinced that the CCF were nearly ready to spring, so his first order to Van Fleet restricted the new commander's offensive action to closing up on Line KANSAS-WYOMING. Ridgway's greatest fear was that the forces would be overextended when the blow fell. Although he was confident that the Eighth Army could repel the attack, he specified that no large enemy units were to be bypassed and that lateral contact within and between corps was to be close.

The Eighth Army was still edging toward Line KANSAS-WYOMING when the Chinese attacked on the night of April 22. (*See Atlas Map No. 35.*) The initial drive was mounted from the Iron Triangle, and was delivered by three CCF armies west of the Hwach'on Reservoir. The main attack came later, farther west through Munsan-ni, and was aimed at Seoul. To the east of the reservoir, in the X Corps and ROK sectors, a third drive, mounted by North Koreans, advanced on Inje. Although the Eighth Army held firmly on both flanks, an ROK division broke in the center and fell back about 20 miles. To maintain the security of his line, Van Fleet ordered Plan AUDACIOUS (the withdrawal scheme) into effect, and the army retired in an orderly manner back to Line KANSAS. The enemy strength, however, amounted to some 337,000 troops in the west, driving toward Seoul, and another 150,000 troops in the center. Followed closely by this formidable force, Van Fleet had to abandon Line KANSAS and withdraw well into South Korea, halting finally a bare five miles north of Seoul. By the end of April, the Communist logistical system was again in a depleted state, and the first phase of the CCF offensive subsided.

In early May, Chinese and North Korean units fell back to prepare for the second impulse of their spring offensive. During the lull, they replaced losses and moved supplies forward. Their aim was to take advantage of their numerical superiority by resuming the attack as quickly as possible. Ridgway and Van Fleet agreed that the best way to minimize the effects of a renewed drive was to keep the enemy off balance through aggressive offensive action. Van Fleet sought, therefore, to retain the initiative by establishing patrol bases, each manned by a complete regimental combat team, forward of the frontline divisions. He established the bases some seven to eight miles in advance of the UN main battle position. From them, tank-

infantry patrols probed even deeper into enemy territory in search of CCF and North Korean covering forces and assembly areas. Simultaneously, Van Fleet began planning a renewal of the UN offensive. But before he could turn north, intelligence reports convinced the army commander that the CCF were ready to launch another drive. Van Fleet thought that the Chinese would again strike at Seoul, but between May 10 and May 16 they shifted their main attack to the east. (*See Atlas Map No. 36.*) Late on the sixteenth, five CCF armies attacked across a 40-mile front extending from Hangye to Taepo on the Sea of Japan. In the week that followed, the CCF drove the X Corps and the two ROK corps on the right flank well south of the 38th Parallel.

Once the latest enemy drive was under way, Ridgway sensed that the concentration of seven armies in the central and eastern sectors indicated an imbalance of Communist strength across the front. He calculated that there were probably no more than four armies covering the remaining front to the west. If this were true, Van Fleet should be able to strike north of Seoul before the CCF could redeploy. After reconnoitering the front, he ordered Van Fleet to attack north through Uijongbu with at least two divisions. Such an action would relieve the pressure on the IX and the X Corps and open up possibilities for further exploitation should the Chinese be caught off guard. (*See Atlas Map No. 37.*) The rest of the army was to attack simultaneously across the entire front.[57] Accordingly, while the enemy was still driving across the east-central front, the Eighth Army moved north in a sudden counteroffensive. The effect was immediate and dramatic as the enemy was caught by surprise. UN units advanced quickly against weak resistance and inflicted the highest casualties the enemy had yet experienced. By the end of May, the Eighth Army had almost regained Line KANSAS, and the Chinese appeared to be routed in confusion. Not only were the enemy dead stacked up on the battlefield, but nearly 10,000 prisoners, mostly Chinese, had been captured. So great were the estimates that Ridgway was hesitant to accept the reports of enemy dead, and could only guess at the number of wounded who would probably die for want of adequate care. Moreover, UN troops seized quantities of enemy weapons and other supplies at a far greater rate than ever before. Chinese prisoners complained of having to eat grass and roots because of short rations. In all, Ridgway concluded, the outlook for Eighth Army was excellent:

I, therefore, believe [he reported to the JCS on May 30] that for the next sixty days the United States Government should be able to count with reasonable assurance upon a military situation in Korea offering

Infantrymen of the 3rd Division Cross an Enemy-Made Footbridge

optimum advantages in support of its diplomatic ne-gotiations.[58]

By mid-June, Van Fleet had gained a line, except in the central sector, that was about where the contending forces would fight until the end of the war, two years later. While Van Fleet wanted to undertake further offensive actions, he was ordered by his superiors to stop his advance at Line KANSAS-WYOMING, as the prospects of a negotiated settlement had improved greatly.

Negotiations

For some months, American policy planners had recog-nized that the Korean War was unlikely to end in a decisive victory for either side. The spirit of determination among UN members, so strong the year before, had ebbed; the American public had lost its enthusiasm for a limited war ever since the Chinese victory in November–December of 1950; and political leaders in Congress and the administra-tion were anxious to begin negotiations to end the con-flict.[59] By April, the JCS had advised the National Security Council that American forces should continue limited mil-

itary operations in Korea only until a political settlement could be reached. They spelled out what they wanted in a May 31 directive to General Ridgway. In essence, Ridgway was to inflict maximum losses of men and materiel on the Communists, operating within the geographic boundaries of Korea, "in order to create conditions favorable to a settlement of the Korean conflict. . . ."[60] Ridgway was also charged with terminating hostilities by concluding an ar-mistice and withdrawing non-Korean forces from the pen-insula. Restrictions on military operations near the inter-national boundaries continued, and now included a limit of advance to a line through the Hwach'on Reservoir—in effect, Line KANSAS-WYOMING. In short, Ridgway's mission became one of ending the war as quickly and pain-lessly as possible.

Communist forces were also under strong pressures to stop the shooting. Losses sustained during the May with-drawal had been painful. Morale of both Chinese and North Korean troops was low, and the men needed some respite.

Diplomatically, the war had also begun to go badly for the Communists. On February 1, the United States had gained the support it sought in the UN, branding the Gov-ernment of China as an aggressor. Words—even strong ones—had little effect, however; the real pinch began on

May 18, when the General Assembly passed a resolution demanding that its members place an economic embargo on trade with China. Beyond that, the resolution called for a complete embargo by *all* nations on the sale of arms, ammunition, and other implements of war, including petroleum and other items of strategic value. While it took some time to develop, there was considerable support for the embargo. Even the British curtailed their growing trade with China, reflecting the closer Anglo-American relations resulting from MacArthur's relief. Further, Chinese intransigence toward earlier offers to negotiate alienated members of the UN. At the same time, the United States won support for its policy of applying military pressure while calling for an armistice on the basis of the status quo. Suddenly, a barrage of quasi-official public statements put pressure on the Soviets and Chinese to take realistic measures to end the fighting.

In a UN-sponsored radio series aired during the last week of May, Lester Pearson, Canadian Minister of External Affairs, observed that the object of the war in Korea was to defeat aggression, not to force the capitulation of the North Koreans and Chinese. On June 1, Trygve Lie said that a cease-fire in the vicinity of the 38th Parallel would fulfill the purposes of the UN resolutions passed the preceding June. During the MacArthur hearings, underway at the same time in Washington, Secretary of State Acheson seconded UN Secretary General Lie, and secret talks between the Soviets and the Americans began. Finally, on June 23, Soviet Ambassador Jacob Malik, speaking on the UN radio series, offered real hope by revealing a policy initiative by his government. As a first step, Malik said, "discussions should be started between the belligerents for a ceasefire and an armistice providing for the mutual withdrawal of forces from the 38th Parallel."[61] In the view of the Soviet Government, this was the price to be paid for peace. From this moment on, arrangements for negotiations moved quickly from New York to the Korean battlefield as all principal leaders, except Syngman Rhee, lent their support.

As Commander-in-Chief of the UN Command,

The Conference Site in Kaesong on the First Day of Negotiations, July 10, 1951

The United Nations Command Delegation to the Peace Talks: *(Left to right)* Major General Laurence C. Craigie, Major General Paik Sun Yup, Vice Admiral C. Turner Joy, Major General Henry I. Hodes, and Rear Admiral Arleigh Burke

Ridgway made the first move. On June 29, he broadcast a message to his Communist counterpart, announcing his willingness to negotiate and offering to name a representative upon receipt of a favorable reply. After three days, Kim Il Sung, Premier of North Korea, and General Peng Teh-huai, commanding the CCF, proposed a meeting at Kaesong. Ridgway agreed, and on July 5, liaison officers gathered in a Kaesong teahouse and chose July 10 as the date of the first meeting of the truce delegations.

As it turned out, arranging the first meeting proved to be the easiest part of the whole procedure. Whether to strengthen their negotiating position, to gain propaganda value, or both, the Communists engineered a series of incidents that delayed serious negotiations. Although the negotiations site was to have been neutral, the Communists were in actual control of the Kaesong area. From the first, CCF and North Korean troops created conditions that were far from evenhanded. As the UN delegation drove into the conference site for the first time, carrying the agreed upon white flag of truce, Communist photographers recorded their "surrender." Even worse, no Western newsmen were permitted to accompany the UN delegation, thus depriving the West of a balanced account of the sessions. Ridgway decided to make an issue of the press restrictions. Reacting quickly, he discontinued the talks on July 12 until the neutrality of Kaesong and the admission of Western journalists were guaranteed by the Communists. Even after the first abrasive confrontations eased,

child-like incidents continued to disrupt the negotiations. On August 4, armed Communist troops blocked the entrance to the teahouse and herded UN delegates from place to place, treating them like prisoners. Again, Ridgway withdrew his representatives for six days. Once back at the conference table, Vice Admiral Turner Joy, chief UN delegate, found himself seated on an absurdly small chair under the gaze of North Korean General Nam Il, who towered over him from an equally absurd high chair across the table. A North Korean flag, part of the centerpiece, was fully six inches higher than the UN flag beside it. Discussions between delegates fared no better, and the language of diplomacy degenerated into angry abuse. As the delegates tested each other, the Communists insisted on being called by full, formal titles while referring to South Korea's president as "the murderer Rhee" and to Chiang Kai-shek as "your puppet on Formosa."[62] On August 23, talks were interrupted again when the Communist delegation accused the UN of violating the neutrality of the conference area by dropping napalm. Serious discussions did not really begin until the armistice negotiations were moved to Panmunjom, a site that afforded unrestricted access to both sides.

Finding a truly neutral site removed some of the opportunities for delay, but brought the delegates no closer to agreement. Although the first debates arose over the agenda, they actually reflected the opposing goals of the delegations. The objectives of the UN Command were to agree on a cease-fire along a militarily defensible line of

The Communist Delegation to the Peace Talks: *(Left to right)* Major General Hsieh Fang, Lieutenant General Teng Hua, General Nam Il, Major General Lee Sang Cho, and Major General Chang Pyong San

contact, to establish some kind of commission to supervise the truce, and to exclude all political questions from the truce discussions, deferring their solution to a meeting of interested governments at a later date. The Communists emphasized two main points: that the 38th Parallel rather than the line of contact be the truce line, and that all foreign troops be withdrawn from Korea. Both of these points were seen to be essentially political issues by the UN delegates; the 38th Parallel had never been recognized as an international boundary, and the Communists were not inclined to view the Chinese as foreign troops. In this argument the UN finally prevailed, and on July 26 the two delegations agreed to the following:

1. The adoption of an agenda for future talks.
2. The future establishment of a military demarcation line so as to create a demilitarized zone (DMZ) as the basic condition for a cease-fire.
3. The making of concrete arrangements for a supervising body.
4. The determination of arrangements for prisoners of war.
5. The development of recommendations to the governments of countries concerned with the war.[63]

Considering that the negotiations dragged on until the armistice was signed in July 1953, two years later, the major flaw in the agenda was positioning the demarcation line talks first rather than last. By discussing this issue first, the UN Command permitted itself to be maneuvered into a stalemate condition for the rest of the war.

Ironically, the stalemate emanated from Van Fleet's desire to keep military pressure on the enemy and a UN proposal designed to gain a quick truce. Having been reinforced during the early summer lull and concerned that inactivity would dull the fighting skills of the army, Van Fleet launched a limited offensive beginning in late July. His purpose was to adjust his front and to keep pressure on the enemy by inflicting heavy casualties. Fighting for terrain features such as the Punchbowl, Bloody Ridge, and Heartbreak Ridge, the Eighth Army established a new line on commanding ground, providing a much stronger defensive position. (*See Atlas Map No. 37.*) It is difficult to draw a firm connection between the course of negotiations and military pressure, for on November 12 Ridgway ordered Van Fleet to cease offensive operations and begin what he called an active defense. The active defense limited Van Fleet to battalion-sized operations; anything larger required Ridgway's permission. Its purpose was to avoid needless UN casualties while negotiations reached a conclusion regarding the demarcation line.

On the seventeenth, the UN delegation presented a proposal—drafted in Washington and the UN and vividly illustrating their desire for a quick truce—that suggested designating the current line of contact (*see Atlas Map No. 38*) as the demarcation line, provided that the general armistice be signed within 30 days after agreement to the proposal. Although the proposal provided incentive to achieve a quick truce, it also contained the potential for stalemating the front. The Communists needed a 30-day breather to mend the damage inflicted by Van Fleet's offensive.[64] All they had to do was agree to the present line of contact as the demarcation line—which they did on November 27—and then *not* agree to the remaining three agenda items by December 27. The result was, in effect, a 30-day truce during which the Communists built a defensive system that protected their armies.

Stalemate

For the rest of the war, the two opposing armies dug themselves into the hills along Line KANSAS-WYOMING. The Communists built a defensive zone 14 miles deep—deeper than the German lines in World War I—that was designed to withstand nuclear attack. Tunnels, fighting trenches, and bunkers provided an integrated defense that was supported by large numbers of artillery and mortars. In fact, so deeply was their artillery dug into the hills that it proved unable to maneuver in support of offensive operations thereafter. In an effort to protect themselves from the dreadful effects of Van Fleet's offensive power, the Chinese and North Koreans had immobilized their armies.[65]

Similarly, but for different reasons, the UN Command immobilized itself. First, Ridgway and Van Fleet agreed that they could not advance farther into North Korea without substantial reinforcements. The Joint Chiefs had long since decided that there would be no significant reinforcement in Korea. Although they had sent Ridgway the 40th and 45th National Guard Divisions for the defense of Japan—and for use later in Korea—their first concern was the reinforcement of NATO in Europe. Unable to advance, Van Fleet had halted on the best defensive terrain to await the results of the truce talks. But he had to stretch his troops thinly across the 155-mile front, and accordingly lacked the favorable ratio of men to front that would permit him to crack the formidable defensive zone across the valley. Consequently, for the next 20 months, as the two sides haggled over the truce agreement at Panmunjom, the armies skirmished with each other between their two main lines of resistance.

Across the front, infantry units on both sides waged a strange kind of static war. On the surface, at least, their purpose appeared to be the straightening of bulges in the line, the gaining of better observation posts, and the denial of vantage points to the enemy. For some, the war occasionally erupted into violent battles that consumed men but achieved nothing decisive or even substantial. For others, the war declined into a state of boredom in which engineering skills, rather than fighting spirit, were at a premium. On the UN main line of resistance (MLR), infantry companies organized positions along the fingers of the steep, often barren hills, placing their platoons well forward and maintaining only meager reserves. Along the military crests of the hills and ridges, the infantrymen built log and sandbag bunkers that protected their machineguns and automatic rifles. These fighting bunkers were sited to deliver automatic fire into the most likely avenues of approach and along final protective lines that interlocked the entire company front and tied into adjacent companies. On the higher peaks, overlooking the fingers that sloped into the valley below, larger bunkers provided observation posts for platoon and company commanders and the artillery forward observers. Connecting the fighting bunkers and the command posts were deep, narrow communications trenches that outlined the military crest of the hills, ridges, and fingers in a curious pattern that was reminiscent of World War I. Along the trench lines, riflemen cut individual bays from which they could fight to protect the blind sides of the automatic weapons bunkers. All bunkers and trenches were camouflaged for concealment, the extent of the camouflage depending upon the ingenuity and diligence of the infantry commanders. Small barbed wire entanglements—called hedgehogs—were positioned on the parapets, ready to be dropped into the trenches in order to isolate a portion of the line should the enemy penetrate the position. To further strengthen the position, riflemen constructed protective barbed wire fences sufficiently far down the slopes to prevent enemy troops from advancing within grenade-throwing range. Beyond that, more complex wire entanglements were combined with antipersonnel minefields to obstruct the movement of enemy troops as they approached the killing zone, an area that could be saturated by the fires of artillery, mortars, and automatic weapons. Once constructed, the positions were constantly improved and extended in depth to provide more flexibility in the defense. The more fortunate infantry units shared their positions with hard-hitting tanks whose guns were integrated into the defensive fire plan.

Creeping outward from the fortified zones, the two armies occupied rival outposts over which the remaining war was fought. Breaking the tedium of life in the trenches, battles flared over colorfully named hills such as Carson, Reno, Vegas, the Hook, Old Baldy, Porkchop Hill, the T-Bone, Whitehorse, Outpost Harry, and Sniper's Ridge. Often, these fights—most of which were at night—resulted from the engagement of probing patrols that sought either prisoners or general intelligence, or from contact

M4 Tanks Fire in Support of the 2nd Infantry Division, September 1951

A Patrol of the 35th Infantry Studies a Map Prior to Departure

patrols that were caught in ambushes. Occasionally, as at Porkchop Hill, the UN forces or the Communists decided to capture an outpost to gain a local tactical advantage. When this happened, the other side might be equally determined to hold the position, and the process of "piling on"* would result in a bloody and prolonged fight. More often than not, such battles were related in some way to the difficult negotiations that continued at Panmunjom. Whatever the cause, the battles of the outpost line illustrated the problem of negotiating with the Communists.

As ground action waned, the UN turned to powerful air and naval arms for the military pressure needed to support its negotiating team. In August 1951—before Van Fleet's army adopted the active defense—air, naval, and marine commanders concentrated all available aircraft on the interdiction of Communist-controlled bridges, highways, railroad lines and yards, and supply points. Most of the air assets took part in Operation STRANGLE, a rail-cutting scheme designed by Fifth Air Force to slow down the southward movement of enemy troops and materiel. During the day, fighter-bombers raked the railroad lines; at night, B-26s scoured the countryside for trucks. Approximately 96 fighter sorties a day continued to provide close air support to the static ground war. For most pilots, however, the Air Force theme song became "We've been working on the Railroad."[66] While enemy work details devised ingenious ways to repair the railroad overnight, it was a costly task. The North Korean Railroad Bureau employed three brigades (7,700 men) full time on railroad repair, and, at the height of the air campaign, used as many as

*When an enemy force is encountered, troops "pile on" by bringing overwhelming numbers and munitions to bear against it.

500,000 soldiers and civilians to keep the lines open. At first, Operation STRANGLE also forced the Communist air forces out of their Manchurian sanctuary. Beginning in September 1951, though, Communist MiG-15s became more numerous and more aggressive over North Korea, bringing an end to the Allies' uncontested control of the air. Nevertheless, enemy air forces never achieved their full potential during the war. When Communist fighters chose to challenge UN aircraft, they suffered heavy losses; eventually, UN aircraft once again concentrated their efforts on providing close air support to ground forces along the frontlines.[67]

Paradoxically, the decision to remove ground military pressure from the enemy and pursue an active defense also removed the enemy's incentive to negotiate. This was a serious political error, for while the Americans and their UN allies correctly believed that the enemy wanted to stop the shooting—at least the Eighth Army offensives—they failed to see that the Communists welcomed the opportunity to wage a different kind of war by shifting the fight from the battlefield to the arena of world opinion. American and UN leaders, pressured by growing disillusionment with the war in Western democracies, jumped at the prospect of a truce even after the military situation no longer demanded one. Unlike their antagonists, the Communists were far more concerned with issues than casualties, and as long as they felt no military pressure, they felt no compulsion to conclude a truce. They were perfectly happy to

F-86 Sabrejets Over North Korea

switch from a military struggle to a political one. Thus the war dragged on as the delegation at Panmunjom debated the last three points on the agenda, and the Communists sought to discredit the UN in the eyes of neutral nations.

External Factors

Mixed in with the negotiations on the remaining agenda items was a carefully thought out Communist propaganda campaign. As the talks wore on through 1952 and 1953, the Communists charged the Western powers, and particularly the United States, with imperialism and warmongering. They encouraged a worldwide peace movement that adopted anti-Westernism as its central theme. To make the contrast between the peace-loving Communist states and the imperialist warmongers even more vivid, they mounted an almost believable campaign—employing public testimony by American prisoners of war—charging the United States with waging bacteriological warfare against North Korea and China. While the peace campaign had little direct impact on American policy toward Korea, it would be unwise to conclude that neutral nations, in and out of the UN, were unaffected. At the very least, there was a coincident rise in the clamor for a quick peace.

Even if an armistice could not be concluded quickly, the United States National Security Council hoped to develop the ROK Army to a point where it could take over the war. For his own reasons, ROK President Syngman Rhee called for the immediate arming of additional infantry divisions which, if necessary, would be commanded by American officers. Although Rhee repeatedly returned to this theme, there was little support for this radical proposal among members of the American High Command. Both Ridgway and Van Fleet objected on the grounds that the ROK Army needed not more men and weapons, but long-term improvement of leadership and military training. To achieve this, they advocated a reinvigorated military school system for officers and non commissioned officers, the training of ROK instructor personnel at American Army school centers, and the establishment of effective training programs for the ROK units on line. Van Fleet introduced the latter by rotating ROK units in and out of training camps set up in the corps rear areas. While the American Army staff favored a limited expansion of the ROK Army, it was unwilling to commit additional logistical support if it meant reducing the strategic reserve or depriving NATO. Nevertheless, by the end of the war, there was a moderate increase in ROK divisions, although well short of the number that Rhee wanted. More importantly, under Van

Fleet's tutelage, the ROK Army became a much improved fighting organization, able to stand up to heavy Chinese attacks as the war neared its end.[68]

Logistical constraints not only influenced the expansion of the ROK Army, but also became a serious problem for the United States Army. Ammunition supply was particularly vexing. Following World War II, the Army found itself with large quantities of artillery and gun ammunition stored around the world. For this reason, in the postwar years of fiscal austerity, the Army staff gave little thought to producing new ammunition in great quantities. Further, the lack of an ammunition procurement program caused the major suppliers to discontinue the production of ammunition and convert to consumer goods. After the Korean War broke out, the Army had to draw upon the old stocks, which soon began to dwindle. Congress appropriated ample funds for procurement, but because the lead time for ammunition production was so great—a year to a year and a half—ammunition purchased in January 1951 could not be delivered until late 1952. To complicate matters, as the front stabilized in Korea and the enemy dug into the hills, ammunition consumption rose dramatically. In 1951, one artillery battalion engaged at Bloody Ridge fired 14,425 rounds of 105-mm shells in one 24-hour period. By contrast, the average daily expenditure of a 105-mm battalion during World War II had been 480 rounds. Overnight, commanders in Korea called for increased shipments to replenish their depleting stocks, and shortages developed in depot and theater stocks. This resulted in limitations on daily expenditure rates, particularly in the heavy calibers used to root enemy forces out of their deep tunnels and holes. Generally, however, units under attack or engaged in a critical offensive action were amply supplied by a redistribution of ammunition found in unengaged units and in local supply points.[69] Certainly, the ammunition shortage, while disconcerting at the tactical level, had no important effect on the outcome of the war.[70] That rested on the truce talks at Panmunjom and the election of a new American president in November 1952.

As the election approached, the war saw little activity other than patrolling and the incessant haggling over an armistice. In the summer of 1952, General Mark Clark succeeded Ridgway as Commander-in-Chief, UN Command, and operated under the same policies and restrictions faced by his predecessor. The Chinese and North Koreans seemed similarly restrained, avoiding serious military action, and the Soviets showed no inclination to become involved. Clearly, the American public and Congress were disgruntled and frustrated by the stalemate; ending the war became the major campaign issue. The Democrats were hard pressed to defend the policy that had produced the stalemate, and despite the efforts of President Truman and Adlai Stevenson, the Democratic candidate, the party's popularity dropped before the charm of the Republican standard bearer. Promising to visit Korea, ostensibly to end the interminable war, Dwight D. Eisenhower swung the electorate to a Republican administration. A month after his election, the President-elect traveled to Korea and toured the front, talking to commanders at all levels. He concluded that there was no easy solution to ending the war, and returned to Washington to organize his administration for the difficult task ahead.

Armistice

Discussions concerning the demarcation line were largely concluded in December 1951.[71] The only remaining issues concerning the trace of the line were the width of the DMZ—the Communists wanted a 4-kilometer belt—and a provision for deferring the exact trace of the demarcation line until all other agenda items had been settled. The UN Command agreed to both. Not surprisingly, in late May 1953 the Communists exploited the latter agreement to mount a spurt of offensives against the ROK sector and thereby achieve the illusion of final victory. Although the offensive was expected and the gains were limited, its political effect was much as the Communists had hoped, particularly in the neutral nations that became increasingly anti-Western as negotiations on agenda items 3, 4, and 5 dragged on.

Arrangements for the supervision and control of the armistice agreement proved to be negotiable, but extremely complex. For this reason, the UN delegation was slow in developing a position, and ended up debating a Communist initiative. The United States Government had two fundamental goals: a supervisory armistice commission with free access to all of Korea, and an agreement that there would be no reinforcement of personnel, equipment, and supplies. Ridgway thought that the Communists would not agree to free access by any inspecting body—he was not too happy with the idea himself—so he proposed inspections at selected ports of entry. Vice Admiral Joy wanted to prevent the construction and repair of airfields in North Korea, so he favored including provisions for photo reconnaissance. As enemy air activity increased in the winter of 1951–1952, Ridgway added his support to Joy's proposition, and the prevention of airfield construction and maintenance became a major issue; indeed, it was considered necessary to insure the future security of South Korea.

Before the UN delegation could offer a coordinated proposal, the Communists presented their package. Their comprehensive program sounded much like the developing UN position, but contained some significant differences. Under the Communist plan, not only were there to be no reinforcements, but there was no provision for replacing the troops and equipment in Korea. This was unacceptable to the UN, as agreement would lead to the obsolescence of equipment and an inability to replace veterans of the war who were scheduled to return home. The Communists also insisted that there be no interference with the construction and maintenance of airfields and other facilities. Regardless of the differences, a compromise slowly emerged. The UN high command realized that it had no practical way of preventing the restoration of airfields, so photo reconnaissance was really not essential; the Chinese agreed that there could be a rotation of 35,000 men a month through selected ports of entry; and both sides agreed that Sweden, Switzerland, Poland, and Czechoslovakia would provide the members of the neutral armistice commission.

Item 5 was settled in recordbreaking time when the Communists proposed to *recommend* to the governments involved that a political conference convene three months after the armistice was signed. At that time, those issues deferred during the truce talks, such as the withdrawal of all forces from Korea, would be discussed. After suggesting minor changes for clarification, Vice Admiral Joy agreed so quickly that the Communists paused to re-examine their text for fear they had made a mistake. The fact was that Joy was satisfied with the proposal as long as its provisions were kept vague and were offered in the form of recommendations. In all, agenda item 5 took only 11 days to complete; the delegations were not prepared to deal so quickly with the remaining item—arrangements for prisoners of war.

The handling of prisoners turned out to be the most difficult problem faced at Panmunjom. Fundamental differences between Western and Communist attitudes toward both the process of negotiations and the humane treatment of prisoners underlay the issue. The UN sought voluntary repatriation in which those prisoners who did not want to return to China or North Korea could remain in the south. The UN delegation believed that a significant number either had been captured early in the war and forced to serve in the North Korean Army or had served in the Chinese Nationalist Army before its defeat in 1949 and did not want to live under Communist rule. The Communists wanted all prisoners returned to the losing side, even if it meant forcible repatriation. They wanted neither a public testimony of the unpopularity of Communism nor the loss of trained manpower for the armed forces. They saw voluntary repatriation as a UN ploy to hold on to the prisoners. To break the deadlock, the UN Command suggested that the prisoners be polled by the International Red Cross to determine how many wanted to go home and how many wished to stay where they were. The Communists agreed. By April 5, 1952, 132,000 Communist prisoners and 37,000 civilians had been screened, and the results were shocking. Among the soldiers, 54,000 North Koreans and only 5,100 of some 20,000 Chinese chose to return home. The Communists immediately accused the UN of duplicity and refused to moderate their position. For fifteen months, the prisoner question remained the only major unresolved issue.

Organization of the prison camps by hardcore Communists complicated the problem further and illustrated the totality of the Communist war effort. Operating in communication and coordination with the truce delegation at Panmunjom, Communist leaders gained control of the compounds in which the prisoners were held. Coercion of anti-Communist prisoners and outright resistance to camp command resulted. The influence of the Communist leadership became so strong that the UN Command decided to separate the hardcore Communists from those who did not want repatriation to North Korea or China. During May 1952, in extension of Communist objections to voluntary repatriation at Panmunjom, hardcore prisoners in the camp on the island of Koje-do seized Brigadier General Francis T. Dodd in an unguarded moment and forced him to negotiate with them for future humane treatment and the discontinuation of forcible screening. After Dodd publicly agreed to the prisoners' demands, he was released unharmed. Although Dodd had averted bloodshed in the camp, he had put the UN in a very bad position by implying that the treatment of prisoners had been inhumane. The Communist press made much of the incident as they tried to discredit the concept of voluntary repatriation. It was at this time that General Mark Clark replaced Ridgway as Commander-in-Chief, UN Command, and the Koje incident was his introduction to the war. Believing that strong measures were needed to restore discipline to the camps, Clark relieved Dodd and others above him in the chain of command. He appointed Brigadier General Haydon L. Boatner as the new commander at Koje and reinforced his command with troops from the 2nd Infantry Division and the 187 Airborne Regimental Combat Team. Boatner stormed the compounds with tank-infantry teams and literally dragged the leaders out by the seats of their pants. As his men later bragged, they "Boatnerized" the hard core and restored discipline. All in all, the prisoner affair had an adverse effect on the UN negotiating

position; America's allies disapproved of the handling of the prisoners, and Communist opposition to voluntary repatriation hardened.

A break in the deadlock finally came in the winter of 1952–1953. General Clark suggested that the two sides exchange their sick and wounded prisoners. At the end of March 1953, the Communists agreed, and on April 20, Operation LITTLE SWITCH began. This seemed to trigger a softening of the Communist position, for while the exchange of the sick and wounded was underway, the negotiating teams agreed in principle to a solution of the larger problem. Repatriation was to be offered to all who wanted to go home. Those who did not want to return were to be handed over to a neutral repatriation commission that would hold the prisoners until they could be interviewed by representatives of their armies. If they still did not change their minds, the repatriation commission would release them to whichever government they chose. All seemed to be moving to a final agreement on the terms of an armistice when President Syngman Rhee became a formidable obstacle.

Rhee had always insisted that there could be no armistice without unification. He was equally adamant about voluntary repatriation. As agreement on a truce neared, Rhee announced that the settlement was unacceptable to the Korean people. Although he knew that South Korea would have great difficulty should the UN withdraw its support, he undertook a great gamble that in the end the United States would not abandon him. American leaders saw the reality of the situation as well; there was little they could do to make Rhee observe a truce he did not want. They were just not sure if Rhee was bluffing. He was not. On June 18, he opened the gates of prison camps and released some 25,000 North Koreans who wanted to live in the south. In spite of UN efforts to tighten camp security, Rhee's men continued to aid the escape of anti-Communist prisoners.

The United States finally bought Rhee's support of the armistice. The price was high in terms of dollars, but it paved the way for a final settlement. The Truman administration offered Rhee a mutual security pact; long-term economic aid, beginning with a $200 million installment; expansion of the ROK Army to 20 divisions; and coordination of their goals and actions in the international conference to follow the armistice.

While Rhee was winning his diplomatic victory, the Communists sought one more military triumph upon which to end the war. Beginning on July 13, elements of five CCF armies attacked an ROK Army salient on the Kumsong front. The CCF broke through the frontline divisions and forced a withdrawal. General Maxwell D. Tay-

General Mark Clark, Commander-in-Chief of the United Nations Command, Signs the Armistice Agreement, July 27, 1953

lor, commander of Eighth Army since the spring retirement of Van Fleet, was concerned, and reinforced the threatened sector with the 187th Airborne Regimental Combat Team and the 3rd Infantry Division. By July 15, the line had been stabilized and the attack stalled. Taylor then ordered the ROK II Corps to counterattack. Although the ROK corps recovered some ground, it could not regain all that had been lost. As the action subsided on the battlefield, the commanders and delegations of the contending powers gathered to sign the truce. At 10:00 p.m. on July 27, 1953, the Korean War ended after over three years of hostilities, two of which were spent trying to bring it to an end.

How could a war conducted with inspirational generalship and brilliant maneuver—such as that displayed by Walker in the Pusan perimeter, MacArthur at Inchon, and Ridgway in the "meatgrinder"—have ended in negotiations, with a stalemate on the battlefield? There is no single answer to this complex question. First, it is clear that in June 1950, the United States was neither conceptually nor organizationally prepared to fight a limited war. Success was the result more of rapid crisis management than military readiness and deliberate planning. Once the enemy had been driven out of South Korea after Inchon, the

President and his advisers seemed incapable of resolving the conflicting demands of successful operations on the battlefield and worldwide coalition goals. Having assumed the leadership in both arenas, they allowed the battlefield objective, which was to uni_y Korea by force, to coexist with the broader goal of avoiding a wider war while rearming the United States and her Western allies. After the Chinese intervened, and the risks and costs of unification became too great to accept, the high command changed goals once again, settling for a limited war along the 38th Parallel while negotiating an end to the conflict. Coincidentally, disagreement between MacArthur and his superiors exposed a serious failure of command. MacArthur and the JCS tried to practice traditional command relationships in a situation that would not permit the wide latitude normally given to a local commander. When MacArthur tried to change his government's war policy by taking his case to the Congress and the people, he was relieved, and a new chapter in American civil-military relations opened. Finally, the eagerness of the Western powers to end the war led to miscalculations that permitted the Communists to stalemate the battlefield, prolong the war, and seek a propaganda victory on the world stage.

What then were the significant consequences of the war? South Korea remained free of Communist domination, but the peninsula remained divided. The Chinese Communists ascended to a position of great influence in the world, particularly among the unaligned states, and the Soviet Union appeared more threatening than ever before to the Western powers. The leadership of the United States reacted by committing the nation to military preparedness. The draft and large defense budgets became an important part of American life; Europe and some Asian powers, including former enemies, were rearmed; multinational and bilateral treaties enmeshed the nation in a complicated network of alliances designed to insure security; and a military-industrial complex maintained permanent readiness for war. In short, the Korean War intensified the Cold War by redefining the struggle between the non-Communist and Communist powers in global and military terms. Containment by political and economic measures was no longer the only option for the United States. The long march to Vietnam had begun.

Notes

[1] J. Lawton Collins, *War in Peacetime: The History and Lessons of Korea* (Boston, 1969) pp. 197–198; James F. Schnable, *Policy and Direction: The First Year, United States Army in the Korean War* (Washington, D.C., 1972) pp. 221–222, 228–229.

[2] Disposition Form, G4 to G3, October 25, 1950, subject: "Policies Governing Redeployment of Ground Forces from Korea," in DA File G3 091 Korea (C); Summary sheet, G3 Plans Division to Chief of Staff, October 27, 1950, subject: "Procurement of Additional UN Ground Forces for Use in Korea," in DA File G3 091 Korea (S); Summary sheet, G3 to Chief of Staff, October 19, 1950, subject: "Readjustment of FECOM Forces Following Cessation of Hostilities in Korea," in DA File G3 320.2 Pacific (TS), all in National Archives. See also Schnable, *Policy and Direction*, pp. 223–224, 229–230.

[3] Handwritten note, [Ridgway] October 10, 1950, subject: "Info furnished by Col. Duff, G2," Box 16, Ridgway Papers, U.S. Army Military History Research Collection, Carlisle Barracks, Pa.

[4] Schnable, *Policy and Direction*, p. 236.

[5] Dean G. Acheson, *Present at the Creation: My Years in the State Department* (New York, 1970) p. 585; H.A. DeWeerd, "Strategic Surprise in the Korean War," in *Orbis*, 6 (October 1962), 446.

[6] Acheson, *Present at the Creation*, pp. 585–586.

[7] DeWeerd, "Strategic Surprise in Korea," p. 446.

[8] Acheson's testimony in U.S., Congress, Senate, Committee on Armed Services and Committee on Foreign Relations, *Military Situation in the Far East and the Facts Surrounding the Relief of General of the Army Douglas MacArthur from His Assignments in that Area*, pt. 3, 82nd Cong., 1st sess., 1951, p. 1833; hereafter cited as *Military Situation in the Far East*. Also see David S. McLellan, "Dean Acheson and the Korean War," in *Political Science Quarterly*, 83 (March 1968), 19.

[9] Schnable, *Policy and Direction*, p. 233.

[10] Collins' testimony in *Military Situation in the Far East*, pt. 2, p. 1311; Schnable, *Policy and Direction*, p. 233; Collins, *War in Peacetime*, pp. 217–218.

[11] Collins, *War in Peacetime*, p. 175.

[12] Schnable, *Policy and Direction*, pp. 233–234.

[13] From Walker's memorandum to MacArthur, November 6, 1950, quoted in Schnable, *Policy and Direction*, pp. 235–236.

[14] *Ibid.*

[15] Monograph, HQ U.S. Eighth Army, Korea, July 11, 1952, subject: "Logistical Problems and Their Solutions," in DA File G4 51-52 (S), National Archives, pp. 62–63; Roy E. Appleman, *South to the Naktong, North to the Yalu* (Washington, D.C., 1961) pp. 638–639.

[16] Monograph, "Logistical Problems and Their Solutions," pp. 70–72; Appleman, *South to the Naktong*, pp. 668–669.

[17] Letter, Brigadier General K.L. Hastings, QM, HQ FECOM to Major General H. Feldman, QMG, November 3, 1950, subject: "Informal Report on Logistics Situation in Korea," in DA File OPS 091 Korea (C), National Archives.

[18] "Record of Actions taken by the Joint Chiefs of Staff Relative to the United Nations Operations in Korea from 25 June 1950 to 11 April 1951," prepared by the Joint Chiefs of Staff for the Senate Armed Forces [*sic*] and Foreign Relations Committees, April 30, 1951, CCS 013.36 (4-20-51), Bulky Package, National Archives, pp. 53–56. Hereafter cited as "Record of Actions."

[19] *Ibid.*

[20] Marshall's testimony in *Military Situation in the Far East,* pt. 1, p. 360; Bradley's testimony in pt. 2, pp. 372, 896.

[21] Memo, Major General Bolte to Chief of Staff, December 3, 1950, subject: "Use of Atomic Bomb," in DA File G3 091 Korea (TS), National Archives.

[22] Maxwell D. Taylor, *Swords and Plowshares* (New York, 1972), p. 134. Taylor's discussion of this matter is confirmed by classified documents in the National Archives.

[23] Transcript of the third interview with General Matthew B. Ridgway, conducted by Colonel John M. Blair, January 6, 1972, "Conversations with General Ridgway," Box 51, Ridgway Papers, U.S. Army Military History Research Collection, Carlisle Barracks, Pa., pp. 67–69.

[24] Testimony in "Transcripts of Hearings Held by the Committee on Armed Services and the Committee on Foreign Relations: Inquiry into the Military Situation in the Far East and the Facts Surrounding the Relief of General of the Army Douglas MacArthur from His Assignments in that Area," Records of the Senate Armed Services Committee, Vol. 15, pp. 2450–2457. This is the original 28 volumes of testimony taken during the MacArthur Hearings and classified Top Secret until declassified in April 1972.

[25] Bradley's testimony in "Transcripts of Hearings," Vol. 14, p. 2321; Vandenberg's testimony in Vol. 20, p. 3704.

[26] Bradley's testimony in "Transcripts of Hearings," Vol. 14, p. 2311; Vandenberg's testimony in Vol. 21, p. 3952; Marshall's testimony in Vol. 5, p. 930 and Vol. 8, p. 1301; Collins' testimony in Vol. 18, p. 3124.

[27] "Record of Actions," pp. 60–61, 65–68.

[28] *Ibid.* p. 61.

[29] Collins' testimony in *Military Situation in the Far East*, pt. 2, p. 1205; "Record of Actions," p. 63.

[30] Collins, *War in Peacetime*, p. 209; "Record of Actions," pp. 62–63.

[31] "Record of Actions," p. 66; MacArthur's message is quoted in U.S., Congress, Senate, Committee on the Judiciary, *Interlocking Subversion in Government Departments. Hearings Before the Subcommittee to Investigate the Administration of the Internal Security Act and Other Internal Security Laws*, 83rd Cong., 2nd sess., 1954, p. 2084.

[32] "Record of Actions," p. 66.

[33] *Ibid.;* Bradley's testimony in *Military Situation in the Far East,* pt. 1, pp. 1145–1146.

[34] David Rees, *Korea: The Limited War* (Baltimore, 1964) pp. 165–166; "Record of Actions," pp. 78–79.

[35] "Record of Actions," p. 69.

[36] Rees, *Korea*, pp. 168–172.

[37] "Record of Actions," pp. 70–72, 80.

[38] *Ibid.*, pp. 81–84.

[39] *Ibid.*, p. 85.

[40] Rees, *Korea*, pp. 181–182.

[41]*Ibid.,* p. 183; "Record of Actions," pp. 87–88.

[42]Matthew B. Ridgway, *The War in Korea* (Garden City, NY, 1967) p. 83.

[43]*Ibid.,* p. 89.

[44]Schnable, *Policy and Direction,* p. 326.

[45]*Ibid.*

[46]*Ibid.,* p. 327; "Record of Actions," p. 89.

[47]R.O. Holles in *Now Thrive the Armourers,* quoted in Rees, *Korea,* p. 186.

[48]*Ibid.,* p. 187.

[49]*Ibid.,* pp. 189–190.

[50]Schnable, *Policy and Direction,* p. 360.

[51]"Record of Actions," pp. 94–95; Schnable, *Policy and Direction,* p. 360.

[52]Schnable, *Policy and Direction,* pp. 368–369.

[53]*Ibid.,* p. 372.

[54]*Ibid.,* p. 373; "Record of Actions," p. 74.

[55]"Record of Actions," pp. 100–103.

[56]Schnable, *Policy and Direction,* p. 358.

[57]Collins, *War in Peacetime,* p. 297.

[58]Schnable, *Policy and Direction,* p. 390.

[59]Collins, *War in Peacetime,* p. 303.

[60]The entire text of Ridgway's new directive is quoted in Collins, *War in Peacetime,* p. 301.

[61]Rees, *Korea,* pp. 259–263.

[62]Walter G. Hermes, *Truce Tent and Fighting Front* (Washington, D.C., 1966) p. 22; Rees, *Korea,* p. 293.

[63]Hermes, *Truce Tent,* pp. 31–32; Collins, *War in Peacetime,* p. 330.

[64]Rees, *Korea,* pp. 299–301; Hermes, *Truce Tent,* pp. 118–121.

[65]Hermes, *Truce Tent,* pp. 180–181.

[66]*Ibid.,* p. 105.

[67]*Ibid.,* pp. 325–328; Collins, *War in Peacetime,* pp. 312–313.

[68]Collins, *War in Peacetime,* pp. 314–318.

[69]Ridgway, *War in Korea,* p. 87.

[70]Collins, *War in Peacetime,* pp. 318–322.

[71]The discussion covering the conclusion of negotiations comes from Collins, *War in Peacetime,* and Hermes, *Truce Tent.*

Selected Bibliography

The Arab-Israeli Wars

Allon, Yigal. *The Making of Israel's Army*. New York, 1970. An account of the evolution of the IDF from the *Hashomer* to 1969, by the former *Palmach* commander. Emphasis is on the 1948 War.

Badri, Hassan-el, Taha el Magdoub, and Mohammed Dia el-Dinzohdy. *The Ramadan War, 1973*. Dunn Loring, VA, 1978. An Arab account of the 1973 War written by three Egyptian officers.

Dayan, Moshe. *Diary of the Sinai Campaign*. New York, 1966. An account of the 1956 War by the Israeli Chief of Staff.

Dupuy, Trevor N. *Elusive Victory*. New York, 1978. The best one-volume coverage of the conflicts from 1948 to 1973 from both Arab and Israeli perspectives.

Herzog, Chaim. *The War of Atonement: October, 1973*. Boston, 1975. An Israeli account of the 1973 War by the former Israeli Intelligence Chief. Includes a revealing analysis of the early Israeli failures.

Insight Team of the *London Sunday Times*. *The Yom Kippur War*. New York, 1974. The first full account of the war; excellent color and insights.

Luttwak, Edward and Dan Horowitz. *The Israeli Army*. New York, 1975. An institutional history of the Israeli Army through 1973. Excellent insights.

Marshall, S.L.A. *Sinai Victory*. New York, 1958. An excellent account of small unit actions in the 1956 War.

O'Ballance, Edgar. *No Victor, No Vanquished*. San Rafael, CA, 1978. The definitive work on the 1973 War.

Tal, Israel. "Israel's Defense Doctrine: Background and Dynamics," *Military Review*, 58 (March 1978), 22–37. A concise summary of Israel's unique security problems and military doctrine.

The Chinese Civil War

Boorman, Scott A. *The Protracted Game: A Wei-ch'i Interpretation of Maoist Revolutionary Strategy*. London, 1969. A controversial but challenging conceptual model for understanding Maoist revolutionary strategy as it was developed and applied during the Chinese Civil War. If Boorman is right, the only way to defeat this strategy is to apply it in reverse.

Feuerwerker, Albert. *Rebellion in Nineteenth Century China*. Ann Arbor, MI, 1975. A concise description of the causes and defeats of the shattering rebellions that helped lay the foundation for the Chinese Civil War.

Jansen, Marius B. *Japan and China: From War to Peace, 1894–1972*. Chicago, 1975. A college text that provides an unusually balanced account of Japan's role in the Chinese Civil War.

Liu, F.F. *A Military History of Modern China, 1924–1949*. Princeton, NJ, 1956. A well-researched and very balanced history of the internal development of the Nationalist Army during the Chinese Civil War.

Morwood, William. *Duel For the Middle Kingdom*. New York, 1980. An extremely readable and balanced account of the Chinese Civil War that stresses the personalities and roles of Mao and Chiang. Superbly done.

Sheridan, James E. *China in Disintegration*. New York, 1975. An excellent general account of the Republican era in Chinese history—the period from 1912 to 1949 that encompassed the Chinese Civil War.

Smedley, Agnes B. *The Great Road: The Life and Times of Chu Teh*. New York, 1956. A useful if slightly romantic biography of the military architect of the Communist victory in the Chinese Civil War.

Sun Tzu. *The Art of War*. Trans. Samuel B. Griffith. London, 1971. A polished, annotated translation of a work that underpins Chinese strategic thought. It was on this book (originally written about 350 B.C.), rather than the works of Clausewitz or other Western thinkers, that both Chiang and Mao based their strategies.

Tuchman, Barbara W. *Stilwell and the American Experience in China, 1911–1945*. New York, 1972. Excellent, perceptive coverage of the very limited American role in the Chinese Civil War.

Wilson, Dick. *The Long March, 1935*. New York, 1971. A fast-paced narrative of one of mankind's greatest epics—the escape and rebirth of the Communist armies during the Chinese Civil War.

The Korean War

Official United States Army Histories

Appleman, Roy E. *South to the Naktong, North to the Yalu (June–November 1950), United States Army in the Korean War.* Washington, D.C., 1961. An account of ground operations from the outbreak of the war until the Chinese intervention.

Hermes, Walter G. *Truce Tent and Fighting Front.* Washington, D.C., 1966. Covers the war during the months of negotiation.

Schnable, James F. *Policy and Direction: The First Year, United States Army in the Korean War.* Washington, D.C., 1972. An overview of the formulation of military policy from the outbreak of the war to the beginning of negotiations.

Other Book-Length Monographs

Collins, J. Lawton. *War in Peacetime: The History and Lessons of Korea.* Boston, 1969. An excellent account of the war from the viewpoint of the Joint Chiefs of Staff by the Army Chief of Staff.

Goodrich, Leland M. *Korea: A Study of U.S. Policy in the United Nations.* New York, 1956. For those interested in this particular aspect of the Korean War, it is the only worthwhile work.

Haynes, Richard F. *The Awesome Power: Harry S. Truman as Commander in Chief.* Baton Rouge, 1973. A good overview of Truman's entire record as military chief. A big subject for a single volume, but well done. Contains data on the Korean War found in no other secondary account.

Joy, C. Turner. *How Communists Negotiate.* New York, 1967. A firsthand account of negotiations with the Chinese by the first chief representative of the United Nations.

Paige, Glenn D. *The Korean Decision (June 24–30, 1950).* New York, 1968. The best analysis of the American decision to intervene in Korea. An hour-by-hour account of the week of crisis.

Rees, David. *Korea: The Limited War.* Baltimore, 1964. This is the best one-volume coverage of the war yet written.

Ridgway, Matthew B. *The War in Korea.* Garden City, NY, 1967. A good military analysis of the generalship of the Joint Chiefs and MacArthur, as well as a firsthand account of "Ridgway's war" by the architect himself.

Rovere, Richard H. and Arthur Schlesinger, Jr. *The MacArthur Controversy and American Foreign Policy.* New York, 1965. A view of MacArthur's relief based on the MacArthur congressional hearings. Largely favorable to President Truman.

Spanier, John W. *The Truman-MacArthur Controversy and the Korean War.* Cambridge, MA, 1959. A valuable discussion of command relationships and the preservation of civilian control in a limited war.

Whiting, Allen S. *China Crosses the Yalu: The Decision to Enter the Korean War.* New York, 1950. The standard and best analysis of Chinese policy in regard to the Korean War.

Index